Quintin Jardine was a journalist before joining the Government Information Service where he spent nine years as an advisor to Ministers and Civil Servants. Later he moved into political PR, until in 1986 he 'privatized' himself, to become an independent public relations consultant and writer.

D1152443

Skinner's Ghosts

Quintin Jardine

headline

First published in 1998 by
HEADLINE BOOK PUBLISHING

First published in paperback in 1998 by
HEADLINE BOOK PUBLISHING

15 17 19 20 18 16 14

ISBN 0 7472 5665 9

Typeset by Avon Dataset Ltd, Bidford-on-Avon, Warks

Printed and bound in Great Britain by
Clays Ltd, St Ives plc

HEADLINE BOOK PUBLISHING
A division of Hodder Headline PLC
338 Euston Road
London NW1 3BH

This book, like those which went before, and those which will follow, was inspired by my wife.

Catherine Campbell 'Irene' Jardine

1946–1997

Kate, my lovely Kate.

1

The woman walked, at a steady unhurried pace, down the middle of the village road.

She was wearing the wig and gown of one of Her Majesty's Counsel, a formal, enveloping uniform which served to emphasise, rather than mask, her advanced years. She was small, and bird-like in her features, with a few grey whiskers sprouting among her wrinkles; clearly, she was very old.

Yet for all that, she walked straight-backed and steadily in front of the hearse, and its burden, as she led it down the main street, down the short distance from the great grey castellated house to Aberlady's churchyard, and to the grave which awaited. As she approached, in the doorway of the church a lone piper played a lament.

'Who is she?' asked Pamela Masters.

Beside her, at the wheel of the white BMW as they sat at the head of the queue of waiting traffic, Deputy Chief Constable Bob Skinner smiled.

'Don't you know, Sergeant?' He paused. 'But then I don't suppose you would. It's been a long time since even I've seen her in action.

'She is Christabel Innes Dawson, QC; in her heyday, the only woman silk in Scotland, and one of the very finest too.'

'And who's . . .'

'Who's in the chest? That is Lord Orlach, Senator of the College of Justice, and Lord Justice Clerk for what seemed like about a hundred years. Old Orlach was the last of the Supreme Court judges not to be subject to compulsory retirement. He finally did step down though, last year.'

'And Christabel's his widow?'

Skinner drew in his breath, and shook his head. 'Christ no! Orlach's wife died donkeys' years ago, but he and she never married. He had his town house in Heriot Row, and latterly his country seat out here, while she had her establishment in India Street, with the brass plate on the door saying "Miss Dawson, Advocate". They had a relationship though, that lasted fifty years, until the old boy died last week.

'When he was plain John Stevenson KC . . .'.

'KC?' Pamela interrupted.

'Aye, King's Counsel; it was that far back . . . and she was a junior, admitted to the Faculty of Advocates almost over the dead body of the Dean of the time; he took her on to assist him in a capital murder trial. Their affair began back then.'

He glanced across at the pretty, dark-haired woman in the passenger seat. 'It was never admitted, or discussed, though.' He smiled, at a memory. 'They really did think they were being discreet, too. There's a story about Orlach, that once, in the New Club, an Outer House judge asked him how Christabel was . . . as innocently as that. Orlach froze him with a look, and afterwards, every time one of that judge's decisions came before him on appeal, the old boy would reverse it.'

'Why didn't they marry?' she asked him.

Skinner laughed again, softly. 'Well at first, Mrs Stevenson wouldn't have approved. Then, by the time of her death, Orlach was on the Bench. It was never said of course, but the feeling was that if they had got hitched,

Christabel would have had to leave the Bar. The rules were such that you could never have been sure that she wouldn't have wound up pleading a case before her husband, and that wouldn't have done at all.'

He smiled at the black-gowned figure as she drew nearer, then suddenly and spontaneously stepped out of the car and stood beside it. As she turned to lead the hearse into the churchyard, Christabel Innes Dawson, QC, glanced sideways and gave him the briefest nod of recognition.

'Of course,' he said as he folded himself back into the driver's seat, 'the fact that they didn't marry meant that she could and did appear before him without restraint.' He laughed again, out loud this time. 'I remember she crossexamined me once in a criminal trial, with Orlach as presiding judge. Andy Martin too. He was raw at the time and she knew it. At the end she was screaming at him like a banshee, and old Orlach let her get on with it.'

'Did she try it on with you too?' Pamela asked.

'No, fortunately. She had a degree of respect for DI rank and above, but detective constables and sergeants . . . she chewed 'em up and spat out the bits.'

He looked at her mischievously. 'She still appears, you know. A few times a year she'll take on the defence in a High Court trial. More often than not she gets an acquittal. Maybe we can fix it for you to be a police witness in one of them.'

She snorted, and flounced her dark hair. 'No thank you!'

As the hearse passed through the churchyard gates, the uniformed police officer who had stopped the traffic turned to Skinner, saluted and waved him on. The DCC nodded an acknowledgement and slipped the car into gear.

He glanced to his left as he passed the church, as the old lady moved to join the congregation inside.

'All these years maintaining their discreet front,' he murmured, 'yet when the time comes she leads him to the grave. There's a nobility about that, though, Pam, is there not?'

She looked at him, as the BMW snaked though the chicane exit from Aberlady, heading for Gullane. 'Maybe there is. What I can see though is a situation that's a bit close to home. I'm as big a secret as old Christabel there . . . or so you think.'

'What d'you mean . . . so I think? I haven't told anyone, not even Andy. So who would know?'

'Ruth McConnell, your secretary, for a start. D'you think she hasn't guessed? DCI Rose for another. God, her eyebrows went up when you made me your Exec six months ago!'

Skinner shrugged his shoulders. 'But I replaced you with Neil McIlhenney after two months.'

'Sure, and DCS Martin was delighted to have me added to his personal staff, wasn't he?' she said ironically.

He raised his eyebrows. 'He never said a word to me. I told him that we had agreed you'd be better working for him and he accepted that at face value.'

She twisted in her seat to look at him. 'Okay, so tell me why, when she called into the office two days ago to see Mr Martin, your daughter . . . his fiancée . . . froze me like a block of ice with a single look. Not, I suggest, because she thinks I fancy Andy.'

Skinner frowned at her. 'You don't think Ruth's been talking, do you?' He sounded genuinely shocked.

'Of course not,' she said at once. 'DCS Martin's figured it out, and told Alex. He'd do that, wouldn't he?'

Her companion sighed. 'Well they live together, so I guess so. Those two have no secrets from each other. But,

4

hold on. Even if Andy and Alex have guessed, they wouldn't let on to anyone else.'

'Mmm,' said Pamela, demurely. 'But are you as confident of Sergeant Boyd, from the Haddington nick, who stopped the traffic back there in Aberlady, and recognised both you and me: in casual clothes heading towards Gullane, where you have a cottage . . . and on a Friday afternoon to boot? Even a plonker like him will have put two and two together from that. Jesus, he's probably been on the radio to HQ already.'

He nodded. 'Touché. You've got me there.' He fell silent as he swung the car round a long left-handed bend, and drove them past the small stone cairn, marking the entrance to Luffness Golf Club, settling deep into brooding thought, until long after he had closed the door of the cottage behind them.

Finally, as they sat on wooden chairs in the secluded garden, enjoying the warm summer sun, he turned to her.

'So,' he said, with the beginning of a frown, 'are you giving me the message, Pam, love? Do you want me to put us on an official footing? Or do you just want out?'

She shook her head. 'No, out is certainly not what I want . . . unless you've decided you want your wife back. If that's the case then I'm off like a shot. To tell you the truth, when you went off to the States in May for your wee boy's first birthday, I was more than half expecting you to bring them back with you.'

Bob frowned more heavily, and fell silent once more. 'To be as honest with you,' he said at last, 'I thought that might have happened too, despite what you and I have together. Coming home and leaving the wee fella behind was one of the toughest things I've ever had to do. But there's a wall between Sarah and me that we couldn't break down. I guess she's gone native again, gone back to being an American. Somehow she isn't the woman I met and married.'

Pamela laughed, suddenly and with a trace of mockery. 'Nonsense!' she said. 'Of course she is. It's just that you've never seen her in her native environment before. Also, for the first time in your lives you're seeing her take up a position which isn't exactly in support of yours. You can add to that the fact that she's probably never seen you on the defensive before.'

'Well okay,' he said, wearily. 'So we've both seen each other in a new light, and neither of us could handle it. Whatever the case, I won't get back together with her just for the baby's sake. That wouldn't be right for any of us. Anyway, she's made it clear where she wants to be. Remember what she said in her goodbye note about not wanting to be stuck in Edinburgh for the rest of her life. She has a hospital job in the States now, and she's doing scene-of-crime work for the local police.'

'Is she seeing anyone, do you think?' she asked, softly.

The question took him by surprise, so much that he was unable to keep the hurt from showing in his eyes. 'Possibly,' he said, quietly. 'I'm not sure, but I think she could be.'

'But you didn't tell her about us?'

'No. Like I said, I didn't. I thought it was maybe too soon for that.'

'You mean you thought you'd keep your options open?'

'No! I didn't want to kick her in the teeth, that's all.' He drew a deep breath. 'Or maybe I was just chicken.'

She raised an eyebrow, a gesture denoting scepticism. 'Chicken? The great Bob Skinner was chicken?'

He shrugged his shoulders. 'We all run from something,' he said quietly.

'Come on, what are you saying to me, Pamela? Like I asked you before. Is all this too heavy for you? Do you want us to chuck it?'

She pushed herself out of her chair, knelt on the concrete paving, at his feet, and laid her head in his lap for a few seconds, rubbing her face from side to side against his thighs. Finally she looked up at him, still shaking her head. 'No I don't want that . . . although God knows I should. You're the DCC; I'm a sergeant. You're married, even if you are legally separated. Madness, sheer madness.

'But no, what I am saying is that you and I don't have the option of being like Old Christabel and Lord So and So. We can't keep that sort of secret.'

He frowned at her again, knitting his brows heavily, accentuating the deep vertical line above the bridge of his nose, and the scar which ran alongside it. 'Why not? I always tell my troops that their private lives are their own as long as it's consistent with duty and discipline. We're not working together any more, so why are we different?'

She squeezed his thighs, hard. 'Because we are, man! Look, are you or are you not the Secretary of State's security adviser? Were you or were you not a candidate for the top job in the Met until Sir Derrick Raymond agreed to do another two years? Do you or do you not want Chief Constable rank somewhere? Three Yes's: don't you tell me differently.

'Bob, you've got that ambition, and that potential, and here you are, sleeping with a detective sergeant under your command!'

'Not in the office, I ain't,' he said doggedly. He almost added, 'Besides, maybe I care more about you than about all that stuff,' but something held him back.

She shrugged her shoulders. 'Fine. So why haven't you

told your daughter about me? Or Andy Martin? Or the Chief? Or am I wrong? Have you briefed the Command Corridor, off the record?'

He threw up his hands. 'Okay! Okay! Okay!'

'Well!' She sighed, and paused. 'Look, I'm not asking for a public declaration of undying love. I like it the way it is, as long as you're completely and genuinely separated from Sarah. I love being with you. You excite me more than anyone I've ever known. But your companionship . . . and great sex, of course . . . for now that's enough for me. As long as it doesn't do you harm, and as long as it doesn't compromise your future career. So think about it, eh?'

Skinner sighed. 'Okay sweetheart. I know you're right, and I'll do something about it. I'll tell the Chief, Andy and Alex . . . probably in reverse order. But in my own time . . .' He pointed a finger at her, suddenly, '. . . and mind, I won't be seeking their advice or approval.'

'What if Andy Martin wants me off his staff once you've told him?' she asked him.

'I'll deal with that if it happens.' Abruptly he stood up, gathering her in his arms. 'Meantime . . . what was that you were saying about great sex?'

2

The telephone rang four times, before the automatic answering machine picked up the call. As she heard Bob's recorded voice giving the response, Pamela sat up in bed, a sheen of perspiration glistening lightly on her back.

A few seconds later, the caller left the invited message. Neither she nor Bob could hear what was said, but both recognised the inflections of Detective Chief Superintendent Andy Martin's even, steady baritone.

She nodded in the direction of the bedside telephone. 'Go on, pick it up,' she urged him.

He grinned at her, tugging at her arm to draw her back down beside him. 'Later. Chances are it's work. If it is, I'm not letting it in here.'

She pulled herself free from his light grasp, shaking her head. 'No! It's as if he's in the house with us. If you don't answer it, I will.' As the muffled voice continued to float through to them from the living room, she twisted and threw herself across the recumbent Skinner, reaching out with her left hand. She was smiling, but he took her threat seriously enough to grab her and pull her neat little body back down towards him, holding her away from the phone.

'All right,' he said. 'But you keep quiet. I've said I'll tell him, but in my own time.' He reached behind him with his free hand and picked up the telephone.

'I'll try the mobile,' he heard Andy Martin say, 'but if you get this first, call me . . .'

'Andy! Sorry, mate. I was in the garden. What can I do for you?'

'Did you get any of that?'

Involuntarily, Skinner shook his head. 'No, not a bit of it.' The coiled-spring tension in Martin's voice grasped him at once. Releasing Pam from his grasp, he swung his legs from beneath the duvet and sat on the edge of the bed. 'What's up?' he growled.

'Bob, you're going to hate this. I'm at Leona McGrath's place, down in Trinity.' There was a pause. 'Leona's dead. She's been raped, battered and strangled.'

'Jesus!' Skinner shuddered, so suddenly and violently that, to Pamela, the bed seemed to shake. He ran his fingers through his tousled, steel-grey hair, grasping a clump as he fought to control his shock. Behind him, the mattress squeaked as Pam sat up once more. He waved her to silence over his shoulder.

'When?' he asked, hoarsely.

'She was found about an hour ago. She'd been due to attend a constituency event. When she didn't turn up, the local party chairwoman called round to ask why. There was no reply to the bell, but the back door had been forced. The woman had a look around, and found Mrs McGrath upstairs.'

Skinner sat stunned. As she looked at him, wondering and fearful, Pamela saw that the battle scars on his back and thigh were standing out vivid purple, and realised that he had gone pale. She gripped his arm again, squeezing.

'And her son?' the DCC asked at last. 'Wee Mark. What about him?'

'There's no-one else here, Bob. Neil McIlhenney, Sammy Pye and I have been over the place ourselves. We've been everywhere. There's no sign of the kid.'

'Mark!' said Skinner sharply. 'His name is Mark.'

He squeezed his eyes tight shut, partly to stem the hot tears which he felt springing up, and partly to try to stop himself shaking with tension.

'After what that woman's endured, and done,' he murmured, when he had calmed himself. 'For it to end like this . . .'

He stood up, still holding the phone and turned to face Pam, his back to the muslin-draped window. 'You say Neil and Sammy are there?'

'That's right. Sammy was with me when the call came in. And I thought you'd want the big fella here.'

'I tried to raise Sergeant Masters, but she's on a day off.' Skinner searched for an undertone in his friend's remark, but found none.

'Forget Pam,' he said. 'She doesn't need to be there. I'll be with you in Edinburgh inside an hour. Meantime, I suggest you contact the grandparents. Mark's very close to Roland's father. Let's pray that he's with him.'

He replaced the phone in its cradle and looked down at Pamela.

'What . . .' she began, before Skinner forestalled her question.

'A very good friend,' he said. 'Leona McGrath. The MP for Edinburgh Dean. You must remember her. Her husband was killed in the plane crash last year. She fought the seat, and won it.' Pam nodded.

'Well, now it's her time to die. She's been murdered.'

He stood there before her, naked, and heaved a huge sigh. 'Oh my girl,' she said, 'when you live with me, you find that some terrible things force their way into your life. Even in the quietest moments, you're never safe from them.

'Think you can cope with it?' He reached for his clothes and began to dress.

3

The house was so familiar to him. He walked past the uniformed officers who stood guard at the head of the driveway, his sandals crunching their way up the narrow gravel path which led from the gate.

The front door was open. He stepped into the hall, pulling on a white scene-of-crime tunic and overshoes before venturing further.

Properly clad now and knowing exactly where he was going, he strode into the drawing room, then through to the wooden conservatory. Around him, specialist technicians were bent over their work, dusting down doors, windows and furniture for fingerprints, in the hope that one – even a fragment of one – would have been left by the intruder rather than by Leona or her son. Skinner nodded approval of the team's tenacity, even though experience told him that the chances of their work being rewarded were around one in five.

As he stepped back into the hall he collided with another white-suited figure, three or four inches shorter in height than his own six foot two, but distinctive, with his shock of red hair.

'Hello Inspector,' he said grimly. 'How's it going?'

'All the mess is upstairs, sir. It looks clean as a whistle down here,' said Arthur Dorward, confirming Skinner's pessimism. 'The back door's been jemmied, but other than that, nothing's disturbed. Mrs McGrath's in the front bedroom, top of the stairs.

'That's where you'll find Mr Martin.'

The DCC nodded. 'Come with me then. I'll welcome your insight. ME still here, is he?'

Inspector Dorward nodded. 'Aye, sir. Dr Banks as usual.' He paused. 'He's not a patch on his predecessor, if you don't mind my saying so.'

He did mind, very much, but he let it pass. There was no point in taking his bitterness out on an honest soldier like the scene-of-crime Inspector, especially when he knew that he was speaking no more than the truth. Dr Sarah Grace Skinner was the best murder-scene examiner he had ever encountered, gifted with an uncanny ability to paint compelling pictures of events from the very slightest of clues. As he and Dorward climbed the stair a huge pang of regret shot through him.

Detective Chief Superintendent Andy Martin, Head of CID, was standing in the doorway of the bedroom as they reached the upper landing, leaning against its upright, his broad back to them in its white suit.

Skinner stepped up behind him and placed a hand on his shoulder, drawing him out into the hall. 'Hi, son,' he said quietly. 'Is Banks nearly finished?'

Martin nodded. 'You know him. He's taken forever, but he's just about done now.'

'Mmm,' said the DCC. 'I suppose I'd better take a look then.' He made a conscious effort to brace himself as he stepped into the room.

Skinner believed deeply that every good police officer had a tolerance limit when it came to viewing the bodies of murder victims. He knew that he had passed his own a long time before. One of the benefits of Chief Officer rank was the ability to delegate, to opt out personally from the messy end, where once he would have attended automatically.

Yet some circumstances, like the murder of a public figure, and this, the murder of a woman who had come to be a very close friend, still demanded his presence. And of course, once there, on view himself, he could show no weakness.

He thought that he had prepared himself mentally for what he would see, but a moan still escaped his lips as he looked at the body of Leona McGrath.

'Oh, no,' said Bob Skinner, out loud for all to hear. 'You poor wee lass. What bastard did that to you?'

And then the rage – cold, blind, savage rage – took over. 'When I lay hands on you, whoever you may be . . .' he hissed.

'I think we all feel like that, sir,' said Martin, his green eyes narrowed slightly and his shoulders bunched.

Skinner knelt beside the body. The little woman . . . she had been not much over five feet tall . . . lay on her back. Her arms were twisted under her and the policeman knew without looking that the wrists were bound together. She was naked, save for a brassière, still fastened, but forced up above her breasts. She was covered in blood. From her vagina, it was matted in her thick growth of pubic hair, and smeared across her thighs and belly. From her nose and mouth, it was spread across her face, shoulders and chest, staining the white bra. From her left ear ran a single crimson line. Before her heart had stopped pumping, it had flowed into a puddle, congealed now on the fawn-coloured carpet.

Great vivid bruises and welts showed all over her pallid, yellowish skin. The most vivid were on her face, and on her side, just below her left breast, as if a fist had pounded on her, time and time again.

Her face was swollen grotesquely, from the beating and from the white garments – panties, he guessed, possibly

15

more than one pair – which had been stuffed into her mouth. A single black nylon stocking had been wound around her neck, more than once, as a strangling ligature, then tied off, ferociously tight. The flesh around it was blue and puffed.

Finally, when he could avoid them no longer, Skinner looked at her eyes. They were bulging, staring up at him, and so full of anger and remonstration that he winced and looked away for a second, before closing them, almost reverently, with his right hand.

Gently, he turned her on to her side. Her wrists were indeed bound, with the electric cord of a black hair-dryer. Just above the blood which was caked on her buttocks, there were vivid red marks where its plug had been crushed into her flesh. He leaned closer, to look at her hands. Her fingernails were long, and appeared to be painted with a hard clear varnish. On the tips of three, on her right hand, he could see what appeared to be blood.

He glanced up at Martin. 'Andy,' he said. 'Untie her hands, while I hold her, would you.' Without a word, the grim-faced Head of CID did as he was asked.

'Plastic bags on the hands please, Doctor,' said Skinner to the Medical Examiner, who stood a few feet away. 'There's blood on her nails, and it might not be hers.' He rolled the body over, and laid her face down, partly to help Banks cover her fingers and partly to hide her poor battered features from the others in the room. Almost without thinking, he unfastened the bra.

The doctor set the clear plastic covers in place over the dead fingers, securing them with elastic bands, snapped into place around the weals left in the wrists by the binding cable. He stood up, beside the DCC.

'Well?' asked Skinner.

'Whoever did this wasn't messing about,' said Banks. 'She was raped, and sodomised, pretty savagely, thumped around a bit, then strangled. Don't worry about fingernail scrapings,' he said dismissively. 'You'll find all the DNA you need in other places.' Astonishingly, he smiled at the detectives, from one to the other. 'The press'll have a field day with this. I expect I'll be all over the telly when I come to give evidence at the trial.'

Skinner felt himself come to boiling point, but it was the normally unflappable Andy Martin who exploded first. 'Are you enjoying this, Banks?' he shouted. The DCC stared at him in surprise, unable to remember ever having heard his friend raise his voice in anger.

'You know something, you little shit,' barked the Head of CID. 'I've never liked you; nor has anyone else on our team. You turn up late at crime scenes, then you give us half-arsed reports which don't usually help us one bit. But the worst thing about you is your total lack of respect.

'We knew that lady lying there, Mr Skinner and I. This is a personal tragedy for us. She was worth a dozen of you, and in death she *will* be treated with honour, not as a vehicle to advance your personal reputation.'

He stepped close to the doctor and prodded him in the chest with his broad right index finger. 'You can bet on this, Banks. You will not be called as a witness in the trial of Leona's killer. The pathologist's evidence will be enough. And you can bet on this also. You're at your last crime scene in this city, and with this force.

'First thing tomorrow, I will see to it personally that your name is removed from our list of medical examiners. Now, I think you'd better leave . . . before you make me lose my temper.'

Doctor Banks' face went from white to red in a couple

of seconds. 'You can't do that,' he spluttered.

Skinner leaned forward, took him by the arm, and led him towards the door, past an astonished Inspector Dorward. 'Too fucking right he can, mate,' he said. 'Too fucking right.' He eased the doctor out on to the landing. 'Send the mortuary people up as you leave,' he ordered, and closed the door in his face. His mouth was set, tight and grim, as he turned back to Martin. 'Good for you, son,' he said, softly. 'Couldn't have done better myself.'

He glanced across at the red-haired Inspector. 'Right, Arthur. Let's have your observations.' A sudden thought struck him. 'No, before that. Where are McIlhenney and Pye?'

'I sent them off to see the grandparents,' said Martin, 'to check whether Mark's with them.'

Skinner nodded. 'Good. You could hardly have telephoned, right enough. Okay, Arthur, sorry. Carry on.'

Dorward coughed, clearing his throat. As he did so, the door opened, and two dark-uniformed mortuary workers, a man and a woman, entered, carrying a brown plastic coffin.

The three policemen stood aside. As the bloody, naked body of Leona McGrath was lifted and placed gently in its makeshift container Skinner turned away and looked out of the bedroom window into the street, lit by the summer evening sun, which shone on a small crowd of around a dozen onlookers, and on a larger number of reporters, photographers and television cameramen. Their number had doubled since his arrival. He guessed that the tip-off industry had done its stuff once again. As he watched them he saw a camera raised and trained upon him. Quickly he reached across and pulled the curtains closed.

When he turned back the coffin was gone. 'Arthur,' he said. 'At last.'

'Yes sir,' said Dorward. He paused for a few seconds, then went on. 'The only relevant comment I have to make is that Mrs McGrath must have been surprised in this room. Look over there.' He pointed to a wardrobe door, which lay open. 'And there.' He pointed to a dressing-table drawer from which items of underwear hung. 'And there.' He pointed to a chair, across which denim jeans and a white blouse had been laid neatly.

'There are no signs of a struggle downstairs,' said Dorward, 'and precious few in here. No torn clothes, nothing like that. If you look in the *en suite* bathroom, you'll find a damp towel. I'd guess that Mrs McGrath was getting ready to go out when she was attacked.

'Her assailant burst in on her and found her virtually naked. Maybe rape wasn't on his mind till then.'

'Or their minds,' Martin interrupted.

'That's true, sir,' Dorward agreed. 'But semen testing will tell us whether there was more than one rapist.'

'So what was on the killer's mind . . . singular or plural?' asked Skinner. 'Robbery?'

Dorward shrugged. 'It doesn't look like it, boss. There's a handbag downstairs, in plain view on the kitchen table, so that the intruder must have walked past it. There's about a hundred and fifty quid in there, in cash. There's an antique clock on the mantelpiece in the living room that's worth a couple of grand. There was a diamond engagement ring still on her finger, and more jewellery on the dressing table. There's a briefcase in her study, but no papers seem to have been disturbed.

'No sir. Not robbery. That's pretty certain.'

'Then what?' Skinner barked the question, not at Dorward, but at the ceiling, feeling an uncomfortable nagging knot forming in the pit of his stomach as one possible answer grew larger in his mind.

He glanced across at Martin. 'Who was it found her?'

'Her constituency chair, a woman called Marks. She was just babbling nonsense when I got here. Banks gave her a sedative, and I had her taken home. With luck we'll get sense out of her tomorrow.'

'Let's hope so. We've got people interviewing neigh-bours, yes?'

'Yes. Dan Pringle's people are doing that.' Skinner nodded approval. Detective Superintendent Dan Pringle was Divisional Head of CID for the greater part of the City of Edinburgh. With him in charge there would be no chance of sloppiness.

'Where will you base the investigation?'

The DCS shrugged. 'Headquarters, I thought, rather than the Divisional Office. We've got everything we need at Fettes, plus we have more room to handle the press. With the political involvement, this will be no ordinary murder enquiry.'

'I can't argue with that,' said Skinner. 'When are you going to see the press?'

'I've told Alan Royston to set up a briefing for seven thirty. Do you want to take it?'

The older man shook his head. 'No. You're Head of CID. That's your job.'

'They'll expect you,' said Martin doubtfully.

'Well they're not fucking having me, and that's an end of it. You take the first press conference, then leave the later briefings to Royston. That's what he's paid for.'

'Okay.' The DCS paused. 'Here,' he asked, casually, 'd'you know if Royston's still involved with Pam Masters? I know he was for a while. Did she mention anything when she worked for you?'

Inwardly, Skinner gulped. He stared at Martin, looking for anything devious in his eyes, yet seeing nothing. 'That finished a long time ago,' he said at last. 'What made you bring that up?'

Martin smiled. 'Plain old-fashioned curiosity, that's all. I've never known an officer who keeps her private life as private as she does.'

'So much for Pam's notions about Alex and Andy's shared conclusion,' he thought. He might have told his friend the truth there and then had not Neil McIlhenney's shout drifted up from the hallway. 'Sir? You still up there?'

'Yes,' Skinner called out in reply, suddenly relieved by the interruption. 'We're on our way down though.'

Leaving Dorward to carry on his painstaking work in the bedroom, the two senior officers descended the staircase. Detective Sergeant McIlhenney, Skinner's personal assistant, stood waiting in the hall with Detective Constable Sammy Pye, one of Martin's staff officers. The two flanked a tall man in his seventies, silver hair, pale and shaking.

'Hello, Mr McGrath,' said the DCC, advancing on him with hand outstretched. The two had met for the first time at the scene of the death of the old man's son. On that occasion he had been dignified and purposeful. Skinner guessed that this would prove one bereavement too many. Harold McGrath seemed overwhelmed. Gently the tall policeman slid an arm around his shoulders and led him into the living room.

'Neil,' he said quietly, over his shoulder. 'Whisky. Over there, on the sideboard.' As the heavily built sergeant picked up decanter and glass, the dead woman's father-in-law lowered himself carefully into an armchair.

'Sergeant McIlhenney has obviously told you what happened,' said Skinner, glancing across at his assistant as

21

he spoke and noticing for the first time the strain in his normally jolly eyes.

'Yes,' the old man whispered.

'There's nothing I can say to lessen the shock, or the horror of it,' said the detective. 'We all knew your daughter-in-law; we admired her tremendously. We're stunned too. But believe me, we will catch whoever did this, and we will put him away for the rest of his miserable life.'

'It was a man then?' asked old McGrath, bewildered, seeming to age before their very eyes. Skinner guessed that McIlhenney had spared much of the detail. 'Beyond a doubt,' he replied, gently.

'Where's my grandson?' said the old man suddenly, urgently.

A sudden desperation hit the DCC, the earlier pang of concern gripping him now with a fierce certainty. 'He's not with you, then?'

The silver head shook. 'No. Leona said she would bring him over before she went to her constituency meeting. When she didn't turn up, my wife and I assumed that she had taken him with her after all. She did sometimes, like a sort of mascot.

'So where is he?'

'That's just the thing, Mr McGrath. We don't know.' The old man looked up at him, his mouth slightly open.

'Look,' said Skinner. 'Does he have any pals around here? Could Leona have taken him somewhere else, before she was attacked?'

'No,' said the grandfather. 'I don't think so. All Mark's friends are away on holiday just now. We were supposed to be going too, on Sunday, now that the House of Commons has risen.'

'You're sure there's no-one still at home, no pal where he could have gone?'

'Quite sure. Leona remarked on the fact just last night, on the telephone.'

'How about Leona's parents?' asked Martin. 'Are they still alive?'

Mr McGrath looked round at him, over his shoulder, clutching the whisky which McIlhenney had pressed into his shaking hand. 'Her mother is. Her name's Mrs Baillie, Mary Baillie. She lives in Broughty Ferry. But she's on holiday as well, in Greece with a friend. They left last Sunday, from Glasgow Airport.'

Skinner turned to his assistant. 'Neil,' he said. 'Fast as you can, get on to the tour operators and trace Mrs Baillie. This is going to break very fast through satellite television. I don't want the poor woman to hear of her daughter's death from a Sky newscaster.

'Andy,' he said quickly to Martin. 'You'd better postpone your briefing till we've contacted the mother. Meantime, we'd better mobilise every available officer, CID and uniformed. I want an inch-by-inch search of the surrounding area. If Mark escaped from the house he could be hiding out somewhere. Whatever, if he's anywhere around here, we've got to find him!'

He stabbed the air with a finger. 'Every available officer remember, whether they're off duty or not. I'll even call the Chief and ACC Elder. You turn out all your team.' He paused, then added as a seeming afterthought, 'Try and raise Pam Masters again. You never know. She might be home by now.'

4

'At this moment,' said Andy Martin, surveying a hushed gathering of reporters and cameramen in the main briefing room of the police headquarters building in Fettes Avenue, 'every available police officer in the City of Edinburgh is involved in an intensive search of an area within a three-mile radius of Mrs McGrath's home.

'That amounts to over a thousand officers, including Chief Constable Sir James Proud, Deputy Chief Constable Bob Skinner and Assistant Chief Constable Jim Elder. We're searching public parks, railway embankments, unoccupied houses and other properties. Everywhere.'

'Are you asking for volunteers to help widen the search area, Chief Superintendent?' The question came from a reporter in the front row of the audience, representing the city's cable television channel.

'No,' he told the woman, 'because we have to keep things under control. But you and all the other broadcast media can help us by asking your viewing and listening audiences to search their own premises right away, just in case a very frightened wee boy might be hiding there.'

'What can you tell us about Mark, Andy?' asked John Hunter, a freelance, and the senior member of the Scottish Capital's media corps.

'Well for a start, you can all collect his photograph on the way out, although I suspect that most of you will have him on file from the time of his father's funeral.'

He paused. 'Mark is six years old, and beyond doubt

24

he's the most remarkable wee boy I have ever met. As you all know, undoubtedly, by a miracle he survived the plane crash in which his father was killed. Not only that, he was instrumental in helping us catch the man whose bomb brought the aircraft down.'

Roger Quick, of Radio Forth, raised a hand. 'Mr Martin, do you suspect any link between the murder of Mrs McGrath, and her husband's death?'

The Detective Chief Superintendent looked at the reporter for a moment, then shook his blond head. 'No, none at all. We said at the time that we were satisfied that the bomber had acted alone, and that we knew what his motive was. As the man was shot dead at the scene of his subsequent crime, we have to regard the fact that both of Mark's parents were murdered as no more than a particularly brutal coincidence.'

'So,' asked Hunter once more. 'Do you see any motive for Mrs McGrath's killing?'

Martin shrugged his shoulders, rippling the cloth of his navy blue blazer.

'John,' he said, slowly, speaking clearly for the microphones massed around him, 'I've told you all we know for sure at this moment. I'm not going to speculate on anything else, nor would you expect me to. Motive – if there is one – is anyone's guess. I have to deal with established fact. Our thinking might crystallise once we trace Mark, but until then we're throwing everything into the search.'

'D'you think the boy's been kidnapped?' asked the old reporter, bluntly.

'Possibly, but I don't know,' snapped the detective. 'What I do know is that we are involved in the biggest search this city has ever seen. If it proves fruitless, then that possibility would harden into a probability.' He picked up the notes on the table before him. 'Now, let's get on with it, shall we?'

As Martin stood up, a hand was raised at the back of the room. The policeman's eyes narrowed as he recognised Noel Salmon, a tabloid journalist recently declared *persona non grata* by Skinner.

'Chief Superintendent . . .'

The Head of CID turned to Alan Royston, the force's civilian media relations manager, who was seated at the table beside him. 'How did he get in here?' he growled, with unaccustomed menace.

'I had to let him in,' Royston whispered. 'He's been accredited by that sleazy new Sunday, the *Spotlight* – you know, the rag they sell through supermarkets.'

'Chief Superintendent,' Salmon called out once more, a shout this time. 'On behalf of the *Spotlight*, I have a personal question about DCC Skinner. Is it true that his wife has filed for divorce?'

Every head in the room turned towards the untidy little journalist; then most swivelled back towards Martin, waiting for his reaction. The detective's green eyes were like ice as he stared at the reporter.

'Not to my knowledge,' he said loudly and clearly. 'Congratulations, Mr Salmon,' he went on. 'You've just been barred from this building yet again. You and your paper.'

'Do you expect her to?' the man shouted across the room.

'No,' Martin barked, losing his temper for the second time that day, just as a photographer rose from the seat next to Salmon and snapped off a series of motor-driven shots. 'Now get out of here, before I run you through the door myself!'

5

'Royston did *what*?'

Skinner roared his incredulous, rhetorical question across the floor of the Chief Constable's office in the Fettes Command Corridor. 'I'll have the stupid bastard's balls for paperweights! I personally banned that little shite Salmon from this office. For life, I said, yet our press officer lets him back in – and to represent that bloody downmarket rag at that!'

He turned from Martin to Neil McIlhenney. 'Sergeant, first thing tomorrow morning, I want you to find out for me all about the procedure for firing a civilian employee. Meantime, Royston's suspended. By the time I'm done with him, he'll be glad of a job on the fucking *Spotlight* himself.'

It was fifteen minutes after midnight. Skinner, Chief Constable Sir James Proud, ACC Jim Elder, Martin and McIlhenney had gathered in the Chief's room to review progress – or lack of it – in the fruitless search for any trace of Mark McGrath, or of his mother's murderer. There had been no easy way for Martin to break the news of Salmon's intervention in the press briefing. Even so, he had anticipated his friend's reaction, and with the Chief's support had told Royston to stay away from the office until further notice.

'Bob,' said Sir James, as Martin had guessed he would, 'don't you think you should pause for thought, before taking action?'

Skinner looked at him, a thick vein standing out on his

27

right temple. 'Jimmy, Royston reports directly to me. Right?'

The Chief nodded, waiting as his deputy took a deep breath. 'Okay,' Skinner said at last. 'In deference to you, I'll think about it. Once I have, chances are I'll still sack him, but at least I won't have done it in the heat of the moment.'

Proud Jimmy grunted. 'That'll be some consolation to him.' He paused. 'Bob, why would that bloody man Salmon ask such a question? You and Sarah aren't . . .'

Skinner shook his head, emphatically. 'Sarah hasn't raised the subject of divorce with me, nor I with her. Now, can we please talk about police business?'

'Of course,' said the Chief, as keen as Skinner to change the subject, and ushering his colleagues to chairs. 'You too, sergeant,' he said to McIlhenney.

'Will I sort out some coffee, first, sir?'

'Good idea, Neil. Good idea.' The big man left the room, leaving the door slightly ajar.

'Well,' said Sir James. 'No luck with our search.'

Skinner shook his head. 'Not that I expected it. I know that wee boy too well. Chances are he'd have defended his mother. If not, and he'd escaped from the house, Mark wouldn't have hidden in fright. He'd have raised the street.'

'D'you think the kid's dead, then?' asked ACC Elder.

Andy Martin answered for Skinner, reading his mind as he had done a thousand times before. 'No, sir. It's likely that he's alive, still. If he'd been killed, he'd have been left at the scene. Why should the murderer take him away, to kill him later? There's a better than even chance that he's been kidnapped.'

'Why would anyone in his right mind . . .' Elder began.

'Who says he is?' Skinner growled. 'Andy's right. We have to look at this as a kidnapping.'

'How did he get away with it, then, in broad daylight?' asked Proud, shifting uncomfortably in his uniform and running his fingers through his silver hair. 'Did none of the neighbours see or hear anything?'

'No, Chief,' Martin replied. 'The fact is that with the time of the day and the holidays there were damn few neighbours about. There were none on either side of the McGrath house, or across the street, and only a few at the end of the road. One of them thought he saw a silver or grey car in Leona's driveway, but that's the only lead we have. Leona's car's grey so when he drove past, the man thought nothing of it. Only the McGrath car was locked in the garage at the time.'

The DCS paused. 'As I see it, the killer drove right up the driveway. Unlike the footpath to the front door, it's tarmac, so he wouldn't have made much noise. In any event, Mrs McGrath was in the shower, getting ready for her afternoon meeting.

'Once he'd jemmied the back door, I suspect that the intruder made sure of Mark right away. When the first officers arrived they found the television on in the living room. It was tuned to the Cartoon Network, on cable, the sort of stuff that kids watch all day, when they're not at school.

'After he had secured the boy – tied and gagged him, maybe – I guess the man went upstairs, for the mother. As Arthur Dorward pointed out, she must have been taken completely by surprise in her bedroom, still barely dry from the shower, wearing her bra and nothing else.'

Sir James Proud frowned. 'If kidnap was his motive, why would he do that? If he could have got away quietly, why attack the mother as well?'

Skinner sighed. 'There's a difference between purpose

and motive, Chief. This bastard may have gone there with the purpose of kidnapping the child. Or he may have gone there with the rape and murder of the mother on his mind.

'In either case, the kidnap, or the killing, may have been spur-of-the moment action. Alternatively there could have been a single game plan from the start. But none of that takes us any nearer the killer's actual motive. It still doesn't tell us why.'

'What do you think, then, Bob?' asked the chief. 'Do you have any notion of what's behind this?'

The DCC looked at his only superior officer. The closer he had come in rank to James Proud, the more he had come to value the man, and to appreciate his humanity. He knew how much the brutal death of a woman, and the disappearance of her child, would be affecting him, and the effort he would be making to keep his emotions in check. He knew also, and made allowances for the fact, that the Chief Constable's career path had been one of administration rather than investigation, and that, as good a leader as he was, he lacked the detective's instincts.

'Maybe we coppers place too much stress on motive sometimes,' Skinner replied, eventually. 'Genuine evil doesn't need reasons to be. Sometimes it just is. That's a difficult concept for normal, balanced people to grasp, and so it's easy to discount it.

'But it could be that all this man sought was gratification; from the rape, torture and murder of a vulnerable, defenceless woman, and from the taking and terrorising of a child. If that's the case it's awful.' His voice rose suddenly and he slammed his right fist into his cupped left palm. 'Not just for what happened to Leona, but for what could be happening to that poor wee boy right now.'

'And presumably,' continued Proud Jimmy, in an

ominous tone, 'because he could do it again.'

Skinner shot him a quick glance. 'Not could, Jimmy,' he said, quietly. 'I'd say will.'

He paused. 'And of course, he may have done it before. At the moment, our best hope is that DNA sampling will give us a match to a known offender, a sociopathic rapist, perhaps, with a previous conviction, who's done his time but hasn't exhausted his urges.'

The Chief shook his head. 'It's a nightmare, right enough.'

'But there's something else that we mustn't forget,' broke in Andy Martin, as McIlhenney returned with a tray of steaming mugs. 'This was no ordinary single parent, but a very high-profile lady. A Tory MP. That gives us the possibility also that this crime could have political involvement.'

'Terrorism?' said ACC Elder.

'Who can say at this stage?' growled Skinner. 'The only certainty just now is that here we all are, as we've been a hundred times before, in the middle of the night, without a bloody clue.'

6

Pamela stirred and looked at the bedside alarm. Its red digits told her that it was 1.34 a.m. as Skinner slid into her bed.

'Sorry, pet,' he whispered. 'I didn't mean to wake you.'

She kissed him, feeling the harsh stubble on his chin. 'That's all right. I wasn't sure whether you'd come here.'

'I almost didn't. I thought of going to Fairyhouse Avenue. I even thought of crashing out in the office. But then I thought of you, and I realised that I needed to be with you.'

In the dark, she stroked his cheek. 'Was it bad? In the house, I mean.'

She felt him shiver, although the summer night was hot. 'I've never been good at a murder scene,' he muttered. 'But this one – someone I knew; someone I admired; someone who's had enough tragedy in her life.' She felt the touch of his forehead on hers, and his arm slip around her.

'I tell you, lover. When we catch this guy, I hope I'm there, and I hope he resists arrest. Because I want the privilege of personally tearing out his heart.'

'Shh! Shh!' she whispered, quickly. 'Don't say that. I hope you never get near him, in that case. You're too good a man to have anyone's blood on your hands, even his.'

She was shocked, even a touch frightened, by his sudden ironic laugh in the darkness. 'You think that, do you, Pammy? God, lass, but you don't know me as well as you think!

'Andy, now. He's shot someone dead, and it's broken his heart. Brian Mackie: he's had to do it, and never given an emotional twitch. But me, now: I've had to kill in the course of my career, more than once. And each time, when I've looked at the body at my feet, this person inside me, this voice, has said clear as you like, "Quite fucking right too!"

'Believe this, if you've ever believed anything. Whoever killed poor wee Leona had better never give me a clear shot and legal justification, or I'll shoot him like a dog and say "Got you, you bastard".'

She leaned away from him, trying to see his face in the faint light which crept into her bedroom from the city outside. 'Bob,' she said, with surprise in her voice. 'I'd never have put you down for a supporter of capital punishment.'

She saw the gleam of his white teeth as he smiled. 'That's the thing,' he muttered, more gently now. 'I'm not, in the judicial sense. I couldn't hurt a fly in cold blood. But in the heat of action, there's something in me that takes over. Between you and me, it scares me shitless. I'm just glad I'm on the right side of the fence.'

He drew her to him once more. 'But enough of this black talk. Let me feel the warmth of your body, and let's both get some sleep. For at six thirty, we're both off out again, in the vain hope of finding wee Mark.

'I saved his life once before, you know. I pray that I or one of Skinner's finest gets the chance to do so again.'

7

'I've sent Pamela to be an observer at the post-mortem,' said Martin, casually. The search for Mark McGrath had just been declared exhausted, and the Head of CID and Skinner were sharing an early lunch in the senior officers' dining room.

The DCC felt his stomach churn, involuntarily, but all that his colleague saw was the raising of his eyebrows.

'It's part of the job, Bob. She has to take her turn. Young Pye's gone with her.'

'Fair enough,' said Skinner. 'She's on your team.' He took a deep breath.

'Listen Andy,' he began. 'Will you and Alex be free this evening?'

Martin looked at him. 'Aye, sure. Are you fed up eating alone? Is that it?'

The DCC shook his head. 'No. There's something I've got . . .'

'Excuse me, sir.' The voice came from the doorway. Both detectives glanced across, to see a tall thin man in a sergeant's uniform. 'You told me to let you know, Mr Martin, when the media were ready,' said William Rowland, Alan Royston's deputy.

The DCS stood up at once. 'Yes, thanks Bill.' He looked down at Skinner. 'I'm going to carry on taking the briefings, sir, until you've resolved the Royston situation. It wouldn't be fair to leave it to Sergeant Rowland.'

'Fair enough. Listen, will you get someone to tell

Royston to be in my office at ten on Monday morning. I'd better have it out with the guy.'

Martin nodded. 'I think that's best.' He headed towards the door, where Rowland still waited.

'Come to dinner tonight, why don't you?' He paused, and said, 'Our place; make it around half-seven. That'll give us time to get ready. To tell you the truth, I think Alex has been working herself up to talk to you about . . . well, everything. I know she's not happy about the situation between you and Sarah. Those two are like sisters, you know.'

Skinner grunted. 'Tell me about it! That's part of the problem. But my daughter's right, I haven't been talking to her nearly enough.' He picked up his coffee. 'Okay. I'll see you then.'

8

'What are the chances of finding the child alive, Chief Superintendent?'

The radio reporter looked barely more than a child himself. Looking at him, Andy Martin wondered whether he might be on a work-experience placement, used by the station as a cheap way of providing Saturday news cover.

'There's every chance, Mr . . .?' His voice tailed off.

'Braden, sir.'

'. . . Mr Braden. In fact, we're very hopeful of finding Mark alive. Our ground search has run its course, and so far we've had plenty of support from the public. Sooner or later we'll get a lead.

'What I am doing today is renewing my request to property-owners to check garages and outbuildings – anywhere that a frightened child might be hiding. Also, I'm asking everyone who was in the Trinity area of Edinburgh on Friday afternoon to think hard, just in case they saw anything unusual, particularly if it involved a child and a grey car.'

The boy looked eagerly at the detective. 'Is that your most positive lead so far, a grey car?'

'To be unusually frank with you, it's our only lead so far.'

John Hunter waved a hand. 'So kidnap's now becoming a probability, is it, Andy?'

Martin nodded. 'With every passing minute. We're being as positive as we can in our search, of course. If you're an innocent motorist in a grey car, I apologise in advance for the inconvenience of being stopped by the police. But I'm sure you'll realise that we're only doing what's necessary.'

He looked at the assembled media. 'That's all I have for you today, folks. Same time tomorrow, unless anything breaks. If that happens you'll be contacted.'

John Hunter fell into step with the detective as he left the room. 'Where's Royston?' he muttered.

'Don't ask,' Martin whispered in return.

'Oh. I see.' The old journalist paused. 'Listen, Andy. I saw that wee shite Salmon in the bar of the Bank Hotel last night, after you had flung him out of here. He wasn't letting on why, but he looked as happy as a two-cocked dog in a stand of trees.

'He's up to something, and whatever it is, I have a feeling that your lot aren't going to like it.'

9

Joseph Hutchison, Professor of Pathology at Edinburgh University, knew Deputy Chief Constable Skinner well enough to know of his loathing of post-mortem examinations. So when he recognised the big policeman, despite his surgical gown and cap, as soon as he stepped into the theatre, it was natural for him to look up in surprise.

'Hello, Bob,' said the twinkling-eyed little scientist. 'This is a rare honour, having you visit my workshop.'

Skinner grunted a response, as he strode over to stand between Pamela Masters and Sammy Pye, who seemed to be positioned as far as possible from the post-mortem table. Clearly, the examination had been under way for some time. He glanced down at Pamela: she was slightly pale, and her cheekbones stood out a little more than usual, but otherwise she was impassive.

'Any surprises for me, Joe?' Skinner asked. 'Or haven't you got that far yet?'

'Oh yes,' said Professor Hutchison, 'I've got that far. As even the good Dr Banks could work out, death was due to strangulation by ligature. The hyoid bone was crushed. The ligature was so tight that the blood supply to the brain would have been cut off at once, causing unconsciousness, prior to death.' He paused, coughing suddenly.

'I've examined the major internal organs. All healthy and undamaged. I'm just looking at the brain now.' He held it up, so that the police observers could see its swirling surface patterns, slicked with blood and fluid. In spite of himself, Skinner looked away. 'As you can see,' continued the Professor, 'no obvious damage here either, other than that consistent with a sudden stoppage of the blood supply.' He paused again.

'There were other injuries, of course. Four broken ribs, all left side, ruptured left eardrum, left zygotic bone fractured – all indicative of a severe beating by a right-handed attacker, pounding on her face and body repeatedly with his fist. However, none of these would have contributed to death. They were either gratuitous, or they were an attempt to subdue the victim, prior to the sexual assaults.

'I'd say they were simply sadistic, actually, because the first thing the man did was to tie up the victim. There's a big bruise to the small of her back, consistent with the attacker having thrown her to the ground, knelt on her, really hard, as he bound her wrists securely with the electrical cord your people say was used.'

'How about the blood on her fingernails, Joe?' Skinner asked. 'Will we get any joy there?'

'Hah,' said the Professor. 'My first piece of bad news, I'm afraid. The lab will have to confirm this, but I surmise that those samples were from the victim herself. There are marks on her back, near those made by the electrical plug, which conform to her nails having been crushed into her own tissue.'

'Damn it!' said the policeman. 'Still, there'll be other traces.'

There was a long silence. 'That is the really bad news, my friend. There aren't.'

'Eh? But what about the sexual injuries? Surely to Christ he . . .'

The little pathologist shrugged his shoulders. 'It's frustrating, I know.

'The woman was sexually attacked, by a fairly large man, and repeated penetration took place. She was sodomised first, I'd say, very painfully. Much, but not all of the blood came from the rupturing of vessels around the anus, the rest from tearing around the vagina. The muscles in these areas were all cramped and constricted, indicating that the victim resisted throughout every attack, even at the cost of added suffering, and even if ultimately unsuccessfully.

'Yet there are no traces of semen.' The little pathologist looked up and across at Skinner. 'That's the trouble with the information superhighway, I'm afraid, Bob. There's far too much information about. Even the stupidest criminals know about DNA tracing, and can work out some fairly obvious ways of avoiding it.

'This one probably used a condom.'

Skinner slapped the wall behind him, in sudden fury, causing both Pam Masters and Sammy Pye to start in surprise. 'Bastard,' he shouted, ripping off his mask. 'The cold-blooded bastard. You sure, Joe? Not a single smear?'

Hutchison shook his head. 'Sorry chum. I understand your anger, but there it is. When you catch the guy, you may find that he has sexual injuries. This was a sadistic attack, extremely vicious, and the perpetrator is likely to show the effects upon his, er, person, for some time.

'Even then, of course, it would be virtually impossible to link such injuries to this attack.'

'*Sshitt*!' hissed the DCC.

'Is there nothing at all you can do?' Detective Constable Pye asked the Professor, breaking, if not clearing, the tension in the room.

It was Skinner who answered him, suddenly and forcefully. 'Yes,' he said, 'there is. And you're going to do it, Joe, aren't you?'

The pathologist sighed. 'Yes. You know we are. We will search the victim's body minutely, Constable, looking for just one hair that doesn't belong to her. We will go though the areas in which it could be lodged with, literally, a fine-tooth comb, and we will examine everything that isn't actually rooted.

'That will be a lot, but there is the real possibility that we will not find a single hair out of place, to be literal about it.' He paused, to look up at Skinner.

'Mind you, this is knock for knock, Bob. You'll have to send Dorward's team back to the murder scene to do exactly the same thing, to collect every loose hair for testing. Then you'll have to eliminate her son, her housekeeper, her late husband, of whom traces will undoubtedly remain in the room, and any casual callers Mrs McGrath may have had ... sorry to be so blunt ... before and after her widowhood.'

The big detective nodded. 'We'll do all that, Joe, and any more that's necessary, don't you worry. Just you go and get out your fine-tooth comb.'

10

'Can I ask you something, Bob?'

Skinner turned to Pamela and smiled. 'When couldn't you?'

'Oh come on! When I went to work for you at first; I couldn't then. And now, when I see shadows cross your face when you don't know I'm looking at you.'

'That happens a lot, does it?'

'Yes it does. For example, every time I find you looking at your son's photograph, your eyes are thousands of miles away.'

He grimaced. 'Allow me that, Pammy, please. I miss wee Jazz every moment of every day. Missing him's become a part of me, but it doesn't affect our relationship. Come on, what did you want to ask me?'

She looked around the kitchen of Skinner's bungalow in Fairyhouse Avenue, not far from the police headquarters building. 'Why have you never brought me here before?'

He looked her straight in the eye as he replied: 'Because this is the home I made with Sarah. The furniture in it we bought together. The swing on the tree outside I made for our son.

'Gullane's different. That's the home I made with Myra, years ago. You know about her, all about her life and death. It seems natural for you and I to be together there, or for that matter at your place. But I haven't felt right about bringing you here, not until now. That's the truth of it.'

She looked at him, solemnly, and nodded. 'Yes, I thought

you'd say that. And I understand it. So why have you brought me here this afternoon?'

He smiled back at her. 'Because this evening I'm going to begin to do what I promised you. I'm going to have dinner with Alex and Andy, and I'm going to tell them that you and I are seeing each other.

'Then tomorrow, I'm going to have lunch with the Chief in the New Club, and tell him the same thing.

'Finally, tomorrow night, I'm going to phone Sarah and talk things though with her. I'm going to ask her if she wants a divorce.'

'What if she says no?'

'At that point, I'll tell her about us. I'm sorry if that seems devious or even cowardly, but I'd sooner that Sarah and I divorce because she's thought it through and wants to than because I'm putting a gun to her head.'

He saw her eyes narrow. 'You're guilty about me, aren't you?'

He shook his head at once. 'I have a clear conscience. My mother might not have seen it that way, but I do. Sarah and I had parted before you came on the scene. But I do care for her, and I want to be as gentle on her as I can.'

'What if she tells you she has another man?'

'I'll say, fair enough.'

'But you'll hurt inside.'

'If I do, love, that's where it'll stay. Now, let's talk about something else.'

To his surprise, she frowned, and a different shadow crossed her face. 'Remember when I dropped my car off at my place, I went up to check the flat?'

Bob nodded.

'There was a message on the answering machine. From Alan Royston.'

He snorted. 'Royston? Your ex? Did he want you to ask me to let him off the hook?'

She shook her head, vigorously. 'Don't be daft. He doesn't know about us, any more than anyone else does. No, he didn't leave any message, other than for me to call him as soon as possible. He sounded funny, though – anxious, I mean. What should I do?'

'Nothing!' said Skinner, vehemently. 'Don't call him back under any circumstances. I'm interviewing him on Monday morning, to give him a chance to explain himself. I'm still undecided what to do about him. If you speak to him at all there's a danger that you could compromise both of us.

'In fact, till I have dealt with him, don't even mention the bugger's name to me. For now, Royston's another subject that's off limits!'

11

The Saturday evening traffic in Leith was unusually heavy, a result in part at least, Skinner guessed, of the police flagging down and questioning the driver of every grey car in sight.

Having dropped Pamela at her home, after promising to return to tell her of his confession to his daughter and her fiancé, he was fifteen minutes behind schedule when he arrived at the flat near Haymarket which Andy Martin and Alexis Skinner now shared.

As he reached for the bell, the heavy front door swung open, and Alex appeared. She was wearing light cotton jeans, a yellow teeshirt, and a very serious expression.

'Hello darlin',' said Bob, holding out a bottle of red wine, wrapped in green tissue. 'Sorry I'm late. The traffic was murder. Did you see me arrive, then, from your perch over the street?'

She nodded, kissed him on the cheek as he entered the hall, then put a hand on his chest, to stop him. 'Pops,' she said. 'There's someone here to see you. He wouldn't say what it's about, till you got here, but I think it's a problem.'

Skinner frowned. 'Who is it?'

'Come on through. You'll see.' She led her father into the living room of the second-floor flat, with its bay window overlooking the street. Andy Martin was standing at the fireplace, looking down in silence at a man seated on the couch, his back to the door. Even from that angle, hunched nervously in his seat, Skinner recognised Alan Royston.

He glared across the room. 'What is this, Andy?' he asked, with an edge of menace.

'Search me, Bob,' said Martin, as Royston rose to his feet. 'Alan phoned about three-quarters of an hour ago, to ask if I knew where you were. He said that it was very important that he saw you at once. So I told him that if he was prepared to risk being chucked out of the window, he'd better come here.'

The media relations manager turned, nervously, to face Skinner. He was clutching a document case, fashioned of supple, black leather. 'I'm sorry about this, sir. I had no choice, even allowing for my situation. There's no way I could have referred this to Bill Dowling, or anyone other than you.' He paused. 'Look, could we speak in private?'

The DCC shook his head. He had no idea what the man wanted, but all of a sudden he felt as if a black cloud was gathering above him, and preparing itself to rain, very hard. 'No way, Alan. If you've got bad news for me, it won't be anything my family can't hear. But if it is about your situation, as you call it, my daughter will show you the door.'

Royston shook his head, and began to unzip the document case. Instinct, as much as anything else, made Skinner hold up a hand.

'Wait just a minute, please.' He looked across at Alex, standing now, by Andy's side. 'Before we hear anything, there's something that I have to say. I came here this evening to tell you something that I should have told you both before. For the last couple of months, since just after Sarah and I separated formally, I've been having a relationship with Pam Masters.'

As he looked at his daughter, she gazed at the floor and nodded. 'I know, Pops,' she said, as though they were the only people in the room. 'I drove out to Gullane one Friday night, about three weeks ago, to surprise you; to cheer you up. I was just turning into the Green when I saw Pamela jump out of her car and run into the cottage, carrying what looked like an overnight bag.'

'Och, love, I'm sorry,' Skinner blurted out. Glancing at Martin, he saw that his friend was stunned. 'So why didn't you tell Andy . . . for I can see you didn't?'

'Because I knew that you'd tell us both, if and when you were ready.'

He grinned, but without humour. 'You knew better than me, then.'

Abruptly, he turned to Royston. 'Right Alan, now that's said, please carry on.'

The man nodded, and finished unzipping his case. 'That's why I'm here, sir, I'm afraid.

'Noel Salmon came to see me at six o'clock. The little bastard was almost chortling with glee. He gave me this, and asked if you would care to comment on the story for his next edition.'

Slowly he withdrew, from the document case, a copy of the *Sunday Spotlight*. 'This will be on sale in all of its supermarket outlets around Britain tomorrow morning. They've labelled it exclusive, but they'll release copies to television and radio at nine this evening, to promote their sales.'

His hand shook as he handed Skinner the newspaper, and he winced as the policemen unfolded it and saw the front page.

'*Top Cop and Sexy Sarge*,' the headline blared. '*Naked romps shock police force . . . Exclusive, by* Spotlight's *top reporter Noel Salmon*.'

Skinner felt his spine stiffen as he stared at the tabloid,

his eyes widening. Beneath the headline most of the front page was taken up by a colour photograph. It had been shot with a long lens, and through a muslin-draped window, but it was clear enough. It showed a tall, naked man, standing with his back to the window and the camera. Beyond, sitting up in bed and staring at him, as if in awe, the head and shoulders of a woman, recognisable clearly as Pam Masters.

'Holy shit!' Skinner whispered at last, as he stared at the picture. It took a while, before he was able to shift his gaze to the story beneath. He began to read, aloud, in a strained voice.

'*Top Detective Bob Skinner, Edinburgh's famous deputy chief of police, has been enjoying a steamy affair with his quote personal assistant unquote, Sergeant Pamela Masters, while his beautiful doctor wife Sarah has been staying in the US, with her parents and year-old baby son, James.*

'*Only last year Mrs Skinner, 32, spent a week-long vigil at her husband's bedside as he lay critically wounded in an Edinburgh hospital after being stabbed by a young girl.*

'*The two-timing detective, 46, thought to be a serious candidate for the post of Commissioner of the Metropolitan Police, and the stunning Sarge have been enjoying raunchy romps at Skinner's luxury seaside cottage in Gullane, Scotland – one of his three homes – and at 34-year-old Masters' penthouse pad in Edinburgh's trendy Leith district.*

'*This week, Detective Chief Superintendent Andy Martin refused to answer* Spotlight *questions on his boss's indiscretion, or on the likely reaction of Mrs Skinner, angrily ordering that your reporter be thrown out of an open press conference at which he tried to raise the issue.*

'Martin, 37, is engaged to Skinner's lawyer daughter Alexis, 22, and is known throughout Scottish police circles as his personal protégé.

'The high hopes that Masters, a one-time marketing whizz-kid, clearly entertained for a similarly rapid rise through the ranks, look like disappearing even more rapidly as Skinner's own career is thrown into doubt.

*'*Spotlight *readers must ask whether the two-timing 'tec can be trusted in one of the country's top police positions, and whether he can continue in his other post, as security adviser to Bruce Anderson, the new Secretary of State for Scotland.*

'Read next week's Spotlight *for Sarah Skinner's reaction to her husband's betrayal. More exclusive pics on pages 4 and 5.'*

'Would you credit that?' said Skinner hoarsely as he looked up from the newspaper. 'The miserable, snooping, duplicitous little creep photographed me through my bedroom window. And the story's a fucking travesty.

'Sarah and I are formally, legally separated, both here and in the States. "Holidaying with her parents" for Christ's sake! She has a job over there. She took my son over there – without my agreement at that.

'What the hell else have they done? Let's see.' He lifted the paper again and tore it open at pages four and five. As he did so Alex and Andy came to stand with him, scanning the pages from either side.

The spread showed an array of photographs. One showed Sarah, white-tunic-clad at an open-air crime scene, frowning at her husband. 'Last year, at Witches Hill, I guess,' said Skinner. Others showed Martin, at the press conference, pointing to the door as he ordered Salmon from the room, then glaring angrily at Alan Royston. A fourth, taken in the street below, showed Alex and Andy leaving home, casually dressed.

Finally there was a series of three photographs, in colour like the rest. They had been taken from a high vantage-point looking down into the garden of the Gullane cottage. The first showed Bob and Pam, kissing. In the second, she was kneeling before him, her face buried in his lap. In the third, he had gathered her up in his arms, and was carrying her towards the house.

'The dirty little sod,' Alex cried out. 'Imagine photographing us in the street like that. And those in Gullane . . . How could they have taken them?'

Icily calm now, Skinner shrugged. 'The window shot, that's obvious. They waited outside and they got lucky. The others . . . they could only have been taken from one place. The big house at the top of the Green, the one that belongs to our chum. He's in the Seychelles just now and the place is empty. They must have climbed on to the roof.'

He crumpled the tabloid in his hands, twisting it in his fury and tearing it to pieces. Throwing it into a corner, he turned to his daughter, putting his hands on her shoulders and looking her in the eye. 'I am so sorry, my love, that you and Andy have been mixed up in this. It's not right, it's not fair, and it's all down to me.'

She looked at him solemnly. 'Dad,' she began, 'I've only got one thing to say to you.'

He waited, looking at her anxiously. 'Go on.'

'If the *Spotlight*'s done nothing else, it's proved to the world that you've got a nice bum for a forty-six-year-old.'

She smiled at him, suddenly and brightly, and hugged him. 'Pops, if you think for one second that I won't stand by you in this . . .

'You, Sarah, and Pam, you're all grown-up people. Just do what's best for my wee brother, that's all I ask. But I know you will.'

Bob heaved a great sigh of relief. He turned to Andy Martin, who was smiling also.

'Right, people,' he barked. 'What am I going to do about this?'

Martin answered him at once. '*We*, Bob. What are *we* going to do? I for one am going to have that little bastard Salmon arrested and charged with breach of the peace. I reckon we might be able to make that stick, on the basis of that bedroom shot.'

'I'd love to let you, Andy,' Skinner replied. 'You know that. I'd love to use all my power to have this little man broken like a butterfly on a wheel. For Pam's sake, I'd like personally to knock ten bells out of him in a quiet room somewhere.

'But none of that is going to happen.' He turned to his daughter.

'Alex, right now, you get on the phone to the chairman of this new law firm of yours, my football-daft chum in North Berwick. I know you're only a raw new apprentice there, but in this you're acting for me. I want an opinion from him on whether we can go to court to secure an injunction stopping publication of this crap. If it's possible, do it.

'If he says it isn't, I want him to issue through the firm a statement on my behalf saying that my relationship with Miss Masters is an entirely private matter, setting out the legal position between Sarah and me, and saying – if he thinks that we have a case – that writs for defamation will be issued on Monday morning by both Pamela and by me.

'Any press statement from me should issue through your firm, not the force. Got all that?'

Alex nodded. 'I've got Mr Laidlaw's number too. I was given a list of senior partners' contact numbers. I'll call him now from the bedroom.' She rushed off to make the call.

Skinner turned back to Royston. 'Alan, I should crucify you for letting Salmon back into Fettes against my orders, but I'm not going to. For the Chief's sake, you need to be back on the job now: and anyway, I was only going to chew you out on Monday, nothing worse.

'Unless an injunction sticks, Sir James will be asked tonight for a response to the story. He'll need your objective guidance and support. I want you to come with me now, to see him. I have to tell him about this, personally. Once I've done that, I'll withdraw so that he can't be accused of acting under pressure from me.'

Royston nodded. 'I agree with all of that, sir. But there's someone else involved. What about Pam?'

Skinner could see his anxiety. 'Look, Alan,' he said. 'I know that you and she were close once, but don't worry. I'll look out for her in this.'

He turned away from the press officer, took out his mobile, and dialled Pamela Masters' number. She answered, sounding hesitant and a little afraid.

'Listen love,' said Bob, 'to what I have to say. We've got a media problem, and it could be messy. Stay where you are for now. Don't answer the phone, and don't answer the door until I get there. I'll give four quick buzzes so you know it's me.

'Before then I have to see the Chief, and I have to go back to Fairyhouse Avenue.'

'Why do you have to go there?' Her tone was one of bewilderment.

'Because I have to phone Sarah, and it just seems right to me that I do it from there.'

'Bob. This problem involves me, yes?' She sounded completely scared now.

'I'm afraid so, honey. You and I will be all over the scandal sheets tomorrow, thanks to a wee man with a grudge. But don't you worry: things are under control, and hopefully we can nip it in the bud.

'I'll be with you as soon as I can.' He ended the call just as Alex reappeared in the doorway.

'Dad,' she said. 'I've got Mr Laidlaw on the line. He wants to speak with you.' Skinner nodded and followed his daughter through to the flat's main bedroom. The telephone was lying off its cradle on a bedside table. He sat down and picked it up. 'Mitch, hello. Sorry to break into your Saturday evening, but this fucking scandal sheet's left me no option.'

Skinner had known Mitchell Laidlaw socially for twenty years, as a fellow member of an informal group who gathered together on Thursday evening in North Berwick Sports Centre to play enthusiastic, if largely unskilled, indoor five-a-side football. However this was the first time the two had ever spoken on a professional footing. Laidlaw's career had paralleled that of Skinner, as he had risen through the legal ranks to become Scotland's leading litigation solicitor, and finally, head of its largest law firm, Curle, Anthony and Jarvis, which Alex had joined a month earlier on leaving university.

'So I gather from your daughter, Bob.' Skinner was struck at once by his friend's tone. There was no hint of the normal Thursday-evening banter. Mitch Laidlaw sounded solemn and totally professional.

'Alex has read the article to me, and described the photographs. I admit that charging the people involved with breach of the peace is a nice idea, but even if the Sheriff convicted, he'd be overturned at appeal for sure, and your force would be open to an action for malicious prosecution. So you were right to veto that.

'As for an injunction, I'm afraid that we just don't have time to injunct successfully. By the time we had drafted it, and rounded up a judge, the article would be in the hands of the broadcast media, and I suspect in the hands of the *Spotlight*'s sister publications.'

Skinner growled. 'You mean there are more of these damn things?'

'Oh yes. This isn't the first time I've had to deal with this magazine on behalf of angry clients. There's an American version, one in Australasia, and issues in French, German, Spanish and Japanese. The chain is US-owned, and each version is marketed purely through supermarkets, at checkouts and at in-house news-stands.'

'Okay, if we can't stop them, can we sue the bastards?'

On the other end of the line, he heard Laidlaw take a deep breath. 'Can I ask a very delicate question, Bob?'

'If you have to.'

'I do. Are you completely confident of Miss Masters' integrity?'

'One hundred per cent,' the policeman replied without hesitation.

'Good. In that case, I'd say that she has a very strong case in an action for defamation. The paper implies beyond challenge that her relationship with you is motivated by a hope of personal advantage. Tell me Bob, what was the sequence of events here? How did the relationship – which Alex says you don't deny – how did it develop?'

Skinner reflected for a few moments. 'Let's see. The first time I ever met Pam was when I chaired a promotion board for prospective sergeants. It was a twenty-minute interview and she passed unanimously.

'A few months later, my Executive Assistant was promoted and I was looking for a successor. I remembered Pam, interviewed her and gave her the job. My marriage was in trouble before that. In fact her appointment virtually coincided with my moving out.

'We worked together well and amicably for a while. We had a few late shifts, which led to a few meals together. I realised early on that I was attracted to her, but our physical relationship didn't develop until after Sarah had taken our son to the States. We spent two nights under the same roof, once at her place when I was snowed in, and once in Gullane. But we didn't actually sleep together until my separation from Sarah had been legally recognised. I can give you dates later, Mitch, but that's the sequence of events.'

'That's good,' said the lawyer. 'Now what about Miss Masters' post as your assistant?'

'As soon as I saw how things would develop, I moved her out of my office. I transferred her to Andy Martin's personal staff, and took Sergeant Neil McIlhenney as her replacement.'

'Ah!' said Laidlaw. 'So because you and she were entering a physical relationship, Miss Masters actually lost her important, fast-track job as your Executive Officer?'

'Absolutely.'

'Then all she has to do to pursue a defamation action is to decide on the quantum of the claim. That is, how much the accusation that she was prepared to sell herself for advancement is worth to her, or at least how much a court is likely to think it worth.'

'What do you think?'

'Hmm.' Mitch Laidlaw contemplated. 'She has good career prospects, yes?'

'Yes. She was a late entrant, but she can expect to make Chief Inspector, as a minimum.'

'Well in that case, I think they'd settle out of court for at least a hundred and fifty thou. Maybe two hundred. Plus costs, of course.' The solicitor paused again. 'She'll need to instruct me personally if she wants to proceed, but that can be done tomorrow.

'Now. About your own case. That's not so clear-cut, I'm afraid.'

'Why not?' Skinner protested.

'For a couple of reasons. First, you are a very senior officer. Even if Miss Masters sues successfully, the defence against an action by you could be that you used your position, a glamorous and powerful position, to turn the lady's head, or to pull her, if you want a Thursday-night term. Second, you may be separated legally, but you are still married.'

'Hold on, Mitch,' Skinner protested. 'The article says that Sarah went to the States on holiday and that I've been having it off behind her back.'

'No, Bob. You read it that way, but it didn't actually say so. The phrase used was "staying in the US with her parents". In any event, their defence would be that an action for adultery would succeed, and if one was lodged and decree granted before your case reached the Court of Session we wouldn't have a chance.

'To sum up, if you instruct me I'll lodge a writ for defamation on Monday, but with no great expectation of success. In that case, any short-term benefit which may accrue to you would be lost when you were forced to drop your action and meet defence costs.'

The big policeman sighed. 'So what do you recommend?'

'I will issue a statement on your behalf, saying that your relationship with Miss Masters is private and personal, with no professional overtones, and that it began after you and your wife entered a formal separation agreement. I will say also that I have advised you of the potential for an action for defamation, and that you will consult with me on Monday to determine the course of proceedings.

'That'll put the *Spotlight* thing into some sort of perspective, and it'll make the rest of the media think carefully about carrying on the story.'

Skinner grunted agreement. 'Okay. I know I couldn't be in better hands, Mitch. So you do as you advise. How will you go about it?'

'I'll give the statement to our marketing officer, and tell her to issue it in an hour. We'll say that you have nothing to add to the statement, but you'd better make sure anyway that your force press people are briefed to refer to us all callers who come on looking for you or Pamela. If Alex has my home number, she'll have the marketing lady's as well.'

'Okay,' said Skinner. 'I'll alert everyone. Look, thanks again, Mitch. We'll speak on Monday.'

'Earlier if necessary,' said Laidlaw. 'Incidentally, Bob,' he added. 'I'm very impressed with that daughter of yours. We haven't allocated her to a department as yet, so I think I'll take her into mine.'

Skinner smiled across at Alex, who stood by the window, watching him. 'Be careful about that, mate. She could wind up ruling your life too.'

12

'My goodness, Bob, what a position to find yourself in. Mind you, I have to say – as I'm sure no-one else will have – that you've only got yourself to blame.'

'What for, Jimmy? Not pulling the bedroom curtains?'

Skinner and the Chief Constable were alone in the Proud sitting room. Lady Proud, at her husband's suggestion, had taken Alan Royston to the kitchen, to make coffee. The DCC had watched his commander's face grow increasingly red as he had studied the *Spotlight* exclusive.

'Don't be flip with me, man. You have to know that public figures are always in the spotlight . . . no pun intended.'

The big detective growled. 'But not to that extent, surely.'

'Obviously they are, Bob,' said the Chief, waving the newspaper. 'Much as I regret it, this sort of media behaviour is still legal in this, and in most free countries. However much I might deprecate this man Salmon and his rag, you were there for him to see, and to photograph.

'I have nothing against Sergeant Masters, Bob, but I am very fond of Sarah, as you know, and I am heart sorry to think of her on the other end of this situation.'

'So am I, Jimmy, but at least I've got time to warn her.'

'Confession rather than warning, I think,' said Proud, sadly now. 'Tell me, Bob, why? What did you see in this lass?'

Skinner sat in one of the Chief's big armchairs. 'Have

you ever been lonely, Jimmy?' he asked, then continued, without waiting for an answer. 'Well I have. For about fifteen years, after Myra was killed, I had this big, cold streak inside me. I brought up my daughter, I did my job as hard and as best I could, I socialised with the lads. But always it was there – that big, cold lump that set me apart from the rest.

'I know now what it was. It's called bereavement, and all widowed people carry it around inside them. Some have faith that helps them to handle it, that even lets them draw strength from it. But I lost my wife young, and I never came to terms with the fact. At least not until Sarah came along. When I met her, that coldness began to disappear, until at last, it was gone altogether, and I was really happy again, after half a lifetime.'

He leaned back in the chair. 'Then, out of the blue, it seemed, things went pear-shaped between the two of us, very suddenly and completely unexpectedly. I'd just assumed that we'd be happy ever after.

'It doesn't matter whose fault it was, whether I was wrong or whether she was, or whether, as is most likely, we both were. We had just lost the way. We were broken asunder. And with that, and no doubt with my uncovering the circumstances of Myra's death as well, that big, cold beast of bereavement was back with me.'

He looked up at Proud. 'Loneliness is the only thing in life that really scares me, Jimmy. The prospect of it makes me crazy.

'Fortuitous or whatever, Pam was there for me when I needed her most, to help me fight off my fear. I believe that everything I've done since then has been proper, except that I chose to be secretive about it. I should have told my family, I should have come clean with Sarah when I saw her in May, and I should have taken you into my confidence.

'For all of that, I apologise to you.' He stopped.

'First time in my life I've ever had to say that to you, and it'll be the last. Like Pam said to me, it's a bugger when you discover you ain't the person you thought you were.'

The gruff old Chief Constable stood over him. 'Apology accepted, son,' he said, and sat down, facing Skinner. 'Don't be too hard on yourself.

'Now' he muttered, grimly, 'what are we going to do about this bloody man Salmon?'

'That's the point at which I have to leave you to make your own decisions, sir. If nothing else, I have caused embarrassment to the force. It's for you to determine your course of action without input from me. That's why I've brought Royston with me.

'He'll brief you on the questions that are likely to come up, and advise you on the shape of your responses. The content is up to you. If you want to suspend me forthwith, I'll respect that and make no public reaction myself.'

'Hah!' the Chief roared. 'Suspend you! Do you think I'd let a wipearse like Salmon, and his paper, deprive this city of its finest police officer? I'm going to stand by you, just as you've always stood by everyone under your command.'

The silver-haired Sir James paused, and his expression became serious once more. 'There is one thing, though, of which we should both be conscious. We have a new government in power, elected on the crest of a wave of concern about probity in public life. Its party members are in the ruling majority on the Joint Police Board.

'The one area in this job where I'm still ahead of you, Bob, is in the politics of it. For you they don't exist, but believe me, they do. I can hold the Chair of the Board in line, but some of the members, as you've seen for yourself, are unpredictable. A few are downright anti-polis! We even know of a couple with criminal records.'

Proud rose, walked over to Skinner and laid a hand on his shoulder. 'I have friends in the Scottish media that even you don't know about. Most of the press won't run with this story. Unless, that is, the Board gives them no option. I'll do my best on that score, I promise.

'Now, let's see what advice Master Royston has to give me.'

13

There was a long silence at the other end of the line. 'Let me get this straight,' said Sarah at last, her New York tones more drawn-out than ever. 'You're telling me that you're having an affair, and that because of it, our lives, our child, and the state of our marriage are going to be all over the gutter press.'

'I can't soften it, love,' said Bob. 'That's what's happened.'

'This woman, the Pamela creature. Were you screwing her before you visited with Jazz and me in May?'

'Yes. I'm sorry: I should have told you back then.'

A snort bounced off the satellite, and crossed the Atlantic. 'Oh no you shouldn't! With my folks around, while you were under their roof! That would not have been the time to tell me I'd been traded in for a younger model.'

'Pam's older, actually,' said Bob, automatically, cursing himself at once. 'Oh darlin', I'm sorry. Listen it's not like that. My world was upside-down at the time. I'm not making excuses, but it just happened.'

'What?' There was a hitch in Sarah's voice, the sound of a suppressed sob. 'You just fell in love with another woman, with the ink barely dry on our separation?'

'No!' he protested. 'Listen . . .'

'Shut up for a minute, Bob, please. Let me get my head round this a piece at a time.' She paused, and he could hear her fight to calm her breathing, to calm herself.

'That explains the phone call, anyway,' she said finally, in an even tone.

'What phone call?'

'This afternoon. I had a call from a guy in Scotland. He said his name was Salmon. He said that he was researching for a series on your career, and that he needed medical background on some of your investigations. He asked if he could come to Buffalo to visit me.

'I thought it was a little odd, but I said okay, if he was prepared to pay the airfare, then I was prepared to see him next Tuesday. I take it that . . .'

'Yes,' muttered Bob, grimly. 'He's the shit who broke the story.'

'And he expects still to be alive next Tuesday,' Sarah responded, with a faint hint of mockery.

'Andy was going to lock him up. The trouble was he hadn't broken any laws. Pam may be able to sue him, but that's it.'

'Pam may be able . . .! What, you mean she isn't a man-grabbing little opportunist?' Her voice rose once more.

'No,' said her husband quietly. 'She isn't.'

'Okay,' said Sarah, more calmly. 'I'm sorry. I shouldn't have got down to that level. What does this man Salmon want?'

'Some photos of the wronged wife and baby, I guess. Plus confirmation from you that I'm a shit and that you can't wait to divorce me.'

'None of that sounds too tough,' said Sarah.

'So you'll see him?'

There was another snort, with a laugh in it this time. 'Like hell I will! Do you think for one moment that I'd involve myself, or my baby, with a rag like that? I've seen the US *Spotlight*, and I can think of half-a-dozen congressmen who're trying to have it banned. If you can get word to this guy, let him know that if he sets foot on my dad's doorstep, he'll have him arrested. And in this city, my dad could probably do that!'

'I'll have Royston pass that message on,' said Bob.

'Sarah,' he went on, strangely hesitant. 'I have to ask you this. Do you intend to divorce me?'

He heard her gasp slightly. She was silent for several expensive transatlantic seconds, until finally she responded, very quietly. 'Do you want me to?'

'I've no right to expect otherwise.'

'But is it what you want?'

This time it was Bob's turn to fall silent. 'No,' he said, at last. 'Ask me now and the answer's no.'

'Do you and Pamela love each other? Like does she want to have your babies?'

Another pause. 'No. I don't think we do. I don't think she does. We've avoided discussing anything so heavy.'

'Then get yourselves sorted out. I'll give you three months. If, after that, you're no longer involved with this woman, and you tell me that you love me and want me back, I'll decide how I feel. If you can't make me believe all that, I'll know it's over.'

'Don't we have to say those things to each other?' he asked.

She chuckled, and in his mind's eye he could see her shake her head. 'Not from where I'm standing, we don't.'

The big policeman, alone in his sitting room, heaved a sigh and nodded. 'Okay. That's how it'll be.

'Before I hang up, can I speak to Jazz.'

'He's out with Granddad, I'm afraid.'

'Okay.' He was about to say goodbye, when something struck him. 'Sarah, one thing you should look out for. This bastard Salmon isn't going to like it when we blow him

64

out. Be careful that he doesn't try any *Candid Camera* stuff on you.'

'Okay, but how could he?'

'Well . . .' Skinner gulped, and took the plunge. 'If you were seeing anyone, however innocently . . .'

'As opposed to guiltily, you mean?'

'Aye, okay . . .' he grunted.

There was a pause at the other end of the line. 'Well . . . I have had a few dinner dates with a single guy around my own age, on the medical staff at my hospital. Dinner dates, though, that's all.'

He felt a tug in the pit of his stomach. 'So you haven't . . .'

'No I have not!' she cried. 'Sure, the thought has crossed my mind: I'm as human as you, but maybe just a bit more restrained. The invitation's been extended, too, in a very gentlemanly, diplomatic fashion. Till now, I've thanked him, but declined, as a lady should. After this, though, you can work out for yourself how I'm likely to respond.

'However, my dear, there's one thing that I will promise you.'

'What's that?'

'When I do decide to let Terry and me enjoy the good honest fuck to which he's probably entitled, and which I *undoubtedly* deserve, I'll make bloody sure that the drapes are drawn tight!'

The sound of a phone being slammed down crashed in his ear.

14

Skinner sat on the edge of the couch in the curtained living room in Gullane, drawing listlessly on a bottle of Beck's. It was just after ten thirty.

'Sarah gave you a hard time, did she?' asked Pamela. 'Come on, tell me about it. You've been silent as the grave on the subject.' It was true. Skinner had eaten before picking her up from the Leith apartment, principally to allow him to recover from his conversation with his wife.

As they had driven to East Lothian – having decided to ignore any paparazzi who might be on their trail next day – he had told her of his instruction of Mitchell Laidlaw, and of his conversation with the Chief Constable. From the cottage, he had made phone calls to Royston, and to Alex to confirm that both the force and the solicitor's spokeswoman had been bombarded with press enquiries since the *Spotlight* story had broken.

But he had said nothing at all until then of his telephone call to Sarah, or of her reaction. 'What is it?' asked Pamela once more. 'Has she asked for a divorce?'

He took another swig of his beer. 'She's stopped short of that, but let's say she's reserved her position.'

'Did you ask her if she has someone else?'

Pamela's eagerness irked him. 'Yes. And she has. Platonic so far, but I've driven her into his bed, I'm sure.'

'What makes you think that?'

'Christ, she more or less told me so! Anyway, you've

been in her place. How did you react when you found out about David?'

She pouted. 'Just hold on! David was living with me when he had his affairs, so the situation isn't the same. I certainly didn't respond in kind: not for a while, at least. It was almost two years before I fancied anyone else.

'We're dodging an issue though. If you're jealous of Sarah's new man, real or not, I don't like that. In fact you can either get over it, or do without me. Which would you prefer?'

Bob laid the beer on the floor and took her by the hand. 'Calm down, Pammy. It's just that I'm an old Presbyterian at heart. I'll get over it.'

'Take me to bed, then,' she said, teasingly, reaching for the buttons of his shirt.

'I might consider it,' he said, managing a weak smile, but feeling a pang of doubt inside. Just in time the ring of the telephone took him off the hook.

'Sod it,' he said, reaching across to pick it up.

'Good evening, Mr Skinner,' said a smug voice, raised slightly over a background of conversation. 'I hope you enjoy your weekend reading. If you switch on the telly at eleven o'clock, I think you'll find that *Sky News* give you a good show too.'

'Salmon, you little cunt,' the policeman snarled. 'How did you get this number?'

'I have friends. Despite what your lawyer said, I felt I had to give you the chance of coming clean for my readers. Can they expect your resignation within the week?'

'You can expect my hand on your collar, you slimy wee toad,' Skinner exploded. 'Plus, we're going to sue you till your fucking eyes pop. You can forget going to see my wife too. She has nothing to say to you, and if you push your luck over there, I have friends in the FBI who'll slam you right inside.'

'Nice one, Bob,' said Salmon, with a disturbingly calm assurance. 'I've got that all noted down, and, it'll read well in next week's *Spotlight*. You and Pamela have a nice night, now. But think on this: I haven't finished with you yet – not by a long way.'

As the call ended, Skinner hurled the phone across the room, tearing the flex from its socket and smashing it against the wall. He turned to Pam, who sat shocked and drawn. 'He got my number!' he said, incredulously. 'I'm on the MI5 network, yet he got my ex-directory number. Some shit sold it to him.'

She stood up and held him to her, feeling him tremble with rage. 'Control yourself, love,' she said. 'Every point that nasty little man adds to your blood pressure is a victory for him. Remember the rule. Don't get mad, get even.'

He shook his head. 'I've never been any good at that. Some guys, like Andy, can count up to ten, and by the time they get there they've cooled down. I've never made it past three.' Nevertheless, his breathing did begin to steady as she drew his face down to hers and kissed him, and as she stroked his hair.

'That's better,' she whispered, with a smile. 'Forget Salmon, and come with me. Come on. I drew the curtains earlier, but we'll keep the light out as well, just to be safe!'

Gradually his expression softened, until finally he allowed himself to be led through to the bedroom. Slowly she undressed him in the dark, peeling off her own clothes more quickly, and climbing on top of him as he lay on the duvet. He felt her tongue in his mouth, flicking, seeking his; then it moved, as she did. He felt it lick its way along his chest, playing lightly with its curly hairs; felt her lips move on him kissing, puckering, felt himself growing huge as she made her steady way down, until . . .

The only functional telephone in the cottage seemed to scream at the night a few feet from his ear. 'No!' It was Pam's turn to shout her frustration. 'If that's him again . . .'

'Then he's a goner,' said Skinner, quite seriously.

He picked up the phone. 'Now listen, you,' he began in a deadly tone.

'Good evening, Mr Skinner.' The voice cut across his: not Salmon, another man; a quiet, even and controlled tone, without accent.

'Who . . .'

'I have the child. He is alive, but at my disposition. You will hear from me again.'

For the second time that evening a phone line went dead, leaving Skinner staring ahead into darkness.

15

'British Telecom couldn't help, then, Andy, I take it?'

Martin shook his head. He and Skinner sat grim-faced at the kitchen table in the cottage, china mugs of coffee steaming before them. It was twenty-five minutes past midnight, and the Head of CID had just arrived from Edinburgh, leaving Alex alone in the Haymarket flat.

From the living room, the faint sound of the television carried through, as Pamela watched, for the fourth or fifth time, a video of the carefully worded *Sky News* précis of Noel Salmon's *Spotlight* exclusive.

'They did their best, of course, Bob, but without exceptional luck – such as the guy forgetting to disable 1471 – or advance warning, there wasn't much chance that they'd be able to trace the origin of the call.'

Skinner grunted. 'Come on, Andy, d'you think that I didn't try the automatic number trace? "You were called today at . . .",' he mimicked. ' "The caller withheld his number." '

Martin glanced at him. 'Maybe he used a payphone. Did you hear coins drop?'

'No, but that's not a give-away any more. They did away with "Press button A" years ago, on most of them.'

The younger man raised an eyebrow. 'Hey, maybe he used a credit card.'

Skinner glowered across the table. 'Andy, son, I know it's past midnight, and that we're clutching at some very short straws, but really . . .'

Martin sipped his coffee. 'Miracles happen.'

'No they bloody don't!' Skinner slapped the table, gently. 'Look, it's been a mind-fucker of a night, but let's get a grip of ourselves and start thinking and acting like the serious coppers we are.

'I asked you out here so that the two of us could have a brainstorm, before we call in the Cavalry, so let's get on with it.'

'Can I join in too?' asked Pamela from the doorway. 'Or is this for General Staff only.'

Bob grinned at her, as she leaned against the jamb wearing a teeshirt and his long towelling bathrobe. 'Aye, come on in, Sergeant, even though you're out of uniform.'

She looked at him in football top and shorts, then at Martin, in denims, raised her eyebrows in a gesture which said 'Oh yes?', then joined them at the table.

'Right,' said Skinner. 'There are all sorts of potential implications which we can draw from this call. Let's see if we can nail them all down.'

'A question first, surely,' Pamela interrupted. 'Was the call genuine? Could it have been a crank?'

'That's possible. But if it was a crank, bear in mind that the call was made to an ex-directory number. That means that the perpetrator is either one of my inner circle, with access to that number, or he's gone to some trouble, and possibly some risk, to get it.

'No,' he said, emphatically, 'I've no doubt that the call was genuine. Anyway we have to assume that it was, until we know otherwise. So okay, not a hoax. Next?'

'Why to you?' asked Martin. 'Why did the guy give a personal message to you? I've been the front man in this investigation all along? You've never been involved publicly.'

Skinner nodded. 'Good one. Ideas? Pam?'

She hesitated. 'Well, you are pretty well known. Think police, think Edinburgh, think Bob Skinner. It could be no more than that, except . . .'

'. . . except,' said Martin, 'that it's public knowledge that you have a special connection with this child. After the Lammermuirs air disaster, when wee Mark was the only survivor – which proves incidentally,' he interjected, triumphantly, 'that miracles *do* happen – it was you who rescued him from the sinking cockpit of the plane, in the middle of a reservoir.

'That was all over the papers at the time. Everybody knows about you saving that wee boy's life.'

'So?'

'So . . . It could explain why the kidnapper would choose to make contact with you.'

Skinner smiled, and his eyes narrowed. 'And could it explain why he took the child?'

Martin stared at him. 'You mean, could he have taken the child as an act of revenge against you?'

'Well? Could he? You'll concede I've made a few potential enemies over the years.'

Martin nodded. 'Even leaving out the ghosts of the dead ones.'

'Okay, suppose someone wants to hurt me,' the DCC went on. 'What are his choices?

'He could come at me in person. But maybe he lacks the physical capability, the resources, or just the bottle for that. He could target my daughter. But she lives with you, and you're as dangerous a customer as I am. He could target my wife and son. But they're a long way off, in the States.

'So, how does he do something that's going to hurt me

72

to the heart?' Skinner paused. 'Maybe, just maybe, he remembers last year's publicity; he remembers the bond between me and wee Mark, and he says, "That's the way." So he keeps Leona's house under observation; he traces her movements; he waits, and he waits; he picks his time, and he kidnaps Mark. Not Skinner's son, but a surrogate.'

Pamela touched his arm. 'But why kill the mother?'

He turned and looked at her. 'Not Sarah, but a surrogate,' he said, quietly, then paused. 'What do you think of the proposition, Chief Superintendent? Sergeant?'

Martin frowned, then rose from the table. 'Let me think about it for a minute,' he said, moving towards the living room. 'Pam,' he smiled over his shoulder. 'How about some more coffee? You are on my staff, after all.'

'Yes sir,' she said smartly, as Skinner followed his friend out of the kitchen.

In the other room, Martin was waiting, his smile gone. 'Bob, I accept your theory. Not as a main line of investigation, perhaps, but as a credible scenario. However, should you be right, have you thought of another implication which flows from it?'

'What's that?'

The younger man paused. 'The proposition that Leona might have been attacked instead of Sarah. After this weekend's publicity, if that is true, the killer has a new target.' He jerked a thumb towards the kitchen.

Skinner's face darkened. 'Whistling Christ, Andy, you're right!' He nodded, absently, to himself. 'From now on, she'd better not leave my side.' And then, like sunlight over a field as a cloud blows away, his expression changed as a new thought came to him.

'Unless,' he said, his voice rising. 'He's already using Pam to hurt me. Think of it. For the past few months she's hardly been out of my sight while we've been off duty, or out of yours while she's been at work. In reality, that would make her an even tougher target than Sarah or Alex. But suppose, my enemy's been watching me, he's seen the two of us together, and made the connection.'

'Yes,' said Martin, comprehending, racing alongside Skinner's thinking. 'We know all about Salmon and his story, but we don't know his source. Suppose the kidnapper tipped off Salmon, put him on your trail.'

'That figures, Andy. The wee bastard's never had a decent exclusive of his own before. He could even have used it to land his job on the *Spotlight*.'

'And something else,' added the Chief Superintendent. 'Salmon called you tonight, and so did the kidnapper; both on your ex-directory number. Is it possible that the kidnapper gave Salmon the number?'

It had become a game now, one they had often played before, chasing an idea, worrying at it, throwing in possibilities, adding tints and colours until a picture emerged. Skinner beamed. 'Or did Salmon give it to him,' he asked, 'even without knowing why he would use it?'

His friend shook his head. 'Don't let's stop there, Bob? Let's give that slimeball the benefit of no doubt at all. Or did Salmon know why he would use it?'

'I couldn't believe that,' said Skinner, doubtfully, 'not even of him.'

'Neither do I,' said Martin, as Pamela came into the room carrying a cafetière, 'but it gives us all the reason we need, and more, to arrest the wee bastard. And in the process to leak – accidentally of course – the name of the man who's assisting us with our investigation of a murder and kidnap.'

Bob threw back his big grey-mopped head and laughed,

heartily, for what seemed to each of the others to be the first time in an age. 'Oh yes,' he chuckled. 'I'm going to love that. Especially when I play my tape back to him.'

Andy and Pamela stared at him. 'What tape?' asked Martin.

'Something even you didn't know, mate ... and, incidentally, which the pair of you still don't know, even after tonight.

'It's an open secret now that, as the Secretary of State's security adviser, I'm part of MI5. But the fact that all MI5 officers' home phones are tapped: that's a very closed secret indeed!'

He punched Martin gently on the shoulder. 'Let's nick him, pal. I suggest that you have McGuire do it: he's hard enough to frighten stone, and besides, being lifted by Special Branch always concentrates the mind.' He smiled, as an afterthought came to him. 'Tell Mario to take McIlhenney with him, just for added effect.

'Have them pick him up, tomorrow morning, over breakfast. Then you and McGuire chew him around good and proper. Lean on him, pressure him for the name of the person who gave him my unlisted number. Let him think we're after him for bribery; don't tell him about the kidnapper's call.

'I want to spring that on him myself. After an hour or two, I'll come in and play my tape. I can't wait to see the look on his face when I ask him to convince us that he isn't in cahoots with a killer.'

Martin nodded. 'Okay, save for one thing. I don't think it would be wise – or even proper – for you to take part in any interview with Salmon. You've got a personal involvement with him and a very public grudge against him. I'll play your tape to him, don't worry about that.'

The big DCC grunted. 'Yes, I suppose you're right. It's a pity though. I really want to see that wee sod piss his pants.'

16

The building in which Salmon's flat was located was a dingy affair, in a part of Leith which seemed to have escaped the process of yuppification by which much of the old port has been transformed. The door to the street was unsecured and the wide, dusty stairway smelled strongly of urine.

'Jesus Christ, Mario,' muttered McIlhenney. 'Places like this make a case for more public lavvies.'

Mario McGuire shook his dark Latin head. 'People who pish up closes will always pish up closes, you know that.' He paused, and grinned. 'What happened to the "sir" by the way?'

'Fuck off, Inspector. That's for when there are people around. Don't let this SB stuff go to your head. I suppose you call your wife "ma'am" all the time, eh?'

'What else would I call a senior officer? You know DCI Rose: she's a stickler for formality. "Excuse me, ma'am, would you please pass the marmalade." That's normal across our breakfast table. Or "Excuse me, ma'am, is there any chance of a shag?" That's for after dinner.'

The big sergeant chuckled. 'It's lucky you're not in Admin, then, or you'd have to fill out a requisition.'

'Aye,' said McGuire, laughing himself. 'Another fuckin' chitty!'

'Married life's agreeing with you, then?' said McIlhenney, as they climbed the dirty stairs, away from the rankness of the street level.

'To my slight surprise, it is. I'll tell you, as an old pal, I was a wee bit scared when we tied the knot. The Italian side of my lineage isn't big on divorce. I needn't have worried though. Mags is one in a million.

'We're a couple of lucky bastards, you and I, Neil. All those fish in the sea yet I land her, and you land Olive; exceptional women both of them.'

The Sergeant nodded thoughtfully. 'It's true what you say; about my Olive too,' he said at last. 'Exceptional. Out of every million fish or so, you can expect to find a Great White Shark.'

'Aw come on, Neil,' McGuire protested. 'You can kid the rest of them, but not me. I remember those Sunday lunches Olive used to cook for me when I was young, free and single. And I remember she had you eating them out of her hand.'

McIlhenney shrugged his shoulders and smiled, sheepishly. 'Fair enough,' he chuckled, 'but don't tell anyone else, okay. I've got her image to protect, ken.'

In the seconds of silence which followed, as they climbed past the second floor, scanning the nameplate on each door, his smile faded. 'It's a shame about the Big Man though, Mario, isn't it?' he said at last.

'Depends what you mean,' replied McGuire. 'I know a few guys would give their back teeth to be banging Pam Masters. It's a shame about them being all over the papers though . . .

'As this guy Salmon's going to find out,' he added, grimly.

'No,' countered the Sergeant. 'I mean it's a shame about him and Sarah. I thought that pair were set for life. I just can't imagine what happened to split them up.'

'Him bangin' Pam Masters could have had just a wee bit to do with it!'

'Maybe now it could, but I'm pretty certain that didn't start till after they separated. There was some other reason for him moving out when he did. Don't know what it was, though.'

McGuire drew a deep breath as they reached the fourth, and top, floor of the tenement building. 'Did you know about him and Masters?' he asked at last.

'I suspected. Being his PA and all, I picked up the odd hint.'

'What's she like? I don't really know her.'

McIlheney shrugged again. 'Pam? She's okay. She's bright, although I wouldn't put her in Maggie's league. She's efficient too. I know that, having taken over from her. It's just . . . Och, she's no Sarah, that's all.' He glanced at his colleague. 'What does Maggie think of her? She worked for her for a while, didn't she?'

McGuire nodded. 'She hasn't said much. I just get the impression that she doesn't think she's a real copper – know what I mean? Mags isn't too struck on late entrants to the force. She definitely doesn't approve of her and the boss, though. I can tell you that. When she saw the paper this morning, she'd a face like thunder.'

The Sergeant winced. 'A few folk'll think that way, I fear. Tell you what I think, Mario. It's the first wrong move I've ever known Big Bob make.'

He glanced across the landing, lit by a glass cupola above, to a mauve-painted door. 'There,' he said, pointing. 'Salmon. That's the boy's flat.' He looked at McGuire once again. 'Quiet or noisy?' he asked.

The black-haired policeman grinned, wickedly. 'What do you think? Let's give the neighbours something to talk about!'

He stepped up to the door and pounded on its wooden

panel with the side of his heavy fist. 'Police,' he roared. 'Open up!'

McIlhenney leaned against the door, listening. 'He's switched the tranny off.' The two policemen stood, waiting.

After almost a minute, the Inspector thumped the door again. 'Come on! Open up or we'll kick it in.'

The Sergeant pressed his ear to the panel once more. 'He's coming,' he said, suddenly leaning back.

They heard the rattle of a security chain being slipped, then a key turned in the lock, and the mauve door swung open.

'What d'youse . . .' The words died in the woman's throat as she stared at McIlhenney, in recognition. She was tall and blonde, in her mid-thirties. Her face was not unattractive, but bony, and the lines around the eyes had been carved not by laughter but by life. Her hair was dishevelled, and her make-up only a memory of the night before. As she looked at McIlhenney, her right hand rose involuntarily, clutching the long teeshirt which she wore and pulling it up, in the process, to the edge of immodesty.

'Oh, no,' she said, in a resigned tone. 'No' you again.'

'Well, well, well,' said the Sergeant. 'If it isn't Joanne Virtue, lady of the night. The Big Easy herself. And what, my good woman, would you be doing here?'

The blonde struggled to recover her composure. Belligerence flickered in her eyes. 'Ah live here,' she said, with an attempt at boldness.

'Like fuck you do, Joanne,' said McIlhenney, patiently. 'You live down by the waterfront, as you and I both know. Now go and tell Mr Salmon that – like you – the polis await his pleasure.'

'Who's Mr Salmon?'

'Your punter,' said McGuire.

'Aw. Is that his name? He just telt me it was Noel.'

McIlhenney's patience, a scarce and fragile commodity at the best of times, ran out. 'Bugger this for a game of soldiers,' he said, marching past the prostitute and into the flat.

'Salmon! Where are you?' he bellowed, throwing open the nearest door, to the right off the hallway. He looked quickly into an untidy, stale-smelling bedroom. A black dress, bra and tights were thrown over a chair and men's clothing lay strewn across the floor, but the room was empty.

The big detective looked over his shoulder at Joanne Virtue. She shrugged her shoulders and pointed, briefly, at a door on the other side of the hall. McIlhenney nodded, and with a grim smile, stepped across and threw it open.

A naked man stood, with his back to him, bent over the toilet bowl, pumping at the handle as if that would make the cistern refill faster. 'Whatever you're doing, Salmon,' said Mario McGuire from the doorway, 'stop it right now!'

The man turned and looked at the two policemen, then grabbed a towel and fastened it round his middle. 'What do you want?' he shouted, his face contorted with a mixture of fear and frustration. 'What do you think you're doing? You've no right!'

McGuire smiled. 'We're here to see you, Mr Salmon, in connection with a potential security leak, which we have reason to believe may involve the corrupt obtaining of an unlisted telephone number. As for our entering your premises, Miss Virtue invited us.' He looked over his shoulder at the woman. 'That's right, isn't it?'

Joanne Virtue nodded, avoiding Salmon's glare.

'You having trouble wi' your bog, Noel?' asked McIlhenney. 'Isn't it flushing properly?'

He stepped across the small bathroom and peered into the toilet bowl, with an expression of distaste. 'There's nothing I dislike more than skidmarks in the lavvie,' he said. 'You're a dirty wee bastard, aren't you . . . in every respect.'

His eyes narrowed, and he shook his head. 'That's pretty pathetic, chuckin' talcum powder down it to freshen it up.

'It is talcum powder, isn't it?'

Oblivious of his covering towel, as it unfastened and fell to the floor, Salmon spun round and grabbed the handle of the cistern. But before he could twist it to flush, McIlhenney seized his wrist in a grip like a vice. 'Let go,' he said, in an even tone, 'or I'll break your fucking hand off.'

The man, white-faced, released the handle. The sergeant spun him around and propelled him out of the bathroom and through to the bedroom. 'Get dressed, friend; we can hardly take you out like that.'

'Noel Salmon,' said McGuire, 'I am arresting you on suspicion of being in possession of a controlled substance. You do not have to say anything . . .' He administered the rest of the formal caution in a stiff, formal tone, speaking clearly and ensuring that he was word perfect, in the form the law required.

Reaching for his underwear, the journalist looked up at him. 'This is a fucking fit-up,' he shouted, almost in tears.

'No, mate,' the Inspector replied. 'It's just your unlucky day, that's all.' He turned to McIlhenney, who was holding Joanne Virtue by the left arm, gently but securely. 'Neil, call Fettes for a team of technicians. We'll need to find out what that talc really is. Tell them to get a formal search warrant too: we'd better take the place apart just in case Mr Salmon has any other goodies hidden away.'

The Sergeant nodded. 'Very good, sir,' he said with a

grin. 'I'll ask for some uniforms to stand guard at the door till they get here. That way we can take these two back to the shop quicker. Wouldn't do to keep Mr Martin waiting.'

'Martin?' Salmon bleated. 'He's behind this?'

'What dae youse mean, take us both back?' Joanne Virtue protested. 'Ah'm an innocent bystander.'

McIlhenney laughed out loud. 'Joanne,' he boomed, 'you haven't been fuckin' innocent for about twenty-five years!'

17

Even before his appointment as Head of CID – indeed, from his days as Bob Skinner's Executive Officer – Detective Chief Superintendent Andy Martin had come to know the Edinburgh press corps well. He had seen them amused; he had seen them bored; he had seen them at their most cynical, and at their most constructive.

But in all that time, he could not recall ever having seen them on the edge of their seats. On his instruction, Alan Royston had called a press briefing, to announce 'an important development in the McGrath case'.

Sunday or not, 10.30 a.m. or not, the conference room was full. As Martin, impassive, sat down at the blue-covered table, facing the cameras, the room fell silent.

'Thank you, ladies and gentlemen,' he began. 'Late yesterday evening, at his home, Deputy Chief Constable Bob Skinner received a telephone call from a man. The caller did not identify himself. He said simply that he had the child and that he was alive. Then he ended the call.

'Our telecommunications experts have been unable to trace the phone from which the call was made, so we have no way of identifying the caller, or of knowing for sure whether the message was genuine. However, we are proceeding on the basis that the anonymous man was indeed the kidnapper. If we take his statement at face value, then Mark McGrath is alive.'

As he paused, a forest of hands shot up. As always, he took John Hunter, the senior journalist, first.

'Andy, did he say anything else?' asked the veteran.

'He said that we would hear from him again, that's all.'

'He made no ransom demand then?'

Martin shook his head. 'None at all. The call lasted seconds, and that's all there was to it.'

From the side of the room a woman, brandishing a television microphone, broke in. 'Did Mr Skinner take the call himself, or was it Ms Masters?'

The detective frowned at her, but answered. 'He took it himself. And his recollection is quite clear. A record was made there and then.'

'Do you have any clue at all about where the call came from?' called a man from the back of the room.

'Not much, I'm afraid. We do know it didn't come from a mobile, and we know that it wasn't international. But other than that, it could have been made from any telephone in the UK.'

'Are you expecting a ransom demand, eventually?' asked John Hunter.

The Head of CID raised his eyebrows. 'It's a possibility. If the man had a reason other than money for abducting the child, there's no indication of it.'

'D'you think you'll find the wee boy alive, Andy?' Hunter sounded weary, as if he had been at too many briefings such as this.

'We can only hope, John. We can only hope. Meantime, every police force in the country is taking part in the search. There are no available resources unused. If this man has any compassion, or any sense, for that matter, he'll simply release Mark. If he doesn't, he'll be hunted down like a rabid animal.'

He looked round the room. 'Ladies and gentlemen, I don't think there's anything I can add, so if you'll excuse me . . .'

The woman with the television mike raised her hand. 'Mr Martin, can you tell us if there are any developments on Mr Skinner's situation?'

The blond detective took a deep breath, and clenched his teeth. 'As you must know, the Chief Constable issued a statement last night, deprecating the conduct of the *Spotlight*, and saying that the DCC's private life was his own business.'

'Well,' she persisted, 'do you or he have any response to the statement issued subsequently by several members of the Police Board saying that they intend to bring the matter up at the next meeting, and to move that Mr Skinner be disciplined?'

'Sorry, lady,' said Martin, evenly and emphatically. 'Mr Royston will deal with your questions from now on. I have to be off. I have business in another part of the building.'

As he strode towards the door, he caught the eye of John Hunter, and nodded, so quickly and unobtrusively that no-one else saw. The old man rose and followed him from the room. Quickly, before any other reporters emerged, Martin ushered him up the short flight of stairs which led to the command corridor.

'I thought you might like to know, old pal,' the detective said, as the door clicked shut behind them. 'We've got Noel Salmon in custody, under investigation for corruption. Also, when we lifted him, the silly wee bugger had in his possession something which I'm sure that tests will prove to be cocaine.'

Hunter whistled. 'What a shame, eh? What's the corruption about?'

'Bob had another call last night on his unlisted phone number, as well as the one from the kidnapper. It was from Noel Salmon. We want to know how he got the number.

Specifically, whether he bunged anyone to give it to him.
And we want to know whether he gave it to anyone else.'

The old reporter was quick on the uptake. 'Jesus wept!'
he whispered. 'You don't think . . .'

18

Joanne Virtue looked up as the door of the interview room opened. In a corner stood a female officer in uniform, staring fixedly at the wall opposite. As Detective Chief Superintendent Martin entered, with Inspector McGuire following behind, she stiffened and came to attention.

'You can leave us, Constable,' said the Head of CID, quietly. The woman nodded and slipped out, closing the door behind her.

'Hello, Jo,' the blond detective began, with a smile. 'Don't take this personally, but I'd hoped I wouldn't see you again.'

The prostitute snorted as he sat down. 'Nobody's forcin' yis tae see me, Mr Martin,' she said, in a heavy Glasgow accent, still hard at the edges despite her years in Edinburgh. 'There's nothin' ah can tell yis about that fella.'

'Let's just see about that. When did you meet him?'

'Last night, in a boozer off Constitution Street.'

'You'd never met him before?'

She shook her head firmly. 'Okay,' said Martin, believing her. He had known the big blonde whore since he was a beat constable, and had a policeman's grudging respect for her as a basically honest working woman.

'What was he doing when you bumped into him?' he asked.

'Waving his wad around. Ah got talkin' tae him and he waved some of it in ma direction.'

'Didn't you think it was a bit risky, going to his place?' asked McGuire.

'Naw. Nae danger. Ah've been on the game long enough tae ken the dodgy ones. Wee whit's his name's hermless.'

The Inspector looked her in the eye. 'Did you do any coke?'

She glanced from McGuire to Martin. 'Don't be daft,' she said. 'Ah'm a tart, no' a dope fiend.'

'Did you see Salmon using?' asked the chief super-intendent.

Joanne nodded. 'Aye. We were hardly in the door before he got out his wee poke and cut himself a line.' She snorted. 'Just as well ah didnae fancy ony. The stingy wee bastard never even offered!'

McGuire leaned across the table. 'Did he tell you anything about himself?'

'Did he no' just! He said he wis a reporter, wi' a big international magazine.'

'Anything else? Anything about his work?'

She looked at the detectives, a little cautiously. 'Aye,' she said at last. 'He kept goin' on about this big story he was workin' on. He said it was about your boss, Mr Skinner, and that once it was all out he'd be out of a job, and more.'

'Give me that exactly, Joanne,' said Martin. 'The actual words he used.'

'That's whit he said, Mr Martin. "He'll be out of a job, and more." And he smiled when he said it, real nasty like. Usually ah don't chat tae the punters, not at all. Ah'm there for copulation, no' conversation. But even so, ah asked him what he meant. He wouldnae tell me though. "Buy my paper for the next couple of weeks and find out." That wis all he'd say.'

'Did he let slip anything else?'

The Big Easy leaned back in her chair, knitting her brows. 'He did say that once it was all done, his source would be very happy.'

'His source. No name?'

She shook her head. 'Naw. And he only said it the once.'

'When did he say all this?'

'Once we got back tae his place.'

'Did he say anything in the pub?'

'No' much.'

'How did you meet him?'

Joanne grinned. 'He came over tae me and started chattin' me up. He thinks he's God's gift, even though he wis at the end o' the queue when the looks were handed out. I let him go on for a bit, then Ah told him that Ah took neither Bullshit nor Barclaycard, and spelled things out for him.'

Martin looked at her. 'I thought you only worked the saunas, Jo.'

She laughed, a short, hard laugh. 'Aye, but Saturday's ma night off! What d'ye think ah do in ma spare time, ori-fuckin'-gami?'

The Chief Superintendent grunted. 'Nothing you do would surprise me, Miss Virtue. Did Salmon do or say anything in the pub?'

'Just before we left, he went off tae make a phone call, but that's all.'

'D'you know how many calls he made?' asked McGuire.

'Just the one. I could see him from where Ah was standing.'

Martin nodded and leaned back. 'Okay, Jo. Nearly finished. There's just one other thing. When Mario banged the door, what happened?'

The woman frowned again, ransacking her memory.

'Well he jumped off me, for a start, and switched off the radio. Then he grabbed his notebook: it's one of those Filofax things. He took something from it, real quick like. After that he picked up what was left of the coke and dived intae the bog.'

'And that's all?'

'Everything,' she said. 'Honest.'

The Chief Superintendent leaned back from the table. 'Aye, Jo, I know you are. Okay, you can go. We'll let you know if we want a formal statement.' He pressed a buzzer on the wall. 'Meanwhile, the WPC outside will see you out. D'you want a lift back to Leith?'

She drew him a frosty look. 'Me! Going hame in a polis car! That'll be the day.' She stood up picked up her red plastic handbag, smoothed her dress, and strode from the room.

'Well,' muttered Martin, as the door closed behind her. 'That was interesting.' He looked round at McGuire. 'You sure there was no scrap of paper floating in the bog when Neil looked at it?'

'Ask him, sir, but you know big McIlhenney. He wouldn't have missed it if there had been.'

'Mmm. That's what I thought. So Mr Salmon was even more interested in flushing that page from his notebook down the toilet than he was in disposing of his cocaine. Why d'you think it was so important, Mario, eh?'

'Maybe it was the name of his source, sir.'

'That, or a phone number. It's too damn bad. That piece of evidence will be out at sea by now! We'll just have to see if we can frighten it out of him.'

19

'No! I won't tell you who my source is. The first rule of reputable journalism is to protect the integrity of your informants.'

'Salmon,' said Andy Martin, shaking his head in disbelief. 'You could barely spell "reputable".

'Okay,' he went on, 'let's try another tack. Last night you called Mr Skinner. Agreed?'

The man shook his head, dark stubble showing on his chin. 'No. I agree nothing.'

'Have it your way, chum,' retorted Martin. 'We know you did.'

Noel Salmon scowled. 'What's the point of all this anyway? I've been here for nearly four hours already, waiting for you lot. I want to go home.'

'The point . . .' said the Head of CID, pausing and looking hard across the table, '. . . the point is that Mr Skinner's number, like all his telephone numbers, like mine, like Inspector McGuire's, is ex-directory. We don't like the thought of people – especially people like you – having open access to them, and we want to know who gave DCC Skinner's to you.'

He glanced at the tape recorder, at the side of the table, its red record light shining in the dim interview room. 'Now, I ask you, formally. How did you come by Mr Skinner's unlisted number, at his Gullane address?'

Salmon looked up at him from behind furrowed brows. 'I can't remember.'

'Oh, come on. You have the Deputy Chief Constable's ex-directory number in your possession and you can't remember how you got it! Who gave it to you!'

'I can't remember.'

'We don't believe you, Mr Salmon.'

'Tough!'

'That could be,' said Martin, quietly. 'Let's get this straight. You recall very clearly who gave you that number, but you don't intend to tell us. That's the truth of it, isn't it?'

'Have it your way.'

'We will. Did you pay someone to give it to you?'

'No.'

The DCS paused. 'Think carefully about that answer. If we find out later that you did, it'll go hard for you.'

Salmon paled slightly, wringing his hands together. 'Look, I didn't pay anyone for the number, okay. It was given to me.'

'By the same person who gave you the information on Mr Skinner on which your story in the *Spotlight* is based?'

The little reporter opened his mouth to speak, then clamped it shut.

'Mr Salmon refuses to answer,' said Martin in an aside to the tape. He glanced at McGuire. 'But let's make the assumption that the sources are one and the same. I ask you again, who was your informant?'

Salmon stared down at the table. 'Nothing to say. Can I go now?'

'No, sir, you may not. In case you've forgotten, you're being held on suspicion of being in possession of a Class A drug.'

'Aw come on,' the man whined, 'a wee bit of coke!'

Almost as soon as the words left his mouth he turned and stared at the tape.

Martin smiled. 'That's right, Noel.' He nodded. 'A wee bit of cocaine . . . but enough to land you in front of the Sheriff. How do you think your many friends in the media will handle your court appearance? D'you think they won't report it because you're one of their number? I don't think so.'

The detective paused for a second. 'And what about your new employers at the *Spotlight*?' he continued. 'I've been reading some back numbers. Know what your magazine's official policy is? That all drug traffickers should be executed, and that all users should get five years. Do you think you'll be working for them after you're convicted for possession? Do you think you'll be working for anyone?

'All I have to do is file a report to the Fiscal, and professionally you're a goner.'

He paused again. 'Of course, if you were to tell me who gave you Bob Skinner's ex-directory number, maybe I'd think twice about it.'

For the first time, a trace of desperation showed in Noel Salmon's expression. He chewed his lip for a second or two, weighing up his options. Finally he sighed. 'I don't know who my source is,' he said. It was almost a moan.

'Sure you don't,' said Martin, easily.

'It's the truth,' the man protested. 'I had a letter, a few weeks back. It was anonymous. All it said was that if I kept an eye on Skinner, I'd find that he was straying from the straight and narrow. I thought it was crap at first, but just for fun – and because I hate the big bastard – I followed him. It didn't take me long to find out about the Masters bird.

'She was staying at his place in Gullane most nights.

94

When they weren't there, they were at hers. I kept an eye on them, looking for some juicy pictures to back up the story. Eventually I got them. Juicy was hardly the word – him in the buff, and her bent over him like she was sucking his cock.'

Suddenly Martin was grim-faced. 'This anonymous tipster. Ever had anything from him before?'

Salmon shook his head. 'Not that I know of.'

'What did you do with the letter?'

'I binned it, long ago.'

'So what was the piece of paper you were so keen to get rid of when I thumped on your door?' asked McGuire.

The man's eyebrows narrowed for a second. 'Ah, the tart told you that, did she?' he said. 'That had nothing to do with Skinner.'

'So what was it?'

Salmon shook his head. 'Nothing to say.' A gleam came into his eye, developing quickly into a smile. 'Did the tart tell you it was her coke?'

Martin laughed; short, sharp and hard. 'No, she did not. She said it was yours, as we both know it was.'

The little man spread his palms wide. 'And I say that it was hers; that she brought it into my flat and offered me some before we had it off. I refused, of course.'

The Head of CID sighed. 'And you'll say that when Mario thumped your door you panicked and flushed it down the bog.'

Salmon nodded. 'That's right. So charge me. I'll plead not guilty; she'll tell her story and I'll tell mine. Is a jury going to convict me on the word of a prostitute?'

The reporter was recovering his confidence rapidly – and, as Martin knew, with justification. His scenario had a loud ring of credibility about it.

'So,' said the dishevelled little man. 'Can I go now?'

'Oh no,' replied the blond detective. 'Not so easily. Besides, there's a tape I want you to hear.'

'What sort of tape?'

'In a minute. Let's go back to Mr Skinner's phone number. Was that included in your anonymous note?'

'I'm not saying any more about that.'

'We'll see.' Martin reached into the pocket of his jacket and took out a small tape player. He pressed the 'play' button. A few seconds later, Salmon heard his own voice, echoing from the speaker with a metallic tone. The two policemen gazed at him, as he sat back in his chair, surprised and slightly shocked.

'*But think on this: I haven't finished with you yet – not by a long way.*' As the recorded conversation ended with a click, McGuire reached across and switched off the tape.

'How did . . .' Salmon began.

'Work it out for yourself,' said Martin. 'Did it never occur to you that it was a bit dangerous to call a senior police officer on an unlisted number and to make threats.'

'What d'you mean, threats?'

'What else would you call that last comment of yours?' The policeman paused. 'But wait. There's more. A few minutes after you phoned him, Mr Skinner received another call on his unlisted number. If you'd been at our press briefing this morning, instead of being banged up in here, you'd know about it already.' He switched on the tape once more.

'*I have the child. He is alive, but at my disposition. You will hear from me again.*'

Salmon sat bolt upright in his seat at the sound of the smooth, controlled voice. His eyes widened. 'Was that . . .?'

'The man who murdered Leona McGrath, and kidnapped

her son? We have to believe that it is. Which throws up a pretty big coincidence. Two men, in possession of a very confidential telephone number, using it within minutes of each other.'

Martin leaned forward, his forearms on the table. Suddenly, although his expression was as affable as ever, there was an air of menace about him.

'Now, Salmon,' he said, in a clear, formal voice, 'do you know that man? Did you give him Mr Skinner's number or did he give it to you?'

The dishevelled reporter gulped, fear showing in his eyes. 'I've no idea who he is,' he protested. 'No, I didn't give him Skinner's number! No, I didn't get it from him!'

'How did you get it, then? No more bullshit, friend. You are in very dangerous waters, and way out of your depth.'

Noel Salmon slumped back in his seat. 'It was in the second message,' he whispered.

'What second message?'

'I got it last week. It was anonymous, like the other one.'

Andy Martin fixed his green eyes on the man. 'So how do you know that it didn't come from the man we've just heard on that tape?' he asked, in an even tone.

His quarry looked down at the scratched tabletop. 'I don't,' he muttered helplessly.

'No, you don't, do you? Not if you're telling the truth, you don't. For if we believed that you were lying to us, in any way, we'd have to look at the possibility that you were this man's accomplice.'

'Wait a minute . . .'

'So prove yourself to us. Let us see the second letter.'

'I can't,' said Salmon, plaintively. 'That was what I flushed down the toilet.'

The detective whistled. 'I see. You are in deep shit, aren't you?'

'Appropriate, in the circumstances,' said McGuire, beside him.

'Help yourself, then,' offered Martin. 'Tell us what was in the letter.'

Salmon turned his face away from them, towards the wall of the windowless interview room, his fingers twisting, intertwined, in an unconscious show of indecision.

'Come on, Noel,' said the Head of CID.

Salmon turned back to face them, nodding slightly as if he had reached a decision. He looked up in the silence which filled the room and opened his mouth as if to speak.

There was a knock on the brown-painted door. The handle turned. The door swung open, revealing the bulky frame of Neil McIlhenney. A tall, dark-haired man stood behind him.

'What the hell is it?' snapped Andy Martin, in a rare display of annoyance.

'I'm sorry, sir,' said the Sergeant, 'but I had no choice.' He nodded over his shoulder, towards the man who followed him into the room. 'This is Mr Alec Linden. He's a solicitor, retained by the *Spotlight* to represent Salmon. He demanded that I bring him in here.'

The Chief Superintendent sighed heavily in his exasperation, and nodded, standing up as he did so and reaching out to switch off the tape recorder. 'You're right, Neil, you didn't have a choice. Thank you. Interview suspended.'

He turned to the lawyer, as McIlhenney withdrew. 'I don't think we've met, Mr Linden.'

The man shook his head. 'No. I'm senior partner of Herd and Phillips, in Glasgow.' Martin recognised the name of the biggest criminal law firm in Scotland. 'I was instructed by Mr Salmon's employers immediately after they heard of his arrest on a radio news bulletin. They are naturally concerned that he is being persecuted because of the story in today's issue of their magazine. So am I.

'I understand from your Sergeant,' said Linden, brusquely, 'that you are questioning my client over his possession of an unlisted telephone number.'

'That, and his possession of a quantity of cocaine.'

The solicitor frowned. 'I wasn't aware of that. You'll do me the courtesy of allowing me a few minutes alone with my client?'

'Of course. Give us a call when you're ready.' The two detectives stepped outside, into the corridor, where McIlhenney waited. 'What do you think, sir?' asked McGuire.

'I think he'll piss all over us,' said Martin glumly. 'Fuck me, Neil, if you'd only stopped to tie your shoelace before you knocked on that door. We had Salmon by the stones right then.'

The Sergeant looked crestfallen. 'Christ, boss, but I'm sorry.'

'Ach, never you mind, big fella, you weren't to know.'

They stood silent in the corridor for almost ten minutes, before the door opened, and Linden's face appeared. 'Gentlemen, we're ready for you now.' Martin and McGuire re-entered the room, and resumed their seats across the table from Salmon and his new adviser.

'I'll come straight to the point,' said the solicitor. 'On the matter of the cocaine, my client maintains that it was introduced to his premises without his knowledge by his lady-friend. On the matter of the telephone number, it is not an offence simply to possess such information, and you have no evidence whatsoever that it was obtained corruptly. Also, my client denies any knowledge of, or co-operation with, the person who made the second telephone call to Mr Skinner.'

He paused. 'I have advised my client that he should answer no further questions. Obviously, it is up to you to decide how to proceed on the matter of the cocaine, but in the meantime, I insist that Mr Salmon be released.'

Andy Martin glanced at the journalist, who sat relaxed, beaming back at him, all his arrogance and cockiness restored. In his mind he weighed the options of the situation, realising that, with his solicitor by his side, Salmon would not budge from his story. He knew that he had no practical choice.

'Okay, Mr Linden,' he sighed, at last. 'You can have him. A report will be submitted to the Procurator Fiscal. It'll be for him to decide whether your client will be charged with possession.

'In the meantime, I suggest that you advise him to be very careful of the people with whom he associates, and to be wary of any further anonymous information he might receive. Now please, take him away, so that we can have this place fumigated.'

20

'Don't take it to heart, Andy. You did well do get anything out of the wee shit. I know Alec Linden. He's an honest operator, but very sharp. If he'd turned up earlier you'd have got sod all.'

Martin's face twisted into a grimace. 'I know that, Bob, but I was so nearly there. He knows more than he told us. Plus, he's got something else up his sleeve, I'm sure. And he was that close to spilling it, when that bloody lawyer turned up.

'When he made the arrest, Mario offered him the chance to call someone, but he turned it down. We reckoned he was wetting himself so badly about the cocaine, he wasn't thinking too straight.'

'So how did Linden know about it, and where to find him?' asked Skinner.

'Sheer bad luck. Salmon's boss was trying to find him. One of the people he called was John Hunter. Old John laughed, and told him where he was. The *Spotlight* guy called his Scottish lawyer, who happens to be Linden.'

'Damn it,' said the DCC. 'And Linden happened to be available and not on the golf course. Life's a bugger at times.

'Here, you don't think it was Big Joanne's stuff, do you?'

'Not a chance. It was Salmon's, okay, but he's right. It'll be his word against hers. The Fiscal won't proceed against him. He's off every single hook, and free to carry on persecuting you.'

101

Skinner reached across the wooden garden table and slapped his friend lightly on the shoulder. 'Fuck him, Andy. He's not worth the bother. Let's concentrate on the main event; not on my self-inflicted troubles, but on finding poor wee, stolen Mark McGrath, and the evil bastard who took him.

'You say Salmon told you that my number was included in the second anonymous letter he received?'

'Right.'

'Did you believe him? I mean, he can't produce either letter. He could be lying.'

Andy Martin shook his head, taking a bite from one of the thick ham sandwiches which Skinner and Pamela had prepared. 'I believed him,' he said, after devouring the mouthful. 'The second phone call on your tape knocked the feet from under him. He knew that it looked bad for him. Just at that moment, he'd have shopped his granny to get off the hook.'

Bob stood up from the table, sandwich in hand, and began to pace, backwards and forwards across the slabbed area of his cottage garden. 'So what have we got?' he began. 'A mystery informant slipping Salmon damaging information about me, and giving him my phone number as well, so that he can really wind me up by calling me at home to rub it in.

'A second man with my unlisted number, who calls me, specifically – not the Press Association, or the telly, or even our headquarters, but me – to tell me, in person, that he has Mark.' He stopped his pacing and looked back towards the table, first at Pamela, then at Martin. 'What are the chances, do you think, given the connection of the number, that our killer is also Noel Salmon's anonymous source?'

'Pretty good, I'd have thought,' said Pamela.

'Could be,' said Martin. 'But in a sense that's irrelevant. The best lead we have is the number itself. If we can find out how our man came by it then we're close to finding him.'

Skinner chuckled. 'Unless he broke into Fettes to get it! That's been done before.' He sat down once more. 'No, but you're right. Have a blitz on Telecom, and on our own telecommunications room. Don't ruffle any feathers, but if there's anyone there who might be making a bit of extra cash by selling restricted numbers, find out.'

The Head of CID looked at his chief, as Pam Masters carried the empty plate back into the kitchen. 'Don't worry. It's already under way. If there's a bad apple in there, anywhere, I'll crush the last drop of juice out of him . . . or her, if it comes to that.'

'I'm sure you will, Andy, I'm sure.

'Meanwhile, there are people down in London who are listening to that tape as carefully as they can. Not to the Salmon bit, but to the kidnapper's call, analysing every fragment of sound on it, seeing if there's anything in the background that they can locate.'

'What are the chances?'

'To be truthful, not very good. I've listened to my copy time and time again, but I can only hear the guy's voice. Mind you, our London friends are working with the original, and can amplify sound to levels that only a very sharp-eared dog could pick up. If there's anything there, they'll find it.'

He stopped and looked towards the cottage. 'You did tell Alex you were coming out here again this afternoon, didn't you?' he asked, suddenly.

Andy nodded. 'She said she had some work that needed doing.'

'On a Sunday? Christ, she's only just started with that law firm. They can't have her working weekends already, surely?'

'No, I think it was housework.'

Bob raised his eyebrows and stared across the table. 'Alex? Housework?' He pointed upwards to a V-shaped formation of geese, flying westwards. 'What d'you think those are, Andy? Pigs?'

He shook his head. 'No, my daughter just didn't want to come. Alex doesn't approve of Pam and me, does she?'

'Bob, that's between you and her.' Andy hesitated. 'But if I were you, I'd just let it lie for a while. She's said she'll support you, and she will, but she's very fond of Sarah, and she was gutted when you two separated. She won't give you any more grief, but it'd be best if you let her come to terms with things in her own time.'

The older man stared at the sky again, back towards the geese as they wheeled round towards Aberlady Nature reserve, their nesting ground. 'Aye, you're right,' he murmured at last. 'The last thing I need is to fall out with our kid as well.'

Suddenly he glanced back across the table. 'And what about you, Andy? What about you? Do you approve of my new relationship? After all, you've got a double interest, personal and professional.'

Abruptly, Martin stood up from the table. 'Let's go for a walk,' he said.

Skinner shook his head. 'I don't want to leave Pam. Not after Leona, and everything that's happened. Not with a madman on the loose.'

His friend smiled. 'Don't worry. You have very discreet protection.'

The DCC looked at him, surprised. 'I didn't ask for . . .'

'Well you bloody should have. My operational decision. End of story.'

'I'm still not sure. There might be photographers out there.'

'Fuck 'em if there are. Let's go for a walk.'

'Yeah. All right then.' With a last show of reluctance, Skinner rose also and took a few paces across to the open back door of the cottage. 'Pam,' he called, 'Andy and I are off for a stroll. Back in half an hour or so. Remember. Keep the door shut, and let the machine answer the phone.'

There were no photographers in sight outside the cottage. As he closed the gate behind him and stepped between Andy's silver Mondeo and his own BMW, Bob glanced across the Goose Green. At its lower end, near the back entrance to the Golf Inn hotel, a single car was parked; a nondescript, grey Escort, with a figure in the front passenger seat seemingly reading a newspaper.

'I've got another officer positioned round in the paddock,' said Martin quietly, catching the look. 'Between them they cover all approaches to the cottage.'

'Yes, that's enough. What are their orders if they see someone approaching the house?'

'They're to radio in and alert you, rather than tackling the suspect and risking him getting away. Unless Pam's there alone, of course. Then they'd go in.'

'What, you mean your game is to let him come at me?' asked Skinner, a grim edge to his voice.

'Yes,' said his colleague, with a quick grin, 'to give us the best chance of catching him. Not that I think it will happen, but if it does, try to leave the guy in one piece. Please.'

They strolled out of the green taking a narrow pathway beside the Episcopalian church, which led them through the golf club car park to the slopes of Gullane Hill. They trudged in silence up the steep road towards its summit, until at last they stood on a grassy knoll which overlooked the club's three courses, and all of the wide Forth estuary.

The two friends sat side by side on a memorial chair, gazing out to sea.

'Well, Andy,' said Bob at last, breathing only slightly heavily from the climb, 'what about it? What do you think of my indiscretion? Give it to me straight.'

Martin hunched his broad shoulders, within his roomy sports jacket. 'If you insist. But first, tell me again how it came about. I don't mean the situation between you and Sarah: I know that arose out of your extreme views on questions of trust. I mean the thing between you and Pam.'

Bob leaned against the back of the bench seat. 'Like I said,' he began, 'it just happened. I was lonely, so was Pamela. We were thrown together by the job, and we were attracted to each other. Pam's divorced, I'm separated. When I realised how it was heading I transferred her out of my office . . .' he paused for a second, '. . . and into my bed.'

'How do you feel about each other?'

'Fond covers it, I think. Somehow, Pam seems to feel . . . safe. She doesn't ask or threaten. D'you understand what I mean?'

'I think so. A once-bitten, twice-shy career woman. I can see why you'd feel safe with her.'

'Mmm,' Bob grunted. 'So come on, out with it.'

Andy drew in a deep breath of the fresh afternoon air, looking out at the grey sea, beneath the blue sky. 'Remember when I was younger – not that long ago. I was a serial shagger, and no mistake. You used to tell me I had had more women than cooked breakfasts, and you were right.

'I always had to have a girlfriend because that was part of me, but as soon as I started to feel safe with them, I ran a mile in the opposite direction. Safety, in my view, is no basis for a relationship. Mere contentment shouldn't be enough.'

He glanced round, towards Skinner. 'Bob, you were never like I used to be, nor will you ever be. You couldn't philander to save your life. When you met Sarah, I was pleased for you. After more than fifteen years of widowhood you'd finally found a woman who was made for you. And I was as jealous as hell. All of a sudden my own life seemed hollow, and I wanted so much to be like you.

'As you'll remember, that led me into one disastrous situation, before I realised that the only woman for me was right before my eyes. I just hadn't noticed that she'd grown up.'

He laughed, but sadly, without humour. 'So look at us now, you and me. My dream's come true. I've become like you were. I'm in love, settled and happy for the rest of my life. You? You're stumbling about like a lost soul.

'You talk about feeling safe, my old friend. Well, I think that's cobblers. I think you're on the fucking rebound, that's what. And I should know. It used to happen to me all the time. I rebounded from one to the next so often that I felt like a human pinball machine.

'You ask me what I think? Well here it is. I've nothing against Pam. She seems like a nice woman, and a couple of years back I'd probably have fancied her myself. But I love Sarah, and I think it's fucking tragic that you and she, between you, are in the process of tearing apart one of the best marriages I've ever seen.

'I don't often presume to speak for Alex, Bob, but I'll

tell you that if you asked her, she would tell you that she feels exactly the same way.'

Skinner sat motionless on the bench, staring out across the wide Firth, over to the Fife coast, towards the string of one-time fishing villages, transformed by fashion and affluence into holiday resorts. He sat there for minutes before responding, still without looking round.

'You're my best pal, Andy. Truth be told, one of the very few real friends I've ever had. I value your opinion, and I'm sorry that Sarah and I have caused you distress. You're right about our marriage; it seemed perfect. But remember that it's possible to shatter even a diamond into smithereens.

'However, as for Pam and me, we're sort of tied together now, by the *Spotlight* thing, and by this killer's possible focus on me. I do care for her too, make no mistake.

'I couldn't just abandon her, even if I wanted to. I accept what you say, about my being on the rebound. Sure, I know that I let my cock do my thinking for me. I suppose I just needed to be told, and only you could do that. But it's happened, and things may have gone beyond redemption now, between me and Sarah.'

He looked around, at last. 'Right, that was your personal view. How do you see it professionally?'

Martin frowned. 'You sure you want to hear?'

'Aye, Chief Superintendent. I can take it. Fire away.'

'Very good, sir.

'You used the word earlier: indiscretion.

'However you justify it, and however properly you think you acted, by transferring Pamela out of your office before your slept with her, I believe that you've laid yourself wide open to accusations of indiscretion . . . at the very least.

'I know you've said in the past that your officers' sex lives are their business, as long as it's legal, but you're no ordinary copper. You're going to be accused of abuse of your position, and maybe even sexual harassment, by at least two female members of the Police Board that I could name, and the Chief is going to have some bloody job defending you.'

Skinner sighed. 'You saying I should resign, Andy?' he asked, sombrely.

'Like hell! If the Board asks for your resignation they'll have mine too, not to mention the Chief's and those of half a dozen senior officers. No, you'll ride it out. Your real worry should be Pamela.'

The big DCC frowned. 'Tell me why.'

'Think about it. Is this relationship going to last for ever, or will it come to an end? Any way you size it up, she has no future in our force. Working in my office, she's just about okay as the DCC's girlfriend, as long as you keep your private lives miles away from Fettes. But she can't stay there for ever. How would she survive in a division? Who among her colleagues would trust her with a confidence?

'Suppose in the future you were to marry? No, Pam's position would be completely untenable.'

Martin paused. 'On the other hand, what will happen if it comes to an end? How do you expect the girl to survive as the Deputy Chief's cast-off mistress?'

'Jesus,' said Skinner loudly enough to draw a frown from a golfer on the seventh tee, thirty yards away. 'I really have made a nonsense of things, haven't I? So what do we do to protect her?'

'You know the options as well as I do,' said Martin. 'If you and Pam decide to marry, I expect she'd want to resign. If that doesn't happen, if you carry on as you are, inform-ally, shall we say, and she wants to stay in the police, we should offer her a transfer to another force – Central, maybe, so she could still live in Edinburgh. Should you split up, the same would apply.'

There was a renewed silence at the other end of the bench. 'Let's not discuss the first option, Andy,' the DCC responded finally, this time in a quiet voice. 'Put feelers out regarding the second, once this *Spotlight* business has blown over. I'll talk to Pam about it, in due course.

'Meantime, I'd be grateful if you'd give her a week's leave, as of now. I'll take her back to her place in Leith tomorrow. It'll be easier for the watchers, and more discreet.'

'Do you want to take some time off yourself?'

'Do I bloody hell! The media would say I'd been sent on gardening leave. Anyway, I'm going nowhere till we've nailed down the bastard who killed Leona McGrath, and till we've got wee Mark back safely.'

Skinner stood up, looking down at his friend. 'You know, son,' he chuckled. 'I'm generally reckoned to be quite a smart guy, ace detective and all that; but over the last few months of my life, I've been made to realise that when it comes to women, I just haven't a bloody clue!'

21

Ruth McConnell was at her desk when Skinner arrived at 8.20 a.m. on Monday, for his first morning in the office since the *Spotlight* story had broken.

'Good morning, sir,' she said, with exactly the same friendly smile to which he had become accustomed.

The DCC glanced at his watch. 'Jeez, but you're early, Ruthie,' he said.

'I thought it might be a good idea,' she replied, standing up from her typist's swivel chair, elegant as ever, the slimness of her long legs accentuated by her tight skirt and her high heels. She picked up a pile of newspapers from her side table. 'There's fresh coffee in your filter machine.'

'I'll need it, when I go through those. Come in and have some with me. I should talk to you anyway.'

'Have you seen any of the papers yet?' asked his secretary, as they crossed the corridor to his office.

The big policeman shook his head. 'No. We left Gullane before mine arrived.' His expression changed for a second as a thought struck him. 'That reminds me. Would you call my newsagent, please, and cancel them till further notice. He's in the book. Surname's Hector.'

He took off the jacket of his dark blue suit and draped it round the back of his chair, while Ruth poured coffee into two mugs.

'So,' said Skinner as she sat down, facing him across the rosewood desk. 'What do you think of my new-found notoriety?'

'I think it's absolutely disgraceful, sir,' the woman exploded, her full lips pouting in her anger. 'I think it's offensive, intrusive, and damned unfair. Even if I've never said it to you, I'm as sorry as everyone else in here about your marriage breaking up, but that's your business.

'To have your private life poked into like that . . . Well, it's intolerable!'

'I have to tolerate it, Ruthie. No choice. I can roar on about what I'm going to do to the so-and-so who put that wee swine Salmon on my trail, but I just have to bear it.'

'Yes,' she said, 'but it's the double standards that get me. I mean, if it had been Neil McIlhenney having an affair with Sergeant Masters, he wouldn't have been all over the front page.'

Skinner surprised her, with his sudden laughter. 'Oh yes he would!' he said. 'Because Olive would have killed him, stone dead.'

His smile faded as quickly as it had appeared. 'No, you're right. But that's the way it is. Sergeant and Sergeant; so what? Deputy Chief and Sergeant, and the press eat it up. I'm a daft bastard. I should have known better.'

He looked across the desk. 'Tell me something, Ruthie, had you guessed that something was going on?' To his surprise, she gasped as a mixture of shock and fear flooded her eyes.

'Sir you don't think I . . .' she began.

He threw up his hands instantly, in horror which matched hers. 'No, no, no!' he insisted. 'Not for one second have I thought that. I trust you absolutely. No, I just want to know how stupid I've been. Alex guessed, and so did McIlhenney, I think. Did you?'

She dropped her gaze from him. Her long hair fell over the shoulders of her blue business jacket as she nodded.

'As soon as you transferred Pamela out of here, I knew exactly why you were doing it. I remembered those late nights when you were chasing Jackie Charles; that time you were snowed in. I could tell from then that something was cooking.'

'And you never said anything.'

'Of course not. I'm your secretary, not your chaperone.'

The policeman grinned at her once more. 'Maybe that's what you should have been. Seriously, though, I'm sorry I kept you in the dark along with everyone else. You have my confidence in every other area; I should have trusted you with that too. Come to think of it, if I had asked your advice, I probably wouldn't be in this mess now.'

Ruth shook her head. 'You have too much faith, Mr Skinner. I've been living with a separated man for the last month. Mine's a doctor, a country GP. We're the talk of the community too, although on a smaller scale than you.'

He looked at her in surprise. Ruth was in her late twenties, and when it came to men, she had always led him to believe that she sought safety in numbers. 'I wondered why you'd changed your contact number,' he murmured.

'And I didn't tell you,' she countered. 'Which, if you want to look at it that way, puts us both at fault.

'Now, are you ready for what the papers say?'

The Deputy Chief Constable nodded. 'As much as I ever will be.'

'I've been through them already. I've marked the pages you should look at. The red numbers are the stories about you. The blue ones are about the McGrath investigation.'

Skinner picked up the paper on top of the pile. As always in Ruth's arrangement, it was the *Scotsman*. His heart sank as he looked at the lower part of the front page, from which his likeness gazed out at him: at once he knew what the tone of the coverage would be.

Rather than recycle the *Spotlight*'s sensational scoop, the responsible *Scotsman* had taken as its front-page lead the announcement by five members of the Police Supervisory Board that they intended to raise the Deputy Chief Constable's conduct at the next meeting of the Board on the following Wednesday. The Chair of the Board had agreed to accept an emergency motion of censure for debate.

Skinner scanned the rest of the story. In careful terms, clearly legally approved, it sketched out the allegations about his private life, naming Pamela Masters, and carrying the statements released by his solicitor and the Chief Constable's office. It closed with a footnote directing readers to Page Sixteen.

He leafed through the pages until he arrived at the Editorial column. There were two leader articles. The second was headed 'Morality and the Media'.

The detective scanned it through then read it aloud.

'If it is to be of true value to society, and ultimately to protect its freedom, the media as a collective entity must never be afraid or reluctant to comment critically on one of its own, when condemnation is justified.

'It is with that in mind that we deprecate the conduct of Spotlight *magazine in its invasion of the private life of Deputy Chief Constable Bob Skinner, and in particular the methods which it chose to adopt. This newspaper disapproves thoroughly of the surreptitious photographing of honest citizens within their own homes. That is why we will not reproduce the photographs which appeared yesterday, although*

we were offered publication rights, at a price.

'Spotlight *is a publication without any perceptible moral standards, driven only by the greed of its owners, and restrained only by the civil law of defamation. Your publishers find it distasteful whenever this newspaper occupies the same shelves in the relatively few outlets where they are sold together.*

'*Nevertheless, when questionable behaviour comes to light, the fact that its exposers are beneath contempt themselves does not make it any less questionable. Mr Skinner occupies a high-profile position which demands exemplary standards of personal behaviour. We will not pass judgement on the motion which will be put before the Joint Police Board on Wednesday. All we will say is that the Deputy Chief Constable, despite his great service to the city, is not above personal censure. On this occasion, if his professional and moral conduct is called into question, then in the circumstances, it seems that he cannot blame the* Spotlight, *however unprofessional and immoral a rag it might be. He can blame only himself.'*

He folded the paper and laid it aside. 'I can't disagree with much of that,' he said. 'Who could, given that it's so circumspectly written?'

He gave a wry smile. 'Mind you, for all its position on the high moral ground, I can't help noticing that the *Scotsman* still manages to put my private life on its own front page.

'Is all the rest of it like this?' he asked.

'Yes,' Ruth replied. 'There are no other leaders, and no-one else has used the photos, but all the stories lead on the censure motion. Everyone's used it. Even the *Telegraph*.'

'Let me guess. On Page Three?'

'Right first time.'

Skinner picked up the *Daily Record* and turned to page seven, as Ruth's red number indicated. 'Five Hunt Top Cop!' he read. He waved the newspaper in the air, indicating a row of head-and-shoulder photographs.

'There they are, the Famous Five. Unreconstructed Lefties, all of them; every one of them keen to take any opportunity to put their own party on the spot.'

His secretary looked across at him. 'Will you go to the meeting on Wednesday?'

'I've thought about that. I'll go only if the Chair guarantees me the right to a personal statement, after the discussion but before the vote.'

'Do you think she will?'

'It won't be her choice. It'll be a group decision. My bet is that she won't be allowed to.'

He rearranged the newspapers into a pile.

'Will you issue any more statements before the meeting?'

Skinner shook his head. 'No. Pam might, though. She's been advised that she has a case for defamation against the *Spotlight*, since they suggested that she slept with me to get on in the Force. I'm telling her to sue.'

He saw Ruth wince. 'You don't agree?'

'If she was sure they'd settle out of court,' she said, 'yes, I'd agree. But if it goes to trial, she could be hammered in the witness box. I wouldn't fancy being cross-examined about my sex life.'

'They'll settle, Ruth. Sooner rather than later too. That rag's used to paying off libel suitors.'

He slapped the papers on his desk, in a typical gesture. 'But enough of that,' he said, suddenly grim again. 'Let's see what the press say about the McGrath case. That's my priority, and the thing that makes me most angry about the *Spotlight* is the fact that they deflected me from it!'

22

'The media gave my Saturday phone call quite a show, Andy. Lead story in three tabloids, and page one in every other.'

'I'm not surprised, sir,' said the Head of CID, always more formal in the office, at least in the company of others. He and Neil McIlhenney were seated with Skinner on the low leather sofas in a corner of the DCC's big office, drinking still more coffee. 'All they've had to report since the murder is a succession of fruitless searches. Did you see the *Herald*? It commissioned a psychological profile of the killer.'

'Yes, I saw it. It says that he's a highly intelligent psychopath, aged between twenty-five and forty. Probably the son of a widow, divorcee or single mother. I'm glad we only paid forty pence for that opinion. I don't know who they got to do it, but they'd have been better with Mystic Meg.'

'Aye, boss,' grunted McIlhenney. 'She might have given us a name to go on, at least.'

Skinner grinned. 'We're going to have to dig that out for ourselves, Sergeant,' he retorted.

'If they did use a professional, I'd have thought he'd have focused on the real give-away from the call; the fact that the man chose to call me, and went to the bother of getting my home phone number, presumably so that he could do it without being tied on the Fettes switchboard long enough for his phone to be traced.

'It's me he wants. It's me Salmon wants. Salmon claims his source could be anonymous. Could the killer be his informant? If so, how did he know about me and Pam? Come to that, who else knew about me and Pam?'

He took a sip from his mug. 'Let's try and answer all those questions, lads, but let's begin by looking at my former clients. Names, you said, Neil. Let's start with a few of them, those still alive, and at liberty. Put some people on to it, Andy. Draw up a list and start checking on current whereabouts. Discreetly, though. If our man is one of them we don't want to tip his hand.

'We're already checking out known rapists and paedophiles. Add this lot to them and spread the load among the officers deployed already.'

'How far back should we go?' asked the Head of CID.

'As far as you have to. Meanwhile I'll see if the clever people down south have had any joy with that tape.'

23

Martin and McIlhenney had barely left Skinner's office before he picked up his secure telephone and dialled a London number.

'This is Skinner, in Scotland,' he said, curtly, to the man who answered his call with a simple 'Yes?'. 'The technical people are analysing a tape for me. Have them call me back with a progress report, within ten minutes.'

Six minutes and four seconds later, the direct line rang. He picked it up quickly, laying down the file he was reading. 'Skinner.'

The voice on the other end of the line answered in a middle-American drawl. Skinner knew that the special relationship which had sprung up between the new Prime Minister and the US President had led to promises of greater co-operation between the security services for which each was responsible. He wondered if the caller was early evidence of their sincerity.

'Good morning, sir,' said the woman. 'My name is Caroline Farmer. I've been working on your tape.'

'Good to hear from you, Ms Farmer. Been with us long?'

'Three weeks, sir, on secondment from Langley.' The Scot smiled, his supposition answered. 'What's your background?' he asked.

'I'm a graduate of Massachusetts Institute of Technology, been with the Company for four years. I'm over on the new information exchange programme.'

'That's good. How about my mystery voice, then? You got anything for me?'

Caroline Farmer hesitated. 'Yeah, we've got something,' she began. 'I'll start with the accent. We have people here who reckon they can place the origin of UK citizens by the nature of their speech.'

'Yes, I know. What are they saying?'

'They believe that your caller is Scottish, sir.'

'Hah,' laughed Skinner, 'that's very good. Now carry on please: Scotland's quite a big place.'

'That's it, sir,' said the American. 'They can't do any better than that. They say that the basic cast of the voice indicates that the caller is Scottish. But his speech is absolutely flat, other than that. Listening to you, sir, I can detect a pronounced accent which I assume is regional Edinburgh.'

'Mostly Lanarkshire, actually,' the DCC grunted.

'Okay, but distinctive none the less. This guy is either disguising his voice, or he's been subject to so many influences that he cannot be pinned down. They did say, though, that he could have spent some time outside Scotland, or have a non-Scottish parent.'

'That's something at least. Now how about the tape itself: any joy from that?'

Caroline Farmer paused once more. 'I'm not sure whether you'll find it joyful, sir.'

'Try me.'

'Okay,' she said, 'but first I have to ask you something? When the call came in, was there an open door or window in your home.'

Skinner frowned, searching his memory. 'Yes,' he said at last. 'It was a warm night. We had the window open a little.'

'Good. Now think again. Can you remember, as you listened to the man, whether you could hear anything else?'

He closed his eyes, and tried to place himself back in the bedroom. His anger still burning over Salmon's taunting call. Undressing in the dark, beginning the process of unwinding, of relaxing, of making love. Then the ringing of the phone, and his fury erupting once more. He stopped and concentrated on the moments before the interruption. Pamela, kissing, licking, nibbling her way down his body . . .

'Geese!' he said suddenly. 'Through the window I could hear geese. It's no big deal for us, part of the sound furniture, you might say. There's a wildlife sanctuary near my house. In summer, they go over in flocks at all hours.'

'Okay,' said Caroline Farmer. 'That was on the tape: the sound of geese. You couldn't hear it on the cassette we sent up, but when we built it up, it was there.

'Now to the interesting part. The equipment that we use to tape telephone calls records each half of the conversation on separate tracks. This is the sound we took from the background of your track. Listen.'

She broke off, and suddenly Skinner heard in the earpiece the familiar squawking sound of a large flight of wild geese, as he had heard it thousands of times, as he had heard it less than forty-eight hours before. There was a click as the player was switched off.

'Now,' the woman resumed. 'Hold on while I switch cassettes. Okay, ready. This is the background from the caller's track.'

Another pause. Another click. Once more the sound of flying geese filled Skinner's ear. He listened, puzzled, for a few seconds. 'Wrong tape,' he said, at last. 'You're playing my track again.'

No sir,' said Farmer, emphatically. 'I am not. That is the background from the caller's track.'

'Well, surely the sound from my phone must have fed through to his.'

'It did. There was feedback sound on both tracks. We've stripped that off. You, and this guy, sir, you could both hear the same flight of geese, at the same volume, at the same time. Which means that the call was made from very near your home.'

Skinner sat at his desk, stunned. 'There's no possibility of the equipment being faulty?'

'No, sir, there is not. You live in a village, I understand.'

'Right.'

'That might make it easier for you. We were able to match the sounds on each track exactly. The recording levels on each were almost exactly the same. I would say that you and your caller were no more than a quarter of a mile apart.

'Can I ask you, sir, in which direction do the geese fly?'

'Westward; by evening and night, they fly westward.'

'Good, that tells me from the sound pattern that the caller was to the east of your home.'

'Anything else?' asked Skinner, eagerly. 'Was there anything else on his track? Can you tell what type of telephone it was?'

The American chuckled on the other end of the secure line. 'We ain't that good, sir. It was a touchtone telephone, and the caller disabled your 1471 tracing service, but you knew that already. There were other sounds though, faintly, beneath the geese. An automobile passed close by during the call travelling in a straight line at about forty miles per hour. And there was music playing nearby. Further away, there was the sound of a woman, shouting angrily. Does any of that help?'

Skinner grunted. 'It might. Listen, Agent, or whatever I should call you, that's great work. I want copies of all these tapes sent up here for my people as soon as possible, like today. Can you isolate that woman's voice?'

'Sure. I'll put that on a separate tape. I'll have everything with you by courier by mid-afternoon. Meantime, we'll keep on working. We can take resolution up practically to the level of an individual goose. You never know what else we might turn up.'

24

Detective Chief Superintendent Martin was seated at his desk as Skinner rapped on his door and burst into the room. Detective Constable Sammy Pye, with his back to the door, looked over his shoulder and sprang to his feet.

'I'm just getting young Sammy started on that list you ordered, sir,' said the Head of CID.

'Good,' said Skinner, closing the door behind him, and waving Pye back to his seat, 'but put it on hold for now. Our Friends in the South have come up trumps. We know where the caller was when he phoned me, and you're not going to believe it. The cheeky bastard was within a quarter of a mile of my bloody house!'

Martin's eyebrows rose. 'You what?' he gasped, incredulously.

'That's right. The background noise gave him away. From what I've been told, my guess is that he called from the phone box outside the Post Office, across the road from the pub. However we can't be certain of that. Chief Superintendent, I want to know, from British Telecom, the location of every telephone in Gullane that was used at ten fifty last Saturday night, and I want every one of those subscribers checked out.'

He paused. 'I can't believe that the guy would actually hide Mark in my home village, but it's the first lead we've had and it must be followed. Unless we turn up something from the telephone check, I want a house-by-house check of the whole place. You can leave mine out, but I want every other door in that village knocked.'

'What are we looking for?'

'We're looking for a lucky break, Andy.'

The Head of CID grunted assent. 'Yes, like the guy still being around. It beggars belief, though, to think that he actually lives there.'

'Sure, I agree. But he phoned from there. It's not beyond belief that he might be hiding out there. Remember, there are still weekend cottages and holiday homes in Gullane . . . my own among them, till recently at any rate.'

'Do we know which they are?'

'A few, through Neighbourhood Watch, but not all, not by any means. Quite a few are just left from one visit to the next. Some have private caretaking arrangements.'

'How do you want to play it? What line should our officers take with the householders when they knock their doors? These people are your neighbours, after all.'

Skinner pondered the question for a while. 'Simple is best,' he said. 'Let's have them say that we're extending our enquiries out from Edinburgh. Ask each occupier if he's seen anything out of the ordinary in the area, and ask those with substantial outbuildings – and there are some; you've seen them, up the Hill – whether they've checked them lately.

'Where a house is unoccupied, see if the neighbours know anything about the owner.'

Martin nodded. 'Let's think carefully about all this,' he said. 'We've got an advantage, here. Our man can't know that we're on to the fact that he called from Gullane. We want to keep that information secret for as long as we can.'

'Fine. In that case let's keep it literally to ourselves. Other than you, me, and our staffs, the people doing the rounds can simply be told what we've just decided to tell the punters; that the search is being widened. They'll be all the more convincing if they don't know any different themselves.

'You'll need more leg-power for all this, so you'd better mobilise Brian Mackie and Maggie Rose. All of a sudden this investigation has spilled over into their area.' Skinner nodded to himself, as if in satisfaction. 'How quickly can you get it done?'

'It'll be done within forty-eight hours.'

'Quicker, if you can. Start today. While that's happening, there's something else we should do. I want officers in all five pubs and hotel bars in Gullane this evening, checking on everyone who was out for a bevvy on Saturday.

'Someone may have seen our man in the phone box, and may be able to give us a description.' He paused. 'We'll need a cover story for that too. Tell our troops that we're looking for someone who's been using the box to make obscene phone calls. Christ,' he added grimly, 'that's true, in a way.'

Skinner turned to leave. 'There'll be another line of investigation to be followed up also,' he said, 'but I can't do anything about that until a certain tape arrives from London.'

He opened the door, then stopped, and spun round to face Martin and Pye again. 'Call box. Coins. Sammy, get on to Telecom and have them empty the cash from that phone box. You never know, maybe my caller left a thumbprint on a ten-pence piece that'll help us put a name to his voice.'

25

Pamela frowned at him across the kitchen, as she ladled soup into two shallow white bowls. 'Is this how it's going to be? You nipping home at lunchtime to check up on me?' She handed him a bowl and a plate of thick-cut sandwiches, and gestured him towards the door.

'Don't be daft,' he protested, carrying his snack though to the big living area of her top-floor flat, and sitting on the couch which faced the big W-shaped window, draped with white muslin now, where once it had offered an uninterrupted view of the Water of Leith as it coursed towards the sea.

'I'm here because I want to be. On top of that, I had that news for you about the phone call.'

Unsmiling, Pam set about her lunch. 'Look,' she said, finally, 'how much longer do I have to stay here? I feel like a hostage. If I'm supposed to be on leave, can't I at least go out?'

'Yes,' said Skinner, 'if you take your escorts with you.'

'Oh really! This man won't come after me.'

In shirtsleeves, he shrugged his shoulders. 'If there's only one chance in a hundred of that,' he said, 'I'm still not going to take it. Whoever this guy is he certainly identifies with me. Maybe it's purely because I'm a high-profile police figure that he can thumb his nose at, but my publicised connection with wee Mark McGrath makes that unlikely.

'Against that background, in the light of the *Spotlight* story, you have to be protected.'

128

She looked at him, as he devoured his last sandwich. 'Should I really be scared, then?' she asked, quietly, when he was finished.

'Not while you're here, with protection outside. Not while I'm here. Women and kids are this man's size.'

She looked at him again, sulkily. 'But couldn't you protect me in the office? After all, I'm sure this leave I'm taking will come off my annual allowance . . . don't try and tell me different. I can see the *Spotlight* headline now: "Skinner's girlfriend gets extra holidays!" '

'It's because of *Spotlight* that we . . . okay, I . . . thought you'd be better away from the office for a few days.'

'What!' She sat bolt upright, sulking seriously now. 'I thought this was all about security. But you mean you and Andy decided I'd be better kept out of the way for a while to save embarrassment. Whose, in that case? Mine, or yours?'

His eyebrows came together in a single heavy line. 'I'm still there, remember,' he growled.

'Oh, so you are embarrassed!'

'No, I didn't say that. It's you that I'm concerned about.'

Her expression softened. 'Yes,' she said, 'I suppose you are. But, please, don't make decisions about me without involving me. Even if you are my commanding officer.' She hesitated. 'Let me come back, please. If people point fingers at me it'll be behind my back, and I can take that, I think. Let's do what we've done up to now, travel to and from work separately, and steer clear of each other in the office.'

She slid across beside him on the couch, and poked him in the ribs. 'Come on, I'll bet you need me, too. Don't tell me that the Head of CID isn't short-handed just now. It isn't right to keep me here, when I could be out helping you catch the man who murdered Mrs McGrath and stole her son.'

He laid his plate and bowl on the floor, and turned towards her, his hands gripping her upper arms, gently. 'Okay,' he said, smiling. 'I give up. You can come in tomorrow. But either we go in together or you get a lift from the protection people. Deal?'

'Deal.' She nodded, and slipping free of his grasp, threw her arms around his neck and kissed him. 'Now,' she whispered, 'since this is a one-off occasion, what say we take full advantage of it?'

He disengaged himself, still grinning. 'One triumph per lunch hour's enough for you,' he said. 'I have to get back to the office. There's a hot tape coming up from London. Meantime, you can spend the afternoon deciding whether you intend to sue the *Spotlight* for defaming your impeccable character.'

26

Sammy Pye was waiting in the Command Corridor as Skinner bounded up the stairs from the small entrance hallway. The DCC knew at once that, whatever news he had brought, he would not be starting his afternoon with a smile.

'What's the damage?' he asked the glum young detective.

'It's that phone box, sir,' said Pye, heavily. 'The cash compartment was emptied at half past nine this morning. By the time I spoke to Telecom the money was back at their regional office, mixed up with the takings from about thirty other kiosks.

'I've told them not to bank it till they hear from us.'

Skinner shook his head. 'Sam, with that number of boxes, even if we had enough technicians to dust all those coins, we'd be cross-matching prints from now till Christmas. You tell Telecom they can bank their cash. Let them concentrate on giving us that list of numbers in use last Saturday night, at eleven.'

The young man's earnest face brightened. 'I've got that already, sir. There were six phones used in Gullane at that time, as well as the call box.' He caught Skinner's expression and nodded. 'Yes, sir, BT confirmed that it was used at the time in question.

'Mr Martin told me to give the list to Superintendent Mackie,' he went on, quickly, 'for him to check it out.'

'That's good. Thanks, Sammy.'

The young man nodded and made to leave, but hesitated.

131

'Yes?' said Skinner. 'Something bothering you?'

The constable took a deep breath. 'Well, sir, couldn't we just check the subscribers and see who they are? I mean most of the folk in Gullane are . . .' He stopped, sensing a chasm before him.

Skinner smiled. 'Are old bufties, you were going to say? Like me, you mean?'

'Well, eh . . .'

'You're right, of course. I'll probably know most of them. No, Sam, the main reason for checking every call is to prove beyond doubt that it was the phone box that was used.'

Pye nodded, and headed off, back to the CID suite to pass his message to BT. Skinner stepped into his secretary's office. 'Any deliveries?' he asked.

Ruth nodded and picked up a tape cassette box from her desk, waving it in the air. 'Ten minutes ago,' she said.

'Excellent,' said the DCC. 'Let's hear it. Full blast.'

On her side table, his secretary kept a radio cassette player, which was used mainly for monitoring radio news bulletins. She took the tape from its box, inserted it in the slot and pressed 'play', twisting the volume control to a high setting.

At first they heard only hissing, but after thirty seconds or so, the sound changed. There was no background noise at all, only a woman's voice, shouting but slurring, her words insistent, but thick, as if with alcohol. 'Lemme go, lemme go,' she called out.

Then a man's voice – not so loud, flatter, but sounding just as drunk. 'Fuckn' bitch,' he said.

'Lemme go, ya bassa.' Another slurred shout. Then a sound, a crack, the noise possibly of palm meeting cheek.

The hissing resumed once more. Ruth pressed the stop

button and rewound the tape. 'There's a note with it,' she said, handing Skinner a folded sheet of paper. He opened it and read.

'*This is what we were able to do. The man's voice was a bonus. I guess your caller used a phone box and that he had the door open.*' Skinner smiled, guessing why he would choose to do that at such an hour on a Saturday night. '*The mikes on your public phones are very good. The people you hear on the tape could have been up to twenty-five yards away. Good Luck, Caroline Farmer.*'

He looked at Ruth. 'Some bonuses from my Saturday call,' he said. 'It was made from the phone box near my cottage.'

'Mmm,' she said. 'You do have the nicest neighbours, don't you?'

Skinner grinned at the waspish dryness of her humour. 'Aye,' he nodded, 'and I'm going to find out who they are too. Have a copy made, and give it to me. I'll send McIlhenney out to Gullane to play it, discreetly, to the pub owners and bar staff in the village.

'He should get a laugh from them, at least, and maybe, a couple of names.'

27

Detective Superintendent Brian Mackie's expression was usually deadpan, and so, as the McGrath investigation team filed into the conference room at the St Leonards Divisional Police Office at exactly 9 a.m. on Tuesday morning, Andy Martin was surprised to note that he looked a shade nervous.

He strolled up to the head of the table, where Mackie stood. 'Chin up, Thin Man,' he whispered. 'You should be pleased that the boss asked me to have you run the morning briefing, and on your turf too.'

'Sure,' said the newly promoted divisional CID commander, 'but it'd be easier if he wasn't here himself. This is the first time I've done something like this, outside Special Branch, and that wasn't the same at all. You know what the boss is like. He can't stop himself from jumping in, even when he isn't in the chair.'

The Head of CID grinned. 'Don't I bloody know it. But don't worry. I've asked him to be on his best behaviour.'

Mackie, his shiny bald head adding to his cadaverous look, looked unconvinced. 'Aye, but even at that. I really feel in the spotlight here, considering who I've taken over from.'

'You put that right out of your mind. With hindsight, you should have been in this job before him anyway. If you hadn't been so valuable in SB, you probably would have been.'

For the first time, the slim detective looked reassured.

'Kind of you to say that, Andy, true or not.' He paused, and looked around the room as if searching for a face. Skinner, making his way along the far side of the room, caught his eye and nodded.

'The boss is here, but is your sergeant coming?' the Superintendent murmured.

'No way,' replied Martin, quietly. 'He's let her come back to work this morning, but I'm going to make sure that they're never in the same room, not with other officers around anyway.'

Mackie nodded. 'Good. Especially not with Maggie Rose. She's good at studied disapproval, is my second-in-command.'

He looked up to see Skinner reach Detective Chief Inspector Rose, his Executive Assistant before Pamela Masters' brief tenure in the post. 'Mornin' Mags,' said the DCC. 'How's the new boss?'

Rose looked over her shoulder towards Mackie. 'Strict but fair just about covers it, sir,' she said with a faint smile. If Skinner noticed that it was less warm than usual, he gave no sign.

'Bit like me, you mean?' He reached out to shake the Superintendent's hand. 'Mornin' Brian. Christ,' he said suddenly. 'Look at the three of you. All graduates from my private office. A certain route to the top, indeed.' Skinner rarely said anything simply to make conversation, but the words were out before he could stop them. Had he not known Maggie Rose so well he would never have noticed the slight change in her expression.

'Anyway,' he said, quickly. 'Let's get on with it.' He nodded towards a chair at the side of the table. 'Brian, I'll sit over there, and I'll try to keep my mouth shut, honest. Arrange the rest as you like.'

Mackie nodded and rapped the table. 'Okay, ladies and gentlemen,' he called out, 'if you'll all take seats, please.' He looked around the room. In addition to Skinner, Martin and Rose, by his side, Sammy Pye and Neil McIlhenney faced him across the table, together with three other officers, two men and a woman.

Quickly, the room came to order.

'Very good,' said the Superintendent, flanked in his seat by his deputy and by the Head of CID. 'This briefing has been called to review progress yesterday in our enquiries in Gullane, where a lead has developed in the McGrath Murder investigation.' He glanced round at Martin. 'Of the officers involved in the investigation, sir, only the people in this room know the full story, that Mr Skinner's call on Saturday was made from Gullane.'

Briefly, but comprehensively, Mackie related the developments since Skinner's unexpected telephone call, and since the discovery of its point of origin.

'First of all,' he said, once everyone was up to date, 'let's deal with the follow-up visits to the six telephone subscribers on that BT list. Sergeant Reid, you handled that . . .'

The second female officer in the room nodded, and sat straighter in her chair. 'Yes, sir. They've all been checked out, as far as possible.'

'How did you go about it?' asked Martin.

'Discreetly, sir, as ordered. Mr Mackie said that what we really wanted was to get a look at these people. So I told every person I visited that I was investigating reports of nuisance phone calls in the area, and was checking to see whether they'd had any. Just to make it convincing, sir, I called on all the homes around each of the names on my list.'

'Have you excluded everyone?' asked Skinner from the

side. Mackie glanced at Martin and raised an eyebrow, slightly.

'No, sir. One subscriber wasn't in. However the folk next door told me that he was a seventy-year-old widower, who'd gone off in a hurry on Sunday to visit his sick grandson. Other than that, though, I've seen them all. Of the other five, four were middle-aged couples, and the fifth was an old lady in a retirement community.'

'Very good, Janice,' said Mackie, hurriedly taking back control of the meeting. 'Sergeant Spring, will you please report on the house-by-house check.'

Spring, the older Sergeant, nodded. 'We're going as fast as we can, sir. Some of the houses we know are a dead loss, but like Janice, we have to be seen to be calling on everyone, so it's taking a while. There's been nothing suspicious so far.'

'How about empty houses?' asked Martin. 'Have you encountered any?'

'Seven, so far,' said Spring. 'Five of them have no known local key-holder, two have a key-holder known to us, and the other is believed to have a local caretaker, but the neighbours don't know who that is. They keep themselves to themselves in Gullane, right enough, sir.' All at once the Sergeant gulped, visibly, and glanced across at Skinner.

The DCC himself broke the ensuing silence. 'What have you done about the empties, John?' he asked.

'Had a good look round, sir, as far as we could. There didn't seem to be anything out of the ordinary, anywhere.'

Skinner nodded and leaned back in his seat.

Mackie looked at the officer beside Spring. 'Sergeant Carney, you've been doing the pubs. Any feedback?'

'Some, sir. It's a pity it was a Saturday. During the week the firemen from the Training School would have been around, and they'd have been going home around that time, sober mostly, and potentially good witnesses.

'As it was we found a couple of guys who admitted they were passing the phone box, just before eleven. They were a bit shifty like, so we pressed them. One of them finally admitted that he had a piss in it on the way past.'

'And presumably, Phil, there was no-one else in it at the time,' said Maggie Rose, with a grim, disapproving smile.

'Not that he mentioned, ma'am.'

Mackie clasped his hands together and leaned forward. 'So that's it then, is it? Phone subscribers clear; nothing from the house-to-house; nothing from the pubs. Blanks all round.'

He looked round the table, from face to face. 'In that case, we'd all best go back and get on with the house-to-house, as quickly as possible.'

He was almost in the act of rising, when Skinner leaned forward. 'There is just one other thing, Superintendent,' he said. Martin, Mackie and Rose looked at him, their surprise undisguised. 'McIlhenney has something to report. Go on, Neil.'

The bulky Sergeant shifted uncomfortably in his chair. He looked along the table at Mackie. 'We had a tip, sir,' he began, 'that two people, man and woman, were near the phone box when the call was made.' The Superintendent looked back, stone-faced. His Special Branch experience still fresh in his mind, he knew better than to ask where the information had come from if Skinner's aide had not volunteered the fact.

'On the boss's instruction, I did some asking around. I'm assured that they're a couple called Grayson, Michael and Rose, of 12 Carnoustie Terrace, in the village.'

The DCC leaned forward again. 'I know you're hard

pressed with the house-to-house, so I thought Neil and I would check them out. Just to keep our hands in, so to speak. That all right with you, Brian?'

'Of course, boss,' said Mackie, managing to suppress his sigh.

28

'Watch this bend, Neil.'

Sergeant McIlhenney believed that, if you were any good at the business of life, you would learn something new every day. For him, Tuesday's unexpected lesson was that Bob Skinner was a nervous passenger in a motor car.

All the way along the coast road, the DCC had shifted uneasily in the passenger seat of the unmarked car which his personal assistant had drawn from the pool, the DCC having reasoned that his own car was too well known in Gullane not to be noticed if it was parked outside a strange house. It was the first time that the Sergeant had ever driven his commander.

Now, as McIlhenney took the Luffness corner at scarcely more than fifty miles an hour, he pointed at the curve of the road, and barked his warning.

'No problem, boss. I've driven this road before, you know.'

'Of course you have, Neil. Sorry. I just have this dislike of being driven, that's all. Especially there. It's where my first wife was killed.'

'Ah,' said McIlhenney, understanding at once. 'You should have said. I just assumed that I'd be driving.'

'Quite right,' grunted Skinner. 'It's what personal assistants are for. Anyway, you have to confront your dislikes every so often, or they can become phobias.'

As the police car swung round the right-hand bend into Gullane, he began to give the Sergeant a series of directions.

Finally, they turned a corner, into Carnoustie Terrace, McIlhenney crawling along the kerbside until he spotted Number 12. 'There we are, boss,' he said cheerily. 'Ordeal over.'

The two policeman stepped from the car, into the warm sunshine of the summer day. There were no more than two dozen hoses in Carnoustie Terrace, linked, as its name suggested, in groups of six. From the roughcast exterior Skinner's assistant guessed that they were Council-built, although he guessed by the variety of window and door styles that most were now in private ownership.

Number 12 did not have new UPVC windows. Its were wooden, modern enough, but matching only a few others in the street. He held the rusty metal gate open for Skinner and followed him into a short driveway. The house was fronted by a dark green privet hedge, in need of a trim, and by weedy grass on either side of the path, in need of cutting. The blue-painted, half-glazed front door was scratched, and marked at the bottom, as if it was kicked regularly.

'No' exactly house-proud, sir,' muttered McIlhenney, as he pressed the white plastic bell-push.

They saw the figure approach through the obscured glass, seeming to shamble rather than walk. The door opened, slowly. Although the name had meant nothing to him when he had heard it first, Skinner recognised Rose Grayson at once. Part of the street furniture of the village; a presence on his occasional visits to the local pubs.

She was a big woman, aged anywhere between forty and fifty, five feet eight and fat, hipless, with a thick waist. Despite the fine weather, a nylon housecoat hung loosely round her shoulders, covering a dirty pink sweater and a crumpled grey dress. On her feet were carpet slippers, trimmed with grey-pink artificial fur. A cigarette hung loosely between the first two fingers of her right hand. At once Skinner formed a mental picture of her husband, Michael, skinny, badly suited, with a shock of greasy dark hair, and the permanent scowl of an evil disposition. The Graysons were a couple whom the rest of the village left to themselves.

Rose Grayson sighed, as if the unannounced appearance at her door of two strange men in suits was not an unusual occurrence. 'Aye?' she asked, wearily, with a permanently defeated tone to her voice.

'Police, Mrs Grayson,' Skinner announced. 'We'd like a word. Is your husband at work?'

'You must be fuckin' jokin', mister. He's out the back. Yis'd better come in.' She turned and led them into the house. The embossed wallpaper in the hall had been painted over, but a long time before. Dirty curls made their way up from the skirting board. The living room looked like a war zone, littered with discarded newspapers, empty beer cans and full ash trays. Automatically the policemen breathed as gently as they could, trying to deflect the smell of the woman and of her shabby surroundings.

'Haud on a minute,' she said. 'Ah'll get Mick.' She stepped across to the window, white on the outside with what looked like a seagull's message, and rapped on the glass. Outside the policemen saw a man in a deck chair, as he started, as if from sleep. He was wearing the crumpled trousers of a dark suit, braces and a blue-striped shirt. He was barefoot. Rose Grayson waved her husband into the house, and turned towards her visitors. In the light from the window, they noticed for the first time a bruise beneath her left eye.

A few seconds later, Mick Grayson came into the living room, tripping over the frayed edge of the carpet and stumbling as he entered, cursing softly. 'Who're you?' he began, then looked at Skinner for the first time. 'Here, don't ah ken you? What d'yis want?'

'You might know me by sight, Mr Grayson,' said the DCC, 'but that's all. My name is Skinner, and this is Sergeant McIlhenney. We're police officers.'

The man's chest puffed out aggressively. 'Ah havenae done anything.' He turned suddenly on his wife. 'You havenae been nickin' fae the Co-op again, have ye, ya bitch?' he said, loudly. He made towards her, raising his right hand, as if to hit her. Before he had taken more than two steps McIlhenney grabbed him by the wrist and swung him round.

Grayson made the merest of gestures towards him with his free hand, bunched into a fist, but stopped abruptly, as common sense, or self-preservation, took over. 'Wise man,' said the sergeant, giving the wrist a quick, painful squeeze before releasing it.

'Look,' said Skinner, 'for once we don't want to talk to you about anything you've done. We're looking for help with an investigation.'

Mick Grayson, subdued, looked at him. 'That's a'right then,' he said, managing, amazingly, to sound condescending. 'Whit is it?'

'We're told that you two were out on Saturday night, and that at around eleven you were having an argument just outside the village hall.'

Grayson looked blank. 'Were we?' he said.

His wife narrowed her eyes, her hand going to the bruise on her cheek. 'Aye,' she muttered, fiercely. 'We were.'

Her husband's eyes dropped. 'Oh aye, so we were.'

'What was the barney about?' McIlhenney asked.

Rose Grayson glowered. 'That yin bought himself a pint

and . . .' Her voice soared with indignation, '. . . a whisky wi' the last of our money, and never got anything for me. Honest tae God, he's a miserable wee toerag wi' a drink in him, so he is. Come tae think of it, he's a miserable wee toerag a' the time.'

'Aye,' said Skinner, 'but he's *your* miserable wee toerag, isn't he?'

He went on quickly. 'Right, we've got you two at the foot of the hill between the Post Office and Bissett's, having a ding-dong. Now think carefully. On your way past, and while this was going on, did you see anyone in the phone box?'

Mick Grayson shook his head. 'Naw,' said his wife.

'Think carefully, I said. This is important.'

Husband and wife, reproved, knitted their brows. But eventually, they shook their heads. 'Naw,' said Mick, 'Ah honestly cannae remember.'

The DCC sighed. 'Well, did you see anyone at all in the area?'

There was a pause. Rose looked at her spouse, a new hesitant look in her eyes. 'Well,' she said finally, more to Mick than to the policemen, 'there was yon man.'

Grayson nodded, briefly, but it was enough. She looked back to Skinner and McIlhenney. 'We were havin' a barney, like you said. I shoved Mick and he hut me. Just after that, this man appeared, doon the hill, well-dressed like. Ah said tae him, "Did you see that, mister?" He nodded his head and just went on. "Some fuckin' gent you," Ah shouted after him.

'He stopped at that, and he said tae Mick, "Don't hit the lady, then." He'd have walked on again, but Mick took a swing at him.'

'So what did he do, this man?' urged Skinner.

Grimly, unexpectedly, Rose Grayson smiled. 'He flattened the wee toerag, didn't he? Only hit him the wance, but he laid him as broad as he was long.' The smile broadened into a grin.

'Then what?'

'He turned away, got intae a motor in the village hall car park, and drove off, back up the hill. He just missed runnin' Mick over. More's the pity,' she added, sincerely.

Skinner looked at McIlhenney, and shook his head. 'Describe him,' he snapped.

She shrugged. 'Wee bit smaller than you, slim like, dark hair.'

Mick Grayson shook his head. 'Naw, he wisnae like that. He was taller than yon man, and he had fair hair.'

'Come on,' McIlhenney barked, 'make up your minds. Fair hair? Dark hair? Tall? Short? Which is it?'

'Ah'm right,' said Rose.

'Naw ye're no'!' her husband insisted.

'Jesus Christ!' shouted Skinner, exasperated. 'We're agreed, then, that he wasn't a bald-headed dwarf.' He looked at Rose. 'How about his car? What colour was it?'

'Light,' she answered. 'But it was shining orange under the street light, so a couldnae tell for sure.'

'What make?'

She shrugged. 'Ah dinnae ken things like that.'

The DCC sighed. 'Okay, one last thing. When the guy got to the top of the hill, did he turn right or left?' She looked at him, befuddled. 'Towards North Berwick, or towards Aberlady?' he asked, patient once again.

She paused, then nodded. 'North Berwick. He wis heading for North Berwick,' she announced, with a smile of satisfaction.

Skinner nodded. 'Good. Something at least. Right, that's

as far as we can take it. Come on, Neil.' The policemen headed for the doorway, until Skinner turned. He pointed at Mick Grayson. 'You,' he said, evenly. 'If I ever hear that you've hit your wife again, I'll have you barred from every pub in East Lothian.' He strode off, leading McIlhenney out, into the fresh air.

'What a pair of disasters,' the Sergeant exploded, outside.

'Say that again,' Skinner agreed.. 'Still, we've got something at least. Assuming it was our man, he was heading out of Gullane. There's nowhere beyond the Post Office where he wouldn't stick out like a sore thumb.'

29

'Does it take you any further?'

Skinner shook his head. 'Not really, Pam. I had hoped that we'd come up with a description of the guy, but not a double dose. That's worse than useless. We can hardly announce that we're looking for someone who's either tall and fair or stocky and dark, or issue two photofits.'

'Which one do you think is most likely to be accurate?' she asked.

'Hah! Take your pick on that one. The Graysons were both pissed as rats. The only thing she was certain about was the direction he took away from the scene.'

'And does that help?'

Skinner knitted his brows. 'Maybe it does. It tells me that if he does have the boy hidden, it isn't in Gullane itself. As I said to Big Neil, most of the holiday houses are to the west of the village. The eastern part was built much later. The houses are closer together, on smaller plots, and nearly all of them are occupied.'

'So what do you do next?'

'I've spoken to Andy. We've pretty well decided to tell the press tomorrow that we're widening the search to East Lothian. We can't knock on every door in the county, but there are quite a few empty properties in North Berwick. We can check them, at least.'

She looked at him doubtfully. 'Is there much chance of a result?'

He smiled, sadly. 'Next to bugger all,' he admitted. 'But

what else can we do? Andy'll set the ball rolling at his press briefing tomorrow.' He leaned back on the couch, the remnants of his late supper still on a tray in his lap, and sighed. She leaned over and kissed him on the forehead.

'Cheer up, love,' she said. 'At least the investigation's still doing something.'

'Yes, but to what purpose? It's been three days since that phone call: three days since the guy said that we'd hear from him again. Three days with that wee boy at this nutter's mercy. "At my disposition," he said. It chills my blood, to think what might be happening to him.'

She stood up, took the tray from him, laid it on the floor, and tugged at his arm. 'Bob, enough,' she said. 'You look knackered and you sound depressed. It's almost eleven. Let's go to bed, even if it's only to sleep.'

He nodded. 'Yes, okay.' He rose, wearily, taking her hand as she led him through to the bedroom.

The bedside lamp was still on as she slipped in beside him, naked. 'Of course,' she said. 'We don't have to sleep.' He reached across, without a word, and switched the light off. They made love silently. Pamela, inventive as always, took the initiative, allowing him time to settle his mind and drawing his attention towards her. And yet, even as he climaxed, with his lover bucking and writhing astride him, there was a part of his mind that was somewhere else.

She knew it, too. She was barely finished, before she rolled away and lay with her back to him in the dark. 'That was a new twist,' she said. 'It's usually the woman who fakes it!'

He was moved by the hurt in her voice. 'No, Pam, I didn't, honest. It was good, great, like always. I just wasn't really in the mood. I'm sorry, honey.' He put a hand on her hip, and leaned over her, kissing her neck. She turned

148

on to her back, and looked up at him.

'What is it, then?' she asked. 'Second thoughts?'

He shook his head. 'Nothing to do with you and me,' he promised. 'I just can't get this man out of my mind. He's singled me out to be contacted. He killed Leona, and she was my friend. He kidnapped her son, the wee boy I rescued last year. It's as if he's speaking directly to me, and there's a taunt in it. He even came to my home village to call me.

'It's as if he's challenging me to guess where he's hiding the kid.'

He stopped short, and she could see his eyes, gleaming in the light from the window. 'Can you imagine how angry that makes me? And how frustrated?'

Pamela propped herself up on her elbows, the edge of the duvet falling around her waist. 'Yes,' she said softly, 'I can imagine. I'm sorry I'm such a petulant bitch.'

He laid a hand on the flat of her stomach, rubbing it gently. 'You're not,' he murmured. 'Not at all. You're under pressure too, with the *Spotlight* article, and those appalling photos. With one thing and another, it's as if we're drowning, you and I.'

She laid her hand on his, half a second before it suddenly clenched, tightening on her belly. 'Drowning!' he hissed, suddenly.

30

When the telephone rang, Alex and Andy were watching a video. One of the *Batman* series with interchangeable heroes and big-name villains, was reaching its conclusion.

'Damn,' said Skinner's daughter, freezing the frame and picking up the telephone, to find her father on the other end. 'Pops, really,' she said. 'We were just getting to the good bit.

'Of the movie, I meant!' She passed the phone to her fiancé.

'Yes, Bob,' said Martin. 'What's the panic?'

'No panic, but a sudden thought. Quite clearly, this guy is thumbing his nose at me, with a call to my private line from my home village. This guy doesn't want to get caught, but he does want to show us how clever, resourceful and daring he is. You agree with me?'

'Yes, I'll go along with that.'

'Good, now try this one for size. If this guy is an expert on me, and knows about my connection with Mark, don't you think he's bound to know where I first encountered the child?'

Martin whistled. 'You think he might be hiding him up on the moors, where the plane went down?'

'I don't think, I wonder. Let's postpone the press briefing tomorrow, and take a look up there.'

'Okay,' said the Head of CID, shifting his position against the back of the sofa, as Alex stood up to go into the kitchen. 'I'll do that, first thing. I'll put men on all the roads, then get a helicopter to take a look at all the sheds and bothies scattered about up there.'

'It makes sense, Andy,' Skinner stressed. 'We're pretty certain that he took the laddie out of the city, yet he wouldn't have risked being too long on the road, not with him in his car. Those moors aren't much more than half an hour from the McGrath house.'

'Sure, I agree. We'll do it, first thing. Now you get some sleep and let us finish our video.'

He replaced the phone just as Alex came back into the living room, carrying two cans of Diet Coke. 'What did Pops want?' she asked.

Andy grinned. 'He's had a hunch. You know what he's like when he gets one of them.'

'Do I! Is it a good one?'

'Could be. They usually are.'

Alex handed him his Coke, and sat beside him once again. He picked up the video control, but she put her hand on his before he could press the play button. 'Andy,' she whispered. 'Do you think my dad's losing it?'

He looked at her, surprised. 'Bob? Never. He's still firing on all cylinders. What made you ask that, anyway?'

She leaned her head on her shoulders. 'Oh, I don't know,' she said, sadly. 'He just seems like such a lost soul just now.'

Andy touched her chin, gently, and tilted her face towards him. 'Love, you can see how much he's missing Sarah and Jazz. So can I. So can the Chief. Your dad's the only one who doesn't realise it.'

'No.' She was suddenly indignant. 'Because he's shacked up with this Pamela woman!'

'Maybe. She was there for him when he had his bust-up with Sarah. She helps him ward off the loneliness. Maybe he does the same for her.'

'Is she a gold-digger, d'you think? Does she have an eye for the main chance?'

He shook his head, after a few seconds' thought. 'No. I wouldn't say so. I don't think she sees herself as your next stepmother, if that's what you mean.'

'Do you like her, Andy?'

He pondered her question again. 'Yes, I reckon I do. She's bright, intelligent and she seems to care for Bob a lot. She had nothing to do with his marriage break-up, remember.'

'Maybe not, but with her around there's no chance of it being mended.'

Andy sighed. 'That, my darling, is something your dad's got to figure out for himself. Always assuming that he wants to mend it, that is.'

'And his judgement, in sleeping with this woman? What do you think of that? Honestly?'

He looked her in the eye. 'We're all entitled to make mistakes, love.'

Alex grunted. 'Let's hope the Police Board take that view tomorrow,' she said, gloomily.

31

The press benches in Edinburgh's ornate Victorian council chamber had never been more full for a meeting of the Joint Police Board, made up of elected members of the local authorities whose areas the force covered.

The Chair of the Board, Marcia Topham, a Labour councillor from Midlothian, was regarded by Sir James Proud as a moderate, and someone with whom he could work. Or as Bob Skinner often put it in private, someone whom he could twist round his little finger.

Today was different. In the ante-room, outside the chamber, the Chief Constable saw that Councillor Topham looked tense and nervous. As he had anticipated, Skinner's request to address the meeting at the close of the discussion had been rejected, after consultation by the Chair with her senior colleagues.

'Like I said,' the DCC had growled. 'She's had her orders.'

A buzz went round the press gallery as the members and officials filed into the chamber, and as they saw that Bob Skinner was not in attendance. Marcia Topham frowned in their direction, but her disapproval was ignored.

She called the meeting to order quickly, pounding on the old mahogany desk with her gavel. 'Ladies, gentlemen,' she said loudly, to mask the tremor in her voice. 'Let us proceed.'

She looked around the members, and nodded to the Chief Constable, who was seated in the well of the chamber, alongside the Board's solicitor. 'Item One,' she announced.

Bob Skinner grudged every minute of the time that he was forced, occasionally, to spend at Board meetings. It was an advisory body, but under the previous administration it had become a vehicle for political speeches. However, on the basis of a few months' evidence, the change of government had seen little change in the nature of the meetings.

'It still sounds the same, Jimmy,' Skinner had grumbled. 'Different bloody axes being ground, that's all.'

The Chief Constable on the other hand, appreciated the Board. He focused on its advisory status, deciding arbitrarily which parts of its advice he would reject, and which he would accept. He understood too that the police service benefited from the lack of significant political interference with its work, and had no intention of rocking that particular boat.

'Indulge them, Bob,' he always advised his deputy. 'Let them have their say, then let them go away home. They don't have any weight, so they can't throw it about.'

Today, though, the normally benign Chief was in no mood to be conciliatory.

The listed items on the agenda were eliminated with unprecedented speed, until, fifty minutes after opening the meeting, Councillor Topham announced: 'We now come to other business. I am advised of a motion by Councillor Agnes Maley, of Edinburgh City Council.'

Sir James looked around as Councillor Maley rose to her feet. He knew her well: a self-confessed enemy of the police service, she owed her position of power within her party to her ability to mobilise the enlarged group of women members in her support. As she stood, short, squat and denim-clad, she was flanked by five of her colleagues.

'Thank you, Chair,' she began, but had gone no further before the Chief Constable thrust himself to his feet.

'If you will excuse me, Councillor Maley,' he boomed. He glowered at the Chair. 'Councillor Topham, I had assumed that you would instruct that this motion, if it has to be heard at all, should be stated without the press and public being present. Standing orders allow you to declare that sensitive items be discussed in private. I have to insist that be the case here.'

Marcia Topham stared at the silver-haired policeman. This was not kind, benign 'Call me Jimmy' Proud. This was someone she had never seen before, fierce, bristling, formidable and on battle bent. For several seconds her mouth formed sounds, but none emerged.

She was beaten to it by a shout from the left. 'I protest, Chair. The Chief Constable's right out of order. He's responsible to this meeting. He doesn't run it.'

Sir James rounded on Agnes Maley. 'As usual, Councillor, you're mistaken when it comes to police matters. I am not responsible to this Board. It advises me. Now I am advising it that it is not appropriate for the private business of a senior serving officer – any serving officer, for that matter – to be discussed in public session.'

He looked back towards Councillor Topham. 'Madam Chair, you may wish to consult your solicitor.'

Grateful for the escape route, Marcia Topham nodded. 'Mr Wanless,' she asked, quickly. 'What's your guidance?'

The solicitor took a deep breath and looked up at her. 'The Chief Constable is quite right: you have the power to order this matter heard in private. However, you do not have an obligation in this case.'

A murmur of satisfaction sped along the benches behind Proud. 'That said,' the solicitor went on, his voice rising in emphasis, 'I am bound to remind you that no form of privilege attaches to this body. Should anything be said in discussion which was held subsequently to be defamatory of Mr Skinner, or Detective Sergeant Masters, then the Court would undoubtedly find that defamation to have been aggravated by a decision by you to hold the debate in public. This would be in addition to the personal responsibility for such defamation which would probably attach to you.

'The decision is yours, Madam Chair.'

Councillor Topham's gaze settled on the lawyer, as if she was trapped by the headlights of an oncoming car. At last she glanced helplessly across towards Councillor Maley. 'Will the press and public please leave,' she said.

Before her, on the members' benches and in the public gallery, cries of protest rang out. However, with council attendants and two police constables acting as ushers, the room was cleared relatively quickly.

'Very good,' said the Chair, as the door closed on the last journalist. 'Now, Councillor Maley, do you wish to proceed?'

'One moment more, please!' Proud's voice boomed out even more loudly. 'Before the lady begins, I have something else to say.'

For a moment, Councillor Topham looked as if she would use her gavel to intervene, but the Chief froze her with a glare and a dismissive wave of his hand.

'I want it recorded in the minutes of this meeting that I believe that it is absolutely disgraceful for this motion to be entertained. It relates entirely to matters which are within Mr Skinner's private life, and which are no business of this Board in any way.

'I believe that the proposer and seconder are motivated by malice against the police in general, which has been evident before at meetings of this Board. They have seized on the disgraceful publicity attaching to Mr Skinner's private life as a means of damaging my service, even if it means the further public humiliation of one of its finest officers.

'The days in which personal relationships between serving police officers were forbidden are long gone, as the proposer and seconder, and their supporters, know well. Indeed were I to propose their reintroduction, they would be the first on their feet in protest.'

He turned and looked at the benches behind him. 'On a personal level, rather than professionally, I do not believe that by today's standards Mr Skinner and Miss Masters are wrongdoers. By my own standards perhaps, but the world is changing.' He stared hard at Agnes Maley. 'I am prepared to bet you,' he said, 'that among the members of this Board, there must be at least one who is living in what some might call sin, with a person separated and not yet divorced.' The councillor's face flushed beetroot red.

Sir James turned back to the Chair. 'I am no great Bible scholar,' he said, 'but I do remember well the story of the woman taken in adultery.

'I will say just this. Before anyone casts the first stone at Bob Skinner, they should remember that no-one in this room is in a better position than me to know which of you is without sin. And before this matter is put to a vote, Councillor Maley and her friends would do well to bear that in mind.

'Now I will leave you to your discussions.' He picked up his papers and strode from the chamber.

32

Andy Martin had only one phobia: heights. He also possessed an inherent will to win which had made him a feared opponent on the rugby field, and which would not allow him to be overcome by anything, not even mortal terror.

He had tackled his secret enemy head-on by joining a rock-climbing club in his senior year at high school, and had taken this further at university by joining the mountaineering club. It had been hard, all the way through, but he had kept his jaw tight and his hands strong in a domestic climbing career which had taken in some of the finest climbs in the Cuillins, the beautiful mountains of the Island of Skye, and in the spectacular, craggy Lake District.

Yet a true phobia is never banished; it is only overcome moment by moment. And so, as the police helicopter swept over the purple heather of the moorland, Martin, in the co-pilot's seat, still felt a lurching in his stomach as he looked down, and still fought to master the panic at the back of his brain.

'Okay, John,' he said to the police pilot through his head-set, essential equipment given the booming noise within the cockpit from the engine behind them, and the whirring of the rotors above. 'That's the fifth sector on this map covered, and no sign of any recent activity up here, other than bloody sheep. One more to go: bank south please, down towards Longformacus.'

The pilot nodded in confirmation and swung the craft

round. They were flying at a height of around three hundred feet, high enough not to be easily identified from the ground, low enough to allow Martin to scan the area beneath with powerful wide-field binoculars. They flew on for ten minutes, sweeping the sector in swathes, east to west, west to east, as if they were mowing it from a great height.

'There's a bothy down to the right,' Martin called out at last. 'Drop us down a bit and let's take a closer look.' The pilot obeyed, dropping the helicopter by around fifty feet and slowing their steady speed still further.

Martin peered through the glasses. The bothy, a stone-built shelter, was in poor repair. At one corner, its slate roof had collapsed. There had once been glass in its single window, but now its panes were smashed, and its door hung by a single hinge. All around, the grass stood high, and the narrow worn path which led to the door from the heathery pasture was overgrown and barely discernible.

The Chief Superintendent shook his head. 'No,' he called, into his microphone, 'another dud. There's been no-one there for years by the look of it. Pick it up again.'

The pilot flew on as ordered, through one swathe, then another, until finally they were almost over the village of Longformacus, beyond which the character of the land changed. They were to the west of the tiny community when Martin spotted the caravan. 'What's that doing there?' he asked himself.

It was a touring van, still shiny and new. Yet it was well away from the roadway, parked on the bank of a small, fast-flowing stream feeding into a small loch, over which they had just flown. There was no car alongside it, but the grass around it was crushed and torn, as if a vehicle had turned and reversed there, recently and frequently.

'Where are we?' Martin muttered again. He looked at

his map, tracing their progress with a finger. The loch was marked as the Black Water reservoir, but there was no carriageway shown at all.

'Know what that road is down there?' the detective asked the pilot. 'Either I'm misreading the map, or it doesn't exist.'

'That's the Southern Upland Way, sir, the walkway that crosses the country from the Solway Firth to the East Coast. There's going on for a hundred miles of it. You can manage a car along part of it . . . just about.'

'Let's see if we can find out who owns that caravan, then. We came over a farmhouse a couple of miles back. Put me down near there and I'll see if anyone knows.'

The pilot nodded and swung the helicopter around. He found a flat spot in an empty field just over a quarter of a mile from the house and set it down. Martin jumped out, gratefully, and set off across the dry grass. The gravelled road to the farmhouse ran beside the field, turning through a high-pillared gateway. As the detective slid through a gap in the beech hedge which served as a boundary, a man appeared at the head of the driveway.

'What's up?' he asked, cheerfully. 'Mechanical trouble?' He stood around six feet four, and despite the warmth of the day he was dressed in country clothes: twill trousers, heavy shirt and tweed jacket. But Martin noted his hands before anything else. They were, he thought, bigger than any he had ever seen.

He smiled at the man, shaking his huge right mitt. 'No,' he replied. 'Nothing like that. I'm a policeman, from Edinburgh. We're looking for someone, and we thought that he might just have a hideaway up here on the moors.

'My name's Martin, by the way. Detective Chief Superintendent.'

'Robert Carr,' said the ruddy-faced man. 'I own this land. Thousand bloody acres of it, much of it useless for anything but sheep.'

'Does that extend up there – ' he pointed westwards – 'past the reservoir?'

'Yes,' replied Carr, 'and a damn sight further.'

'There's a caravan up there, beside the stream.'

The farmer looked surprised. 'Is there? Still?'

'You know about it?'

'Yes, but I'd assumed that the fellow would have been gone by now.'

'What fellow?'

Robert Carr turned towards his big grey stone farmhouse, beckoning Martin to follow. 'Chap rang the doorbell about a week ago. Said his name was Mr Gilbert. He told me that he was planning to do some walks along the Way, and that he had a caravan as a base. He asked me if he could park it somewhere out of the way.

'He seemed like a decent chap, so I said okay, and gave him directions up the road. Told him he could set up by the stream, and take fresh water from it . . . just as long as he didn't put anything back in! He offered me cash, but I told him I wasn't that strapped.'

'Have you seen him about much?'

'I haven't seen him at all, not since then. I'd thought he'd moved on.'

Martin looked up at him as they reached the farmhouse's kitchen door. 'Can you describe him for me, this Mr Gilbert?'

Carr ushered him indoors. 'Mary!' he bellowed. 'Tea for two, lass!' As he led the policeman through to a comfortable study, a small grey woman scurried in the opposite direction, smiling and nodding. 'Housekeeper,' he said. 'I'm a widower.'

161

He paused. 'Gilbert,' he went on. 'Description. Right. Same height as you, few years older maybe. Clean-shaven, fair hair, though not as fair as yours. Short and very well cut. Slim build, but not skinny, if you know what I mean. Wearing light cotton trousers and a red teeshirt, with a badge saying Reebok or something. Also, wore sports sandals, without socks.'

'What about his accent?' asked the policeman.

For the first time, the farmer looked puzzled. 'Haven't a bloody clue,' he said eventually. 'You know, I don't think he had one.'

'No? You sure? Scottish, English, Irish, Welsh?'

Carr's eyes narrowed, as he tried to hear again the sound of the man's voice. But eventually he shook his head. 'Sorry. Not Welsh or Irish: that's all I can tell you with any certainty.'

The study door opened, and the housekeeper appeared with tea and biscuits on a tray. She filled two cups and handed one to each of the men before leaving, still without having uttered a word.

Martin declined milk and sugar. Actually, he disliked strong tea, but was too polite to say so. 'What about his car?' he asked.

'Never saw it,' his host retorted. 'He left it at the foot of the road and walked up the drive. I could just see the top of the caravan over the hedge.'

The tall man beamed. 'So, could he be your quarry, my Mr Gilbert?'

'No idea,' Martin lied. 'But I would like to talk to him.' He smiled across at Carr. 'Can I use your phone? To be on the safe side, I think I'd better call in the Cavalry!'

33

Skinner, from the corridor, leaned into the ante-room to Sir James Proud's office. 'Is the Chief free?' he asked Gerry, his civilian secretary. It was just after midday.

'Yes, sir. He's catching up with his correspondence, that's all. I'm sure he'll be pleased to see you.' The young man looked efficient and crisp in an immaculately pressed short-sleeved white shirt. '*That our officers should be half as smart,*' the DCC mused as he opened the door and stepped into Proud Jimmy's long office.

The Chief Constable looked up from the papers on his desk. 'Oh, hello, Bob,' he said, almost casually. 'What can I do for you?'

Skinner grinned. 'You can give me your version of whatever the hell you said to the Police Board this morning. I've just had a call from Roger Mather, the Tory member from East Lothian; he was laughing so much I thought he'd have a stroke.'

'Was he?' remarked the Chief, blandly. 'What was the outcome? I left before the end.'

'No vote was taken. Apparently Aggie Maley did some ranting, but didn't quite get round to proposing the motion.'

Proud Jimmy nodded. 'That's good,' he said. 'That's good. Best that it ends that way. Best for you and best for the force.'

'Aye,' laughed Skinner, 'but according to Roger, most of the ranting was about you. Christ, Jimmy, did you really accuse Maley of being shacked up with a married man?'

'Certainly not. Not directly, at any rate. But what if I had? It's true.'

'And did you really threaten to rattle all the skeletons in their cupboards if they put the motion to a vote?'

The old Chief leaned back in his chair beaming, now, with undisguised pleasure. 'Too bloody right I did, my son. Too bloody right I did. If those bastards thought that they could have a go at you and I'd just sit there and allow it; or worse, if they thought they could just ignore me . . .

'They fucking well know different now, don't they?'

Skinner shook his head, still laughing quietly. 'You know, Chief. When you drop the old avuncular act you drop it with a real vengeance.'

Gradually, though, his expression grew more serious. 'Mind you,' he said, 'you've made an enemy of Aggie Maley.'

'Nothing new in that. Councillor Maley's the enemy of everyone in a uniform . . . unless it's got a red star on it somewhere. I can handle her, and the troublemakers behind her. Hopefully Ms Topham will have a bit more control over them, now that I've set her the example.'

He slapped his palms flat on the desk. 'You'll find out for yourself at the next meeting. I'm on holiday, so you'll have to be there.'

Skinner scowled. 'Maybe they'll have another go.'

'No danger of that,' said Proud. 'They're paper tigers, with a lighted match held at their tails. They might shout the odds for a day or two, but they won't cross me again . . . or you. No, Bob, you don't have to worry about the councillors.'

He paused and frowned. 'Ministers, though, that's another matter. I don't know this new Secretary of State at all. What's he like?'

Skinner shrugged his shoulders. 'I barely know him either,' he said. 'I've met him twice, to brief him on outstanding matters. On each occasion he just listened, barely said a word.'

'What do we know about him?'

'He's squeaky clean. He's a doctor by profession. He was a GP for five years, till he landed his seat in the wilds of Glasgow.'

'Pro-police or anti, would you say?'

The DCC thought the question over. 'Pro-himself more than anything else. He wants to climb the tree. I reckon he'd step on his own granny to reach a higher branch.'

'Watch him, then,' warned Proud.

He swung round in his chair. 'Bob,' he ventured, suddenly tentative. 'About Pamela. Would it make life easier for you if I gave her a job on my personal staff?'

Skinner looked at him, surprised. 'Yes, Jimmy, it would. But it would make life more difficult for you, so I would be against it.

'The thought's much appreciated,' he said. 'But Andy and I are considering Pam's career options. And soon, I'm going to have to let her in on our thinking.'

34

'This could be nothing, but there is a chance that it could be a life-or-death situation.' Detective Chief Superintendent Martin looked round the group of officers gathered in Farmer Carr's driveway.

There were twenty of them, all but one of them men, and apart from the Head of CID, Detective Superintendent Mackie, and DCI Rose, they were all in uniform. Most were carrying carbines.

'The caravan's in the middle of open country,' he said. 'The chopper's just done another overflight, and there's still no sign of any car. There's no obvious place close by where one could be hidden either. There's an old barn a mile away, but that's been checked.

'Now there is no hard evidence of a connection with the kidnapper. However, Mr Carr's description of the man's featureless accent is in line with the tape the boss received. Added to that is the fact that we've checked the number plate on the caravan. It's entirely fictitious.

'Because of all that, I'm not taking any chances.

'The road approach to the van is blocked off already. Now I want a dozen armed men deployed on vantage points around the area, out of sight in the heather, just in case our suspect is in there.

'The best outcome here will be for the child to be in the caravan, alive and alone. I needn't say what the worst would be, but the most difficult would be if the kidnapper and Mark were both inside.'

He looked around the officers once more. 'So how do we approach the caravan? The thing is bang in the middle of open country. If we try to rush it and they're both inside, chances are we'll be seen before we're halfway there.

'There isn't any way we can sneak up on it safely either. There are windows all around. No,' said Martin, 'I propose that two people, man and woman, should walk right up to it and knock on the door, as if they're hikers asking for directions; water; to use the toilet; anything.'

He looked at Mackie and Rose. 'Brian, Mags, it's down to you, I think. My face has been all over the papers, and the telly, since this started. I can't take the chance that he'll recognise me. You two okay with that?'

Mackie nodded. Rose replied, 'Of course, sir. I've got a better plan than just walking up to the door though.'

'Fine, so just make it work. Now you'll both be armed. If the man does open the door to you, grab him, down him and put a gun to his head until he's cuffed.'

The Superintendent looked up at Martin. 'What if he opens the door with a gun in his hand?'

'If he does that,' the blond detective replied, 'then both of you stand aside. I'll be covering you myself. If he shows a weapon, then he goes down.' He waited for a few seconds, then nodded to one of the uniformed officers. 'Inspector Brown, get the marksmen in position.

'Chief Inspector, fill me in on your plan of approach. Let's get this operation moving.'

35

Skinner picked up the nearest of the three telephones on his desk and punched in an extension number.

'Sergeant Masters,' said the bright voice on the other end.

'Hello, Sergeant. DCC Skinner here. Word from the Board meeting. The motion was not pressed.'

He heard her gasp with surprise. 'That's great. What happened?'

'The Chief read his own version of the Riot Act, and put the fear of God into the enemy. I'll tell you tonight how he did it. So long for now.'

'Bye.'

He had barely hung up, when there was a knock on the door. 'Okay!' he called. It opened and Alan Royston came into the room. He was holding a mini-cassette.

'I thought you might like to hear this, sir,' he began. 'It's a tape of the Radio Forth news bulletin at the top of the hour. Councillor Maley's on it complaining about the Chief bullying the Chair of the Police Board, as she puts it.'

The DCC grinned. 'From what I hear, she's right about that. Does she say anything about me?'

'She says that in the circumstances she didn't press for a vote, because she knew that the Chief would ignore it anyway. She winds up complaining about his generally threatening behaviour . . . her words again.' The press officer paused. 'And she says she still thinks that you should be censured,' he concluded.

What about Pam?'

'Her name wasn't mentioned.'

'How will the written media report her?' asked Skinner.

'I don't think that it'll be too serious, sir. She isn't saying anything about you that she hasn't said before. As for the Chief, he's like Edinburgh's favourite uncle. No-one can really see him as a bully and a tyrant.'

The DCC laughed. 'Apart from the Police Board, that is. So, Alan, are Pam and I yesterday's news?'

Royston's mood changed in an instant. 'I hope so, sir. But I hear from a source that Salmon's still hell of a pleased with himself. He's giving everyone the impression that there's another exclusive coming out this weekend.' He hesitated. 'I'm sorry, sir, but it's my job to ask you this. You can't think of any other potential skeleton, can you?'

Skinner frowned. 'What, you mean like Pam being pregnant?'

Royston reddened.

'Don't worry, Alan, she's not. Bad-taste joke, sorry. No Salmon hasn't been near Sarah . . . nor has anyone else from the *Spotlight*, or I would know about it. So it won't be anything involving her. Apart from my relationship with Pam, I can't think of anything else that Salmon could possibly have on me that would interest his readers.

'But look here, you keep in touch with your sources. Anything you can find out would be welcome.'

'Yes, sir. Equally, if anything does occur to you . . .'

Skinner glowered at him. 'Alan,' he said, in a grinding tone. 'That little bastard of a journalist is not going to make me into a goldfish. There are aspects of my life that are going to stay private, even from you.'

36

Maggie Rose clung to Brian Mackie with her right arm as tightly as she had ever held her husband. The difference was that she was wearing walking clothes and hopping on her left foot.

Together, they crested the rise above the caravan until they were in full sight of anyone who happened to be watching from inside. They were approaching from the opposite direction to the farmhouse, an injured rambler and her escort, in search of help.

The tourer was long and white, with a television aerial on top, and it looked virtually new. Two windows faced them, above the tow-bar and the gas bottle which sat upon it, and on what would have been the off-side on the road. Behind both, curtains were partly drawn.

They looked at the van only occasionally as they approached, but neither could see any signs of occupancy. As they approached, Mackie called out. 'Hello. Anyone there?' He and Rose watched carefully for signs of anyone moving inside, but saw not as much as a tremor.

Soon they reached the door, which was accessed by three portable steps. 'Lean against the van, love,' said the Superintendent, loud enough to be heard by anyone who might be inside. 'I'll knock.'

He stood on the middle step and rapped the door firmly with the knuckles of his left hand. His jacket was open, giving him instant access to his pistol in its holster, beneath his left armpit.

The silence from within the caravan was unbroken. He knocked again. Finally, he waved a hand in the air, as a sign to the hidden watchers, reached up and tried the handle of the door. To his surprise and that of Rose, it swung open, outwards, at his touch.

Instinctively, both officers drew their guns. 'I'm going in, Maggie,' said Mackie, and a moment later launched himself through the doorway, into the living area inside.

The caravan was empty, or so it seemed. There was a toilet cubicle in one corner, and a tall cupboard beside the door. Mackie opened both and looked inside, then checked the sliding doors of the storage areas under the window seats.

'Okay, Maggie,' he called out at last. 'It's empty. Signal Andy, would you please.'

Outside, Rose waved both arms above her head in an all-clear gesture. Twenty-one men, all but one in uniform, stood up awkwardly from their concealment in the heather. Handing his carbine to the man closest to him, Martin bounded down the slope towards her, and together they joined Mackie in the suspect van.

Martin looked round, carefully. 'It's as clean as a whistle, isn't it? There's not a sign of occupancy.'

Mackie lifted the metal lid which covered the burners of the gas hob. 'This has been cleaned,' he said. 'You can still smell the Flash.'

'So have all the other work-surfaces,' said Rose. 'Within the last couple of days, probably. There's barely a sign of dust.' She opened the cubicle door once more and checked inside. 'The chemical toilet's been emptied too, but there's bleach in the pan, so it has been used.'

'Radio communications are hopeless up here,' said Martin, stepping back to the door. 'Inspector,' he called

171

outside. 'Send someone back to the farmhouse. Use Mr Carr's phone to order a team of technicians up here.' He turned back to Mackie and Rose. 'This guy's been very efficient, but let's turn the place over quickly ourselves, just in case he's missed something.'

Each taking one third of the caravan, the three detectives began to search quickly and efficiently, looking inside empty drawers, behind curtains, inside the oven, under the movable squabs of the window seats for any scrap which might lead them eventually to the identity of the man who had brought the vehicle to its isolated parking place.

'Nothing this end,' called Maggie Rose from near the door, after ten minutes.

'Me neither,' said Mackie, from the kitchen area.

'No,' said Martin. 'Nowt here either that I can see.' As he spoke he made to pick up the squab of the seat beneath the end window, but it was secure. He tugged either end to make sure that it was indeed immovable, and was about to turn away when his eye was caught by a glint, just where the upholstery nestled against the wall. He leaned forward and forced a gap with his right index finger, working away until he freed an object.

'What's this, then?' he muttered to himself. It was in fact a piece of foil, folded over double. As he straightened it a slip of brown waxy paper fell out.

He picked it up and spread out the foil. 'Look at this,' he said to his colleagues. 'Transway. It's the cover off a "rich and creamy" yoghurt, complete with best-before date, five days hence.' He looked at the paper. 'Half a Mars bar label. And,' he said, almost triumphantly, 'there's a bar code on it.'

'Where's the nearest Transway supermarket?' asked Mackie.

'Haddington,' said Martin and Rose in unison. The DCS handed over both items to the Superintendent, holding each carefully by the corner. 'I suggest,' he said, 'that you take the wrapper down there, and find out what they can tell you from that bar code.

'I don't imagine it'll identify the transaction, but it should tell you whether they sold it and when. The technicians can have a look at the yoghurt top. If they can get a print off it, I'll bet you it was left by Mark McGrath.'

Maggie Rose looked at him, astutely. 'D'you think Mark planted those deliberately, hoping that we'd find them eventually?'

'God knows,' said Martin. 'He's a clever and resourceful wee boy, no doubt, but that might be expecting too much of him.'

Rose smiled as she remembered her first encounter with the missing child. 'I only hope,' she said earnestly, 'that we have a chance to ask him.'

37

'What's wrong?' Pamela asked from the kitchen doorway. She was leaning against the jamb, wrapped in her short dressing-gown, looking anxiously at Skinner.

He was reading the *Scotsman*, which he had picked up from the corner newsagent's towards the end of his early-morning run. His teeshirt and shorts were plastered to him, soaked with sweat.

'Hey, Bob,' she called, as he failed to answer her. 'Remember me, the woman you sleep with? I live here. Now, what's wrong?'

He glanced over his shoulder at her and smiled apologetically. 'Ach, it's the bloody press again, love. They didn't like being kicked out of the Police Board meeting yesterday, so they're having another indirect pop at me.'

'What are they saying?'

He folded the paper, and threw it down on to the work-surface. 'They've given some space to Aggie Maley's beef about the way the meeting was run, and her criticism of the Topham woman. In the process they've rehashed all that shite from the weekend, and said that my position remains "difficult", as they put it.'

She crossed the kitchen and took his arm, squeezing it. 'Don't let it get to you. It was predictable that they'd carry something. What page was it on?'

'Five.'

'There you are then,' she said, in an encouraging tone. 'Alan was right. The story's running out of steam.

174

We're not Page One news any more.'

He frowned. 'I don't care to be Page Anything news, thanks. Not in this way, at least.'

'I know. I'm sorry.' She took a deep breath. 'Look Bob,' she ventured, hesitantly. 'Would it be better for you if we were to call it a day?'

'No it would not,' he retorted sharply. The frown turned into a scowl. 'That would make me look like an even bigger shit. I run into some embarrassing personal publicity, and I react by giving you the elbow. Even I'd hate me if I did that.'

'We wouldn't need to make a public announcement about it,' Pam argued. 'I could get a transfer to another force, and be gone from out of your hair.'

Skinner looked down at her. 'I agree with you about a transfer. To tell you the truth,' he said apologetically, 'I've already put out feelers in Fife and Central. I was choosing my moment to talk to you about it. It would be much more . . . How do I put it? . . . Much more, comfortable, if we were with different forces, and, frankly, it's easier to transfer a sergeant than a Deputy Chief.'

'I understand that, and I don't mind, really. Make it Central if you can, though. I'd prefer a more urban force than Fife.' She paused. 'But don't duck the main issue. It isn't about how you'd look, it's about what's best. We always said that this arrangement had no strings, and that it was based on mutual physical attraction rather than anything deeper.' She turned him round to face her. 'Would it be better for you then, if I called it a day?'

He smiled at her, lightly, for the first time that morning. 'That's what you want, is it?'

A silence hung between them, as Pam gazed at him, solemnly. At last her eyes dropped to his chest. 'No,' she whispered. 'No it's not. I want you; and I don't feel any guilt about it, either.'

'Then enough of such talk. As for me, I'm not going to do anything to satisfy the likes of Aggie Maley or Noel Salmon.'

She frowned. 'That's your main reason for staying with me? Not giving them satisfaction?'

He growled at her, playfully. 'Don't cross-examine me, lady,' he said. 'More skilled counsel than you have tried and failed. I have many reasons for staying with you.' In a single movement he slid her robe from her shoulders, leaving it lying at her feet. 'Let me show you a couple.' He picked her up and headed for the bedroom.

He was looking down at her, lying waiting for him, and peeling off his shorts when the phone rang. 'For fuck's sake,' he shouted, 'why does this always happen when I've got a hard-on?' He sat, naked, on the edge of the bed and picked up the receiver.

'Yes!'

'Mr Skinner? David Hewlett, here, in Private Office.'

The policeman recognised the smooth tones of the Secretary of State for Scotland's private secretary. 'You're early, David,' he said. 'It's barely gone seven o'clock. Which office are you at?'

'Edinburgh. We took the sleeper up from London,' the civil servant replied. 'Mr Skinner, the boss was wondering it you could come in to see him this morning, to give him a progress report on the McGrath murder investigation. He has a special interest, with Mrs McGrath being a fellow Member of Parliament.'

'Of course,' said Skinner. 'I'll look in before I go to Fettes?'

'That's good. When can we expect you?'

He looked round at Pam. 'Better give me a couple of hours.'

38

'I'm sorry I wasn't available yesterday,' said Graham Ross, the manager of the Haddington Transway supermarket. 'These quality training days are mandatory for all staff. We really are in the most competitive retail environment these days.

'Anyway, I'm here now. What can I do for you?'

'I need any information that you can give me on a couple of items that I hope were bought from your store,' said Maggie Rose. From her pocket, she removed the foil yoghurt top and the portion of Mars bar wrapper which they had found in the caravan, each now encased in a clear plastic folder. She passed them across Mr Ross' small desk.

The balding manager peered at each through his spectacles. He held up the yoghurt foil. 'This is from a multi-pack, rather than an individual item sale. The only thing I can tell you is that from the "use by" date, wherever it was sold, it wasn't any earlier than Tuesday of last week.'

'That's a start,' said DCI Rose. 'How about the wrapper? It has a bar code.'

Ross nodded. 'That's more hopeful. Gimme a minute.' He stood up and strode from the office.

In fact, he was gone for almost ten minutes. By the time he returned, DCI Rose was fidgeting impatiently in her chair, but his smile soothed her annoyance at once.

'Yes,' he said, even before sitting down. 'It is one of ours. It was sold at nine forty-three last Wednesday morning, eight days ago.' He handed over a long slip of paper. 'This is a record of the transaction.'

The policewoman looked at him. 'How did the buyer pay?' she asked eagerly.

'By cash. I take it you were hoping it was by Switch or credit card.'

'Can't have everything, I suppose.' She ran her eye down the slip. 'Tinned soup, corned beef, bread, Flora, tinned meatballs, tinned sweetcorn, four-pack of yoghurt, another tin of soup, milk, eggs, bacon, coffee, six-pack of Coke.'

'It's as if the buyer was going camping, isn't it?' the manager suggested.

'Oh, he was,' said Maggie Rose, forcefully. 'He was.'

39

The zeal that comes from newly acquired but long-anticipated power still shone in the eyes of Dr Bruce Anderson, Secretary of State for Scotland. He stood as Skinner entered his office in St Andrew's House, Scotland's seat of national government, and came towards him, hand outstretched.

'Hello, Bob,' he welcomed him, with a reassuring smile.

'*Wonder if this was his bedside manner when he was in practice*?' Skinner mused. 'Good morning, Secretary of State,' he replied, shaking the proffered hand. He had learned from bitter experience that it was best to keep his relationship with his ministerial boss on a formal footing.

'*Politicians are a bit like rottweilers*,' Proud Jimmy had warned him, when he had accepted his appointment as security adviser to the Scottish Office. '*Just when you think they're domesticated, they can turn round and bite your bloody hand off.*'

'Have a seat, have a seat,' said Anderson, looking fresh despite his night on the sleeper. 'You'll take coffee?'

'No thank you, sir,' said the policeman, sitting on a low chair facing the Secretary of State's desk. He glanced round the wood-panelled room, which he had come to know so well. 'I've just had breakfast.'

'Okay. Then let's get down to business. I'm really asking you this as Deputy Chief in Edinburgh, not as my adviser. What can you tell me about Leona McGrath's murder? It's nearly a week now, and still no arrest. My parliamentary colleagues are badgering me about it incessantly . . . especially the Tories, since she was their last MP in Scotland. So, how are things going?'

Skinner frowned. 'As well as can be expected, I'd say. The killer didn't leave us any forensic evidence at the scene . . . none that we've been able to find so far, at any rate . . . and he's been very efficient in covering his tracks.

'However,' he went on, 'we've had some excellent technical help from an outside agency, and that led to us tracing a caravan where the man held young Mark after the abduction. There was a serial number on the van. It was stolen last week from a dealership near Penicuik.'

'Did it have number plates?' asked Anderson.

'Phoney,' Skinner replied. 'We've put out a country-wide alert for any vehicle with that number, but if the killer had one set of fictitious plates, then he'll have two, and he'll have swapped over by now.'

'How do you know that they were there?'

Skinner smiled, grimly. 'Like the murder scene, the place was wiped clean. However we found two food labels stuffed down the back of a cushion. One of them was foil, and had the boy's right thumbprint on it, very clearly. We're checking, even as I speak, with the supermarket where we hope the items were bought, but I'll tell you now, that it won't help us identify the killer. If he was there, he'll have paid cash.'

'So,' said the Secretary of State. 'Another dead end.'

'Not quite. Now we have an accurate description of the man, and a good witness who can draw a photofit for us. Also, where it's been surmise before, thanks to a fingerprint on an item, we now know for sure that the child was in that caravan, alive. The usual motive for child-stealing is ransom. Whatever the purpose here, I believe that there

181

will be a further message from the man, and I expect that it will be addressed to me.'

'Why do you say that?'

'Because of the lengths to which he went to contact me, personally, on Saturday evening. He could have taken his pick from dozens of working phone boxes all over East Lothian or Berwick, yet he came to Gullane to make his call from my very own doorstep. Whether it was risk-taking for thrills, or simply his way of rubbing my nose in it, it was thought out, deliberate, and directed at me.

'This is personal, I tell you. This man is a ghost from somewhere in my past, only he's a very live one.'

Anderson frowned. 'I take it that you're looking into all the people who might have grudges against you.'

'Of course, but without success so far.'

The Secretary of State nodded. 'I see.' He swung round in his swivel chair and stared out of the window, across towards Calton Hill.

'Bob,' he said, at last, without looking round, 'don't you feel that it would be better if you were able to give one hundred per cent of your time to this investigation?'

Skinner thought of Proud Jimmy, and felt a tightening around his wrist, like the phantom jaws of a rottweiler.

'No, sir,' he replied, evenly, 'I do not. I have an excellent Head of CID, in day-to-day charge and reporting to me. Added to that, if I am a linking factor in this crime, the arguments are all against me being informed personally.'

'Nevertheless,' Anderson continued, 'I might feel happier.'

The detective felt his jaw tighten, and his eyes narrow, quite involuntarily. If Anderson had been looking at him, he might have felt less assured.

'Secretary of State,' he said evenly. 'Please don't play

games with me. And most of all, don't patronise me. I don't honestly give a fuck about your happiness.

'If you've got something to say, then please, as they say in American Football, let's skip the bullshit and go straight to the nut-cutting.'

Anderson stiffened and swung round in his seat. All the earlier bonhomie was gone. 'Very well. I don't have to say, I hope, how much I admire you as a policeman, Mr Skinner. Your record of success speaks for itself. Nor can I fault the advice you've given me since I've been in office.

'However I would prefer it if my security adviser was with me on a fulltime basis.'

'I am honoured to accept your offer,' said Skinner laconically . . . and lying in his teeth.

The Secretary of State reddened, as he took the bait. 'All right,' he snapped. 'Your private life, and the way in which it has become public, gives me a real difficulty. My party has a high moral code, and . . .'

'That's crap too,' retorted Skinner. 'I'm in on the MI5 briefings, remember. The Security Service knows of at least fifteen members of your government who are having extra-marital affairs. Two of them are with people of the same sex, and another of them is a junior minister in your own department.'

Abruptly the policeman stood up, irked by having Anderson look down on him in the low visitor's seat. 'Let's deal with the truth, shall we?' he said. 'Your party still has difficulty in Scotland in keeping your left-wingers under control. You can't afford to give them the slightest weapon to use against you.

'Aggie Maley and her pals – anti-police to begin with – think that my extra-marital relationship with Pam gives them a bit of leverage. She's painting me as some sort of sexual predator, abusing his position within the force, and within your own party circles she's accusing you of being pro-sleaze and anti-women by keeping me in post.

'Being new in office, you don't need that sort of flak. So you want me to let you off the hook by offering my resignation. That's the truth of it, Dr Anderson, isn't it?'

The Secretary of State's face was redder than ever. 'I wouldn't have put it quite so directly,' he spluttered.

'Well,' said Skinner, 'if you're ever going to fill that chair adequately, you'd better learn to. Express it as you will, but I'm right.'

Anderson sighed. 'If that's how you see it . . .' Finally he looked directly at the other man. 'Will you let me have your resignation?'

The detective, laughed: a short, dry humourless laugh. 'I'd rather stick hot needles in my eyes than give Maley that satisfaction. If you want me out you'll have to fire me.'

'So be it,' said the politician, wearily. 'How would you like me to frame the announcement?'

'I don't give a damn. If anything you say is actionable, and not covered by privilege, I'll sue you. Other than that, say what you like.' He smiled. 'There is of course, the matter of my contract.'

'You'll be paid in full, with a termination bonus of six months' salary. My announcement will say simply that you're leaving the job and that I've decided to make a fulltime appointment. Actually, Sir John Govan will take up the post when he retires as Chief Constable of Strathclyde in a few months.'

'Mmm,' Skinner growled, as he rose to leave. 'It was nice of Jock to call and tell me.' He smiled at Anderson's expression of sudden shock. 'Don't worry, Secretary of

State, he didn't. I'm afraid I've never been very good at sarcasm.

'Tell you one thing, though . . . no two. First, if I ever find out that Councillor Maley put the *Spotlight* on to me, I'll fucking crucify her. Second, I had decided not to apply for the Strathclyde job. Now I've changed my mind. If that bastard Govan thinks he can fill my shoes, I might as well go after his . . . even though they might be too tight.'

40

'What's up, boss?' said Detective Chief Superintendent Martin as he closed the door of Skinner's office behind him.

'Fucking politicians, Andy; that's what's up. Never again will I have anything to do with them. Our Secretary of State's concerned about the Aggie Maley Tendency rocking his boat, so he's thrown me to them as a human sacrifice.'

Briefly, succinctly, but explosively, the DCC described his meeting with Dr Bruce Anderson. 'I tell you, mate,' he concluded. 'From now on, whenever I meet someone with the words Right and Honourable before his name, I'll know it's odds on that both are a fucking lie.'

His pointing finger stabbed the air. 'And as for Jock Govan! I never had him down as such a slippery bastard, that's for sure.' He picked up his direct line and dialled in a number. 'Hello,' he barked. 'Is that Sir John Govan's office? Good. DCC Bob Skinner here, Edinburgh. Put me through please, if he's in.'

Martin stared at him, screwing up his eyes, and making 'calm down' signals with his hands, but Skinner turned away.

'Jock. Bob. I hear congratulations are in order.' The younger man waited for the explosion, but none came. Instead, he saw an incredulous look spread across his friend's face. 'You did?' he heard him say. 'He told you that!'

Skinner shook his head. 'Jock, in the time that you've

186

known me, when have I ever walked away from anything?' There was a short silence. 'Exactly, well it's the same this time. I refused to quit, so Anderson fired me.'

The DCC held the earpiece of his phone a little away from his ear. From its bowl, Martin heard the sound of shouting. 'No, Jock,' said Skinner. 'Don't do that, please. Take the job. MI5 must have an experienced hand up here, someone with common sense. Just make sure that you use the power that you'll have to protect yourself against this sort of rubbish.

'Good luck. I mean it. Thanks, I'll be all right.'

Skinner hung up the phone and looked up at his second-in-command. 'Would you believe it! Govan says that when Anderson offered him the job yesterday, he said that I'd asked to be relieved of my duties in view of my compromised position. He says that he told Anderson that he'd only accept after he had made one more determined effort to persuade me to stay on.

'Half an hour ago, Anderson called him back and said that he'd flung himself at my feet but that I was adamant about going.'

Martin looked serious. 'You believe Govan, do you?'

'Come on, Andy. I'd take the word of a chief police officer over that of a politician ten times out of ten. I tell you, I wish I had something on Anderson himself, rather than his sidekick. I'd bloody use it.

'As for Maley! By God . . .'

It was Skinner's friend, not his junior officer, who sat on the edge of his desk. 'Bob,' he said. 'Let it go.'

'Why should I?'

'Because with all this lashing about you're in danger of forgetting one thing. Bruce Anderson didn't walk out on his wife, weeks after she nursed him back to health. You did. Aggie Maley isn't sleeping with Pam Masters. You are.'

Skinner glared at him, ready to erupt once more.

'Sure, Anderson's behaving badly. Okay, Maley's using your situation to score points. But they're only doing so because you made it possible. No-one else did, Bob. Only you.

'I . . . no, not just me . . . Alex and I are begging you to forget all this shit, and get on with your career, before you blow it.'

Gradually, the fire faded from Bob's eyes as he looked across the desk. Gradually, he seemed to sag, to slump back in his chair.

'You're right, of course, Andy,' he muttered quietly. 'I can get as angry as I like with those characters, but I'm really only trying to shift the blame for my problems away from my own doorstep. I'm their architect, beginning to end, not Salmon, Maley, or anyone else.'

He smiled suddenly. 'You know if one of my divisional commanders was in a pickle like this, I'd send him on a couple of months' sabbatical to sort himself out.

'I dressed it up as "irreconcilable differences" when Sarah and I separated, but you're right. I just walked out. I exploded, accused her of disloyalty and manipulation, and didn't make the slightest effort to reconcile anything. Now it's too late.'

He glanced up, suddenly and sharply. 'So what does that make Pam? Are the Maley clique right? Is she a victim?'

Andy shook his head. 'No, she isn't. You're clearly attracted to each other.' He stopped. 'But if you are asking me,' he resumed abruptly, 'I'd say you might be using her as a shield, a barrier to prevent you facing up to how much you've lost in Sarah, and how much you miss her and Jazz.'

Bob rose from his chair, and went to the window. He stood with his back to his friend, looking out, oblivious of the people coming and going below. 'D'you think this is my mid-life crisis, boy?' he asked.

'If it is,' replied Andy, 'I hope it's your first and last, and I hope that it's over soon.

'I can suggest one cure, though. Some good old-fashioned police work. Arthur Dorward called me, sounding fair pleased with himself. He says he's found a potential lead, and he wants to come to see me about it. He's due in my office in ten minutes.

'Want to sit in?'

'Sure,' said Skinner, the DCC once more. 'Why not. You head back along. I'll round up McIlhenney and join you directly.

'Oh, and Andy,' he added, as Martin headed for the door. 'Thanks for making me face up to myself, at last.'

41

The red-haired Inspector was already in the Head of CID's office when Skinner and his assistant arrived. Both men sat relaxed, as if waiting for him, as they had been.

'Morning, Arthur. No, don't get up,' said the DCC, as he and McIlhenney took the other seats that Martin had drawn up to his desk.

'Well,' he said. 'The DCS said you had made a breakthrough. Let's hear about it.'

'Very good, sir,' said Dorward, sitting more upright in his chair.

'The first thing I have to report is that the pathologist's staff have completed their examination of Mrs McGrath's body. There was nothing there, nothing at all, that shouldn't have been. The tissue under the fingernails was her own, right enough, and there were no stray hairs lodged anywhere.'

'Certain?' asked Skinner.

'One thousand per cent, sir.'

'So where's your breakthrough?'

The Inspector fought to suppress a smile of self-satisfaction. 'Well, sir, it started with a bit of luck, really. One of my team was talking to the cleaning woman, and she mentioned that Mrs McGrath's *en suite* bathroom had only been fitted a few months before, with some of the insurance money she received after her husband's death.'

'Yes, that's right,' said the DCC. 'I remember her mentioning that she'd made some improvements to the house. So where does that take us?'

Dorward's smile broke through, irresistibly. 'Well, sir, that made me wonder. Like, how many people would have used the shower, or the handbasin since they were installed? And like, did the killer wash away the blood and stuff after the rape and murder?'

'So I got in a plumber to strip out the piping and examine the traps.' He paused. Skinner and Martin each nodded approval.

'There were some hairs trapped in the shower,' he continued. 'All Mrs McGrath's. Some head, some pubic, but all hers, no doubt about it.

'But in the S-bend of the basin, there we got lucky. We found hair samples from six different people. We've identified four of them. The lady herself, Mark, his nanny, and the cleaner. The other two, we don't know about, other than that they're from different people. With your permission – ' he looked from Martin to Skinner then back again – 'I'd like to start DNA testing.'

'Fair enough,' said Skinner, 'but before you get too excited, remember that Leona had been a widow for quite a few months. There may have been other people in her bedroom, apart from the killer.'

Martin shook his head. 'Not since the new plumbing was installed. We've spoken to the close family members and to her friends. None of them can remember having used that basin.

'As for man friends, we don't believe that we're in the plural there. We spoke to a close woman friend of the victim. She said that the two of them had a drink together on the Sunday evening before the murder, at Leona's place. Once they'd had a few, it got down to girl talk, and Leona confessed to her that since her husband's death she'd had sex just once.'

'Did she mention a name?' asked the DCC.

'No, sir,' Martin answered: 'only that it had happened at her place, in her bedroom, and just on the one occasion.' He smiled. 'According to the pal, she did say that the guy had a bigger cock than her husband, but that's all she told her about him.'

'I don't think that's admissible in evidence,' said Skinner. 'Okay, Arthur. Run your DNA tests. The budget will stand them. It's a long shot, but you never know your luck.'

42

'The cashier remembers him, sir,' Maggie Rose told DCS Martin. 'Youngish men shopping alone early in the morning tend to stand out in supermarkets, so it seems. The girl's name is Lesley, and I'd say she's a reliable witness.

'Her description matches the one Mr Carr, the farmer, gave us.'

'What about accent?'

'Lesley said she doesn't remember him saying anything other than "Thank you" when she gave him his change.'

'Anything strike her as odd about him?'

Martin heard Rose laugh at the other end of the line. 'I asked her that. She said that she noticed that he didn't buy any cat food, or any Beck's. Apparently guys his age shopping for themselves nearly always buy cat food and Beck's.'

The DCS grunted. 'That's the sort of sweeping generalisation that forms gender stereotypes.'

'High rank's teaching you diplomacy, all right,' said Rose. 'A couple of years ago you'd have said, "That's bloody women for you!".'

'That's funny,' said Martin with a smile. 'I thought that's what I just said. Thanks, Mags, see you.' He hung up and turned to Skinner. 'The man bought enough food for two days,' he said. 'Quick-cook, easy-dispose stuff. Corned beef, meatballs, yoghurt, the stuff he'd expect a kid to go for.'

'Two days,' said the DCC. 'So if he brought Mark back

to the caravan on Friday, and called me on Saturday, unless he went shopping again, it's a fair bet that he moved him again on Sunday.'

Martin nodded.

'One thing more,' Skinner added. 'He bought enough tinned food for two days, but he bought it on Wednesday morning. Which tells us . . .'

'. . . suggests to us,' broke in the Head of CID, 'that he didn't live in the caravan between Wednesday and Friday, otherwise he'd have bought more food.'

'Aye. So let's add to our file on this guy the possibility that he has an address in the Edinburgh area. Let's try and read him, this clever bastard who thinks he's thumbing his nose at me. Let's try and picture him planning this crime.

'Forget about motive, for now. He'll tell us what that is, when he's good and ready. Let's try to read his mind. He's very meticulous, is our man. I think he must have watched Leona for a long time. He must have known her routine: when she'd be at home from Parliament, and so on. He must have known that Mark's *au pair* . . .' Skinner paused and smiled. 'The wee chap gets very offended if you call her a nanny. He was thirty when he was born, that one.'

He continued. 'He must have watched for long enough to know that the girl always had Friday afternoon off. Mark might have called her his *au pair* but she's from Perth. She went home to her parents as soon as Leona got back from London on a Friday, and came back on Sunday night.

'He planned everything in the almost certain knowledge that the two of them, mother and child, would be together, and unprotected. He stole the caravan – no big deal, he'd just cut the chain on the gate to the dealership yard and helped himself – then set it up on this man Carr's land in the middle of fucking nowhere, provisioned and ready for a two-day stop-over. Once it was ready, he went home and waited for his moment.'

He paused, his eyes distant. 'So where's home?' he asked himself, aloud.

'The kidnapper decided to take Mark out of town – somewhere near enough so that he wouldn't have to spend too long on the road getting there, but far enough off the beaten track to be safe. The moors are perfect, and they were even close enough to my place to allow him to pull his telephone stunt with me.

'But why did he go to all that bother? Answer, because he wanted to keep the child, to use him for some purpose, yet to be revealed. Next question. Why not just take him home? Possible answer: because he has a family, or lives with a parent. Yet all my instincts are crying out to me that this man is a loner. Better answer: because he knew that in the period immediately after the murder we would make Edinburgh very hot indeed, far too risky a place to hide the boy. I think this guy lives in our city, Andy. Do you agree?'

'Yes,' said the Head of CID, 'I do. I think that's more than likely.

'But Bob, there's one thing that's still eating at me. Clearly this guy knows you, and knows of your bond with Mark. He's targeting you, somehow, through this crime. But to come to Gullane to make that call. Why would he do that?'

'Because he's crazy, Andy, that's why, and he's a gamester. This guy is as mad as a fucking hatter, and he thinks that he can play with the stupid policeman.'

Skinner went on. 'Let's consider something else. He only planned to stay in the van for a couple of days. Why?'

'He wouldn't want to outstay his welcome with Carr, I guess,' Martin offered.

'Right. So where did he go, when he left on Sunday, after he and Mark had finished their food supply?'

'If I knew that,' said the younger man, 'I'd go and get him.'

'If I knew where he lived,' said Skinner, 'so would I. If he guessed that we only have the manpower to keep the real pressure on for a short period, what was to keep him from just going home?'

The Chief Superintendent looked at the Deputy Chief, and simply nodded his silent agreement.

'Are you seeing the press today?' Skinner asked.

'Whenever Carr finishes the photofit.'

'Right, why don't you tell them that we've found the caravan on the moors, that it's empty, and that we believe that the kidnapper, and Mark, may be back in the city? Let's heat the place up again, with a vengeance. If he is here, maybe we'll panic him into making a break for it.'

Martin looked suddenly doubtful. 'Isn't there a danger that if he panics he'll kill the child?'

The DCC looked him in the eye. 'Yes, there's bound to be: yet this man *wants* Mark, Andy. He needs him for something. That risk has existed since the kidnap, but he hasn't done it yet, or I'm pretty sure you'd have found the kid dead in the caravan.

'Look, our man has been setting the agenda all along. Let's make some moves of our own, and show him that we've got some brains after all.'

'Okay,' said the Head of CID. 'I'll play it that way. Now, since you seem to have recovered your powers of deduction and are back in the detecting game, is there anything else that we could be doing that we're not?'

Skinner smiled. 'Since you ask . . .' he said. 'That caravan. It had a phoney number plate, didn't it?'

'Yes. I wonder why the guy didn't take it off. He's blown his cover in a way by leaving it there.'

'Sure, but if he'd removed it he'd have drawn early attention to the van, which he did not want to do. Anyway it doesn't matter. Since we don't know who he is, our man will be using his legal number again.' The DCC paused.

'But still, the phoneys are a potential lead: how about taking the city apart to see if you can find out who made them?'

43

'This is getting to be a habit,' said Skinner, hanging up the phone and turning to choose a tie from the half-dozen or so that he kept in Pamela's wardrobe. 'Telephone calls from David Hewlett two mornings on the trot.'

She stopped in the act of fastening her skirt, and looked across at him. 'That was the Secretary of State's office? D'you think he's changed his mind about . . .' She paused.

'About giving me the bullet, you were going to say? No chance of that. He's already made the announcement, although he may have to find another replacement for me, even after my chat with Jock Govan.'

'He wouldn't offer it to the Chief would he?' asked Pam.

Bob laughed. 'Do not be daft, my dear. Jimmy's a career administrator; never served in CID in his life. He's a better politician than Anderson, but he knows bugger all about security. Anyway, not even our Secretary of State would be crude enough to offer my Chief a job that I'd been fired from. A refusal often offends, as they say: he wouldn't invite it.

'No, if he'd asked my advice, I'd have told him to recruit my pal Haggerty from Strathclyde. Willie's a bit of a hairyback, but he's a bloody good copper, and he knows everything that's going on through in the West, where you'll find most of the organised crime and terrorism in Scotland.'

'What did Hewlett want, then?'

'Anderson wants to see me again, apparently. Ten o'clock this morning, St Andrew's House.'

He looked in the mirror, to straighten his tie, then picked up his jacket from the bedroom chair, over which he had draped it the night before. He was frowning as he followed Pam through to the kitchen. 'Wonder what the hell it could be about?' he asked himself aloud.

'Didn't Hewlett say?'

'He said that he didn't know.'

'And you believed him, after what happened yesterday?'

Skinner nodded, as he poured cornflakes into two bowls, and reached into the fridge for milk. 'David's one of the good guys. He wouldn't tell me an outright lie. He said "I don't know what it's about", not "I can't tell you", and I take him at his word. Anyway,' he said, 'I can usually tell when someone's telling me porkies.'

'So what do you think it might be about?'

'Could be one or two things. A terrorist whisper from down South, although I'd probably have heard about that too. An attack of nerves over arrangements for his Party's conference in Glasgow this autumn, although Haggerty's well in control there.'

Skinner shook his head. 'I could guess all morning and still get it wrong.

'Anyway, enough about me.' He spooned up some cornflakes. 'I've got some news for you. I spoke to Scott Rolland yesterday afternoon, the chief in Central. He has a pregnant detective sergeant in his drugs squad, based in Falkirk. She goes off on maternity leave in eight weeks, and her job's yours if you want it.

'It'd be a secondment at first, but the woman's told him that if everything's all right with the baby, then she'll be resigning. What d'you think?'

She stared at him. 'Why didn't you tell me this last night?' she asked.

'I was too steamed up over Anderson. Also, I thought you looked tired. Didn't want to put you off your sleep.'

She smiled. 'I suppose I was. Probably something to do with the way the day began.' She hesitated. 'It sounds good. But do you think I'm right for drugs work?'

'You want to make a difference, don't you?'

'Yes.'

'Then, you're right for it. Look, this job isn't about going after Colombian cartels. They don't stretch as far as Falkirk. There will be sharp-end stuff, but it is educational too: police–community liaison, schools visits, that sort of activity.'

She pushed her cornflakes to one side, stepped up to him and slipped her arms round his waist. 'What do you think I should do?'

'Not what I think,' he said firmly, 'what you want.'

'But it'd make life easier, long-term, for us both?'

'Yes, but still, the only factor is whether you'd be happy in the job.'

'When do you have to tell Mr Rolland?'

'Today, if possible, but I can stretch it to next week.'

Pam shook her head. 'No. Tell him, "Yes please, thank you very much". And thank *you* very much too.'

He smiled. '*De nada*,' he said.

'No,' she contradicted him. 'It's not nothing. It's a lot.' She looked up at him, her eyes suddenly very serious. 'Bob, I want to be legit, as far as you're concerned . . . as far as we're concerned. The companionship principle only holds good for a while. Like the girl whose job I'll be taking in Falkirk, I want to have a baby too, before it's too late. And I want to have it with you.

'I know this might be breaking an unwritten rule between us, but I have to say it. Anyway, you're a smart guy, you must have figured it out: I love you.'

He stared down at her.

'Taken your breath away, copper, have I?' she whispered.

He nodded. 'Just a bit. I'll tell you what. Tonight, let's ditch our minders, and let's go somewhere different, a hotel, maybe; somewhere down in the Borders. Peebles Hydro, if we can get in. Let's do that, and let's talk about long-term, and what it means.'

'Agreed. I've never been to Peebles Hydro.'

'Okay. Be ready to leave at six. By then, I'll have found out what the bloody hell my ex-boss wants.'

44

Skinner walked into the entrance hall of St Andrew's House at five minutes to ten. It faced north and, even in the height of summer, always extended a cold welcome to visitors to the building. He showed his official pass to the black-uniformed guard who gave him a brisk salute and a 'Good morning'.

The policeman knew that he should have surrendered the pass on the morning before, but he had kept it out of devilment, as a personal security check.

He stepped into one of the waiting lifts and rode it to the fifth floor. David Hewlett, looking as serious as ever, was in his office, with his assistant and his clerk. He was a thin man, in his middle thirties, with receding fair hair and a domelike forehead.

'Morning, Dave,' said Skinner. 'I thought I'd paid my last visit here. Any idea yet what the panic is?'

Hewlett shook his head. 'I haven't been told, Bob,' he replied, sounding concerned and more than a little offended at having been left in the dark. 'S of S came in this morning from Bute House at eight fifteen, a little later than usual. He instructed me to call you, and two other people, and to ask you in particular to be here at ten sharp.'

'Two others?' Skinner repeated, curious.

'They've been here since nine fifteen, with a fourth person.'

'Who are they?'

Hewlett's natural frown deepened even more. 'I'm not

allowed to say, Bob. I'm even disobeying orders by having this conversation. S of S told me to say nothing to you when you arrived, but to send you down to Committee Room One, on the third floor.'

'Fucking nonsense!' Skinner growled, exasperated. 'Time I sorted this lot out. Thanks, Dave. I think I'll go and paper the walls with your boss. I've half a mind to charge him with wasting police time.'

He left the small office and took the stairs down to the third floor. He thought about knocking on the door of Committee Room One, but with a muttered 'Bugger it!' under his breath he opened the door and strode inside.

Four people were waiting, seated with their backs to the window, facing the door, and a single empty chair. The detective scanned them, from left to right.

Councillor Marcia Topham: the usual slightly overawed expression worn by the Police Board Chair had been replaced by one of pure fright.

Lord Archibald of Alva, the Lord Advocate, Scotland's senior law officer: Archie Nelson, QC, Dean of the Faculty of Advocates until his ennoblement, and an old friend, now sat staring at him impassively as he entered.

Dr Bruce Anderson: the Secretary of State for Scotland sat staring grimly at a folder on the desk before him.

Sir James Proud: the Chief Constable sat ashen-faced, more shocked than his deputy had ever seen him.

As he stared across the table Skinner felt a mixture of apprehension and anger welling up within him. As usual, anger won.

'What the bloody hell is this, Dr Anderson?' he said: not quite a shout, but close to it. 'You and I severed our links yesterday, I think.'

The Secretary of State looked up and shook his head.

'Not quite,' he replied. 'I still have certain powers and responsibilities over police officers of executive rank. Until now, I've never had to use them. I hoped it would never be necessary.'

He stopped. 'Oh sit down, Bob, please. This is difficult enough for us all, without you eyeing us up as if you're deciding who you're going to set about first.'

Skinner took hold of his temper, and sat in the vacant chair. 'Right,' he retorted. 'But I warn you now, if this is about my private life . . .'

The Secretary of State shook his head. Lord Archibald sighed. Marcia Topham whimpered slightly. Proud Jimmy moaned.

'It isn't, Bob,' replied Anderson. 'I only wish it was.

'At quarter to eight this morning, an envelope was delivered to Bute House, my official residence in Charlotte Square. It contained a serious allegation against you, and documents pertaining to it. As soon as I had read them, I called the Lord Advocate.'

Skinner's eyes narrowed. 'What is this allegation?' he asked quietly.

'It concerns corruption.' The Secretary of State turned to Lord Archibald. 'Archie, would you, please?'

The Law Officer nodded. 'Bob, we've all discussed this prior to your arrival. We're shocked by the allegation which has been made, and every one of us is loath to believe it. But if there is anything in it, we feel that it is only right to give you an opportunity to explain it at this stage.

'Consequently, I have to ask you one question. Do you admit to having a personal account in the Guernsey branch of the JZG Bank?'

The policeman stared at him across the table. 'What the hell is the JZG Bank?'

'It's a small private bank based in Liechtenstein, with branches in Guernsey and in the Cayman Islands. Now please give me a direct answer to my question.'

Skinner drew a hard, deep, snorting, impatient breath. 'No, Archie, I do not have a personal account there or in any other Channel Island bank.'

'Then we have a problem, Bob, because the Secretary of State has been given evidence that you do, and that you have a significant amount of cash there.'

'That's preposterous,' Skinner protested. 'I'm reasonably well off, but I don't have bank accounts that I've forgotten about. I demand to be told the detail of the allegation made against me and to be shown the evidence that's been presented.'

'In due course, Deputy Chief Constable,' said Bruce Anderson, suddenly formal in tone. 'However, in the light of the information which has been put before me, I must first formally suspend you from duty. I must advise you also that I shall be requesting senior officers from a force outside Scotland to conduct an independent enquiry into these matters.'

Skinner felt the blood drain from his face.

'Secretary of State,' he interrupted, 'did your information come from an anonymous source?'

The Minister looked across at him. 'No. The donor of the material identified himself.'

'Would I be right in supposing that your source is Noel Salmon, of the *Spotlight*?'

'Yes, you'd be correct.'

'And you're putting a senior police officer's career and reputation on the line on the word of that disreputable wee man, are you?'

Lord Archibald replied. 'Bob, you know that we

wouldn't do that. I'm sorry, but they have given us material in support of the allegation.'

'Then let me see it, please, Archie.'

'In due course,' said the Lord Advocate. 'Look, I want to help you clear your name here. We all do. But the Secretary of State can play no favourites. Two senior officers, a Deputy Chief Constable and a Chief Superintendent, are already on their way here from Manchester to begin enquiries into the allegations against you.

'I think it would be best for you to go away and arrange legal representation. Once you've done that, the visiting officers and I will meet with you and your solicitor, and we will show you the material which we hold.' He stopped abruptly, looking down at the table for a second or two.

'The Secretary of State has decided,' he continued, 'and I'm afraid that I have to agree with him, that while the investigation is in progress you should not take part in any police activity. That's why you have to be formally suspended from duty.

'You shouldn't enter Fettes or any other police office, for any purpose not related to your defence against the accusation. Furthermore, I have to counsel you most strongly against conducting any personal investigation.

'The visiting officers will have the brief of enquiring and reporting to me and to me alone. If you approach anyone to whom they wish to speak, you could make yourself vulnerable to accusations of intimidation. And believe me, Bob, that's the last thing you need.'

'Archie,' said Skinner, evenly. 'I'll do what you say, but if that wee shit Salmon approaches me, then you can be damn sure I'll intimidate him.'

'Salmon will be advised not to approach you,' said Lord Archibald, reassuringly. 'We can't order him of course: *sub judice* rules don't apply at this stage, as you know. But we can warn him of the dangers of interfering with a police inquiry.'

'That's all very well,' said Skinner, 'but why should my hands be tied behind my back? If you can't prevent Salmon from approaching me, how the hell can you justify forbidding me from making my own enquiries into accusations against me? If that's what you're saying, then I'd prefer you to charge me with corruption right now. If the allegations are the subject of criminal proceedings, then no-one can publish till the case comes to court, and my team will have the right of access to the prosecution witnesses.'

'Christ, Bob,' spluttered the former Archie Nelson, 'the last thing I want is to charge you with anything.'

He paused as he considered what Skinner had said. 'I take your point, though. Look, let's have an understanding. You stay away from witnesses personally, but your lawyers can approach them. Deal?'

The policeman surprised the Lord Advocate by smiling: an open smile, but with something devious lurking behind it. 'You've got a deal, M'Lud,' he said. 'The first thing I'm going to do, though, is look for an injunction preventing the *Spotlight* from publishing any of his crap.'

The smile vanished as he turned towards the Secretary of State. 'As for you, Dr Anderson, be aware that I'm going to seek advice on the possibility of raising an injunction against you, and having my suspension lifted.'

'You can but try,' said the Secretary of State.

'Before you do, though, Bob,' Lord Archibald interrupted, 'you should be aware that the Court would require you to show good cause why it should injunct. You would be forced to present strong defences against the evidence.

In effect, you would be putting yourself on trial without time to prepare, and based on what I've seen this morning, I have to tell you that I believe you would lose.

'Please, my friend, go and consult your lawyers, quickly, then bring them to Crown Office, and I'll meet you with the Manchester people. Let's make it two thirty. I'll arrange for you to use the back door, to avoid the media. They'll be keeping an eye on the entrance as soon as this goes public.'

Skinner smiled again. 'I appreciate the courtesy, Archie, but bollocks to it. I've never sneaked in the tradesman's entrance in my life, and I'm damned if I will now. The media have tons of shots of me on file. A few more won't make any difference.'

He nodded across the table. 'Thank you, Secretary of State. The next time we meet, I'll accept your apology.'

The big policeman stood up, with the briefest of nods to his Chief Constable, and walked out of the room. Outside, in the corridor, he stood at the lift doors for a few seconds, then headed for the stairs. He stood on the first landing and waited. A few seconds later, Sir James Proud, puffing and blowing, crashed through the double doors.

'Bob, I . . .'

Skinner held up a hand. 'Jimmy, before you say anything: whatever it is that Anderson has on me, I swear to you that I know nothing about any Guernsey money, and that I have never in my life accepted as much as a bent penny.'

'You don't have to tell me that, son. Come on, let's walk.' Side by side they descended the wide stairway. 'Archie will show you the papers later,' said Proud, 'but they've got documentary evidence of an account in your name in this JZG Bank, opened a few months back, in the middle of the Jackie Charles investigation.'

'How much?'

'One hundred thousand.'

'Jesus. But, Jimmy, anyone could open an account in the name of Robert Skinner. I'm not unique. Why should they think it's me?'

Proud shook his head. 'It's not in anyone's name. It's a numbered account, but Anderson said that there was potential evidence which shows that you're the knowing beneficiary. It's a high-interest, long-access job.'

'What bloody evidence can he have? It's all nonsense.'

'I don't know what he has – Anderson wouldn't tell me – but I think it's pretty serious. I tried to get him to stop short of immediate suspension, but he told me that in his view the supportive evidence made it essential.'

Skinner looked round at his friend as they emerged once more into the cold, barren entrance hall. 'I tell you one thing, Jimmy. For our Secretary of State's sake, he'd better pray he's on solid ground. Because if he's playing politics with my reputation again, he'll find it giving way beneath his feet.'

45

'Andy, it's me. Listen carefully. I want you to find Pam. There's some pretty shocking news you're going to have to break to her.'

'Where are you, Bob? I know you can't be in the building, to have come through on this line.'

'I'm in Mitch Laidlaw's office, with Mitch, and with Alex. Now shut up and listen.'

Speedily, Skinner told Martin of his summons to meet the Secretary of State, and of his encounter in Committee Room One. 'Anderson set it up as a real Star Chamber,' he said as he finished, 'roping in Archie Nelson, with Jimmy and the Topham woman as his official observers.

'The bastard didn't have to play it like that. He could have called me in and shown me his evidence informally; given me the chance to knock it on the head before setting up this very public inquiry. This is the second Secretary of State who's crossed me up, Andy. I tell you, if I can, I'll see to it that he goes the same way as the other one.'

'Sure, Bob, but get yourself off the hook before you start to get even. Why's he called in officers from England?'

'He's got to have at least a DCC in charge. I know all the chiefs and deputies in Scotland, so I guess he figured he had to be seen to be setting up an impartial inquiry.'

Martin snorted. 'So he's saying in effect that he has no faith in the honesty of any chief officer in Scotland.'

'That's one way of looking at it. In fact it's a point I should have made to the bugger myself. Tell you what.

Have a word with Royston, and ask him, when this thing goes public, to try and work that line into the media coverage tomorrow. I smell another *Scotsman* leader coming on!'

'When will it go public?'

'Any minute now, I should think. Anderson won't hang about. So please, get hold of Pam, and tell her, before she hears it on the radio. Then you'd better call Scott Rolland for me. Tell him that Pam'll take the Falkirk job, before he changes his mind and withdraws the offer.'

'Okay. Look Bob, I can't think of anything to say, except good luck.'

'Thanks, mate, but I don't need luck. I'm innocent, remember.'

He hung up and turned to face Mitchell Laidlaw. The chambers of Curle, Anthony and Jarvis were in one of Edinburgh's newest and grandest office developments, with a fine outlook across the Castle Rock and up to Princes Street. Laidlaw's room enjoyed the best of it. It was furnished comfortably rather than opulently, but left visitors in no doubt that they were in the nerve centre of one of the country's leading professional firms.

'So, Mitch,' said Skinner. 'I know your firm doesn't get involved in criminal work as a rule, but none the less, will you take me on?'

'Of course we will, Bob,' nodded the ruddy-faced lawyer, looking more rotund than ever in his high-backed leather chair. 'From what you've told me this isn't really a criminal inquiry anyway. It's sort of a half-breed, set up by the Secretary of State rather than the Lord Advocate, even if it does report to him.'

'I take it that Anderson has the power to do that?' the policeman asked.

Laidlaw smiled broadly across at Alex, who sat by the side of his twin-pillared partner's desk. 'What do you think, Ms Skinner?' he asked.

Alex flushed slightly, thought for a few moments, then launched into her reply. 'Basically,' she said, 'the Secretary of State can do what he bloody well likes unless statute or the courts tell him differently.

'From what we know of the way this investigation's been set up, I'd say that you could probably challenge its validity before just about any Scottish judge and win the day. But what would that achieve? You would be seen as trying to frustrate investigation of the complaint against you, and at the end of the day, Anderson would simply turn the papers over to the Lord Advocate and back off himself.

'So any court victory would be Pyrrhic. It would result in you becoming the subject of a full-scale criminal investigation, and possibly even liable to arrest at a fairly early stage. That's what I think.'

'Couldn't have put it better myself,' said Laidlaw. 'Of course, if you could establish malice against you by Anderson, there might be grounds for another form of action. Is there a chance of that?'

Skinner shook his head. 'I can't say so, honestly. Anderson's just covering his arse, playing to his backbenchers.' He snorted. 'If there's any malice in evidence, it's borne by me towards him.'

Laidlaw spluttered. 'Let's not repeat that outside this room.' He swung round in his chair and leaned across the desk. 'Right, Bob. I'll handle this matter personally, with an assistant.'

The policeman nodded, and pointed towards his daughter. 'Yes,' he said, 'and she's sat there. I promised Archie that I wouldn't go near any potential witnesses myself. But I want them to know who they're dealing with.'

'Pops,' Alex intervened. 'Are you sure about this?'

Mitch Laidlaw raised a hand. 'If he isn't, I am. I don't see anything wrong with a bit of personal involvement in these circumstances. Also, if this does require detailed investigation by us . . . well, something of your father must have rubbed off on you!

'One other thing,' he said. 'It may be helpful if we engage counsel at some point. Do you have any preferences, Bob?'

Skinner rocked his head back and stared for a while at the dappled ceiling, as if racking his brains. At last he looked back across the desk. 'You might think her daft, but of all the people currently available, the best criminal silk who ever cross-examined me is dear old Christabel Innes Dawson, QC.

'I often thought that if I was really in the shit, there's no-one at the Bar I'd rather have on my side. Well I am now, she's still listed as a practising member, and she still has all her marbles.'

Laidlaw smiled. 'I've never instructed her,' he said, 'but I remember seeing her in action, when I was a student. A terrifying sight in full cry, as I recall. If you want her, I'll have a word with her clerk today, to put down a warning marker.

'But meanwhile, let's the three of us have some lunch, before we head up to the Crown Office, to find out just what sort of battle the old lady is going to have to fight.'

46

Pamela sat open-mouthed, facing Andy Martin across his desk. 'I can't believe it. Surely this must be a set-up. But how would the *Spotlight* manage to fake evidence so well that it convinced the Secretary of State?'

'Beats me, Sarge,' said the Chief Superintendent. 'Noel Salmon didn't do it all on his own, that's for sure. He could barely forge a betting slip, far less set up a phoney account in an offshore bank.' A light came into his eyes as he said the words. 'That's a thought, isn't it? I think it's time we stopped bothering about the monkey, and found out more about the organ-grinder.'

'Pamela, do you want to help Bob?'

She looked at him with sudden outrage. 'Of course I do.'

'Sorry, that was a silly thing to say,' he acknowledged. 'What I want you to do, then, is dig up Companies House and get hold of the registration details for *Spotlight* in the UK. After that I want you to call a man in Washington. He owes Bob a couple of favours. It's time we called one in.'

He reached into his desk drawer and produced a small notebook. He flipped through it until he found the page he was looking for, then picked up a pen and scribbled on a scrap of paper. When he was finished he replaced the notebook, locked the drawer, and pushed the paper across the desk to Pamela.

'That's a direct number to a desk on Capitol Hill. Once you've used it, burn it. The man's name is Joe Doherty, and he's a top gun on the US National Security Council. Tell him that Bob needs help, and why. Then ask him if he can get for us detailed information on the ownership of *Spotlight*, and on how it operates, internationally. Anything that he thinks is relevant.

'Ask him to call me personally, as soon as he has something for us.' He glanced at his watch. It was ten minutes past midday. 'Go on, then, and get started. By the time you've checked the UK company listings, Joe should be in his office.

'Incidentally, you don't need to say anything to Bob about this. He regards Joe Doherty as his own personal snout.'

Pamela stood up to leave looking shocked and slightly bewildered. For all his personal loyalties to Sarah, Andy felt a pang of sympathy for her. 'Hey,' he said, standing up. He put his hands on her shoulders and turned her to face him. 'Try not to worry too much. This is nothing; at worst this is just some evil sod playing silly buggers. Bob's been in far worse scrapes than this and come through them.

'I often think that he's been in more trouble than even I know about.

'There was one time he was shot in the leg. He told Alex and me that he had been careless and that his own pistol had gone off accidentally. But that same night, a man disappeared right off the face of the earth . . . as far as I know, at any rate.

'I asked about him afterwards, out of curiosity. All I got was silence, and sincere advice through the Special Branch network to mind my own business.'

She looked up at him. 'You're not saying that Bob . . .'

'I'm not saying anything, other than don't be too

concerned about him. He's like a cat, with quite a few of his nine lives left.'

'You know what I like about you, Chief Superintendent,' Pamela said, with a smile. 'You only see one Bob Skinner, and he can do no wrong.'

Martin grinned back. 'I wouldn't go that far. These contact lenses of mine have a green tint, not rose-coloured. Now, on you go. I'll come out with you. I want to see young Sammy.' He ushered her out of his office and towards her own desk in the corner of the CID Command Suite.

'Tell you something,' he said quietly as she took her seat. 'I ain't half going to miss the big fella's presence. Whoever set Bob up has done Leona McGrath's killer a favour.'

'. . . Unless, of course, they're one and the same person.'

He looked down at her. 'The same thought's been niggling away at me. But let's not turn a long shot into a conclusion. The boss would tell you that setting up the McGrath crime was a full-time job. He'd say that the guy wouldn't have had time to spare for him.'

The Head of CID switched his gaze to the far corner. 'Sammy,' he called, 'come through and give me a report on the supplier of those false plates.'

'I've been waiting to do just that, sir,' the young detective constable replied. 'I think I might be on to something.'

Martin had been heading for his office. He stopped in his tracks and turned back to face Pye as he rose from his desk. 'You do, do you? Good work if you are, lad. Come on, let's hear it.' He strode back into his office, with his junior at his heels.

'It's like this, boss,' said the constable, closing the door behind him. 'I was plugging away like you told me to, round the used car network, and round our informants, without getting as much as a sniff about anyone supplying dodgy plates. I thought I had run it dry: then I had an idea.

'Remember those two guys we encountered in the Jackie Charles investigation? Whitehead and Bailey, the two salesmen who worked for him in the Seafield showroom?'

'Yes,' Martin acknowledged, 'I remember we interviewed them. But they were on the up and up, weren't they?'

'That's right. The inquiry concluded that the showroom was the only legitimate part of Charles's business portfolio, and that they were exactly as they seemed, honest car salesmen.'

The Chief Superintendent nodded. 'Go on.'

'Well, sir, I thought, wasn't that a bit unlikely, really? Everything else about Charles was completely bent. Surely some of it must have washed over the car operation. Then I remembered that guy McCartney, the heavy who was nicked in Alnwick with the, eh . . . incriminating cargo . . . in his boot. He was one of Charles's team, and the plates on that big white Rover of his turned out to have been false too.

'So I took a chance. I went down to Seafield, to see Bailey and Whitehead. You know that Jackie's showroom was rebuilt, and that his dad's managing it for him?'

'Yes.'

'The old man was out when I called, so I saw the two salesmen together, without being bothered by him interfering, or intimidating them by his presence. I told them that we were wrapping up the prosecution case against Ricky McCartney, and that we had info that Jackie's workshop, behind the showroom, had put false plates on the Rover. I asked if they could confirm it, but I said that we were pretty sure of our ground. Of course, I sort of pointed out that it would mean the end for the business.

The finance companies would blacklist it; that sort of thing.'

'So?'

'They bought it. Bailey swore blind, and Whitehead backed him up, that nothing dodgy ever happened at Seafield. Then he told me that on the morning of the incident that McCartney was nicked for, Dougie Terry, Charles's minder, called him. He asked him to pick up a parcel from a workshop just off Dalry Road, and deliver it to big Ricky at his home address.

'Bailey said that he didn't look in the parcel, but that it was long and rectangular and was about the right weight for a couple of plates.'

'Could he remember the address of the workshop?' asked Martin, eagerly.

'Yes, sir. He gave it to me. He said the guy who handed over the package was called Eddie Sweeney. I checked, but it doesn't appear that he's known to us.'

The Head of CID smiled. 'Good work right enough, Sammy. Of course, there's nothing to link our man on the moors with Sweeney, but Bailey's information gives us grounds to pull him in. When we squeeze him, you never know what'll pop out.

'I should really turn it over to Superintendent Pringle. It's his divisional area. But what the hell, you did the legwork on this, so let's you and I pay a call on Mr Sweeney ourselves.'

47

As Lord Archibald had anticipated, Skinner's way was blocked by a small group of photographers as he, Mitchell Laidlaw and Alex stepped out of their taxi in Chambers Street. Beside them stood the exultant figure of Noel Salmon.

'Look this way, Bob,' the *Spotlight* journalist called, a triumphant edge to his tone.

'What,' the policeman called out, with an easy contemptuous smile. 'You mean short, cross-eyed and crumpled?' Several of the photographers laughed.

'Sorry about this, Bob,' said one, a bulky, bearded figure whom Skinner knew well, raising his camera to focus on the group.

'That's all right, Denis. I've never objected to being photographed before, so why should I now?' He looked to his left, at Laidlaw and Alex. 'Just walk on,' he said, 'and smile if you look into anyone's lens.'

'How does it feel to have a crook for a father, Miss Skinner?'

Alex stopped in her tracks and turned to face her heckler, the *Spotlight* reporter. She stared at him with something closely related to the unblinking glare with which her father had transfixed a thousand criminals through his career. 'Are you just plain stupid, or can you really stand the cost of a defamation action, Mr Salmon?' she asked him, edging closer to him, as the little man backed off. 'Because when this is over, what you've just said will give us grounds.'

'Come on, lass,' said her father. 'That'll come in due course. Let's not keep Archie waiting.'

The trio strode off through a gateway and towards the entrance to the Crown Office, from which Scotland's criminal prosecution service is run. The photographers watched them leave. They were not allowed beyond the pavement, since the building also housed Edinburgh's Sheriff Court, from whose precincts they were always banned.

Inside the recently built office, Laidlaw headed for the reception desk. His approach was anticipated by a young woman in a smart grey suit. 'Hello,' she introduced herself. 'I'm Susan Shaw, the Lord Advocate's assistant. If you'll follow me, I'll take you straight to Lord Archibald.'

They walked in silence as she led them along a corridor which ended at a light oak door. She knocked lightly upon it, then held it open for Skinner and his companions.

Lord Archibald crossed the room to meet them, small, grey and twinkling, his hand outstretched in greeting. 'Hello Bob,' he said, then smiled as he saw the other man. 'I'm not too surprised to see you here, Mitch.'

'It's an honour to be in your new chambers, My Lord,' Laidlaw responded. He and Archie Nelson had been contemporaries at university, and had served their legal apprenticeships in the same office. He turned to Alex. 'This is my assistant, Miss Skinner.'

The Lord Advocate's eyebrows rose in surprise, as he looked from Alex, to her father and back again. 'We'd better watch our step, then,' he said, managing to sound not in the least patronising.

'Come, let's sit down.' He turned towards a big conference table to the left of his desk. On the far side, sat two men, unsmiling, in dark suits. Neither rose as the others joined them.

'These are the investigating officers,' announced Lord Archibald, briskly. 'Deputy Chief Constable Cheshire, and Detective Chief Superintendent Ericson. They've just arrived.' The men nodded in turn as they were introduced. Cheshire was in his mid-fifties, Ericson ten years younger. Skinner had heard of the Manchester DCC. He had a reputation within his own force as a fierce disciplinarian, and had handled a number of similar inter-constabulary investigations in England for the Home Office.

He gave him an affable, appraising look. The Englishman stared back, with an expression which made the room suddenly colder.

Skinner knew what the eyes said. '*I don't like bent coppers, mate, and when I get finished, you'll know how much I don't like them.*' His own gaze hardened. 'Normally, I'd be pleased to meet you gentlemen,' he began. 'But in these circumstances, I can't honestly say that I am. However, I recognise that you have a job to do, and as long as you approach it fairly and impartially, we'll co-operate in any way we can.'

Cheshire shook his bullet head. His greying hair was cut so close that it almost seemed shaved, and he wore the deep tan of an outdoorsman. 'Let me disabuse you of that notion, Mr Skinner,' he barked. 'Presumption of innocence is all very well for an ordinary criminal investigation. This isn't. In investigating allegations against policemen, I begin with a presumption of guilt. This time, it'll be up to you to prove yourself innocent.'

Mitchell Laidlaw stiffened, and seemed about to intervene, but Lord Archibald forestalled him with the slightest wave of a hand. 'If that's the approach which the Home Office has allowed you to take in the past,' he said, in his light, lilting accent, 'I'm afraid you'll find that we do things

221

differently in Scotland. I think it best if I begin by setting out, for everyone's benefit, the basis on which this enquiry will proceed.' He leaned forward, linking his short stubby fingers together, and looking directly at Cheshire.

'This is, in law and in fact, my investigation. You are here to look into the allegations which have been made against Deputy Chief Constable Skinner, and to report to me on the weight of the evidence. If your findings are that there is a criminal case to be answered, the precognition of witnesses will be undertaken by the Procurator Fiscal of Strathclyde, and his deputies, all members of the Crown Office staff.

'You and Mr Ericson will not take formal statements from potential witnesses, nor will you be permitted to interview Mr Skinner under caution. In all of this, I must insist that you adopt a neutral attitude. You will make no suggestions to witnesses, and you will conduct all your interviews together, never individually.

'You are not witch finders, gentlemen; you are simply my agents.'

He switched his gaze to Laidlaw. 'Do those ground rules seem fair to you?'

'Perfectly, with the proviso that we have access to any notes taken by Mr Cheshire and Mr Ericson in the course of interviews.'

'That's fine by me,' said the Lord Advocate, '. . . which means it's fine!'

He reached for a thin green manilla folder which lay on the table and pulled it towards him. 'Right, let's get down to business.' He looked at Laidlaw again. 'Mitchell,' he said, in a quiet, and suddenly very formal tone, 'this is what we have against your client.'

He opened the folder and took out a single document.

222

'That's it?' asked Alex, almost incredulous.

The Lord Advocate looked at her, and nodded. 'For the moment, it is. Uncovering the rest, or discounting it, is what this investigation is about.

'This is a covering letter from Mr Noel Salmon, of the newspaper *Spotlight*. It claims that he received information that a corrupt payment, in the amount of £100,000, was made to Mr Skinner, with a view to securing for the donor a favourable outcome of a case under investigation.

'The money, it alleges, was paid into a new account in the Guernsey office of the private bank JZG. The account is numbered, UK 73461, and the deposit was received in cash.'

'From whom?' asked Skinner, sharply, but his solicitor laid a hand on his sleeve, as if to silence him.

'Patience, Bob,' said the Lord Advocate. 'The sum was delivered by courier, with a covering letter of instruction, unsigned.' He looked across at Laidlaw, who nodded.

'Where is the evidence linking this payment to Mr Skinner?' he asked.

'Mr Salmon's letter advises me that he is informed that with the covering letter was a note saying that the bene-ficiary of the account was Mr Robert Morgan Skinner, of Edinburgh. The note, it is alleged, identified you spec-ifically by giving your birthplace and your date of birth. Further, it is said that there was a separate sheet of paper with the note, which bears a sample of Mr Skinner's signature.'

Mitchell Laidlaw rocked back in his chair, looking up at the ceiling, and took a breath so deep that for a second or two, it seemed that the buttons on his waistcoat would pop. 'I see,' he boomed at last, as his explosive exhalation subsided. 'But you are only speaking of allegations, Archie.

Allegations, if I may say so, from a very disreputable source, with a known grudge against my client.

'If the Secretary of State has suspended a senior police officer based purely on what you've told me, I'm going straight to the Court of Session; I'm going to rouse the Lord President himself and have that suspension lifted.'

Skinner looked at his friend, seeing him once more in a new light.

But Lord Archibald shook his head. 'No, no, Mitch,' he retorted quietly. 'I wouldn't have let him do that, and you know it. Salmon's letter says that the manager of the bank refused to discuss the matter with him. Quite right too, and beneficial. Not even the *Spotlight* would dare run the story this Sunday without corroboration from him.' He paused.

'However, the same manager was pragmatic and wise enough to agree to discuss it with me.'

'Why should he do that, with respect?' asked Alex.

'Because I'm a member of the Government, and because JZG has a banking licence in the UK. I didn't have to spell anything out to him, once I'd convinced him who I was.

'I called him this morning, from the Secretary of State's office, and established my *bona fides* simply by having him call me back through the Scottish Office switchboard. His name is Mr Medine: French influence, I suppose.

'He confirmed to me that account number UK 73461 does exist, and that the substance of the allegation is correct. He's awaiting the arrival of Mr Cheshire and Mr Ericson. He doesn't normally go to the office on Saturdays, but he's making an exception tomorrow.'

Skinner leaned forward, looking up the table towards

the Lord Advocate. 'We've got access to this man too, Archie, yes?'

'In principle, you have. I can't order him to see you, of course.'

'Can we make life easier for him, then?'

'What do you have in mind?'

The policeman smiled. 'Well, since this is an informal enquiry, and since we'll have access to witnesses and interview notes, how about letting one of my team accompany your men to Guernsey to sit in on the interview?'

Cheshire snorted. 'Nice try, Skinner.'

Lord Archibald frowned at first at the investigator's comment, then smiled as he began to think the request through. 'As an observer, you say? Not to conduct the interview in any way?'

Skinner shook his head. 'No, but with the right to ask supplementary questions at the end.'

The Law Officer turned to the investigators. 'Apart from there being no precedent, can you give me a good reason why I shouldn't allow this?'

'Potential intimidation of witnesses, sir,' said Cheshire, aggressively.

'Indeed? I'd expect a witness to be intimidated by two senior police officers, but hardly, if I read Mr Skinner's mind aright, by a legal apprentice just out of university.'

Alex looked round at her father in surprise. He grinned at her and nodded.

'All right, Bob,' said Archibald. 'I agree. But your representative must not interrupt Mr Cheshire's questioning, mind.' He turned to the men from Manchester. 'You will allow Miss Skinner to ask supplementaries, though.'

Cheshire sat silent and grim-faced, a flush showing even through the heavy tan. It was Ericson who broke the silence.

'Very good, sir,' he said, turning to Alex. 'Leave me your office number, Miss Skinner, and I'll advise you of our travel plans, once they're made.'

48

Even with the aid of a street map, and even although the Chief Superintendent's flat was less than a mile away, Martin and Pye had trouble finding Eddie Sweeney's workshop. It was tucked away out of sight at the end of one of the lanes which ran off Dalry Road, behind a Georgian town house, a forgotten treasure which had been rescued by an office developer. It was perhaps eight yards across, and twenty deep, a wooden structure with a corrugated iron roof, bounded at the rear and on the right by the high red brick walls of the adjoining building.

Before setting out from Fettes, Martin had called the force's criminal intelligence unit, and the national criminal records department, to check on their target. The second source had yielded a faxed photograph, taken at the time of a conviction in Aberdeen twelve years earlier, for receiving a stolen motor car, an offence which the Sheriff had taken lightly enough to punish with only a year's probation. That had been completed impeccably, and since then there had been no sign of a subsequent transgression.

The policemen drew up in Martin's Mondeo beside big grey-painted double gates which seemed to cover almost the full width of the workshop. The lane was a dead end, and so narrow that the Chief Superintendent had to position the car carefully, to allow both Pye and himself to open their doors.

The gates were secured by a heavy chain and padlock, but inset, to the right, there was a smaller doorway, black-painted, standing out from the surrounding grey, and with a brass nameplate on which the name 'E. Sweeney, Motor Engineer' was etched.

Martin banged on the grey gate. 'Mr Sweeney. Police. Open up, please.' There was no reply, no sound from within. He pushed the smaller door, but its Yale was secure. 'Is there a back entrance to this place, d'you think?' Martin mused.

'Not unless it's through the wall of the whisky bond next door,' Pye pointed out. 'Maybe he closes early on a Friday.'

The Chief Superintendent sighed. 'Well he bloody shouldn't,' he said. 'This week started with a locked door, now it's ending with another. Fuck this, Sammy, I'm fed up being pissed about. I think I feel an accidental stumble coming on.' Abruptly, he lifted his right foot and slammed the door with his heel. There was a crack as the keeper of the Yale gave under the force of the kick.

'Oh dear,' said the young detective constable, 'that was nearly a nasty fall. Are you all right, sir?'

'I've been worse. Thank God that door was there to stop me.'

There were no windows in the workshop; it was in darkness as they stepped inside. The little light which spilled in from the small doorway lit up a red car, jacked up at the front, but beyond the gloom was too deep to make out anything. The place smelled: of oil, of grease, of old leather . . . and of something else. 'Christ,' said Pye, 'd'you think Sweeney just pisses in the corner when he's needing?'

Martin said nothing, but peered around near the entrance until he found a light switch. He threw it, and after a few seconds a sequence of half a dozen neon tubes flickered into life. As they did, Pye had reached the red car, and could see beyond.

He gave a slight, involuntary shout, and started. For a moment Martin thought that the young man would turn and run, but he held his ground. 'Sweeney's in after all, sir,' he whispered.

Quickly, Martin stepped up beside him and together they advanced, into the furthest corner of the workshop.

Clearly, Eddie Sweeney had not been a big man in life. His feet only just touched the ground as he sat in the green, straight-backed wooden chair, his wrists and ankles lashed securely to its legs with heavy black insulating tape. But in death his eyes were huge. They stood out in their sockets, seemingly only a very short step from popping out altogether.

Martin leaned over and stared into the grotesque, purple, dead face. 'Oh, Sammy,' he whispered, 'we're dealing with a very special mind here. This man's an expert. He believes in death as an art form.

'I've only ever encountered one other like him.'

Pye crouched down beside his boss, looking up at the dead, head-lolling Sweeney. And as he did he saw that the man's nose was swollen, with white wisps of cotton wool protruding from the nostrils. His cheeks were distorted too, and something showed between the protruding teeth; something dirty, yellow and furred.

'That's not his tongue, is it, sir?'

Martin chuckled, blackly. 'Not even the most liverish tongue ever looked like that.' He stood up and leaned over the body. 'Yes, there's a grazed lump on his head. Our Mr Sweeney was cracked on the head from behind, then taped into his chair.'

He shook his head. 'What an imagination, and what a way to go. The killer packed his nose with cotton wool, rammed a tennis ball into his mouth, and stood back to watch while the poor sod suffocated.'

Pye shuddered. 'A tennis ball?' He looked closer. 'In the name of . . . So it is.'

'Game, set and match to our man,' said the Chief Superintendent, 'or so he thinks. We'd better take a look around, for the sake of form. But this is a very thorough person. I don't think for a moment that we'll find anything to help us.'

He stepped across to the far side of the workshop, where a grey filing cabinet stood against the wall, with its second drawer slid open. On the floor beside it there was a big brown steel waste bin. Martin looked inside. 'Sammy, forget it,' he called to his young colleague. 'He got what he was after. There's ash in here, and you can bet that once it was the paperwork related to a set of plates, supplied to customer unknown, no questions asked.'

'Are you sure that this was the man we're after, sir? Maybe Sweeney was in bother with someone else.'

The chunky Martin shook his head. 'Forget it, Sam. This was our guy all right. As soon as he saw the photofit which we issued yesterday, he knew that we'd linked him to the caravan. So he went back and covered his tracks. End of story, for Mr Sweeney.'

He looked at the body once more. 'It could be that he's even sending us a message in the way he chose to kill him. All significant openings closed off. Fine, let him be that cocky, for that's how we'll catch him.'

'What do you mean, sir?'

'I mean that when you're dealing with a criminal as arrogant and sure of himself as this one is, all you have to do is wait while his ego and his feelings of infallibility get bigger and bigger, until, sure as eggs is eggs, he makes the mistake which lets you nab him.'

49

Pam woke at seven forty-five on Saturday morning, alone in the bedroom of the Gullane cottage. She was startled at first, until she remembered that she and Bob had decided to leave Edinburgh for the weekend, although not for Peebles Hydro.

They had spent a long, silent Friday evening in the cottage. Skinner was morose, and largely silent, with the telephone set on auto answer, catching calls from a few sympathetic friends. The only calls which he had returned had been from Neil McIlhenney, offering his sympathy, and his total support, and from Andy Martin, telling him of Sweeney's murder.

'Won't that put that farmer in danger?' Pam had asked, as he had explained what had happened. 'Mr Carr, I mean, the man who did the photofit.'

'I shouldn't think so. He'll assume, rightly, that Andy will put a guard on him. So it'd be too dangerous to go back to the farm to take him out. Anyway, what would be the point? The composite picture would be evidence in itself. No, his meeting with Carr was very brief. He must have spent much more time with Sweeney, or maybe Sweeney even knew who he was.'

He had shuddered quite violently, startling her. 'I hate people like him, you know, people who kill with flair, not just with purpose. Murder's murder, I know, always terrible; but usually it's in hot blood. Occasionally it's a commercial transaction, a falling-out among criminals who live by different rules from the rest of us.

'I don't tolerate any of it, but nothing turns my stomach like a man who can kill the way this fellow does. He's so premeditated: the way he just disposed of Sweeney, the way he killed Leona.'

'Leona? Was that necessarily premeditated? Couldn't that have been sexual in origin, with him catching her naked?'

Bob had given her a long cool look, shaking his head. 'Not the way I read it. He didn't have to go upstairs. He could have taken the boy and gone. But he chose to go upstairs to find the mother, to rape and kill her. There was a message there too, I think.'

She had stared at him then, astonished. 'A message? For whom?'

But he had shaken his head and fallen silent once more.

Now, with the soft sunlight of early morning making patterns of the window frames on the bedroom curtains, she rose and, putting on her robe as she went, made her way through the living room to the kitchen. There she found him, sitting at the table, in running shorts and teeshirt, sweating heavily, his shoulders hunched, his head down, caught off guard in an attitude which touched her heart.

She moved silently behind him and ran her fingers through his matted hair. 'Come on, Big Boy,' she whispered, soothingly. 'It's supposed to be darkest just before the dawn, not after it.'

He looked up at her, over his shoulder. 'I'm still waiting for dawn,' he muttered. 'I feel like I'm at war on two fronts. Can you imagine how it feels, to know that my name will be all over this morning's press? I've been a police officer for almost a quarter of a century, more than half my life. In that time, I like to think that I've never done a dishonourable thing.

'Yet here I am, accused of abusing my position through my relationship with you, sacked by Anderson as unsuitable for my security post, under investigation for corruption, stigmatised, suspended, and effectively banned from acting personally in my defence.

'At the same time there's a madman at large with a kidnapped child, with whom I have a strong personal link, and for whom, somehow, I feel a responsibility. Not just that, he's targeting me in some way I don't yet understand. I want to be out there chasing the guy, I ought to be; yet I can't, by order of Dr Bruce Anderson. I tell you girl, there are a few ghosts in my life, and it's as if they're all coming back to haunt me, all of them at once.'

He took the hand which she laid upon his shoulder, and pressed it gently.

'Can't I help, love?' she asked. 'Can I help ease the pain?'

He stood up from the table and turned, looking down at her. 'No, honey. No you can't. I suppose you're a third front, another area of conflict in my life.'

'Is that how you see me?' she asked, quietly.

He shrugged his wide shoulders. 'Oh God, I don't know. Maybe I should have chosen my words more carefully. But our future is something else to be resolved, and right now, I just can't handle any of it.'

He cried out in sudden exasperation. 'When I was out there just now, running along the top of the beach, I remember thinking to myself, "Why stop? Why turn back?" There's part of me that wants to chuck it all in, and I've never felt like that before. It's scary, Pam. It's as if since the stabbing, since my split with Sarah, since my discoveries about Myra, and now with all of this, that I'm just not me any more. There's a bloke inside me, but he's a stranger. Know what else I'm finding out? I don't even like him.'

She pulled him to her, and hugged him, pressing her face against his chest, running her fingers through his hair. But he stood, still and upright in her arms, until finally his right hand came up, and he stroked her cheek with his fingers.

'I'm a real mess, am I not?' he whispered, as she looked up and saw his sad smile. 'Who'd want a future with a crock like me?'

As he spoke, as he asked his despondent question, a face came into his mind's eye, quite unexpectedly: Sarah, looking at him and frowning, with a mixture of surprise and disappointment. He tried to will her away, but her mental image remained. And he knew. At that moment, he knew.

A thump from the hall broke the moment. 'Post lady,' he said, matter-of-fact once more. 'She's always early on a Saturday.' He released himself from her hug, and walked through to the hallway. There were three items of mail lying on the doormat, between the glass and outer doors. Picking them up, he glanced at each in turn as he stepped back into the living room.

He recognised the handwriting on the first, and tore it open as fast as he could. It was a 'cheer up' card from Alex, with a note inside which read, 'Don't worry, Pops, I'll keep an eye on that awful man Cheshire. Anyway, with me on your side, how can you lose?'

He smiled, and positioned the cheery Beryl Cook card, with its voluminous, yet voluptuous ladies, on the shelf above the gas fire, then laid the second envelope, a bill from Scottish Power, unopened beside it.

As soon as he looked at the third item, he felt an old familiar tremor in the pit of his stomach. Policemen, more than any others, have an instinct for danger which is triggered even in the most normal of surroundings.

'Deputy Chief Constable Robert Skinner.' He read his name aloud as he stared at the padded A5 Jiffy bag, the container of choice for many a small letter bomb. He never received official mail at home, but always in the office, where it was X-rayed as a matter of routine. At that moment, Pam appeared in the doorway. He beckoned her into the room. 'Wait here,' he ordered. 'I need to check this out.'

He stepped past her, back into the kitchen, reaching for the cutlery drawer, from which he took a short, but razor sharp, fruit knife. He sat down once more at the table and felt the package with both hands from all angles, pressing gently, and very carefully, lest he should activate a trigger mechanism inside. The only object which he could sense within the bag seemed to be solid and rectangular, a small, firm box.

Relaxing only slightly, Skinner picked up the fruit knife. Slowly, centimetre by centimetre, he began to cut his way into the bag, not along the top, or along the bottom, since letter bombs were often wired at both ends, but along the side, through the outer skin, and into the fibre padding which he pulled out to expose the inner layer. When it was laid bare from end to end of the bag, he carried the parcel over to the sink, which he filled with water, so that he could drop it should it be, after all, an incendiary device.

Finally, when he was completely prepared, with the bag laid on the work surface, he crouched beside it at eye level, and began to make the final incision with the sharp little knife. He worked slowly, ready to stop should he meet any resistance, easing the blade through the paper, until the bag was open.

Leaving it where it was, he reached into the cupboard under the sink, and found a small torch. He fumbled at first with the unreasonably small button, wondering if the batteries were flat until at last its bulb lit up. Pressing the ends of the bag very gently with his broad left hand to widen the opening which he had cut, he shone the beam, undetectable in the daylight, into the gap.

He was looking for wires, but he saw none: only a black cassette box.

He released his breath, which he had been holding, in a loud gasp, and picked up the bag, allowing its contents to drop on to the work-surface. Only then did he look closely again at the Jiffy. It was stamped, with what he took to be the regulation amount, but the postmark was smudged and faint. He shone the torch beam directly on to it from close range, but both the time and postal district were indecipherable.

He swore gently, and tossed the container on to the table, picking up the cassette box as he did so. The lid was clear and showed a shiny new tape inside.

Only then did he look up, to see Pam standing in the doorway, looking anxious. He glowered at her. 'I thought I told you to stay next door!'

'I couldn't. I was worried for you. It's okay?'

He nodded, waving the box as he shooed her back into the living room. 'If this is some direct marketing gimmick, I will personally eat the sender's liver. But somehow, I doubt it.'

She looked at him. 'You think . . .'

'Let's find out.' He stepped across to his hi-fi stack, took out the cassette and slipped it into the play-only deck, which was incapable of erasing tapes, even by accident. Using the remote hand-set, he switched on the amplifier, adjusted the volume upwards and pressed the tape button.

Beside him Pam jumped, as the shouts and background music of a rapper burst from the speakers. Skinner waited, guessing what would come next. 'It's Radio One,' boomed the disc jockey, as the music track faded, 'the Nation's Number One. It's Thursday, it's eleven thirty, and it's time for the news.'

There was a short jingle, and a second voice cut in. 'This is *Newsbeat*, with Mary Slavin. Edinburgh police today released a photofit picture of the man they want to question about the murder of MP Leona McGrath, and the kidnap of her son Mark. It shows a clean-shaven fair-haired white man in his mid to late thirties . . .'

The news announcer was cut off abruptly. 'Uncle Bob! Uncle Bob!' The child's cry which replaced it was unmistakably that of Mark McGrath, but not the self-possessed slightly precocious child whom Skinner knew. It was frightened, shocked and tearful.

'Uncle Bob, Mr Gilbert said that the news would show you when this tape was made and that I'm all right. But he never said what would be on it. What did the lady mean about my mummy? My mummy's all right, isn't she? You wouldn't let anything happen to her, Uncle Bob, would you!' It was not a question, rather a cry for reassurance – a cry for a denial of the horror that the boy had just heard on the radio, clearly for the first time.

He broke off, in a crying and whimpering sound which ended after a few seconds in a loud sniff. 'Mr Gilbert says I've to tell you, Uncle Bob, that he has one more thing still to do, then he'll be ready to tell you what this is about. That's what he said. And he says he'll be in touch again, soon.' There was a click, and the tape went dead.

Skinner, who had been staring at the tape deck as if the child was actually inside it, turned back to Pamela. Her hands were to her mouth, and there were tears shining in her eyes. 'How awful,' she cried. 'For the poor wee boy to find out like that about his mother being dead. You just can't imagine cruelty like that.'

'You can when you've seen it as often as I have,' Bob told her. 'But I doubt if the guy knew that would happen. We didn't release the photofit until eleven. Mr Gilbert would have no way of knowing that it would be the lead item on the eleven thirty news. Mind you, I don't think his conscience would be pricked by the way it turned out.'

'I knew you were close to Mark,' said Pamela, 'but I never knew you were on Uncle Bob terms.'

'I made a point of seeing him a lot after the accident, then later, I would look in to say hello sometimes on a Friday after work, when Leona got back from Westminster.' He sighed. 'He's a very gifted wee boy, but he hasn't half been touched by tragedy. His father, his mother, his mother's best friend: all of them dying violent deaths.'

'What'll happen to him? Assuming we get him back alive, that is.'

'Oh we will, Pam, we will. If you believe in anything, believe in that. As for afterwards, that's a good question. The grandparents are probably too old to take on a six-year-old full-time, and there are no uncles or aunts. If it's adoption, it'll need to be a pretty special home.' He reached down and took the tape from the deck.

'Let's concentrate on the first part for now, though, getting him back safe.

'That means getting this tape down to the technical people in London, to see if Mr Gilbert's given us any more accidental assistance. I'm going to take it up to the office as soon as I'm showered and dressed. You'd better come, for I ain't leaving you here alone. I'm beginning to regret getting rid of our watchers yesterday.'

'But you're not supposed to go to the office,' she protested.

'Fuck that for a game of soldiers. But if it makes you happy, you'll be going in. I'll just be there as your bodyguard.'

'Okay.' She started to say more, but hesitated.

'What is it?' he asked, as they moved together, towards the bedroom.

'Oh nothing. I was just going to teach my granny to suck eggs, that was all.'

'Come on, out with it,' he insisted.

'Well, it was that name. Mr Gilbert. I don't imagine it's for real, but all the same, have you checked?'

Skinner nodded. 'As soon as Carr came up with it, I had big Neil do just that. He checked every case on which I've led the investigation. Way back. No Mr Something Gilberts; no Mr Gilbert Somethings.

'You're right. It was bound to be a phoney. Still, we had to try.'

50

'Bob, I thought the Lord Advocate told you to stay away from here.'

Andy Martin looked up in surprise as the door of his office opened and they entered. Pam had noticed his car in the rear car park, but Skinner had known already that with the search for the kidnapper in full swing, and with his own absence, there would be no more days off for his friend for the foreseeable future.

'He can try having me arrested, or he can sue me, or he can piss off.'

He took a tape from his pocket and laid it on the desk. 'Play this.'

Without a word, Martin picked up the cassette, reached across without standing up to put it in the player, and listened in grim glowering silence to the child's desperate message.

'Bastard,' he hissed, very quietly, when it was finished.

'Another one for the specialists, Andy.' He wrote down a name and a number. 'Here's who to call. That's a copy. I've got the original in an envelope in my pocket.' He patted his jacket. 'Sergeant, would you like to fly it down to London?'

Pam, surprised, nodded.

'Good. I'll drive you to the airport and pick you up. You'll be safe travelling, and in London, I reckon.'

He turned back to Martin. 'Anything strike you about the message?'

'You mean apart from the cruelty of Mark finding out

about his mother's death?' the Head of CID growled. 'One thing,' he went on. 'That's what he said. "He has one more thing still to do", before he tells us what he's up to. That one thing was killing our Mr Sweeney, no doubt. So we can expect to hear from him any time now.'

'No, I don't think that was it. Have you got a time of death on Sweeney yet?'

'About four o'clock on Thursday.'

'That figures. You see, I don't think Mr Gilbert knew that he'd have to take the risk of killing Sweeney until he heard the news bulletin recorded on the tape. He must have known then that only Carr could have given us that detailed a picture, and he must have guessed too that we had the phoney number plate from the caravan. Only at that point did it become a bigger risk to leave Sweeney alive than to kill him.'

Skinner stabbed at the table with a finger. 'So,' he said vehemently. 'Mark's "one more thing" means something else. The guy's going to pull another stunt, maybe an even bigger stunt, and there he is, the cocky bastard, telling us . . . telling me . . . about it, knowing that I haven't clue where to start looking.'

His face twisted into a scowl of frustration. 'You haven't gone public on the link between the McGrath investigation and the Sweeney murder, have you?'

'Christ no. I didn't want to start a feeding frenzy in the media.'

'Quite right: you'd just have added to the pressure on the troops, and on yourself.'

The two detectives sat for a while, staring ahead, neither looking at the other, each concentrating so hard on possibilities that they almost failed to react when Pam broke the silence.

'A bigger stunt,' she said. 'He's killed an MP and stolen her son. What could be a bigger stunt, as you put it, than that?'

The words left Skinner's mouth almost without conscious thought. 'To do it again,' he said quietly.

As Martin looked at him, his initial disbelief faded against his knowledge of a hundred other viable kites that his friend had flown in the time that he had known him. 'How many other MPs have young children?' he asked.

'No idea,' said Skinner. 'But the Special Branch offices around the country should know. I think it's time we got on the phone. You dig up McGuire, and I'll contact Strathclyde.'

51

The two Manchester detectives had flown British Airways to London, for the onward flight to Guernsey. Alex had chosen to travel with British Midland, to minimise the time she would have to spend in the company of the formidable and hostile Cheshire.

With very few business travellers in the air on Saturday, the flights were all on time, in take-off and in landing. As they disembarked through the tiny Guernsey terminal building into the dull, breezy morning, after a cross-Channel hop spent mostly in silence, Alex looked around for a taxi rank.

'It's all right,' said Ericson, coming up behind her as she headed for a white Primera minicab. 'We've arranged transport. I'm sure my boss won't mind if you join us.'

Cheshire looked as if he would be quite prepared to allow her to take the taxi, but said nothing. Alex fell into step beside the two officers as they headed for the police car which waited a short distance from the terminal entrance, a uniformed constable standing to attention by the driver's door.

'First time in Guernsey?' Ericson asked her, in a reasonable show of courtesy, as the car pulled away from its stand.

Alex shook her head, setting her curls tumbling, and smiling at the policeman in a way that made even Cheshire stir in his seat. 'No. Dad brought me here on holiday once, a couple of years after my mum died. I was only about six,

243

but I remember. It rained all the time. We were in the best hotel in town, though, with plenty of covered facilities, so it didn't matter so much.'

Cheshire turned in the front passenger seat. 'Your father could afford good holidays even then?' he asked, his cold expressionless eyes fixed on her. 'He's a man of property, isn't he? Two houses in Scotland, I understand, and two more in Spain. Looking at that, some might say it's hardly surprising that some chickens have come home to roost.'

Ericson looked straight ahead, focusing on the back of the driver's head. She wondered if his question had been a set-up, until she realised that he was embarrassed by his chief's brutal directness.

Quite unexpectedly, Alex smiled. 'Mr Cheshire,' she said, 'if that look is meant to intimidate me, you're wasting your time. When I was a wee girl, if I did or said something I shouldn't have, my dad would let me know just by giving me a long look. It was his worst punishment, almost the only one he ever needed; a couple of seconds, and I'd be saying "sorry". Believe me, when it comes to intimidating stares, you're not in the same class as him.'

Her smile vanished. 'I'm not here to be interrogated by you two, but I am happy to put you right about Pops. He's had three inheritances in his life. When my mum was killed, the mortgage on the Gullane house was paid off, and there were other life policies in his name. That helped him to buy, largely, an apartment in Spain, which we used. He still owns it, but he rents it out to policemen . . . at a very reasonable rate, incidentally.

'Later, an aunt died, and left him a lot of money, the bulk of it in property in Perthshire, which he sold. He only needed part of that to buy the Spanish villa, which we use as a family. The rest was invested.

'After that, when my grandparents died, he and I were the only beneficiaries. Oh yes, and the Edinburgh property is jointly owned by Pops and Sarah, my stepmother. There's a small loan on that, because with mortgage tax relief it was cheaper to borrow than take it all from invested capital.'

Now it was her turn to stare hard at her inquisitor. 'Mr Cheshire, we're all here looking into an allegation by persons unknown that my dad's taken a bung of a hundred grand. If all you've done so far is check up on his assets, without checking how he came by them, you're pretty shoddy detectives. No wonder the crime rate in Manchester is so high.

'The fact is, gentlemen, my dad doesn't need a hundred thousand. He *has* a hundred thousand, and quite a lot more.'

Cheshire's glare had softened, but he was still unsmiling. 'Very good, Miss Skinner. I hear what you say, and if you thought I was trying to bully you, I apologise. The fact is, we know all of your father's financial history. He's been vetted several times in the course of his career.

'But I have to tell you, I don't care how comfortably off he is. I have never met anyone – even my own dear wife,' he interjected, with his first flicker of humour – 'who couldn't use another hundred thousand.

'I once knew a man; neighbour of mine,' said the policeman, in his rumbling northern accent, 'gynaecologist, he was, middle-aged, private practice, very successful, who was arrested for nicking a pound box of Cadbury's Roses from W.H. Smith. His defence was that he was experiencing the male menopause. The prosecution case, which the Bench accepted, was that he was just a thieving bastard.'

As he finished, the car drew to a halt. They had barely noticed their journey through St Peter Port, the island's tiny capital; now they found themselves in what seemed to be a side street, outside a three-storey, white-painted building. As they emerged from the car they saw a single entrance door, with three brass plates and three door buzzers beside it.

JZG Bank was the middle of the three. Cheshire stepped forward and pressed the button. Almost immediately a tinny voice sounded through the small speaker grille which surrounded it. 'Yes?'

'Three visitors for Mr Medine.'

'I am he. Please enter and come up one flight of stairs.' There was a loud buzz, at which the policeman pushed the door open.

Medine was waiting for them on the first landing. He was a small, thin man, aged around sixty, with a sallow wind-burned face and round, rimless spectacles of the type worn almost invariably by Gestapo officers in movies. Alex wondered, fleetingly, if they might be a relic of the days of the German occupation of the island.

'Come in, come in,' said the little man, after Cheshire had made the introductions. 'There is no-one else in the building. It is discreet.' He was dressed, not in a business suit, but in the casual shirt, baggy cardigan and slacks, which Alex guessed he might wear for his weekend gardening. She had been expecting to hear French overtones in the Channel Islander's accent, but in fact there were none. If anything, there was the merest touch of Home Counties South.

He led them into a small office suite, which looked not at all like a bank. He caught Alex's expression and smiled. 'This is not a place where people come to withdraw fifty pounds, or negotiate an overdraft, for all that it says on the sign by the door. Here we handle fairly large amounts of money for people who require offshore banking services.

'Normally they're ex-pat workers, or people who've retired abroad – to Spain, France or Italy, say – but who prefer to keep their main money in the British Isles.'

'For tax reasons?' Alex enquired.

'That's their business. We don't declare interest paid to the Exchequer in London, Paris, Madrid or anywhere else.'

He showed them through a large office into a smaller conference room with a window which looked across the street, to an almost identical, white building as the one in which they took their seats.

'Thank you for seeing us,' Cheshire began, brusque, formal and forbidding once more. 'This is an informal meeting, but Mr Ericson and Miss Skinner may take notes. Miss Skinner is here as an observer, but she may ask a few questions at the conclusion of our discussion, if she feels it necessary.'

Medine nodded, straight-faced. 'I have taken instructions from my head office in Germany. I am cleared to co-operate with you as far as I can.' He rose from the round table at which they sat, and walked round behind Alex to a small filing cabinet.

'You wish to discuss our account number UK 73461, I understand from the call which I received yesterday?'

'Correct.'

Medine took a small folder from the cabinet and resumed his seat at the table. 'It's all in here,' he said, 'all the detail of the instruction. The account details are on computer. I can get you an exact balance, if you wish. It will show the sum deposited, plus interest to date. There have been no withdrawals.

'That would have been unlikely anyway at this stage,' he added.

'Why?' asked Ericson.

'Because the terms of the account specify ninety days' notice of withdrawal. This account was set up only a few months ago.'

'What's the rate of interest?'

'Currently nine-point-seven-five per cent.'

'That's very good,' said the Chief Superintendent.

'That's why we are popular with our customer base. We give that little bit extra for larger deposits. Our minimum is fifty thousand, sterling.'

Cheshire leaned forward. 'Let's get a bit more specific about your customer base, shall we. What types might it include?'

The little manager's eyes narrowed. He pinched his nose, below the cross-piece of his spectacles. 'Most of them are corporate. Our private clients include engineers working abroad, I suppose; retired people, as I said; soldiers.'

'Soldiers? Do they earn that much?' Cheshire looked at him quizzically.

'There are other armies beside ours, sir.'

The policeman nodded. 'You mean mercenaries.'

'Maybe. In my experience, most prefer to be called military advisers.'

'Are all your accounts numbered?'

'Oh no,' said Medine. 'that is simply a service which JZG offers. Most of our accounts are held in the name of the depositor.'

'What about access?'

'Always we require a signature, and proof of identity. We don't go in for codewords or half banknotes or any of that nonsense.' He smiled, thinly.

'Yet if someone comes to you asking for a numbered account, what might that mean?'

The manager leaned back in his chair. 'Who am I to

know?' he countered. 'You tell me of a private bank which asks a customer to provide references when he comes to it with a large sum of money to deposit.

'If I am asked for a numbered account, I provide it without question.'

'And that was how it was in the case of UK 73461?' Cheshire asked.

'Exactly.'

'So how was that account set up?'

Medine opened his folder. 'Around five months ago,' he said, 'a man arrived with a parcel. He didn't give a name, and we didn't ask. He said simply that he was a courier engaged by a third party, and he asked to see the manager.

'I interviewed him, in this same room, and he gave me the parcel. It contained one hundred thousand pounds in sterling, in Bank of England notes of various denominations, and ages.

'With it, there was a covering letter. I have it here.' He took a sheet of paper from the folder, and handed it to Cheshire. 'It instructed me to place the contents of the parcel in a numbered account for the benefit of Robert Morgan Skinner, born in Motherwell, Lanarkshire, on April 7, 1951. Withdrawals from the account could be made only by Mr Skinner, on his signature and on production of a means of secondary identification.

'The letter asked me also to provide acceptable confirmation that the account had been opened. It was unsigned.'

Cheshire read the document which Medine had handed over: once, twice, a third time. Then he passed it across to Alex. She picked it up and stared at it, peering closely. The letter had been typed, not on a word-processor, for printing, but directly on a manual typewriter. It was on a plain sheet of cream A4 paper.

' *"This is an instruction . . .",*' she began to read aloud. It was exactly as the manager had said. Her father's name, his birthplace, his date of birth. 'But anyone could have gone to the General Register Office and looked that up,' she protested, her self-control beginning to slip for the first time that day.

Cheshire raised a hand to silence her, glancing across. For the first time, his eyes were sympathetic, rather than unkind. 'Shh,' he said, 'I know that.'

He looked back at the banker. 'What else, Mr Medine? How was the depositor to know that the courier hadn't just legged it with the cash?'

'He asked for, and I gave him, a signed, numbered receipt from this bank. It bore the number of the account. It's part of our security requirement that account holders must quote the number of their receipt as well as the title of the account when requesting withdrawals.' He took a copy of the slip from the file, and handed it over.

'Of course I have no idea what the courier did with the receipt, but he did ask me also to telephone a UK telephone number and leave a message on its answering machine, saying simply, "Consignment received" and giving the date. This I did.'

'Do you recall the number?'

Medine nodded. 'I wrote it down. Here it is.' He took a slip of paper from the folder and passed it to the policeman. Before he slid it across to Alex, she had seen the first numbers, 0162. Even so, when she saw her father's unlisted Gullane number, a shaft of cold fear swept through her. She wondered if she had gone pale, and if Cheshire had noticed, until she realised that if the investigators had checked his financial details they would also know all of his telephone numbers.

'And finally,' asked Cheshire. 'The signature. How was that to be verified?'

'Easily,' the banker answered. 'This was in the parcel.'

He took the last document from the folder and handed it to the investigator. Cheshire looked at it, his face set once more, and passed it to Alex. It was another sheet of plain A4 paper, cream-coloured. She read, aloud once more. ' *"This is a sample of Mr Skinner's signature. He will also identify himself by producing his police warrant card, issued by his office in Fettes Avenue, Edinburgh"*.'

Below the typescript, there it was, in a clear hand which she knew so well. 'Robert M. Skinner.'

'It's all right, Alex,' said Cheshire, speaking suddenly almost like a kindly uncle. 'I'm not going to ask you.' She found his sympathy so much harder to take than his aggression.

'Are there any questions you'd like to ask?' he offered.

She pulled herself together and nodded.

'The money in the package, Mr Medine. You said that it was in Bank of England notes?'

'That's right.'

'A mix of denominations and ages?'

'Yes, nearly all twenties and fifties. I remember, because I had to authenticate every one of them. Most were in sequence, but not continuous. Not new, but most, if not all, unused. It was as if the whole sum had been gathered together piece by piece, over a period of time.'

'And all of them were Bank of England notes?'

The banker looked at her, puzzled. 'What else? As I said, the deposit was in sterling.'

'Mmm, okay. Can we go back to the courier now?'

Alex asked. 'Can you describe him?'

'Let me think.' Medine knitted his brow in concentration. 'He was tall,' he said at last, hesitantly, 'and slim-built, wearing a grey suit. He had fairish hair, as I recall. I would say that he was in his thirties.'

'How about his accent?'

'I'm bad on UK accents. I can barely tell a Jock from a Geordie. This chap just sounded bland; that's all I can say about him. He didn't give me any regional impression.'

On Alex's left, Chief Superintendent Ericson opened his briefcase, reached into it and, after fumbling with his papers, took out a single sheet which he handed, face-down, to the bank manager. 'Did he look anything like this?' he asked.

As Medine turned the paper over, Alex started in surprise. It was the photofit of Mark McGrath's kidnapper. The Channel Islander nodded at once. 'Yes. This could have been him. I'm not saying that it was, mind you, but in terms of general appearance, yes, that's in the ball-park.

'Apart from the glasses, of course.' He looked up. 'Oh. Didn't I say? The man wore glasses.'

52

'So you do have open minds after all?'

Alex smiled at Ericson as the car moved off. 'Course we do,' said Cheshire. 'It's unthinkable to me that another deputy chief would take a bung from anyone, but in this task, you have to entertain the unthinkable.

'You have, as your dad would be the first to tell you, to look at all the possibilities. Having studied everything about DCC Skinner, we just happened to have that photofit with us. When Medine gave us that description, Ronnie sparked on it right away. Incidentally, I was going to ask him to describe the courier, before we left.

'Pity about those bloody glasses, though?'

He smiled at Alex, suddenly. 'All right young lady. We've given you something, now pay us back. Why were you going on about that money?'

She hesitated, but finally grinned. 'Okay, guv,' she said, 'I'll cough. Those Bank of England notes. If this so-called bung originated from Scotland . . . and where else would it? . . . and it was put together over a period, like Medine said, not in a single wodge of cash, it's very unlikely, to say the least, that there wouldn't be any Scottish banknotes in it. Most of the notes in circulation in Scotland are issued by our own clearing banks, the Bank of Scotland, the Royal Bank, and the Clydesdale. Medine obviously doesn't know that.' She looked from Cheshire to Ericson. 'Neither, equally obviously, do you.'

'Touché, sir,' said the Chief Superintendent to his boss. 'Nice one, Alex.'

The Deputy Chief nodded. 'Yes, it is. But I won't lie to you, lass. Things still look dodgy for your dad. First and foremost, there's his signature. We'll have to check that, but I could tell when you looked at it that you thought it was genuine.'

'It took me by surprise,' she protested, 'but it could still be a good forgery. It must be.'

'Time, and the calligraphy experts will tell. Of course, if it is a phoney, then the whole allegation is a fit-up. But if not . . .' He gave her a meaningful look.

'Anyway, on top of that there's the confirmatory telephone call, to his unlisted number in Gullane. And that receipt: I've got a feeling in my water that it has to be kicking around somewhere.

'You going to let us look for it, or do I get a warrant?'

She nodded. 'I'll ask Pops, but he'll say yes. As for the telephone number, the McGrath kidnapper has that.'

Cheshire looked at her in genuine surprise. 'My fiancé lets me in on some secrets, you know,' she said. 'The first contact from the man was in a telephone call to my dad's unlisted number in Gullane. Andy's people are still tearing British Telecom apart looking for the person who sold it to him.'

The Deputy Chief frowned. 'If I was in my nasty bastard mode,' he muttered, 'I'd say that maybe your dad gave it to him. That maybe the link between them's stronger than we think. That maybe this man's after a king-size ransom, and that your dad's got reasons for making sure he gets it. Maybe the hundred grand was a down-payment from him.'

He saw a look of horror cross her face. 'Of course, that's just my nasty bastard imagination running away with me,' he said, 'but he is facing a divorce petition from your stepmother, and since his assets are mostly in property or long-term investments, maybe another nasty bastard, in the Crown Office, say, might think that he did need some cash in a hurry . . . maybe a bit more than a hundred grand.'

He stopped. 'That's what I really hate about this job,' he said, gloomily. 'It's not just about looking under stones. It's about really rummaging around under 'em, for the most horrible things you could ever imagine.'

53

'How are we doing, Andy?' asked Skinner from the door of Martin's office. He had just returned from Edinburgh Airport, where he had put Pam on the 11 a.m. flight to London, bound for MI5 with the original of Mark McGrath's horrific taped message.

'Just about there. Strathclyde called back a couple of minutes ago. I'm only waiting for Fife.'

'The buggers over there are probably all on the golf course,' the DCC growled. But he had barely spoken before the telephone rang.

'None?' he heard Martin say. 'You sure? Yes, okay, that's fine. Thanks.'

He hung up and looked across at Skinner. 'They only have five MPs. One's a bachelor, another's newly married, a third's getting on a bit, and so on; end result zero. So no additions to my list.'

He picked up a sheet of paper from the desk. 'Seventy-two Scottish MPs, and only nine of them with children under twelve. Twenty-five others have teenagers, but let's discount them, for now at least.'

He handed the list to Skinner, who barely glanced at it. 'How do we go about this?' he mused. 'It's pure speculation on our part. If we act on it, and give them all protection, it'll cost a fortune, and probably start a parliamentary panic.'

'I agree,' said Martin, 'but given the threat on that tape, it's speculation we can't ignore. Look, why don't we ask

Special Branch offices to make quiet contact with all the names on our list, to advise them to keep their kids under constant observation, and to offer them protection if they want it?'

'Good idea. Let's play it that way. You brief Mario McGuire and have him make the calls.' He turned to the list once more. 'Let's see who's here, then.'

He had only just begun to read, and Martin was reaching for his telephone, when it rang. Frowning with momentary annoyance, the Chief Superintendent picked it up.

'Mario,' he said, surprised. 'I was just going to call you.' He fell silent as a look of pure horror crossed his face. 'Oh no,' Skinner heard him gasp. 'Get down there, now,' he snapped. 'The boss and I will meet you there.'

He slammed the phone back into its cradle. 'Let's have it then,' said the DCC quietly.

'See that speculation of ours?' the younger man replied, hunching his shoulders and clasping his hands together. 'I think it's suddenly turned into fact. There's just been a shooting in Abercromby Place. The victim is a Mrs Anderson.

'Mario thinks that it's the Secretary of State's wife.'

54

Abercromby Place is little more than a connecting road, linking Dublin Street and Dundas Street. With few private residences, and much of its town-house office space vacant and available for let, its main value to the city is as a place for shoppers to park.

When Martin and Skinner swung out of Dundas Street, they found the road partially blocked by a police car slewed sideways. The two constables on duty recognised the detectives at once, and waved them through, although one sneaked a second, surprised glance at the suspended DCC.

They drove on but had gone barely any distance before, at a point where the road curved, they came upon two more police cars, an ambulance, and a knot of half a dozen uniformed officers, with men in plain clothes mingled among them.

As they jumped from the car, Mario McGuire saw them and waved them through the crowd.

'Are all these bystanders necessary?' Skinner barked.

'I'm waiting for someone senior from Division to take command, sir,' said McGuire.

'Will we do, d'you think?' said Martin, curtly. 'Senior officer forward,' he called. A uniformed inspector stepped up. 'Get this lot organised and searching. I want spent cartridge cases, and anything else that's lying around.'

He turned back to McGuire. 'Any witnesses?'

'One. She's in the ambulance, being looked after. She was just coming out of her flat in Albany Street when she heard a bang. She didn't react at first, but finally she looked along here and saw something on the ground. She ran along, and realised what it was. By that time the manager of the pub on the corner had appeared too. He called us.'

'How did you get involved?' Skinner asked.

'By luck, Inspector Good was in the first car to respond. He looked in the woman's handbag, found this, and called me straight away.' McGuire handed Skinner a laminated photo-pass, showing a blonde woman in her thirties. It bore a House of Commons crest, and a name: Mrs Catherine Anderson.

'Oh shit,' whispered the DCC. 'It's Bruce's wife all right.

'Let's have a look at her, then,' he said, resignedly.

McGuire led them across the street, towards a car parked nose-in, in the only occupied bay in a group of six. The body lay on the ground beside the driver's door, covered in a grey blanket, emblazoned with the crest of the Scottish Ambulance Service.

Skinner knelt down and lifted it up by a corner, carefully. Two eyes stared out at him, vacantly, looking not in the slightest surprised, just very dead. There was a big ragged hole in the woman's forehead, just at the hairline, from which blood and grey brain matter still oozed. He dropped the blanket quickly, fighting for control of his stomach.

'Shot in the back of the head?' he asked McGuire.

'Yes sir. You can see the exit wound. It looks like he just stepped up behind her and . . . Bang! Poor woman never knew what hit her.' He paused. 'Eh, who's going to tell Mr Anderson?'

'I will,' Skinner answered, 'suspended or not. But we'll need to find him first.' He reached into a pocket of his jacket, to produce a small book. 'I've got his private secretary's home number here.' He began to search again, for his mobile this time, but was interrupted.

'Excuse me, sirs,' said a nervous woman constable, appearing on the edge of the group, 'but there's someone here who says he might know the victim.'

The three detectives looked across, to see a middle-aged man, dressed in a grey shirt, grey trousers and with greying hair and beard, standing with another officer. Martin and Skinner walked across towards him.

'Yes, sir?' the Chief Superintendent began. 'First, can you tell us who you are?'

The man, who was also grey-faced, nodded quickly. 'I'm Charlie Kettles, I have the hair studio on the corner. Look, when I saw the car and heard what had happened . . . It's not Mrs Anderson, is it?'

'D'you know her?' Skinner asked.

Kettles nodded, anxiously. 'She's a customer. She has been ever since her husband became Secretary of State and they took over Bute House. She comes at nine thirty every Saturday morning, for a tidy up usually. She left my place not long ago.'

'I see.' The DCC nodded. 'I'm afraid it is Mrs Anderson.'

'God, that's terrible,' said the hairdresser, his eyes glistening suddenly. 'What about Tanya?'

'What d'you mean?' Martin asked, yet knew the answer. A sinking feeling gathered in his stomach.

'Her daughter. Tanya. She's eight. Every second Saturday, she comes with her mother. She was here today. She's not . . . as well, is she?'

'No,' Skinner replied. 'There's no sign of Tanya. Thanks, Mr Kettles. Someone will take a statement from you in due course. If you'll excuse us, though, for now.'

'Of course.' The man nodded, turned and headed back to

his studio, head bowed, as the DCC took out his mobile phone once more.

He punched in a number. After a few seconds, the Secretary of State's private secretary answered. '247–348 . . .'

'David. It's Bob Skinner here. Where's your boss?'

'Bute House. Why?' Hewlett sounded alarmed.

'Never mind why. Just listen. How long will he be there?'

'Quite a while. He's expecting the Permanent Under Secretary of State and me for a working lunch.'

'Okay. You contact the Permanent Secretary and cancel him. Then get along there yourself. Andy Martin and I will be there before you. This is a real emergency, so no questions for now, Dave. Just do it.'

55

'We spoke to the nearest thing we have to a witness before we came along here. When we pressed her, she said she thought she saw a silver or a grey car heading away from the scene, towards Dundas Street.'

'What does that mean?' asked the Secretary of State for Scotland, ashen-faced.

'We believe that the man who killed Leona McGrath, and took Mark, drives a grey car,' said Andy Martin.

'I see.' Dr Bruce Anderson nodded. He was standing by the tall fireplace at one end of the long, formal drawing room of Bute House, his official residence in Charlotte Square. He started to walk to the window, but Bob Skinner reached out and caught his arm.

'Don't do that. You wouldn't want to be photographed just now.'

'No,' agreed Anderson. 'You're right. Wouldn't do, would it?' His cheeks were still wet with tears as he looked up at Skinner. 'I was surprised to see you here, Bob, but now, I'm glad of your presence; yours and Mr Martin's. Look, let's go upstairs and have a seat somewhere less grand, so we can talk about this.'

'You don't have to do that yet, sir,' said the DCC. 'I mean to say, you've just lost your wife.'

'Yes, and my child has just been kidnapped. I can't do anything for the one, but if I can help you find the other . . . Come on.' He turned to Hewlett who was standing close by. 'David, you'd better find a phone and sort something out with the Information Office.'

'The Director's on his way, sir.'

'Good. You wait here for him, then. I suppose you should get together with the police Press Officer, so that everyone knows everything that's being said.'

He led the way out of the public room and up a narrow staircase, to the floor which had been fitted out as private family quarters in the fine old Georgian House.

'Why did you stay here every Saturday, when your main home and your constituency are in the West?' Martin asked, as the three men entered another sitting room, much smaller than the first, but still finely furnished.

Anderson smiled, as the three men sat. 'Catherine liked Edinburgh. She was like a kid with a new toy when she found that this place came with the job. So every Friday evening, when she had finished teaching and I had done my constituency surgery, she insisted that the three of us pack the car and come through here.

'Normally we stay till Sunday evening. The girls have to be back in Glasgow for school on Monday.' His eyes moistened again, as his out-of-date tenses caught up with him.

'Catherine found the hairdresser, Charlie What's-His-Name, through the wife of one of my colleagues. She was very particular about her hair, and about Tanya's.' He broke off. 'Look, Bob, when can I see her?'

'As soon as possible. Before the post-mortem, certainly.'

'Where was she shot?' the bereaved husband asked, quietly.

'Back of the head, once from close range,' Skinner replied. 'She'd have died in an instant.' He touched his forehead. 'The bullet exited here. It was a medium-calibre weapon; from the cartridge case we found, I'd say nine-millimetre.'

263

'Christ, and I thought we'd banned all handguns,' Anderson moaned.

'You might as well have banned the wheel. In my experience, murderers don't mind using illegal firearms. The fact is they nearly always do. With one or two notorious exceptions, when a person used his own, registered firearm to kill, it was nearly always a suicide.'

He smiled, grimly, for a second. 'See those blokes you've brought up to investigate me? In their home city you can buy a gun in a pub for a few quid. There are so many shootings down there, they barely make the papers now, unless they're fatal. Eastern European weapons usually. Half the Red fucking Army seems to have sold its weapons on the Black Market. Nine-millimetre pistols, many of them are, and they change hands a lot.

'When we find the bullet that killed your wife, Minister, it will tell us whether the gun has been used in an earlier crime, but it's highly unlikely that it will tell us who pulled the trigger.'

Anderson nodded. 'I understand.' He sighed. 'To think that I turned down the chance of Protection Squad cover. What a bloody self-confident fool I am.'

'No,' said Skinner, quickly and emphatically. 'Don't torture yourself with that one, sir. They'd have been with you, not your wife and daughter.'

'Okay. That's some comfort. Now what can we do to catch this man?'

'We've already blocked every main road out of Edinburgh,' Martin replied. 'However, he may have gone to ground in the city itself. Alternatively, he had plenty of time to make it out of the city before our officers were in place.

'To be frank, sir, I don't see this man simply driving up

to a roadblock. He's too thorough.' The Head of CID paused. 'How long had your wife been going to Charlie Kettles on Saturday mornings?'

'About three months.'

'And taking Tanya every second week. The man must have been watching her for all of that time, establishing a pattern, planning. He must have watched Leona McGrath in the same way.'

Anderson twisted in his chair, to look at Skinner. 'Need this be the same man? Couldn't it be a copy-cat?'

'Aye,' said Skinner, 'it could. But it isn't. It's the same man. I received a tape this morning.' He looked round, and saw a midi hi-fi unit on a sideboard behind the couch. 'Listen to this.'

He took the copy of Mark McGrath's message from his pocket, slid it into the tape player, and switched it on. Anderson listened in silence, as the child's voice filled the room. Gradually, his face twisted in anguish, and he began to sob.

The two detectives waited, as he composed himself once more. 'Sorry, gentlemen,' he said at last. 'It's all just too much.'

'I know,' Skinner whispered. 'My daughter was kidnapped once.'

The Secretary of State looked up at him. 'Did you catch the man who did it?'

'Oh yes,' said the detective, even more softly than before. 'I caught him. He won't do it again. I'll catch this bastard too, and neither will he.'

Anderson smiled, weakly. 'I'd better lift your suspension, then, pending the outcome of the enquiry.'

'No. Don't do that. I don't know for sure, but it may be better if this man thinks I'm out of the action.'

'Whatever you want. So how will you catch him, Bob?'

'I'll wait. The next move is his. When he makes it, I'll be ready for him if he makes the slightest mistake. Sooner or later, he will.'

Anderson sighed. 'Oh my God, but I hope so.' He looked at the two detectives, numbly, from one to the other. 'Is this political, gentlemen?' he asked, bewildered

'It has to be,' Skinner replied. 'Two MPs' children snatched. A Member and a Member's wife murdered. And yet it could be personal too in some way. The man chooses to contact me. There's a link between Leona and me, and between Mark and me. There's a link between you and me, Dr Anderson. So it could be aimed at me, somehow. Or it could be all about money.

'We'll know soon, when he contacts us again. For now Andy and I will just have to do the thing we're worst at.'

'What's that?'

'The waiting.' He rose from his seat. 'We'll send a car for you, Dr Anderson, when your wife is ready for a visit. It'll be within the hour, I hope. We'll use the back entrance for your privacy.'

'Also,' said Martin, 'I'll put armed officers in position, front and back.'

'What's the point?' replied the Secretary of State. 'The horse has bolted.'

'Still.' The Head of CID followed Skinner out of the room, all the way down the stairs to the back door at the sub-basement level.

'Here,' he began, at last, as they slid into the Mondeo, 'upstairs, when you were talking about motives, you said something odd: about links.'

'I know,' said Skinner. 'I should have told you before,

and I better had now. Because I'm pretty certain you're going to find out anyway.'

56

It was the most tumultuous press conference that Martin had ever attended, let alone chaired. The murder of a cabinet minister's wife, and the kidnap of a second politician's child.

For the first time in his life, he had felt that the media were out to get him, and although he had been as careful as he could not to allow words to be put into his mouth, he knew that he would be lucky if only a few newspapers questioned his competence and hinted that Skinner's suspension was compromising the investigation.

The DCC was gone when he returned to his office, en route for the airport to pick up Pam from her return flight. Martin sat with his head in his hands, feeling helpless, as the first radio news bulletins were already beginning to say, and very alone.

He was grateful for the sound of the telephone, even though he did not have the slightest expectation that it might be bringing him good news.

He snatched the hand-set out of its cradle. 'Martin,' he said, eagerly.

'Hi, Andy. I like it when someone's pleased to hear from me.'

Such was the clarity of his voice that the man on the line might have been in the next room, but the Chief Superintendent knew that he was calling from Washington. 'Hi Joe,' he responded. 'Yes it is good to hear from you. I feel like I'm running out of friends, and luck, just at the moment.'

'Jesus, kid,' drawled the American. 'What size of dog's crapped on your lawn?'

Quickly, Martin told him of the morning's atrocity, and of the earlier surprise in Skinner's morning mail. 'I see what you mean,' said Joe Doherty, tersely. 'I would say that you are dealing with a real Lulu there. Yes indeed, a real peach. I take it you've looked for a terrorist connection.'

'Joe, we've looked for every sort of connection, and come up blank. Like Bob says, all we can do now is wait for the guy to make his next move, and hope that he makes a mistake. You never know, maybe we will get something from Mark's message tape.'

'Yeah, you never know. But just don't hope for anything; then at least you won't be disappointed.'

There was a pause: as Doherty drew on a cigarette, Martin guessed. 'How's Bob bearing up?' he asked at last.

'He's like a grizzly with a hangover . . . and piles. After all that's happened in his life over the last year or so, he really did not need this nonsense from *Spotlight*. Did you appreciate that Pam, who called you yesterday, is the new woman?'

'I put two and two together. Bob called me, beginning of last week, and asked me to make sure that Sarah wasn't bothered. He told me then about his . . . domestic alterations, let's say.

'What's gone wrong with him, Andy?'

'I don't know, Joe. Truth is, I don't think he does either. Did you speak to Sarah?'

'Yeah, I called her.'

'How did she sound?'

'Hurt and confused. Just like Bob, really.'

'Ahh!' cried Martin, despairing. 'I just feel helpless. And for these corruption allegations to come on top of it all.'

'Yeah,' said Doherty. 'Ms Masters told me about that. What the fuck is that about?'

'Someone's set him up. He has people working on it, Alex among them. I hope she'll bring back some good news tonight. We sure as hell need some.'

He forced himself to sound more upbeat. 'Anyway, why this call at the US Government's expense? Have you got anything for me on this miserable rag that's crucifying my friend?'

'I've got some. *Spotlight* is quite an institution over here you know. It's making inroads in Great Britain too, as you have reason to know. The story about Bob and Pam got it the sort of national attention it's been after.'

'So who owns it?'

'A straight question: not such a straight answer. In the first instance, *Spotlight* belongs to a corporation registered in Chicago. It owns just that one news magazine, but also a string of cracker radio stations, mostly though not all in the South.'

'Radio KKK, you mean?'

'Oh no, nothing so unsubtle. Radio Free America is more like it, the voice of the militants, those backwoods democrats who only like elected government when it does what they want.'

'Who owns the equity in the Chicago corporation?' asked Martin.

'Another corporation, registered in Houston. It's owned in turn by yet another corporation, registered in LA, which also holds a large chunk of the stock of a satellite television news network. Strip the whole thing away, though, and you wind up with a global holding company which pulls together a part of the corporate holdings of a very interesting guy. He's possibly the richest man in America.'

Doherty paused, as if for effect. 'Does the name Everard Balliol mean anything to you?'

'Somehow I feel it should.' Martin scratched his head, and searched his remarkable memory. 'Yes. I remember him. That Pro-Am golf tournament Bob wound up playing in a while back. The one there was bother with. Everard Balliol was one of the leading amateurs.

'As I recall, he didn't like losing.'

Doherty laughed. 'He wouldn't. Mr Balliol doesn't like losing at anything. It's a common trait with billionaires, they tell me.'

'What's his background?'

'His granddaddy was in oil. Everard diversified in a big way. He's still a major player in the oil business, but on top of that he's into computers, telecommunications, air transport, banking, insurance and a few other things.

'Politically, he's way out on the right wing. There was talk a few years back of him going after the Republican nomination, but when he talked about nuking the Colombian coca fields they decided that they didn't want another Goldwater. For a while, he thought of running as an independent, but he decided that he couldn't win under that flag, so he dropped it.

'Instead, he contents himself with backing right-wing causes. He funds but doesn't own one or two militant publications, and gives them air-time on his stations. *Spotlight* is a special toy. He uses it in the States to embarrass federal and state governments if he feels that they're backsliding . . . and he feels that way a lot.

'The international editions run the same way,' Doherty went on. 'Balliol hates every sort of liberalism, anywhere. When your election turned out the way it did, he went ballistic apparently.'

Martin realised that he was frowning, and that it was growing deeper by the second. 'Is this man dangerous, Joe?'

There was a pause, for thought. 'He's dangerous in that he has unlimited resources. He's dangerous in that his political attitudes are shared by a large number of very spooky people, and if he ever gave them serious financial backing, we'd have a real problem.

'But if you mean is he dangerous like homicidal? I doubt it. He's completely ruthless, but I reckon if he really took a dislike to someone he'd prefer to hurt him in a way he'd remember, rather than just by having him made dead. *Spotlight* is the perfect tool for him. Bob should have let him win that Pro-Am, I think.'

'You could see Bob doing that, could you?'

'Maybe not.' He chuckled at the thought. 'There is one other thing about Balliol that should interest you. He's a real Scotophile.'

'Oh yes?'

'Yeah,' said the laconic Doherty. 'He claims Scottish descent. In fact he claims to be the descendant of kings. He owns a castle in your fair land, with an estate. Bought it a year or two back. They tell me he's building a private golf course on the land.'

'It isn't Balmoral, is it?'

The American laughed out loud. 'No, but if that ever comes on the market you can bet Everard will snap it up. His current pile is a place called Erran Mhor, north of somewhere called Fort William, apparently.'

'Does he use it much?'

'He never announces his arrival or departure,' said the American, 'but yes, he does. In fact, he's there right now.'

57

'What about the signature, Bob?' asked Mitchell Laidlaw, holding a photocopy of Medine's sample, which Cheshire and Ericson had given to Alex. 'Is there any chance that this could be genuine?'

Skinner took the sheet from him and looked at it. 'I'd say it probably is. Almost certainly.'

He shrugged his broad shoulders. 'But so what? Mitch, I attend lots of public functions. Quite often I have to make speeches. To Rotarians, for example, or parent groups at schools. I even chaired a reading once at James Thin in George Street, for the publication of the memoirs of a retired copper.

'Frequently I'm asked for my autograph at these events. I always give it, sometimes without even looking at the person who wants it. So getting hold of a sample of my signature would not be a difficult thing to do.

'Don't worry too much about that. Even if the hand-writing gurus insist that it is genuine, we can still defend against it.'

He handed the photocopy back to Laidlaw and looked across at Alex. The three-strong defence team had gathered once more in the offices of Curle, Anthony and Jarvis, as soon as Alex had returned from Guernsey.

'It's some comfort to know that Al Cheshire is a straight-down-the-line operator, after all. I was getting the idea that he'd arrived with his mind made up. When I checked him out, I found that every investigation that he's handled within another force has ended in a prosecution.

'Mind you, in nearly every one of those, he was called in only after preliminary enquiries showed strong evidence of corruption.'

'He'd tell you that's the case here, Bob,' said Laidlaw, quietly.

'Aye, and from what Alex has told us he'd be dead right.' Skinner turned to his daughter. 'That was good work you did though, love, picking up the point about the Bank of England notes and rubbing his nose in it. If the money had been in one big lump of sequentially numbered notes, then fair enough. But the fact that it was put together as it was, that helps us.'

'How?' asked Laidlaw.

The policeman smiled. 'I'm not sure yet. It tells us that it was put together, if not outside Scotland, then probably from an external source. Now the fact is that if anyone had bunged me, it would have been someone within my own patch.'

Alex frowned. 'Yes, that's true, Pops, but that person could have had cash in another country. It's hardly the strongest defence to lay before a jury.'

'I agree,' her father replied, 'but if this thing does get to court, at least it's something for old Christabel to argue.' He chuckled, suddenly, glancing at Laidlaw. 'It's a pity old Orlach's dead. If we'd been able to fix it for him to be on the Bench with Christabel defending . . .'

'Let's look at the courier,' said the solicitor, his crimson, weatherbeaten cheeks indicating that he had spent his morning on the golf course. 'That was a major stroke of luck, surely.'

Beside her boss, Alex nodded vigorously. 'Yes. The man's targeting you in some way through these crimes. He used your private phone number. There's evidence of malice, and a potential identification of him as the courier. Christabel will make hay with that.'

'If we capture the guy alive, maybe she won't have to. But . . .' Skinner shook his head, slightly. 'I'm not so sure. Okay, Medine picked him out from the photofit, and okay, he had my Gullane number, yet there are two major holes in the argument.'

'What are they?' asked Alex, frowning.

'Well it's a mistake, for a start, and this is a very smart guy we're after. If the kidnapper had set me up in Guernsey, I don't see him exposing himself by acting as his own courier.'

'Why not, Pops? You've said yourself that you're waiting for him to make a mistake.'

'Not one as big as this, though. He's better than that.' He stood up from the conference table and walked to the window. 'Anyway, all that's subjective. The other hole in the argument's based on fact.

'The kidnapper made that tape on Thursday. He posted it first class on Friday, although we still don't know from where, the postmark was too badly smudged. So he knew I'd have it on Saturday.'

'So?' asked Laidlaw.

'So if it was him who set me up, through *Spotlight*, he did that on Thursday at the latest. If it was him, he'd have known that by Saturday I'd be under investigation. Yet there was not the faintest hint of that on the tape, not even the faintest hint of him. Through Mark, he was still talking to me as a copper, on Saturday morning.

'No, I'm afraid I need a lot more convincing that the kidnapper is behind this.'

He turned to Alex. 'What's Al Cheshire's next move?'

'He's going to interview Noel Salmon, tomorrow midday. Salmon says he doesn't want me there. He says he'd feel threatened.'

'He's catching on, is he?' scowled Skinner. 'Did Cheshire tell him he had a choice?'

'Well he has, Pops. This is still an informal investigation. No-one's under caution.'

'That's right, Bob,' Laidlaw confirmed. 'However . . . Alex, find out if Salmon would accept my presence. Maybe he'd find me less of a threat.'

He looked across at Skinner, as he resumed his seat. 'Going back to Christabel for a moment, Bob. In the light of the information which Alex has brought back, I think it would be good idea if we arranged a consultation for Monday. If that's okay with you, I'll set it up.'

Skinner nodded, and Laidlaw made a small note on a pad on the table in front of him. He looked up again. 'What about this receipt, Bob? What do we do about that?'

The detective shrugged. 'Alex was right. Let Cheshire search wherever he likes. Any sheriff would give him a warrant if he asked for one, with what he's got. There's no point in putting him to the bother.'

'Pops,' Alex intervened, hesitantly, 'he wants to search Pam's as well. You've been living there.'

'Of course he does. I've already discussed the possibility with her. As long as it's done very discreetly, she's okay with it. To be on the up and up, neither of us should go back to anywhere that's to be searched. So Alex, once we've finished here, you go back to see Cheshire and Ericson and take them where they need to go. I'll give you keys to Pam's place.'

Laidlaw leaned across his desk. 'Bob, I have to ask you this. We've got copies of all the documents. Cheshire was good enough to give us them, while he holds the originals. Looking at that receipt, have you ever seen, however casually, it or anything like it?'

Skinner laughed. 'You asking if I mistook it for one of Sarah's Jenners receipts? Oh yes, a hundred grand. Got off light today, didn't we!

'No, Mitch. I have never seen that receipt in my life, anywhere. Although, the way things are going for me just now . . .' He stopped in mid-sentence. 'What the hell, let Al Cheshire and his pal – but only them mind. Not one of my own officers is to be used – let them go through my socks, Pamela's knickers, and everywhere else. You go along with them though, Alex, and look over their shoulders, just to keep them on their toes.

'They won't like the business any more than I do, I suppose,' he growled. 'Tell you one thing I really don't like, though, and that's Jimmy letting them use my office. I know why he did it, to keep them out of sight of the troops as much as possible, but I don't have to enjoy it, even though I would have done the same thing myself. Because, when this is over and I go back in there, I'll always know.

'It's a bit like someone sleeping with your wife, I suppose.'

'Or your husband,' said Alex, instinctively and as unthinking as her father.

Mitch Laidlaw coughed, to break the silence. 'Look, this will all be over soon,' he said. 'I know it's tough on you both.'

'There'll be more pain,' murmured Skinner, 'before anything starts to heal.' He reached across and squeezed his daughter's hand.

'One thing I was going to ask,' said Laidlaw, casting

around desperately for anything that would change the subject. 'Cheshire. For the record, what is the Al short for? Alan? Alexander?'

Skinner smiled again. 'Hell of a good question,' he replied. 'We've all got a secret somewhere, but in the end no-one's is safe from me. Algernon, that's Cheshire's secret. He's an Algernon. They say that someone called him Algie once, and was never seen again!'

58

Pamela shuddered, in Andy Martin's armchair. 'It makes my flesh creep,' she said, 'to know that even as we're sitting here, strangers are searching my home.'

Skinner smiled, glancing across at Martin. 'I suppose it's a sort of justice for a copper. You and I have done the same thing to other people often enough.' He looked round at Pam. 'Maybe you haven't, honey, not yet at least, but it's part of the career you've chosen, part of making a difference, as you put it.

'Perhaps it's only right that we should have a taste of how our subjects feel, not so much the villains we're after, but their families, when we invade their homes and start tearing the most private parts of their lives apart.

'Remember that Japanese bloke, out in Balerno . . .'

'Talking about private parts, you mean?' interjected Martin, from the kitchen door.

Skinner laughed, short and savage, and in that time a gleam came into his eye. Pam started in her chair as she caught a glimpse of a man she did not know, a glimpse, she realised, of Bob as he had been before life had cut him so deep. She shivered slightly as she realised also that perhaps it was a man she did not really want to know.

'Aye, maybe,' he said. 'But I was trying to be serious. I was thinking of his poor bewildered wife, confronted with a team of hard-faced men and women, bursting into her home armed with a warrant. As far as I know she's back in

279

Japan now, picking up her life, but I bet that's one experience she'll never get over.

'We've got it easy, Pammy, compared to her. Our houses are being gone over by a DCC and a Chief Super, not by Tom, Dick and Harriet, or even Neil, Mario and Maggie.'

'But what about yours?' she said. 'Won't they be tearing up the carpets and everything?'

'Nah. They'll be going through the motions. Algernon knows well enough that if I am bent, I've had time and warning enough to hide the evidence where he'll never find it. In a real search, for a single piece of paper, he wouldn't just be under the carpets, he'd be under the floor, and into the ventilation grilles and damp courses.'

'That's right, Pam,' called Martin, in his chef's apron, quartering a yellow pepper, ready for the food processor. 'Only he doesn't expect to find it, because he doesn't really believe Bob's bent.'

He stepped back into the doorway. 'Where would you hide a piece of paper?' he asked.

Skinner smiled. 'Same place as you, and I'll bet Algie looks there, too.'

Behind him, the living-room door opened. Alex stood there, smiling. 'All over,' she said. 'Congratulations, you two. All three houses are clear. They were very thorough. They even looked among Jazz's nappies down in Fairyhouse Avenue. But they cleared everything up too.'

'Too effing right!' said Bob. 'Did they say anything?'

'About the search, no. Salmon has agreed that Mr Laidlaw should sit in on the interview though.' She looked across at Andy, and at the pepper in his hand. 'Is that as far as you've got with dinner? Here, out of the way.'

The kitchen was too small for four to work together, and

so Bob and Pam went out together, to the nearest Oddbins, to choose the wine for the evening.

They took a conscious decision to talk about golf, music, food and drink over dinner – anything, Bob insisted, but work, politics and sex. But eventually, the meal was over; eventually, the dregs of coffee were drying in their cups.

'I've got something else for you, now,' said Andy to Skinner, at last. 'Something that Pam's been involved in. Joe Doherty called today.'

Bob started in his seat. 'Nothing to do with Sarah?' he asked, but his friend stilled his anxiety with a smile and a shake of the head.

'No, no. This is some checking up we asked him to do under the Old Pals' Act, on the ownership of *Spotlight*. We got a result.

'Remember Everard Balliol?'

Skinner frowned. 'Yank? Golfer? Witches Hill Pro-Am? Bad loser? Am I getting close?'

'Spot on.' Andy launched into Joe Doherty's account of Balliol's interests, of his nature, and of his Scottish connections.

'What does that make you wonder?' he asked, when he was finished.

'A hell of a lot, my son,' said Bob. 'A hell of a lot.

'You know, I was wondering what to do with myself tomorrow. With me having to keep back from the investigations, and away from my own bloody office, I thought that I'd be at a loose end. Not any more. Now my Sunday's laid out for me.'

'How?' asked Alex. 'What will you be doing?'

'I'm surprised you have to ask, daughter. I'll be driving up to Erran Mhor, north of Fort William. Mr Everard Balliol is one bastard that I want to look in the eye!'

59

Pamela was at work at her desk when Martin and Alan Royston returned from the stormy Sunday morning press briefing, held only to record the fact that, twenty-four hours after the murder of the Secretary of State's wife, there was still no progress to report.

Not unnaturally, neither man was smiling.

She had offered to go with Skinner on his search for Balliol, but he had turned her down firmly. 'I can't do anything to help find these kids, Pam, but you can, even if it's only by sitting at a desk beside a telephone, waiting for it to ring.'

And so she had gone to work, to her desk, and the telephone had rung, once.

She waited for Alan Royston to leave the Chief Superintendent's office before knocking on his door. 'Excuse me, sir,' she said, impeccably formally, 'while you were away, there was a call; from a lady. She didn't leave a name, just a number.'

She handed him a note, and left.

Once he was alone, he punched the 0171 number which Pamela had given him into his direct telephone. The call was answered after three rings. 'Yeah?' said an unmistakably American voice.

'Andy Martin, Head of CID, Edinburgh. You rang me?'

'Yeah, hi, I'm Caroline Farmer. I called about the tape you sent down yesterday. No luck with this one, I'm afraid.'

'Is there anything at all that you can tell me?' the Scot asked.

'Nothing that's gonna help you. The message was recorded on some fairly average equipment, a standard ghetto-blaster, I'd say. Apart from the sound of the tape motor itself, and someone breathing next to the mike, there is absolutely no background noise.

'This tape was recorded indoors, for sure. There's no traffic noise, no birdsong, no rustling leaves, just that motor and the breathing, like I said.'

'How about the message? The news bulletin and the child were definitely recorded at the same time, were they?'

'For sure. The radio sound came from another receiver. If he'd been dubbing off the ghetto-blaster itself you wouldn't hear the kid over it as it fades. Also there's a faint click as he switches the other radio off.'

'How about the breathing itself?'

Caroline Farmer chuckled. 'What can I tell you? You breathe in, you breathe out. From the rate of respiration, I'd say that it was a man, but that's all. Sorry to disappoint.'

'Fair enough,' sighed Martin. 'Thanks, Ms Farmer. There's no disappointment; we really didn't expect anything more. Have the tape sent back up with your report, please.'

He hung up, staring out of his window and cursing quietly at the slamming of another door. When he looked round, there was a bullet-headed figure in his doorway. 'Yes?' he asked, curtly, 'Don't you believe in knocking?'

'Not a lot, no. We haven't met. I'm DCC Al Cheshire, and you'll know why I'm here from your fiancée, and from her father, no doubt. I wonder if I could ask you to come with me, Chief Superintendent. I assure you. It's necessary.'

Curiosity overcoming his annoyance, Martin nodded and rose, following his visitor out of the office, past Pamela and past Sammy Pye, both of whom looked up as they passed. 'Have you seen Salmon yet?' he asked, outside in the corridor.

'Yes,' said Cheshire, amicably. 'He is an obnoxious little shit, isn't he? Pity you couldn't make that cocaine charge stick. He didn't tell us anything new, really. Still insists that his sources on both stories about Skinner were anonymous.'

'D'you believe him?'

'Doesn't matter, really. We can't force him to tell us anything, the way we're set up. Do you?'

Martin smiled and shook his head. 'I never believe Salmon, not unless I know he's terrified.'

'Then I suggest you scare him, Mr Martin,' said Cheshire quietly. He led the way into Skinner's office. Chief Superintendent Ericson was waiting inside, grim-faced.

'We wanted you to see this right away,' said the investigator. 'Even though you're Skinner's mate, you're the senior man available.

'As you know we searched his premises yesterday, and Miss Masters' flat. Clean as a whistle, as we'd expected, and frankly as we'd hoped.

'But we were sitting here half an hour ago when Ronnie said to me, "Al, where do you feel most secure?", and I said to him, "In my office, don't I?" So we searched, in here, and I'm afraid we found this.' He walked behind Skinner's desk and pulled out the top right-hand drawer, raising it slightly to free it from its track and lifting it clean out.

He upturned it and held it out to Martin. The Chief Superintendent's heart sank, and his face fell. Taped to the underside of the drawer was a receipt. He looked closer: it bore a signature, a number, the crest of the JZG Bank,

Guernsey, and a second number, UK 73461.

'I'm sorry, Mr Martin, I really am, but we're going to have to see the Lord Advocate at this point, with a recommendation. Can you call in a forensic team for us, please. I want this item removed by them, with the greatest care, then dusted independently for fingerprints.

'I think you should call your Chief Constable as well, as a courtesy. Not Miss Skinner, however. We've reached a stage in this investigation when co-operation with the defence team should be suspended, in everyone's interests.

'I hardly think I need to tell you, Chief Superintendent, but we really are talking about criminal charges now.'

60

It is the variety of landscapes confined within such a small country that makes Scotland a remarkable place.

There is the flat industrial spread of the central belt, ever-changing in character as the blackest of the Black Country disappears to be replaced by new clean sunrise industry. There are the rolling uplands of the Borders regions, with their sheep and cattle grazing on their moors and pastures. There are the fertile coastal plains of the Lothians and Fife, their fields yellow in spring with rape flowers, and golden in summer with wheat, and with barley to fill the maltings.

And to the north, beyond the foothills of the Campsies and the Ochils, there stand the Highlands, the mountain country where some say the real Scotland lies, the land which gave its men to rally behind the banner of the Young Pretender.

Bob Skinner was a cynic when it came to the myths and legends of his own country. As he drove through Glencoe, he recalled that its notorious massacre had been perpetrated by Scot upon Scot, clan upon clan, a family feud reaching a bloody conclusion. He knew that for all of those who had backed Prince Charlie, the Jacobite, there were many others who had maintained their loyalty to the Crown, distant and Germanic though it may have been.

It was the grandeur of the mountains which touched the patriot in him. The suddenness of their approach seemed to give them stature above their measured height. There was no rolling approach to distant heights across a hundred-mile plain, as with the Pyrenees or the Alps. He had seen both, he had walked in both, yet neither impressed him as did the mountains of his home.

There was something great and looming and threatening about Ben Nevis, approached from the south, and about all the other Munros, the Scottish peaks of greater than three thousand feet. It was small wonder, he thought as he drove on, that someone like Everard Balliol, to all intents as American as the Stars and Stripes itself, should be drawn back to roots which had been physically severed hundreds of years before.

He thought of the American as he drove, and their last meeting, under a gathering storm around the eighteenth green of Witches Hill Golf and Country Club: sallow-skinned, mid-fifties, gunmetal, crew-cut hair, tall and lean. Those intense, ruthless, deadly serious eyes. The grudging, resentful admission of defeat. The challenge to another encounter.

'Any time,' Skinner had said. 'Your place or mine.'

Balliol's place, Erran Mhor, was such a significant estate that, unlike most private dwellings, it merited its own entry on the map of Scotland. The policeman stayed on the main road towards Wester Ross for almost thirty miles after passing through Fort William, at the base of the great Ben.

Eventually he came upon a single signpost, pointing westward like a finger and bearing the names Erran Mhor and Loch Mhor. He drove on for miles along the single-track road, with the mountains behind him, and without seeing another car. There were few trees on the peaty plain, and grey boulders and sheep, indistinguishable from a distance, were the only features of the landscape.

He had no clue of whether or not he had passed on to

Balliol's estate, but gradually, the road rose once more towards a horizon above which he could see wheeling gulls. As he crested the rise the landscape changed; before him the land stretched, cultivated and tended, with neat forest plantations, reaching towards the head of a loch. He pulled his car to a stop in a passing place, and climbed out, picking up a small pair of binoculars, to survey the scene.

On the northern shore of Loch Mhor, Skinner could see the turrets of a castle, an impressive structure even from a distance. This was no historic monument built by feudal lords over the centuries, the policeman could tell, but the folly of a Victorian grandee, indulging himself upon money flowing from the sweat of poor people in Britain and around the Empire.

Beyond Balliol's castle, and beyond a helicopter on its landing pad, there was a green area, with a few trees, and familiar golden patches. Skinner smiled, and sharpened the focus of his glasses. Men were working like ants on a determined mission. There were tractors and mowers, and pick-ups loaded with sand: the billionaire's golf course was nearing completion.

He climbed back into the BMW and drove on towards the mock castle. When he was still a mile away, he passed through a large gate, a symbolic gesture really, for the place was too large to be walled in. Beyond the entrance the road widened out, into newly laid, white-lined tarmac. The detective drove on to the very end, which came as a curve opened into a wide area beside a lawn which stretched from the Castle of Erran Mhor down to the lochside.

Skinner, dressed in crisp blue trousers and a matching polo shirt, drew his car to a halt beside a green Range Rover, climbed out and walked across the parking area and towards the house, climbing a wide flight of stairs set into the lawn, and stepping on to a terrace which stretched for the full width of the four-storey building, around eighty yards. He crossed it, passing under a portico which arched over the main doorway.

One half of the great double door swung open before he reached it, and a man stepped out. Korean, Skinner guessed, dressed in a black teeshirt and slacks, balanced lightly on his feet, with brown muscles oiled and rippling. The bodyguard stared at him, impassively, without offering a word.

'I'm here to see Mr Balliol,' said the policeman. 'I reckon he owes me a game of golf.'

The Korean stared back. 'Mr Balliol, please,' Skinner repeated. Still the man did not move or speak.

'Okay,' sighed the detective, at last. 'I'll play the game.'

He took a step towards the doorkeeper. As the man leapt forward to grasp him in what would have been a judo hold, the policeman pivoted with exceptional speed and hit him on the temple. It was a short, hooking, right-handed punch, hard but well short of full force. The Korean's eyes glazed. As he slumped to his knees, Skinner seized his right arm and twisted it round behind him, jerking him back to his feet.

'Did I get the password right?' he asked, looking towards the open door.

'Not bad,' said Everard Balliol, stepping into view. 'Not bad at all for a guy your age.' The policeman had met the American four times, and had spoken to him twice. This was the first time that he had ever seen him smile.

Skinner released the Korean, and patted him on the shoulder. The bodyguard nodded, without any sign of animosity, and went inside.

'Just my rich man's game,' Balliol grinned.

'Pretty risky game. I might really have hurt that bloke.'

The billionaire shook his head. 'Not you. I guessed you wouldn't damage the guy too bad for just doing his job.'

He stretched out his hand in a friendly greeting, which Skinner accepted. 'Come on in.' He turned and led the way into a surprisingly small hallway from which a staircase climbed. 'You want the grand tour?' he asked.

'Maybe not this time.'

Balliol led him through the hall and into a study, behind the stairway. It had a big picture window which looked out across the golf course. Skinner could see two greens, cut and prepared, although only the one on the right had a flag in position.

'So what brings you to see me, Mr Skinner?'

'I'd have thought you'd have worked it out.'

Balliol looked at him, his expression guarded. 'Should I?'

'Come on, now. You going to tell me that though you own it, you don't actually read *Spotlight*?'

'Shit, man,' drawled the Texan. 'Of course I don't read that stuff. Would you?' He smiled. 'But sometimes they do tell me what's goin' in it.'

He walked over to the window. 'You serious about that golf game?'

'I heard you were building a course, so I stuck my clubs in the car.'

'Go get 'em then. I've only got nine holes in play so far, but they're good ones. Tiger Nakamura advised me on the layout. Come round to the first tee, just outside the window. I'll call out the caddies.'

When Skinner arrived on the tee, Balliol was waiting for him, with a huge bag holding a set of brand-new

Callaways, and with two more Koreans, dressed in black like the doorman, but with white golf shoes on their feet. The American handed over a map of the course, and a hole-by-hole yardage chart.

'We're playing ten to eighteen,' he said. 'The earth moving took longer on the front nine. You still off seven?'

'Down to five,' Skinner replied. 'But I'm out of practice.'

'You get a shot, then.' Balliol grinned, hugely. 'The practice is your problem.'

He took out his Great Big Bertha driver and split the first fairway. Skinner took a few practice swings, then tugged his tee-shot left, into heavy rough.

'Let's play for now,' said the billionaire, as they moved off, their black-clad caddies lugging their bags, 'and talk later. Tell me one thing though. How d'you know about the golf course? Only Tiger and me and a few others know about that.'

'More people must know than you think,' said Skinner, 'if a simple copper like me can find out about it. Have you got planning permission?'

Balliol laughed. 'Don't need it. You gotta know that. All I'm doing is landscaping my own back yard!'

They played on, chatting occasionally, but largely in silence. Skinner had been serious about his lack of practice. Putting rather than the quality of his shots kept him in touch with his host's tidy game, but when he missed from ten feet on the seventeenth, the match was over. The sweetness of revenge shone in the American's eye, while the worm of defeat gnawed at the policeman's stomach.

It was late afternoon when they returned to the castle, where sandwiches and drinks were laid out in a great drawing room with a southward view across the loch.

'Okay, Mr Skinner,' said Balliol at last, as he and his

guest looked out across the terrace. 'So you're steamed up at me about that *Spotlight* stuff.'

The policeman shook his head. 'No,' he muttered. 'Not steamed up. That's an understatement.'

The American looked at him. 'This is something you'll never hear me say again, so listen good. I'm sorry.'

Skinner looked at him in surprise, but said nothing.

'A few weeks ago,' Balliol went on, 'the chief editor told me that the British edition had been offered a story about a well-known guy in Britain who was two-timing his American wife and diddling this woman who worked for him.

'The guy who claimed to have the story, Noel Salmon – I thought it was a gal at first with a name like Noel – said he wanted a job.'

'Why did this come all the way up to you?'

Balliol smiled. '*Spotlight*'s kinda like my toy,' he said. 'But I'm tight with my business money, see, and the British edition had been swallowing cash, so I said a while back that all new spending had to be given the nod by me. So I was asked about Salmon, and I said if the story holds up, hire him.

'That was the last I heard till someone sent me a copy, and I saw your beefy ass on the front cover.' Something in the American's tone made Skinner guess that Balliol might be homosexual. He wondered if the FBI had its own suspicions.

'I have to admit I laughed, when I remembered how pissed I'd been with you at Witches Hill. I didn't feel too good about your lady friend bein' in those shots, though, especially the ones where it looks like she could be . . . you know.'

'I'll pass on your regrets,' grunted the detective, sourly. 'She'll be touched.'

Balliol looked away for a second. 'Yeah. Okay. Anyway,' he continued, quickly, 'at the same time as I'm sent the copy, my chief editor says that Salmon has another story, about you, and an illegal payment, a bribe. Our lawyers say though, no way can we use it without more evidence.

'So the chief editor says let's pass the story on to the authorities, announce that we've done it, and act like the good guys. We still sell magazines, but we don't get sued if the story turns out wrong. So I said to go ahead, and that's the way it played.'

Skinner looked at him. 'You know the real reason I came up here, Balliol? I'm a great believer in looking people in the eye. I've never met a man who can do that and tell me a direct lie at the same time.

'So will you look me in the eye, right now, and tell me that it wasn't you who set me up with that rigged bank account, then tipped off your own man about the story?'

The billionaire turned to face him, fixed his gaze upon him, eye to eye, and smiled. 'Shit, son,' he laughed. 'If I'd been going to set you up, it'd have been with a million, not a miserable hundred grand. I'd have set you up so you'd have gone away for life.

'But I didn't, and that is the truth.'

There was a long silence. 'Now,' said Balliol, breaking it finally, 'is that all you came for, or is there something else?'

The big detective nodded. 'Yes, there is. Your creep Salmon says that the information about me came to him from an anonymous source, that he doesn't know who it was tipped him off. We don't believe that, my pal and I. We think that he was about to give it up when your lawyer arrived to get him out of custody.

'I'd like you to order him to come clean now, to tell me

who his source is. Because that's the person who set me up with this phoney bribery charge.'

Balliol sighed. 'Well that's a bastard, ain't it? I'd do that for you, Bob sir, only I can't.'

'Why the hell not?'

'Because Salmon doesn't work for me any more. I told my chief editor to fire him as soon as he had sent his information to your Lord guy.'

'What for?'

Balliol looked at him, genuinely shocked. 'What for? Because he was caught with narcotics in his possession and in the company of a prostitoot. Either one of those things would have got him fired from any one of my companies. Both together! He's lucky I didn't set my Koreans on him.'

'Dammit!' cursed Skinner. 'Now you have to turn out to be a closet moralist! And you the owner of *Spotlight* too.'

'Nothing closet about it, son,' the American protested. '*Spotlight* exposes the private sins of public figures. How can you have a higher moral tone than that?'

Despite himself, the policeman laughed. 'I'll tell you a story, Mr Morality,' he said. 'A couple of years back, we had some really bad trouble at our Edinburgh Festival. Someone was after something very valuable, and went to extraordinary lengths to try to get it.

'They didn't succeed, and the people who caused all that mayhem were caught. But they were only the hired help. They had a paymaster, and we never did find out who that was.

'Funny, is it not, that when I showed up here today, you really weren't a hundred per cent sure what I'd come about.' Skinner leaned over, his face very close to Balliol. 'Am I ringing any bells here?'

The American smiled, coolly. 'Bob, son, I remember

reading about that affair. The people who did those things were completely out of control, and they got their just desserts.

'I tell you now, you can dig all the livelong day, and all of tomorrow, and all of the day after that and so on, but you will never tie me to that one. Believe me on this.'

Skinner stared at him, evenly. 'Oh I do, Mr Balliol, I do. But digging's my job, and when I get started I'm like the seven fucking dwarfs, all rolled into one.'

61

Arthur Dorward stripped the last of the tape from the underside of the drawer. Hands encased in latex gloves, he lifted the receipt very carefully, and slid it into a large plastic envelope, with a fastening along the top.

'We won't do any tests here, sir,' he said to Cheshire, as his sergeant placed the envelope in a document case. 'I'd much prefer to have my full lab facilities available when we start to look for traces.'

'Fair enough, Inspector,' said the investigator, 'but if you don't mind, Mr Ericson and I will come with you.'

Dorward's face set instantly into a frown, as he sensed an implied slur on his integrity. Andy Martin stepped in quickly. 'That's all right, Arthur,' he said. 'It's necessary to the enquiry.'

'Very good, sir.' The red-haired man nodded but his expression remained frozen.

'Before we go to get on with it,' he said, 'could I have a word with you, and with the Chief, in private?'

'Of course,' said Sir James Proud, who was standing near the door of Skinner's office. 'Come across the corridor.' He glanced, unsmiling, at Cheshire and Ericson. 'Excuse us, gentlemen.'

He led his two officers out of the room, and into his own suite. The veteran Chief looked confused, angry and very upset. 'I still don't believe it, you know.'

Dorward sighed. 'Who wants to, sir? But if we find Mr Skinner's prints on that receipt . . .'

'Then you better hadn't!' Proud Jimmy barked.

The Inspector glanced at Martin, with a look of panic, but the Chief soothed him almost at once. 'Oh, Arthur, make no mistake, I want you to do your job as honestly and as well as you always do. I just hate all this, that's all.

'Now, what did you want to see us about? Here, man, sit down, you're not on report.'

As the Chief Constable ushered them to chairs, Dorward's brows knitted. Looking at him, Martin thought that he might be trembling slightly.

'I had a call this morning from a specialist unit which my lab uses on a consultancy basis. They were reporting on a task I'd given them.' His voice was weak, faltering. 'I hardly know how to put this, gentlemen,'

'Try,' said the Chief Superintendent, so tersely that Proud looked at him in surprise.

'Very good, sir. It's like this, then. Remember, we found a number of hair samples trapped in the plumbing of Mrs McGrath's new bathroom?' Martin nodded, almost as a reflex.

'Well, as we thought, we were able to identify four of them very easily. The victim, the child, the nanny and the cleaner: all the people we knew had used the basin. That left us with two hair samples.' He hesitated again. This time it was the Chief Constable who urged him on with an impatient frown.

'We've subjected both of them to intensive analysis. They're both from men, for a start. Also they have different blood groups. One is perfectly common, almost regulation issue you might say. But the other is unusual.

'It's not a one-in-a-million type, but it is very unusual. Now as you know, ordinary medical records don't necessarily include blood type, so we have no way of knowing, other than statistically, how many people have this group, and we certainly can't identify them all. But where a person has been treated in hospital, there you'll find a note.'

Inspector Dorward gulped. 'Naturally, we checked at once with the hospitals in our Health Board area. They gave us a quick response. Five men with that blood group have been treated in Edinburgh hospitals since the beginning of last year. Two of them are dead. One of them is still in the Western. A fourth is seventy-seven years old. The fifth . . .' He faltered once more. He glanced at Martin, but he was looking at the floor.

'The fifth,' he said at last, 'is Mr Skinner.'

Silence has a quality and a value of its own. It may allow time for reflection. Between loving partners, it may contain expressions which need not be committed to words. But the silence which enveloped Sir James Proud's office as Dorward finished his story, was the type which follows the lighting of a fuse.

Eventually, the explosion came. 'Sweet suffering Christ!' boomed Chief Constable Sir James Proud. 'Are there any more rabbits in this fucking hat?'

He glowered at Martin, then looked across at Dorward. 'Thank you, Arthur. Difficult job, telling us that. On you go with Cheshire now. Not a bloody word about this to him, though, not even if he asks you straight out. He does that, refer him to me.'

Neither of the senior officers stood as the Inspector left the room. 'Jesus Christ and General Jackson,' barked the unusually eloquent Proud as the door closed behind him. 'Bob's up to his neck in the shit with this corruption thing. Does this make him a murder suspect now?'

Martin, impassive, shook his head. 'No it doesn't, Chief. He was with Pam at the time of the murder.'

'Could he have left the hair when he visited the murder scene?'

'No. He was suited up then, and he didn't use the basin. He left it there on another occasion.'

'Did you know about this?' the Chief asked, suddenly, his eyebrows rising. 'You were awful quiet when Dorward came out with it.'

The Head of CID nodded. 'Bob told me about it, yesterday. He said that he was pretty certain that one of those hair samples would turn out to be his.'

Proud Jimmy's mouth hung open slightly as he stared at the younger man, with incredulity spreading across his face. 'Oh, in the name of . . . He wasn't screwing Leona McGrath as well, was he?'

In spite of himself, Martin smiled, momentarily, at the Chief's reaction as the truth dawned. 'It happened just once, he told me, before the Pam relationship began, but at a time when he and Sarah were having very real difficulty. Ever since the air disaster, when Bob rescued the wee chap, and with all the things that happened afterwards, he always took a special interest in Mark.

'After Leona was elected, he used to look in on them on a Friday evening, after work, just to say hello, and check that they were okay. The role that Ali Higgins would have filled, had things not . . .' He paused, as he and Proud exchanged glances.

'Well,' he continued, 'there was one Friday when Bob was dropped off there, rather than calling in his own car. He'd been visiting one of the Midlothian offices, I think, and he'd used a driver. Leona invited him to stay for supper. They had a couple of drinks, he was down, she was pretty low too. After wee Mark went to bed one thing led to another, and so did they.

'Afterwards, Bob told me, they agreed that it would be a one-off, for everyone's sake. He started to phone her on a Friday, or at the weekend, instead of looking in. He told me that he was never in the house again until I called him on the day of the murder.'

Andy Martin shook his blond head. 'Think about it, Chief. One evening Bob's in that room, in her bed; next time he's there, he's looking at her raped, battered, strangled body. He said to me that holding it together was one of the most difficult things he's ever had to do.'

'I can imagine,' said Proud. 'Why didn't he tell you about this sooner, though, or tell me for that matter?'

'He didn't think we needed to know, Chief. It was only when he worked out how Arthur Dorward would conduct that investigation that he realised it would come out anyway.'

Sir James stood up, and walked to his window. 'It's a mess, Andy, a horrible mess. I never thought I'd see a day like this. What d'you think Cheshire will make of this development?'

'If we tell him,' said Martin. 'This is part of the McGrath investigation, not his.'

'Careful, son,' warned the Chief. 'You have to remember to think like a policeman here, not as a friend. This has to do with Bob; Cheshire's investigating Bob. We don't have any choice but to tell him. He won't think Bob's implicated in the murder, not for a second, but he'll be entitled to consider it to be evidence of moral instability.' The Chief Constable shook his silver head, wearily.

'I mean, if we look at this thing dispassionately, if we just think in terms of Mr X and do our jobs, what have we got? A secret account for a hundred thousand for the benefit of Mr X. His signature lodged with the bank. The deposit receipt found, concealed, in his office. Against all that, what is there? Alex's point, which you mentioned, about the Bank of England notes, and the fact that the courier may or may not have been Leona McGrath's killer, who may or may not have a grudge against Mr X. Not the strongest defence I've ever encountered.'

Proud Jimmy sighed. 'Let's face it, all we have is the fact that you and I can't believe that Bob Skinner could possibly be corrupt. Yet take your mind back twelve months, and ask yourself at that time whether it's possible that in a year, he'll be split from his wife and son and living with another woman.'

He looked back at Martin, who looked at the floor and shook his head, slowly.

'Anyway, Andy,' the Chief Constable went on, 'none of that is either relevant nor proper. We are senior police officers, with a public duty. If this was anyone else, he'd be charged by now, on the basis of those facts alone.

'See if Cheshire and Ericson are still in the building, will you. We have to tell them what we know.'

62

'It's grim, isn't it?' asked Alex.

'No, love,' Andy replied, sincerely. 'It's much worse than that.'

'What'll they do now?'

'They'll continue to look into every aspect of your dad's recent investigations to try to find a link with the bank account.'

'Okay, and they won't find it. So doesn't that make it a stalemate, at worst?'

He reached out and turned her face round towards his. 'Alex, this afternoon Proud Jimmy had to remind me to think like a policeman. Now I've got to remind you to think like a lawyer.

'Al Cheshire doesn't need to find any more. There needn't be any link to a past enquiry. The Crown can argue that the money was a down payment for future services. Finding that receipt hidden in Bob's desk was a real killer. They can go back to Lord Archibald any time they like and recommend prosecution.

'Cheshire said he'd let me know when they finally decided to do that. He said he'd keep me informed of anything else they turn up.'

'Anything else! Such as?'

'Who knows, after today?'

Tears of helplessness sprang into her eyes. 'Andy, this is a nightmare. I know Pops has had a terrible time over the last few months, but he hasn't changed that much. This is my dad and he's still one of the two best men in the world.'

He drew her to him, and hugged her, as they stood in the window of the Haymarket flat, looking up towards Princes Street, and the Castle. 'I know, sweetheart. The Chief may tell me to think like a policeman, but I just can't in this case. I don't give a bugger about the evidence, Bob didn't do it, and that's that.'

Alex was sobbing now, in his arms. 'But Andy, what if he's convicted?'

'Then I'll leave the force, if necessary, to prove his innocence.'

'You mean because he won't be able to, where he'll be?'

'Shh, wee one. Don't imagine that even for a second.'

'I try not to, but . . . The thing you told me about last night, about Pops and Leona. How much harm can that do?'

'Probably none, in jury terms. I doubt if it would be admissible in evidence. No, its damage is in the way that it makes Cheshire and Ericson see Bob: as being flawed, vulnerable. Open to offers, if you like.'

He squeezed her shoulders again. 'Listen, you're one of his team. You have to keep fear at bay. You're seeing old Christabel tomorrow. She should be good for morale.'

'I never asked you,' said Alex. 'D'you know her?'

Andy smiled. 'I don't know how to answer that. She isn't an acquaintance, yet I know the old witch all right. She cross-examined me once in the High Court. I was only a baby DC then, in some breaking-and-entering thing. I'd only been involved in interviewing the minor witnesses.

'The Advocate Depute took me through it, a bit casually, maybe, then it was her turn. She stood there over her papers, and by God did she put a spell on me. She started going on about Witness A, Witness B and Witness C, and by the time she was finished I hadn't a bloody clue who was who.

'Every question she asked, her voice got louder and louder, until she was bawling at me like an old cow across a field. My mother was there, too, to watch me give evidence in the High Court for the first time. So proud she'd been.' He laughed. 'Afterwards, outside in the corridor, I'd to stop her from tearing into Christabel, for bullying her boy.

'I tell you, with her on his side, Bob's got a chance, whatever the evidence that's been set up against him.'

63

The clock on the BMW showed 1.11 a.m. when Skinner pulled into a vacant parking space outside Pam's converted warehouse. He had expected her to be in bed, asleep, but as he turned his key in the lock and opened the front door, he heard the sound of music, playing softly from the stereo.

There was no light in the living room, other than that of the city outside, diffused by the muslin drapes, but he could see her silhouette as she sat waiting for him in her armchair, her legs doubled beneath her.

She turned towards him as he entered the warm room. From the slope of her shoulders and the swell of her breasts, he could tell, even before his eyes grew accustomed to the dimness of the light, that she was naked.

She rose and came towards him, to wrap herself around him, to press her body against his. 'I was just beginning to worry,' she whispered, pulling his head gently down and kissing him.

'It's been a long day for you. Did you find Balliol? Did he tell you what you wanted to know?'

He swept her up in his arms and carried her through to the bedroom. 'The music . . .' she began.

'Let it play out.'

He laid her down on the bed, and began to undress. 'Yes, I found Balliol,' he said quietly. 'No, he didn't tell me, because he doesn't know either. Salmon's been fired, into the bargain.'

'That's good news, at least.'

Skinner shrugged his shoulders as he stripped off his polo shirt, all in a single supple movement. 'Christ,' he said, 'I hum, what with the golf and the journey. Think I'll take a shower.' He stepped out of his slacks and briefs. 'Salmon was just a commodity to Balliol,' he went on. 'Something to be bought and traded in once it was used up.'

As he headed for the bathroom she rose to follow. 'Incidentally,' he called over his shoulder, his voice loaded with irony. 'Everard sends his regrets for your personal embarrassment. I told him it'd make your day. Over dinner, I told him you were still thinking about suing. Made your mind up yet?'

She nodded, as she watched him step into the bath and twist the shower control, standing back for a few seconds till it reached the set temperature. 'I'm not going to. I just don't need the extra embarrassment it would bring. Even if they settled, the press would still get hold of it.'

He looked at her as the water began to play on his chest. 'We'd be talking serious money, here. From what Balliol said, I suspect he's already told his solicitors to deal if you press it.'

'Still,' replied Pam. 'I want to bring no more embarrassment into your life, or rather into our life . . . because that's the way I want it.'

Skinner frowned, just as he plunged his head into the spray.

'Bob,' she went on, over the splashing of the water. 'I wasn't going to tell you this until morning, but I can't keep it in. Alex called. She said that Andy had gone out, on purpose, so that she could phone.'

'Eh?'

'He's been forbidden to have contact with you on a personal basis.'

'What? Why?' He stepped back, out of the spray.

'Because Cheshire and Ericson searched your office. They found the receipt, taped underneath one of your desk drawers.'

Breath hissed out of Skinner. 'Jesus. Hidden in my bloody desk? And I said to Andy, that if I had hidden it, I'd have put it where I felt most secure. That smart bastard Cheshire must have thought along the same lines.'

He smiled grimly at Pam, completely without humour. 'Commandment number five, Sergeant: thou shalt not underestimate your adversary. I'm always breaking that one. If only I'd had the sense to search my fucking office before he did!

'The bastard who set me up must have broken into Fettes right enough. I tell you, when this is over, I'm going to have such a security blitz on that office!' He snorted. 'Except that if I don't come up with something pretty fast, when this is over I'm going to be the subject of some pretty tight security myself.' He stepped back into the shower.

'I think I'll ask to be sent to Shotts Prison. My friend Big Lenny Plenderleith and I would make quite a team. We'd be running the place inside a week.'

'Don't say that,' Pam cried. She stepped into the shower beside him, rubbing her face in the wet hair of his chest. 'None of that will happen. You will come up with something; you're invincible. Don't think about it. Think about this instead.'

She picked up a hot, wet sponge, ran it up the inside of his thigh, and began to massage him. He grinned down at her. 'You're a bit optimistic, aren't you? Not even I have that good a mental isolator switch. Besides, I've covered most of Scotland today, and back again.' He switched off the shower and reached for two towels.

The smile vanished and the glower was back. 'Be patient. Maybe, after a couple of years they'll allow us a conjugal visit.'

64

Skinner was familiar with Parliament House and with the Advocates Library, headquarters of the Scottish Bar. So was Alex, from student visits, and from occasional visits as a teenager, to watch her father give evidence as a police witness in a significant trial.

But neither had ever been inside the Lord Reid Building, the advocates' consultation centre, until they arrived in its small courtyard off the Royal Mile. Number 142 High Street, in New Assembly Close, was built in 1814 by James Gillespie Graham as the Commercial Bank. Much later, before its acquisition by the Faculty of Advocates, it housed the popular Edinburgh Wax Museum. Skinner guessed that currently far fewer people passed through its doors every year than during its time as a tourist attraction, but that in income terms, its turnover was far greater.

'Consultation with Miss Christabel Innes Dawson, QC,' Mitchell Laidlaw announced to the uniformed Faculty Officer at the small desk in the reception hall.

'Very good, sir,' said the man. 'If your party will please go into the waiting room.' He pointed them towards a large, leather-upholstered waiting room, its walls hung with works of art from the Faculty's extensive collection, and with a large fireplace similar in size and style to that in the formal drawing room in Bute House, and which Skinner guessed at once was original. The policeman in him thought of the profitable trade in stolen antiquities and of the signs posted on several disused Georgian and Victorian offices in and around Edinburgh's Golden Mile which advised potential burglars that all fireplaces had been removed. 'If they ever find out where the store is . . .' he had said once to Andy Martin.

Normally an advocate will arrive to greet solicitors and clients and to take them to their consultation rooms. But Christabel Innes Dawson QC was far too senior and venerable to do her own fetching. After a few minutes, the attendant reappeared. 'If you will follow me, gentlemen, madam . . . Miss Dawson will receive you in Room Five.'

The trio followed him, latterly in single file because of the narrowness of the corridor which led to the rear of the building, until they reached a flight of four steps, with a varnished door at the top. The attendant knocked, opened it and announced them: 'Mr Laidlaw and party, Miss Dawson.'

Christabel Innes Dawson QC did not rise as her instructing solicitor led her client into the room. She was seated at a very ordinary round table, in a very ordinary room, a far cry from that in which they had awaited her pleasure. She surveyed them as they entered one by one, the attendant retreating and closing the door.

Finally she nodded to the solicitor. 'Well, Mr Laidlaw.' The words seemed to roll from her tongue. 'I had begun to despair that you would ever instruct me in a case. I know all about you, mind. When Ken, my clerk, told me you wanted me in this matter, I asked three senior members of Faculty about you. Two of them described you as the best litigation solicitor in Scotland. The third said you were a shark in a lagoon filled with holiday-making children. I think he was saying the same thing as the other two, only in a different way.

'Sit down, sit down please. You're all so tall.'

She turned her attention to Skinner. 'Well, Chief

Inspector . . . or what is it now? . . . this is a sad surprise. I never imagined for one instant that when the great Mr Laidlaw finally called on me it would be to represent you in a criminal cause.

'Last time our paths crossed, literally, was in Aberlady, I think, a couple of weeks ago. Your informal salute was appreciated. So few people pay respects these days to a funeral cortège. There was a time when gentlemen always removed their hats as a hearse passed by. So few gentlemen left now,' she mused.

'Maybe just fewer with hats, Miss Dawson,' said Skinner, gently.

'Maybe, maybe.' Her eyes flashed suddenly, with a cunning gleam. 'If memory serves, you were in your car with the young lady I've been reading about. Well, I certainly won't be the one to criticise you for such a relationship.' She frowned for an instant. 'I'd tell her she's a bloody fool though.'

Beside her father Alex gasped, but Miss Dawson ignored her presence. She guessed that with her apprenticeship completed and two or three years' experience at the Bar, she might merit a nod.

Skinner looked at his Senior Counsel. He had seen her only twice before out of her court dress, each time from a distance. For their meeting she wore a formal charcoal grey suit, and a white blouse, with a ruffled collar. He guessed that she had a dozen such outfits in her wardrobe, and precious little else.

Close to, she really did look old, he realised, but he was not surprised, since judging by the year of her Calling to the Bar, she could not be less than seventy-eight. He had expected her hair to be shorter, and more grey, until he took a second look and realised that she wore a wig not only for court but on all public appearances.

But her voice disguised her frailty and her years. It had kept its strength through over fifty years of practice, and even now, it was only faintly reedy as she spoke.

She addressed Laidlaw once more. 'Thank you for the papers which you sent to my clerk. I have read them.' She glanced quickly and slightly mischievously at Skinner. 'You realise that means that the meter's running, young man.'

Skinner nodded. He knew also that her meter was one of the most reasonable at the Bar. Although her clerk was free to negotiate private fees, she never charged more than the appropriate Legal Aid rate for criminal work.

She looked directly at Laidlaw once more. 'As I say, I've read them, and I've been made aware of yesterday's subsequent development, the discovery of the receipt in Mr Skinner's office. I'm glad at least that there were no fingerprints on it.

'You know I must ask you this. Would a plea of "Guilty" be considered by our client, should the Crown wish to negotiate surrender terms?'

Mitch Laidlaw shook his round head vigorously. 'Under no circumstances. Our client maintains his innocence, and believes that he is the victim of a clever, ruthless and well-planned conspiracy.' He relaxed slightly. 'In any event, given the evidence which they have, it's difficult to imagine how the Crown could come up with a reduced charge, or why it would wish to.'

'Indeed. Very well. Let's look at our cards.' She leaned across the table, her skinny arms folded. 'On the face of it, the signature is a problem. However, I note Mr Skinner's explanation of how it might have been obtained. I find that credible. So, I believe, will the members of the jury, as long as we can sow other seeds of doubt in their minds, in respect of other aspects of the Crown case.'

She glanced briefly at Skinner. 'I like the point about the Bank of England notes. I think that is odd enough to start the jury thinking, also.

'Then there is the bank manager's unwitting identification of the photofit of the suspect in the McGrath and Anderson cases as the courier who delivered the money, a chap with evident malice towards our client. That's a piece of luck.'

'Hold on, though, Miss Dawson,' Skinner intervened. 'That's a coincidence, that's all. Not even I believe for a second that it's the same man.'

The ancient Queen's Counsel gathered her breath and frowned at him, with a degree of outrage. 'What you believe or do not is of no interest to me or relevance to your case. You are the accused here, not the investigator. It is what I can make the jury believe that will determine your future liberty, so any doubts you may have about your own defence arguments would be best kept to yourself.'

The big policeman grinned. No-one had spoken to him in that tone since he was a detective constable.

'We can argue on both those points,' his Counsel continued. 'But for me, the strongest card they have is the Crown's lack of information on who might have paid this money, and for what purpose.'

She looked at Skinner again. 'Now,' she said, 'I'll ask for your professional view. Would you be completely happy to be proceeding in a case with such an omission?'

The DCC considered her question, and as he did, he began to feel optimistic, for the first time in forty-eight hours. 'No,' he answered at last. 'I don't think that I would.' He grinned. 'I certainly wouldn't fancy having you cross-examine me in those circumstances.'

The old lady nodded her gracious thanks for his compliment. 'Very well then, gentlemen. Our best hope is that the donor of this hundred thousand pounds remains unidentified. Who knows, Mr Skinner? Legally, you may even be able to keep it.'

Mitch Laidlaw smiled at the idea. 'What can we expect next, Miss Dawson?' he asked.

'A charge, I should think. The Secretary of State has really set up poor Archie Nelson with his damn investigation. Politics and justice aren't supposed to mix, but in these circumstances, I doubt if the new Lord Advocate can afford not to let this one go to trial.

'So you'd better brace yourself, young man . . .' she addressed Alex for the first time, '. . . and you, young lady. It will probably get worse, before it starts to get better.'

65

'Sir James,' said Cheshire, sitting not in the comfortable suite where callers were usually received, but in a straight-backed chair set in front of the Chief's big desk, 'you really shouldn't be doing this, you know.

'My remit here is to investigate and report to the Lord Advocate, no-one else.'

Proud Jimmy nodded. 'So I've been told, and I've gone along with it for long enough.' He paused and tapped the heavy silver braid on the epaulettes of his uniform jacket. 'But the fact is, I won't have anyone operating as a police officer anywhere in this building, or even in this city, and imagining that I've no jurisdiction over what he does.

'I'm the Chief Constable here, you're out of your own area, and you will answer any question which I choose to put to you. I may have ordered Andy Martin not to see Bob Skinner informally until this nonsense is over, but that's purely because I don't want to take the slightest chance of compromising his career. If you think I'm going to sit on my arse and just watch as my deputy, and one of my best friends to boot, is sent down the Swannee, then think again, sir.

'I know all about the declared and physical evidence that you have. Now, I want to know what you've got on who might have set Bob up.'

'Or bribed him,' said Cheshire, coldly.

'Don't even think that in this office,' barked Proud, 'far less say it. Now, I want to know what you've done to check into people he's put away in his time. You can, and no doubt will, tell Archie Nelson all about this, but I've seen off a right few Lord Advocates in my time, so that doesn't worry me. I've given you an order, now obey it.'

Cheshire capitulated. 'Very good.

'The fact is,' he began, 'the list isn't a very long one. There are very few of Skinner's customers with the means to do something like this, and they're all inside. We've been to see the chap Plenderleith.'

'Mmm, Big Lenny. That was brave of you.'

Cheshire nodded. 'I thought so too. He's bit of a monster, isn't he? However, he does seem to hold Skinner in high regard. I'd expected to find malice there, but when I put the suggestion to him that he might have set this thing up, he took real offence. In fact, he left Ronnie and me in no doubt about what he would do to anyone who was out to get Skinner.'

'You don't surprise me,' said the Chief. 'He was in no doubt about it being a set-up, then?'

'None at all, it seemed. He offered to help us in fact. I gather that Mr Plenderleith is a very important man in prisoner circles.'

'Yes. He's very rich, as well as being very dangerous.'

'I see,' said the Mancunian. 'We accepted his offer in any event, as long as he promised not to have anyone killed. He did. He's putting out feelers, to see if anyone knows anything about it.'

Proud nodded. 'That's unconventional, but go on.'

'Next, we looked at the chap who was arrested after the Witches Hill affair. He hadn't a clue what we were talking about. Apparently he lives in voluntary isolation. He refuses to do prison work, and he hasn't had a visitor, a letter, or received or made a phone call since the day of his sentence. So you can forget him.'

Cheshire went on. 'Finally we looked at the Jackie Charles case. The chap who was arrested at its conclusion . . .'

'Yes, him,' growled Proud.

'You'll recall he hanged himself in his cell, before he could be brought to trial. But then there was Charles himself. We interviewed him.'

'And . . .'

'And, to be frank, Sir James, that is where my suspicions lie. Charles agreed to see us without even asking why but when we got down to the substance of the enquiry, the allegations, he clammed up. He became positively evasive, wouldn't answer direct questions, and finally, he asked for a lawyer.'

Proud scowled across the desk. 'Jackie Charles has been evasive with police officers all his life. It's second nature to him. He knows also that there's no point in refusing to see us. He's always preferred to get it over with quickly.'

'Nevertheless, sir,' countered the Englishman, 'I have to be suspicious. He behaved almost coyly. It was as if he didn't want to incriminate himself, but he wanted us to nail Skinner.'

'Of course,' Proud bellowed. 'He hates Bob. It goes back almost twenty years. Bob arrested him in the end. Why the hell would he bribe him?'

Cheshire paused. 'Well, Sir James, I know you took an interest in the case, so I'll have to be diplomatic here. But didn't it occur to you that after all the time that it took to nail Charles, it was odd that the charges Skinner pressed against him should be limited to tax evasion? Even in England, we were aware of the case. We expected many more serious charges, possibly murder or attempted murder.'

It was Proud's turn to be hesitant. 'There were circumstances,' he said, 'which led Bob to conclude – with the agreement of the Procurator Fiscal, I must stress – that we should accept a plea to the counts we were sure of.'

'Maybe there were, sir. But as dispassionate investigators, looking at the current set of circumstances, we have to look at the possibility that there may have been private considerations, of which you were not aware.'

'Aye, I suppose so,' the Chief agreed, reluctantly. 'So what's your next move?'

'It's being made right now, Sir James, by Ronnie Ericson. We've looked at that case in the most minute detail, and there's one thing we want to check.

'For everyone's sake,' said Cheshire, heavily, 'I really do hope that it draws a blank.'

66

'Maybe I'll be like Christabel in about sixty years,' said Alex.

'What,' cried her father, vehemently, 'a dried-up old dear with nothing in your life except the law? God forbid.

'I hope that in sixty years time you will be secure in the enjoyment of your children and grandchildren, and still gaining pleasure from the care you lavish on your venerable husband.'

'And on my centenarian father, I hope.'

He grinned across the garden table of the Fairyhouse Avenue bungalow, having used his unaccustomed leisure time to shop at the nearby Sainsbury's for a salad-and-sandwich lunch for two. 'No bloody chance of that,' he chuckled. 'I'll be in Dirleton Cemetery by that time.'

'Beside Mum?' asked Alex quietly.

Serious suddenly, he shook his head. 'No. I've bought another lair a bit along from her grave. I won't lie with Myra again, not even in death. You'll have that option, though.'

'With whom will you lie, then? Pamela? Or will it be . . .'

'Time will tell,' he said shortly. 'It won't be my decision, I hope. Jesus, girl, but this is morbid; change the subject.' She tried to catch his eye, but for once he avoided her gaze.

'Pops, are you beginning to . . .'

He cut her off. 'I mean it. Let's talk about something else. So what did you make of our Learned Counsel?'

'She's formidable still, isn't she just?' said Alex. 'She

seems to be as sharp as a tack, still. Mr Laidlaw was certainly impressed by her. I liked her analysis too. Things aren't nearly as black when you look at it from her angle.'

He smiled. 'Sure, but Christabel would be the first to remind you that optimism alone won't make the jury see it her way. Sure, there are holes in the Crown case, but it's still strong. The old dear made me admit that I wouldn't choose to take it to court myself, but if I was forced to it I still reckon I'd have at least an even chance of a conviction.

'Mind you, when you add in the Christabel factor the odds might tilt a bit.' His smile turned into soft laugh. 'I will never in my life forget the doing she gave that fiancé of yours in the witness box. After ten minutes of it, he more or less swore on the Bible that he didn't know his arse from his elbow.'

'Well,' she said, loyally, 'he was only young at the time. What about you? How did you do against her?'

'I think the referee's decision was a draw. She kept trying to get me to say that black might have been a bit grey, if not completely white, but I stuck to the script.'

'How do you think she'll do with Cheshire?'

'She might rattle his cage a bit, but he's a cool one, is Algernon. He'll survive. Anyway, most of what he'll have to say won't be subject to challenge. The question will be what weight the jury gives to old Chrissie's interpretation.'

He frowned. 'No, I'm more worried about what she'll do to Jimmy.'

'Will she call him?'

'Absolutely for certain, she'll call him, unless I forbid it. She'll want him as a character witness, but she'll attack him too.'

'Why should she do that?'

Bob smiled. 'Come on, girl, are you on the team or not? Work it out.'

Alex bit into her last sandwich as she thought the question through. As she chewed she began to nod. 'Yes,' she offered at last. 'She'll have to rubbish the security of the police headquarters building. She'll have to convince the jury that someone could have walked in there and planted that receipt in your desk.'

She looked at him sharply. 'Could they?'

'That's what happened, isn't it?'

'In that case, you're right. To demonstrate that, she'll need the Chief Constable himself to admit it, under oath.'

'Spot on.'

'And will he?' she asked.

'I honestly don't know, my darling.'

Alex slapped the table, wrinkling her forehead in a huge frown. 'None of this should be happening,' she cried out. 'It's just not fair.'

Her father reached across and ruffled her hair. 'Whoever said life was, my angel? Whoever said it was? You go into the house and check your birth certificate. I'm pretty certain that you'll find that it doesn't include any warranties or guarantees.'

'No, I don't recall that it does,' she said, rising from the table, and glancing at her watch. 'Time I was off.'

She helped him carry the plates and mugs into the kitchen. He was walking with her to the door, when the telephone rang. Closest to it, she picked it up.

'Hello,' she said, as if to a familiar voice. 'Yes, he's here.' She handed over the phone, kissed him on the cheek, and disappeared through the front door, with a wave.

'Yes,' grunted Skinner, watching the door close with a surge of pleasure at the woman his daughter had become.

'Hello, boss,' Neil McIlhenney replied. 'How're you doing?'

'Fine, Big Fella, fine.' He paused. 'Well no, I'm not. I'm very, very deeply pissed off, if the truth be told. Is this a social call, seeing as how I'm a non-polisman at the moment?'

'Of course it is, boss. I just wanted to make sure that you're hanging in there.' At the other end of the line, Skinner heard a soft rumbling chuckle. 'Mr Martin specifically didn't tell me to call you. He also told me not to let slip that the McGrath–Anderson team have just had a tip from a woman out in Howgate about a man taking a wee lass into a cottage out there this morning. She was struggling, so the woman said.'

Skinner stood bolt upright. 'Did she know the man?'

'No.'

'Did she give a description?'

'Tall, fair, slim. He took the kid out of the back of a grey Toyota van. With a tow-bar.'

'Who owns the cottage? Anyone checked yet?'

'Sammy just did. It belongs to a Mr George. He gets a Council Tax discount as a sole occupant. But the witness says it's not usually occupied. It's a holiday place, and she hasn't a clue whether the man she saw is the owner or not.'

Skinner took a deep breath. 'When?'

'We're just leaving now. Mr Martin, the boy Pye, Pam and me. We're using two unmarked cars. There's an armed team on the way up now to deploy out of sight.'

'Pam?' said the DCC sharply. 'Why Pam?'

'Don't worry, boss,' the Sergeant reassured him, quickly. 'She'll be well back. Mr Martin wants a woman there to look after the kids if we recover them.'

'Who's carrying?'

'Mr Martin and me.'

'Where's the cottage?'

'You know where the old Inn was?'

'Yes.'

'At the end of a track, just beyond it.'

'And where does the witness live?'

'In a converted steading across the field. There are four houses there. The uniform team has orders to empty them.'

'Very good, Neil,' said Skinner. 'Everything sounds fine. I'm glad the situation's in such good hands. Best of luck.'

'Thanks boss,' said McIlhenney, sounding a touch bewildered.

67

'Fancy seeing you here,' McIlhenney grinned, as he stepped out of the passenger seat of Martin's car, opposite what had once been the Howgate Inn, a popular Midlothian watering place. 'Just for a minute there, I . . .'

'I thought I'd go for a drive,' replied Skinner, casually forestalling him. 'Something going on here?'

An attractive blonde woman, in her mid-forties, stood beside him. Three other people, two more women and an elderly man, residents of the steading, the Sergeant guessed, were gathered a few yards away, with a uniformed constable. 'This is Mrs Christopher,' said the DCC as Martin approached, followed by Pam and Sammy Pye, from a second car. 'Your witness.'

'That's good,' nodded the Chief Superintendent. 'There are a few other questions I wanted to ask.'

Skinner smiled. 'Mrs Christopher and I have had a chat already. The grey van's been around here on and off for two or three weeks. Here for a couple of days, then gone for a couple, then back. She saw it last on Friday night, she says.'

Andy Martin frowned. 'What about the time of the first crime?'

'Mrs Christopher's recollection is that it was gone from the Thursday morning to the following Monday.'

The younger detective turned to the woman, and took two prints from his pocket, a photograph of the kidnapped Tanya Anderson, and the photofit of her abductor. 'The child you saw.' He showed her the print. 'Could these be the man and the girl?'

Mrs Christopher peered at the pictures. 'Yes, it could have been,' she said, nodding. 'They were too far away for me to be absolutely certain, but those are like them. The poor wee thing was really upset. I could tell that. She was crying and struggling when he took her out of the van.'

'From which door did he take her?'

'From the back. That's what really caught me attention in the first place. I mean, imagine, carrying a child in the back of a van!'

'Imagine,' said Martin. 'Now think carefully, please, Mrs Christopher. Have you ever seen another child in this man's company?'

She pointed to Skinner. 'This gentleman's already asked me that. The answer's still no, though. I haven't.'

'Thanks anyway,' said the Head of CID. 'Would you join the others now, please.'

As Mrs Christopher retreated he turned back to Skinner. 'How d'you think we should play this, sir?'

'It's your show, Andy,' the DCC replied.

'Not so as I'd noticed.'

Skinner grinned. 'Well. I did have a quick scout around.' He pointed along the twisting road which led out of the village. 'The track to the cottage is over there, but you're out of its sight until you're almost at the front door. The van's tucked away beyond it, but it's angled so that you can't make out its number, dammit.

'Behind the house there's a wee patch of woodland. The place backs right on to it, with hardly any garden. Some of the armed support is in there already. The rest are in the steading.'

He looked quizzically at Martin. 'Why don't Neil and I

325

make our way through the woods, and you and Sammy go straight up the track?'

'Why don't we call in the SAS?' asked Pye.

'Because there is at least one kid in there that we know of, Sam,' Skinner replied. 'The SAS go in bloody. I don't want any child deafened by a stun grenade or shot by this man in a panic.'

'That's right,' said the Chief Superintendent. 'Let's be gentle about it. I'll just walk up and knock on the front door, with you two out the back, and all that firepower in the woods and across the field.'

Skinner nodded. 'You'd better advise the armed support commander. If he comes out shooting, or even showing a gun, he goes down.' He grimaced. 'I wish we knew just a wee bit more about the situation, but with what we've got, the balance of the risk says we do it now.'

They split into the agreed pairs. Skinner led McIlhenney into the wood, finding a rough path through the trees, trodden down by the armed support officers. A hundred yards or so into the plantation they came upon the four-strong unit, well hidden in the gloom from anyone looking from the bright afternoon outside.

'Seen any movement inside the house?' the DCC asked a uniformed sergeant. The man looked at him, clearly surprised by his presence.

'Only once, sir. A man came into the kitchen, then went out again carrying a can of Pepsi. He was a dead ringer for the photofit.'

The radio which McIlhenney was carrying crackled into life. 'We're in position.' Martin's voice sounded whispered. Skinner and his sergeant stepped across the low wire fence into the cottage's small garden. 'Ready,' said McIlhenney.

A few seconds later, they heard a loud knock. A few

seconds after that, the back door swung open, fast, and a man rushed out: a tall, slim fair-haired man.

His mouth opened in surprise as he caught sight of the two detectives, then panic showed in his eyes at the sight of the pistol in McIlhenney's hand. He started to run for the corner of the house, towards the grey van, the bonnet of which was just visible. He had taken two steps when Skinner hit him, slamming into him with a rugby tackle and bearing him to the ground. Roughly, the DCC rolled the man on to his face and drove a knee into the small of his back, as he reached for his wrists, to secure them.

The girl's voice took him by surprise. 'What are you doing to my Daddy?' she cried.

68

'What have you done with him?' asked Alex.

'He's on his way back to England right now. Pamela and Sammy Pye are driving him and wee Sally down to York. They'll be met at the police headquarters there by two officers from the Suffolk force. They'll hand him over, stay overnight in York, and come back tomorrow morning.'

'Has he done this before, this Mr George?'

Martin shrugged. 'Once is too often for the court's liking. The custody arrangement in his divorce only allows him one weekend a month, and he doesn't like it. He wanted to take his daughter on holiday for a week, but his ex-wife refused. So he turned up at her house yesterday evening, and grabbed the child.

'The mother went to court this morning, and the judge ordered his arrest for contempt. I feel a bit sorry for the guy really. He's just a decent honest soul, a self-employed electrician who works on big projects. That's why his van was away for a few days at a time. The ex-wife's a lawyer, though, and she's got him tied up every way.'

Alex reached across the dining table and punched him lightly on the chin. 'Just you bear that in mind, then,' she laughed.

'Did Pops hurt him much, this poor chap?'

'Not really. He just knocked the wind out of him. He scared the wee girl though; he was a bit upset about that. It would have scared her more if big Neil had shot the bloke, though.'

'Why did he run?' she asked.

'He said that he was going round the side of the house to see who was at the door. When he saw Bob and McIlhenney, pistol drawn, he panicked and tried to leg it.'

'And was it his cottage?'

'His dad's. His wife didn't know about it, apparently.'

Alex frowned. 'Poor sod. It's awful when couples get to that stage. What'll happen to him, d'you think?'

'Ach, the judge'll probably keep him in custody for a week or two, then give him a bollocking and let him go. Hopefully, he'll review the custody deal while he's at it. I think the guy's got a grievance.'

He glanced at her, across the pizzas. 'Your dad's on his side too, of course. I only hope it doesn't come to that with him and Sarah.'

'It won't.'

'How can you be so sure?'

'I know my dad, that's how. And my stepmum too.'

'Mmm,' Andy mused. 'I miss Sarah, you know. Wonder how she's doing?'

'Or who. His name's Terry, I believe.'

'Eh?'

'So Pops told me.'

'Sarah wouldn't.'

She grinned at him again, even more widely than before. 'Maybe she wouldn't. Bloody sure I would though, in her shoes. You can store that away for future reference too.'

'Hey,' he asked her, 'are you trying to talk me out of this engagement?'

'Far from it,' she replied. 'I want to get married.'

His eyes widened with his smile. 'You do? When?'

'As soon as I've got my dad sorted out. Are you game?'

'Need you ask?' He rose, drawing her to her feet also

and pulled her to him, kissing her, running his broad fingers through her abundant wavy hair.

She reached down for his belt buckle. 'Pizzas'll get cold,' he murmured.

'Sod the pizzas.'

From time to time, Andy Martin could convince himself that all telephones show malice towards humans, especially in certain circumstances.

'Sod that!' he growled as it rang. Still, he picked it up.

As Alex watched him, his face grew grim. 'You sure?' he said. 'I see. No, it doesn't. Yes, I'll tell her. She'll have him there.'

He hung up, and turned to her. 'That was Al Cheshire, keeping his word to me. He's fixed a meeting with the Lord Advocate, for ten o'clock tomorrow, and he wants Bob there. They've found something else, and he thinks that Lord Archibald will be forced to place formal charges.'

69

'There's no doubt about this, is there? No chance that your expert could be wrong?'

Deputy Chief Constable Cheshire looked at the Lord Advocate solemnly. 'Sir, we've consulted the manufacturer of the machine. The company's chief design engineer himself will testify that the note which accompanied the deposit in the Guernsey bank was typed on an electric machine purchased five years ago by John Jackson Charles Automobiles Limited, a typewriter seized subsequently by the police during a raid on premises owned by Mr and Mrs Charles.

'Since the day when it was impounded, by Mr Skinner and Sergeant Neil McIlhenney, it has been under lock and key in the production store at Fettes Avenue. Mr Skinner may argue in his defence that someone found their way into his office to hide the Guernsey receipt in his desk. But to argue that the same person broke into the production store, found that machine among thousands of items, plugged it in and typed the note . . . I'm sorry, My Lord, but that is surely stretching credulity.'

Lord Archibald gazed at Skinner across his desk. The detective stared back, impassively.

'I'm sorry, Bob,' he said. 'And I have to say that I'm hugely disappointed. Are you still maintaining your innocence?'

Skinner gave no answer, nor made any movement.

'Mmm,' said Archibald. 'You'd better say nothing

anyway. Look, David Pettigrew, the Fiscal is in the next room. He will caution and charge you, formally. There will be no announcement from this office, but you will appear in the Sheriff Court tomorrow to be formally remanded.

'There'll be no plea taken and of course you'll be released on a simple ordination to appear at a later hearing, but at the pleading diet, it'll be for the Sheriff to decide whether bail should be allowed. I think it's inevitable that the case will be sent to the High Court for disposal.'

He turned back to Cheshire and Ericson. 'You two. Get up to Perth right away and see the man Charles again. I'd like to proceed against him, but I don't have a prospect of success. So, tell him what we've got and see if he'll agree to be a Crown witness, with immunity.'

Mitchell Laidlaw stirred in his seat chair. 'Archie, may I . . .'

The Lord Advocate anticipated the rest of the question. 'Yes,' he said. 'You may interview Charles also, separately. But I mean you, and you alone. Not Bob, under any circumstances, and not Alex either.'

He rose, ending the meeting. 'Now, let's get Pettigrew in here and start putting this most unfortunate business to rest.'

70

'That tears it, Bob,' said Laidlaw.

'Charles has given Cheshire and Ericson a statement saying that he paid you the hundred thousand as a bribe, to secure reduced charges. He says that you gave him a sealed envelope with the destination bank inside, and that he passed it unopened to his associate, Douglas Terry.

'Further, he goes on to say that it was Terry – who is of course conveniently dead – who hired the courier and arranged the gathering in of the money. The Crown will probably argue that Terry may have raised the cash in England, knocking the banknote defence on the head.'

'Does Charles admit to typing the note?' asked Skinner.

Laidlaw nodded. 'Yes, he does.' The lawyer sighed. 'Bob, would Charles have spent a hundred thousand just to frame you?'

The big policeman smiled grimly. 'It sure looks like that, doesn't it?'

The two men, with Andy Martin, were in the living room at Fairyhouse Avenue. 'So where do you think the typewriter thing puts us, Mitch, in terms of our defence?' Skinner asked.

'I've spoken to Miss Dawson about that, by telephone,' the solicitor replied. 'Her view is that it's very serious indeed. It almost completes the chain of evidence. However, she still feels that as long as the Crown can't produce the note which Charles alleges you gave him, she has a slim chance of steering the jury towards a Not Proven verdict, providing she can also convince them that your signature could have been obtained by trickery.'

Skinner turned towards his solicitor. 'The ball's in your court. You go back to see Christabel. Start work on a defence. As for me, I'm going looking for Mr Noel Salmon. I'm going to do something I should have done long ago. I'm going to scare the shit out of that little man, and with it, hopefully, a name.'

He smiled, wickedly. 'You see, the one thing that Jackie Charles would find it difficult to do from his hotel suite in Perth Jail is to make a private, unrecorded call to Salmon, to tip him off about the bank account.

'Jackie's cute. He's turned Cheshire and Ericson back on themselves and got them to buy a statement that could be complete supposition on his part. He's built his story on things that they've told him. The idea that he agreed to pay me off, then turned the mechanics over to Dougie Terry, that's brilliant for two reasons: one, because that's exactly how he used to work, and two, because Terry isn't around any more to contradict him.

'Not that he would have. Dougie the Comedian would have died for Charles. Come to think of it, he did.'

Skinner smiled again, in recollection this time. 'Jackie to Terry, Terry to someone else, and that someone else did whatever needed doing. One to one all the time, so there was never any corroboration. That was the way they worked, and it was the reason why we were never able to nail Jackie for any of the big stuff he was involved in.

'That's why the idea of bunging me to reduce the charges is all so much shite. We always needed Terry's evidence to be sure of convicting Charles, so when he got his head caved in, we were stuffed.

'That's something Jackie's overlooked in his eagerness

to nail me, and Cheshire and Ericson didn't realise. With Terry dead, there were no other charges we could have made stick. Christabel should be able to take him apart in the box with that.'

He turned to Martin. 'Andy, would you do me a big favour? Don't tell anyone about it, just do it, please. Ask McGuire and McIlhenney if they would go up to Perth to question Charles. Tell them to get him to go over his statement again, and again, and again. Tell them also, while he's doing that, to drop in plenty of hints about perjury charges, and the penalties.

'Jackie's out on a limb, you see. I reckon he's seen a chance to get even with me, and he's jumped at it. But if we can undermine his confidence, scare him a wee bit about the risk he's taking, hint that there are one or two things that he doesn't know about, then maybe, just maybe, he'll withdraw that statement.

'Will you do that?'

Martin nodded. 'Of course.'

'Thanks. But explain to Mario and Neil that this isn't an order. If either of them feels uncomfortable about it, I'll understand.'

'You really do think Charles is lying, Bob, don't you?' said Laidlaw. 'That he couldn't be the one who's set you up?'

'I'm certain of it. He had nothing to do with that money. He didn't know about it till Cheshire and Ericson went up to Perth and told him, but when they did, a whole world of possibilities opened up in his devious wee mind.

'The one thing he couldn't do, though, was make that phone call to Salmon.'

'Maybe he had an accomplice?' the solicitor suggested.

Skinner shook his head, firmly, pursing his lips. 'The

only three accomplices Jackie Charles ever had in his life were his wife Carole, Tony Manson, and Dougie Terry. And they're all dead.

'No, the person who gave that information to Salmon was the person who set me up, without any assistance from Jackie, or anyone else.'

He stood, abruptly. 'Right, Mitch, you'd better go and see Christabel again. I'll meet the two of you at the Sheriff Court tomorrow: nine thirty, as Davie Pettigrew asked. Andy, you talk to Mario and Neil about going up to Perth.'

Martin nodded. 'Are you going after Salmon? Because if you find him, I wouldn't want . . .'

His friend laughed. 'You wouldn't want me to damage him, you were going to say? Don't worry, son, I'll get the truth out of that wee man without laying a finger on him. Anyway, he can wait till tomorrow.

'This afternoon, I'm going out to Gullane. I was reminded on Sunday that my golf game's a bit rusty. So just for a break, and to let me do some uninterrupted thinking, I think I'll hit a few balls. When Pam gets back from York, tell her that's where I'll be, and that I'll probably stay out there tonight, if she wants to join me.'

'Sure, I'll do that.' His right eyebrow rose, with a recollection. 'Speaking of your lady,' he added, 'I had a call this morning from the Central Force. The woman she's due to replace has had a complication of pregnancy, so she's gone off earlier than scheduled. They'd like Pam right away if they can have her.'

'How soon?'

'Thursday, if possible?'

'Can you spare her?'

'I think in all the circumstances, it'd be best if I could.'

'Then talk to her about it. And as long as she's happy,

that'll be fine. Then the two of us can get on with sorting out our future. I think I owe it to us both to make an honest woman out of Pamela.'

71

'How long have you got to do, Jackie?' asked McGuire.

John Jackson Charles, managing somehow to look immaculate even in badly cut prison clothes, looked at him coolly. 'I expect to be released in two years and one month . . . as you must know.'

'This story, the one you've told us twice now, about our boss,' said Neil McIlhenney. 'You wouldn't have the idea, would you, that it might get you out a year or so early?'

'I'm not so naive, Sergeant.'

McIlhenney laughed. 'I know that, all right. You're not infallible either though. If you were you wouldn't be wearing that fucking awful suit right now. Daks is your preference, isn't it.'

'Yes,' countered Charles, evenly, 'and Hugo Boss: just for the odd bit of variety you understand. I've got a wardrobe full of them, waiting for me. Dior shirts, too.'

'You might find it easier to put them on when you get out,' growled McGuire.

'Why?'

'You might not have to pull them over your head. Because you might not have a fucking head by then.'

Jackie Charles looked at the silent guards, standing by the door of the prison interview room. 'Are you threatening me, Inspector?'

McGuire flashed his best Latin smile. 'Not at all. I was just hinting at something you might have forgotten.

'Suppose this bright idea of yours actually works, and a

338

jury believes that you bribed our boss. He'll go down, undoubtedly: seven or eight years, probably, while you, as a Crown witness, will be immune from prosecution.

'The Scottish prison network isn't all that big. The odds against big Bob being sent here aren't all that great. Suppose you two wind up in the same nick. Have you considered what he might do to you?'

The first flicker of doubt showed through Charles's confident veneer. 'Why would he do that? He solicited the bribe. He only has himself to blame.'

McIlhenney grunted. 'I know big Bob a bit better than you, Jackie. He might not see it that way. And the Inspector's right, you know. He's got a real nasty streak to him. Christ, if he could put big Lenny Plenderleith in hospital, what's he going to do to you?'

'Let's just go over this story of yours one more time,' said McGuire.

Charles sighed. 'Really!'

'Humour us. Just one more time.'

'Oh, very well. But just once more and that's it. Your great Skinner approached me last year. We go way back, you know, Bob and I. He thought, rightly, as it turned out, that one of your guys might be on the take. I made enquiries about some things that my wife and Dougie Terry were doing, and found that he was right. Into the bargain, I found out that I was in some trouble.

'So I went back to Bob, and I gave him the name of your bad apple. I also suggested, very obliquely, that there might be something in it for him, if he could limit my personal damage.' He looked at McGuire and McIlhenney, his eyes wide and innocent. 'To my surprise, he came back to me and said that his terms were a hundred thousand cash, payable in accordance with instructions in a sealed envelope. He told me that it contained the address of a bank, and a copy of his signature and personal details.

'In return, he said that charges against me would be limited to tax offences, and that I would do a year, eighteen months at the most.'

'And you agreed to pay this backhander?' asked McIlhenney.

'Yes. I decided that it was a worthwhile investment. So I gave the envelope, unopened, to Douglas and told him to make it work. Two days later, he came back to me and told me that the arrangements had been made, and gave me the name of the bank to which the money had been sent.'

'Why did you decide to shop him now?'

Charles smiled, grimly. 'When I heard about the publicity over Bob's private life, it occurred to me that his feet of clay had been exposed. So I decided to drop a word.

'I didn't intend that it should get back to me, of course. I thought that evidence of the payment would be enough.'

McGuire leaned forward, forearms on the table. 'How did you get that word to the Lord Advocate?' he asked. 'We know you didn't phone his office from here; that would have been picked up.'

Charles hesitated, for the first time, taken aback by the question. 'I found someone from Edinburgh who was being released first thing next day,' he replied at last, 'and gave him an anonymous note addressed to the Crown Office.'

'Handwritten? Suggesting that someone should look at the JZG Bank in Guernsey?'

'That's right.'

'What was the name of the man who dropped the note for you?'

Charles shrugged. 'I can't remember. He was just another inmate.'

'His name wasn't Salmon, was it?' asked McIlhenney. 'Noel Salmon?'

The prisoner hesitated again. 'Yes,' he said, finally, 'that was it.'

The two policemen looked at each other, smiling. 'Interview suspended,' said McGuire, reaching across to switch off the tape recorder on the table. 'Jackie,' he grinned, 'you've blown it. Twice. Noel Salmon delivered the message all right, but he was never in here. He should have been, but he wasn't.

'He didn't deliver it to the Crown Office, either, but to the Secretary of State, and because his boss told him to, not you. You're a liar, Charles, and if you go into the witness box to tell that fairy story about Bob Skinner, we'll destroy you with what's on that tape.

'There aren't too many perjury trials, but when they happen, the judges are always tough. We can also charge you right now, through that tape, with giving false information to the police.'

McGuire's smile vanished completely. His eyes hardened, as he leaned forward, and focused on the man across the table. 'This is a once-only offer, Jackie. You may withdraw the statement you gave Cheshire and Ericson, and you withdraw it right now. You may admit that you have no knowledge of and had no involvement in the opening of the Guernsey bank account.

'You can do that right now, and no action will be taken against you. Persist, and I doubt if those suits will still fit, by the time you get out. They'll certainly be well out of fashion. Now, which is it to be?'

Charles looked at him for around ten seconds, unwavering. Then, without warning, his eyes dropped, he sighed and he nodded.

McGuire reached across and switched on the tape once more. 'Interview resumed. Detective Inspector McGuire and Detective Sergeant McIlhenney present in Perth Prison, with John Jackson Charles.'

72

For all her natural confidence and self-belief, and for all her involvement in her father's defence team, Alex still felt slightly overawed when she was summoned to the office of the head of the partnership. The call, from Mitchell Laidlaw's secretary, came just after 4.30 p.m.

The unexpected presence of Christabel Innes Dawson QC did nothing to calm the nerves tugging at her stomach.

'You sent for me, Mr Laidlaw?' she asked.

'Yes, Alex, Miss Dawson thought it would be good for you to sit in on our consultation. I'm sorry, I really should have advised you that she was coming in to see us.'

'I enjoy the odd touch of opulence,' the old lady rumbled. 'Honestly, I only wish I could take all the people who go on about fatcat advocates and parade them through offices like this one.' She glanced at Skinner's daughter.

'D'you intend to come to the Bar, young lady?'

'I've given it some thought.'

'Hmm. Then look around you, and give it some more. Damned hard work, damned little recognition. Of course, I suppose in these times you would have the opportunity to become a judge, if you were good enough. That path was closed to me.' She looked more than a little angry at the recollection, giving Alex a sudden picture of a tiny gimlet-eyed figure in an ermine-trimmed red robe, glaring down at the court.

'Well,' she said, fearlessly, 'I for one am glad that you'll be in the well of the court and on our side, when my dad's case is called.'

The old lady smiled. 'Thank you for that compliment, miss. But you really should say "if", not "when". We've just had a very surprising call.'

Laidlaw nodded. 'That's right. From the Procurator Fiscal, no less. It seems that John Jackson Charles has withdrawn the statement which he gave Cheshire and Ericson.'

She looked at him, astonished and delighted simultaneously. 'He has? But why?'

'It seems that your fiancé sent a couple of heavies to talk to him. "To clear up a discrepancy" was how they put it. It seems that it was big enough to persuade him to alter his recollection of events.'

'I don't suppose my dad had anything to do with it, did he?'

Mitchell Laidlaw smiled, beatifically. 'That's right, my dear,' he said. 'Don't suppose.'

'How did the Fiscal take it?'

'I've known him to be more cheerful,' Christabel Dawson replied. 'He has decided to postpone tomorrow's scheduled court appearance, to allow him to discuss the position with the Lord Advocate. I gather that young Archie is a bit miffed that Mr Martin's persuaders promised Charles that there would be no consequences if he withdrew his statement.'

'Cheshire's furious, too,' said Laidlaw.

'He's got no damn right, then,' barked Miss Dawson. 'The man obviously let slip far too much information about the allegation the first time he interviewed Charles. He let him know the amount, the time, the name and the location of the bank. The awful man was clever enough to build his original story around facts gleaned from them.

'Your fiancé's chaps seem to have been much more subtle.'

'Where will the Crown go from here?' asked Alex.

The ancient silk allowed herself a thin smile. 'Maybe nowhere. Charles's behaviour has attached a bad smell to their side, somehow.'

Laidlaw leaned forward in his chair, smiling agreement. 'Yes. Into the bargain, Alex, I was getting strange vibes from your father today. Even before Charles decided to withdraw his evidence, with things looking fairly black, he was still oddly confident. Although he didn't say anything to confirm it, I felt as if he had something up his sleeve.

'I've no idea what it could be, but I felt that it might be pretty devastating.'

Alexis Skinner laughed, seized by a sudden and almost overwhelming relief. 'Indeed,' she said. 'I rather think I know those vibes. When my father starts playing his cards close to his chest, then it usually means that someone's in for it, and no mistake.'

73

'There won't be any repercussions for you, will there, Andy? After all, the Secretary of State did appoint Cheshire to handle the enquiry. Could you be disciplined for intervening?'

'I suppose it's possible, love, but I hardly think so. Al Cheshire's interview with Charles was downright sloppy work. All he succeeded in doing was getting him to give false evidence against Bob.'

Martin smiled at his fiancée across the table, over the debris of a meal which for once they had completed uninterrupted. 'Mario and Neil did good work though. I played their tape to Cheshire this afternoon, once he'd calmed down enough to listen to it. After a while he conceded that he'd assumed too much when he interviewed Charles, and left himself wide open to being conned.'

'What will he do next?'

'He's doing it already. He and Ericson are writing up their final report to the Lord Advocate. Once it's submitted, they're off home.'

'What do you think it'll say?

'I know from Cheshire what it'll say.' He grinned. 'I shouldn't really tell you, since you're acting for the accused, but I'll chance it. They will report that even without Charles's admission, there's still a strong case to answer. The money exists; the sample signature exists; the note exists. Without using Jackie as a witness, the Crown could try to imply a connection between the

Charleses – either him or Carole – and your dad.'

Alex nodded. 'Fair enough, but we'll be able to introduce Charles's withdrawal of his statement to undermine that.'

'Agreed,' said Andy. 'Yet Cheshire and Ericson will suggest to Lord Archibald that the public interest requires that charges should be brought, and the matter put to the jury, if for no other reason than to try to answer one of the key questions.'

'What's that?'

'Whose is the money? The account is in Bob's name, beyond question. But without the Charles statement or another to replace it, it only becomes a bribe, and thus forfeit, if the jury says it is. If he's tried and acquitted, then I reckon that legally, the money's his.'

She smiled. 'Just as well. He'll need it to pay our fees.

'What's your gut feeling, though, Andy? Do you think the prosecution will still go ahead?'

Martin sighed. 'Yes, on reflection I think it will. The police service cannot afford to be seen to be sweeping anything under the carpet. After all the publicity this business has had, if it was simply dropped, with no prosecution being brought against anyone, that's exactly what would be said.'

74

The post lady was early on a Wednesday also, but Skinner was showered and shaved by seven fifteen, ready and waiting when he heard the loud metallic bang, as the spring-loaded letter-box cover snapped back into place. He was alone, having suggested to Pamela that she should spend the night in Leith, to be in promptly for her last day at the Fettes headquarters.

A bowl, empty save for traces of milk and one sad, solitary cornflake, and a half-finished mug of coffee lay on the table before him as he scanned the *Scotsman* for any reference to the charges laid against him less than twenty-four hours before. To his satisfaction there was none. Both Lord Archibald and Davie Pettigrew had promised him secrecy until the moment of his first court appearance, and they had been as good as their word.

Reading the newspaper, which led with a report of widespread demonstrations against a terrorist murder in Spain, he still felt the cold burning anger which had gripped him as Pettigrew had recited the formal charge, that he had corruptly accepted a payment of one hundred thousand pounds from a person then under investigation in respect of serious offences.

He felt no surprise at all, only an eager satisfaction, when he saw the Jiffy bag, with its handwritten address, a twin of the earlier package, except that this time, the postmark was sharp and legible. He looked at it, and noted with interest that the padded envelope had been posted in

Inverness on the day before. 'So he's taken them north,' he said to himself.

He carried the parcel through to the kitchen, and opened it in exactly the same way in which he had unfastened the first, taking the same precautions. However, when the contents of the bag finally fell on to the counter it was, as he had expected, a second tape cassette.

Quickly he slid it into his hi-fi deck, and pressed the play button. The pips broke the silence of the room. 'This is BBC Radio Four . . .' the announcer began. The Monday news headlines included reports of half a million people on the streets of Bilbao in a mass demonstration, and of the relatively peaceful passage of Orange Marches in Ireland.

As the second story reached its conclusion the radio faded, and Mark McGrath's voice, frightened but controlled, rose once more. 'Uncle Bob,' he shrilled. 'Mr Gilbert says I've to tell you some things. I've to tell you that Tanya's here. She's too frightened to speak, and she cries all the time, but she's here.

'The next thing I've to say is that Mr Gilbert wants a million pounds each for Tanya and me, from the Guv'mint. He says it's to be paid into the bank that you know, the one in . . .' The child paused as the noise of a low-flying aircraft threatened to drown out his voice: '. . . in Gernzie.' He said the name awkwardly and with difficulty, as if he had needed coaching.

'It's to be paid in at exactly ten o'clock on Friday morning.' There was a pause: in the background Skinner could hear a murmur, and the sound of a second child crying. Mark went on. 'Mr Gilbert says I've to tell you that it's money he's owed by the Guv'mint, and that if you ask, you'll find out why. He says that if it isn't paid, you know what'll happen.'

'That is right, Mr Skinner.' The cold, flat voice broke in, suddenly and unexpectedly. 'You know, exactly. And afterwards, there will be more.'

The detective stared at the tape as it went dead. Then he rewound it and searched through it, replaying the same section over and over again, putting a face to a voice, and making certain also that the thing which even he had believed unthinkable must after all be true.

75

Skinner burst into the CID office like an avenging angel, sweeping past Pam with a nod and a wave, and beckoning Sammy Pye to follow.

'It's here, Andy,' he said to the surprised Martin, waving a cassette. 'The contact I've been expecting since Saturday. This has got to go to London too. Sammy, it's your turn for the Shuttle. I'll give you the address and contact name.

'Now both of you, listen to this.' He walked across to Martin's player and put the tape into the slot. Big Ben, followed by Mark McGrath's shrill young voice, filled the office.

'Did you hear?' he asked, when it was finished. 'The bank that I know. The one in Guernsey. I'd thought that it couldn't be possible, Andy, but it's true. The kidnapper and the courier are one and the same man. It has to be. None of that stuff has been in the public domain in any way.'

The Head of CID nodded as Skinner wrote Caroline Farmer's name and the M15 office address on a pad on his desk. 'Has to be, but how about the rest of it?'

'Later, Andy, later.' He handed the note and the original of the tape to Pye. 'Get yourself a travel warrant and get going now, Sam. Tell the lady I want a full analysis as usual – with a voice analysis to confirm that the man at the end is the same as in the telephone call to my house.

'Come on, shift!'

As the young constable bolted from the room, Skinner turned back to the Chief Superintendent. 'There's something else, Andy.' He picked up the telephone and called Ruth McConnell. 'Ruthie,' he barked, without pleasantries. 'Find big McIlhenney, and get him down here.'

Martin looked at him as he replaced the phone. There was a new edge to his friend, beyond the underlying confidence which Mitch Laidlaw had described to Alex, and which he had observed himself. This was cold, hard and lethal, and he had seen it before.

'Mr Gilbert's made a mistake,' said Skinner. 'You heard the plane on that tape? It was a jet, a military aircraft, flying very low and flat out from the noise, and the duration. Yet it was after ten in the evening; gathering dusk if not dead of night.

'There are very few places in Scotland where aircraft are allowed to fly at that height, and that late. Every one of those flights is logged and recorded in detail.' He paused, and smiled. 'When I saw Everard Balliol on Sunday, he went on at some length about low-flying jets over his castle. He told me that the RAF agreed to move the route ten miles to the north. Even so, part of that training run probably still goes over his land.'

Martin started. 'You don't think Balliol . . .'

Skinner laughed. 'Everard needs a million pounds about three and a half thousand times less than you and I. That's how many of them he's got already. Besides, he's a man who thinks that all rapists and paedophiles should be castrated.'

He turned as Detective Sergeant McIlhenney came into the room. 'I owe you and McGuire a big drink, Neil,' he said, 'but it'll have to wait. For now, I want you to get up to RAF Leuchars. Have them plot the route of every plane they had in the air on Monday night, and show you on the map where each one was at exactly fifty seconds past ten.

'Then, I want you to bring that map back here.'

'Very good, boss.'

As the Sergeant headed for the door, Skinner followed, beckoning to Martin. 'Now it's our turn, Andy, yours and mine. Let's leave my lovely Pamela in charge of CID, while you and I go for another consultation with Christabel Innes Dawson, QC.

'She'll enjoy meeting you again, and this time, you might too.'

76

The old advocate looked at Martin. 'You have done well for yourself, young man,' she said. 'I'm willing to bet too that you've never again been as bad in the witness box as you were that day.'

'I hope not, Miss Dawson. You taught me a lesson. It's a long time ago, though. You have a remarkable memory.'

'Not at all, Chief Superintendent. Counsel rarely score such a comprehensive victory over police witnesses. When we do, it sticks in the mind.'

Skinner laughed. 'You didn't get your client off, though, did you? Or had that detail slipped your mind?'

She frowned at him. 'No, it had not,' she snapped. 'You may well find yourself hoping that history does not repeat itself.'

'I do indeed, Miss Dawson. But let's wait and see whether we actually get to court, shall we?' He went on. 'We're not here to talk to you about my case though. I want to search your memory of the trial in which you crucified poor Andy here.

'You see, although I was the chief police witness in that one, I didn't lead the investigation. Andy and I were drafted in to help the burglary unit because of the sensitive nature of the enquiry, and because the Superintendent who ran it, Mr O'Riordan, was on the list for a back operation when it happened. He did the lead work. All I really did was give evidence.'

The old lady nodded. 'I seem to recall that. I tried to

challenge you, but John was forced to concede that you were a competent witness.'

'Your client,' asked Skinner. 'What do you remember of him? Didn't he have a German surname?'

'You are correct,' said Miss Dawson. 'His name was Heuer. That's H. E. U. E. R. His father was German, and his mother Scottish, but he took his mother's nationality. Even served in the British Army for a short while. Strange that he should have turned into a burglar.'

'Yes. He was caught breaking into the Polish Consul General's residence in Edinburgh, not far from our headquarters building. He didn't really have much of a defence, did he?'

'No,' the ancient silk agreed. 'But he insisted on pleading Not Guilty. He seemed to think that the charges would be dropped. Eventually, when he agreed to make a statement, he gave the oddest evidence on his own behalf. He tried to say that he had entered the wrong house, by mistake, as if that would affect the relevance of the complaint.'

Skinner smiled. 'I remember hearing the first part of your examination. You did your best.'

She looked at him frostily. 'As I do always. But he was guilty, and the fact that he was armed added to the severity of John's sentence. Eight years, as I recall.'

The detective produced a tape player from his case and placed it on the table. 'Think of that voice in the witness box,' he asked. 'Could this be him?'

He pressed the play button and the recording of the Saturday night call to his cottage filled the consulting room. Miss Dawson sat up, sharply, her ears twitching like a mouse. 'Let me hear it again,' she commanded. Skinner rewound the tape, and played it once more.

'Oh yes,' said Christabel Innes Dawson QC. 'That's him all right. That's Heuer. Peter Gilbert Heuer.'

77

'I'd forgotten everything about him,' said Andy Martin, back in his office.

'So had I,' Skinner agreed. 'But why should either of us have remembered? Neither you nor I ever interviewed him: we only handled the support players. We were hauled off drugs work to do it, remember, and we were pissed off about it.

'But when Christabel came on the scene as my Counsel, and we started to talk about it, I began to have an itch about something. When I heard his voice on the tape this morning, insistent, angry, as it was in court, I was almost sure. If the old dear hadn't picked him from the first message, I'd have played her the other, but she knew him well, knew all sides of him.'

He looked at the case notes on Martin's desk. 'It reads oddly, doesn't it. He was caught in the Polish Consul's house, with a gun, and some of the Consulate silver in a bag, yet at first he wouldn't make any statement. All the notes say that he was arrogant and confident, yet silent as the grave, until the case was almost ready for trial.

'It reads as if he thought someone was going to spring him.

'He acted that way in court too. But if you recall, my evidence was about how the technicians had found his prints on the disabled alarm, and about how he had activated the second system, linked direct to Fettes, that he hadn't known about.

'When I was finished, he knew that he was done for. Thinking back, I remember the way he looked at me, when I stepped down from the box. Pure hatred. It was as if I had been sent along as his executioner.'

He paused, and picked up the notes. 'When Heuer was arrested, he gave his address as Cromden, in Derbyshire. I'm sure if we had time, we'd find that recently he's been living somewhere in Edinburgh, maybe as Mr Gilbert. You should put Dan Pringle's team on to checking that, but let's not base our hopes on that.

'I left Bruce Anderson to consult the Prime Minister about payment of the ransom. I think that he'll agree.'

'But how will Heuer collect it?' asked Martin.

'He won't leave it in Guernsey, that's for sure. It'll be forwarded to another bank, and maybe one or two more after that, till it reaches its final destination. I'd guess it'll go somewhere we've no jurisdiction, where Heuer can pick it up and disappear for good.'

'And the kids?'

Skinner looked at him. 'You have to ask? He'll kill them, Andy, if he hasn't already. At best – ' he checked his watch – 'we have forty-seven hours to find them. And we can't do anything until Neil gets back from RAF Leuchars.'

Skinner threw open the door of Martin's office. 'I hate hanging around, Andy,' he called from the doorway. 'I'm going off to make a phone call. After that, I'm going to find Noel Salmon, take him into a quiet corner and find out exactly what he knows about all of this.

'Once McIlhenney gets back, with a bit of luck, we'll have a good idea of where to look for Mr Peter Gilbert Heuer. Given that, then tomorrow we'll take him, and pray that the children are still alive.'

'I hate to remind you, Bob,' said Martin, 'but you're still suspended.'

'Bugger that. When we run this bastard to ground, I'm going to be there, and no fucking politicians are going to stop me.' He paused. 'Anyway, I called in to see Bruce Anderson, just after eight, on my way in here. I played him that tape, and this time I let him lift my suspension when he offered.'

He looked across the room. 'Before I forget, Pammy, come out to Gullane tonight. After all, you start your new job tomorrow. Somehow or other, we must fit in dinner to celebrate that.'

78

Skinner sat behind his desk for the first time in days. It felt secure and comfortable as always, not defiled at all by its temporary occupancy by Algernon Cheshire.

He picked up the telephone, and dialled McIlhenney's mobile number. Road noise almost drowned the Sergeant's voice as he answered.

'Neil,' he said, in something approaching a shout. 'A slight change of plan. If you get a result up at Leuchars, meet me at Fairyhouse Avenue. Got that?'

'Understood, sir.' There was not a hint of a question in his assistant's voice.

Skinner replaced the phone and picked up another. From a book which he never left in the office, he selected another number. 'Yes?' said the voice at the other end of the secure line, knowing that wrong numbers can happen anywhere.

'Adam,' snapped Skinner tersely. 'It's Bob here.'

'Hello mate.' All of a sudden, the Derbyshire accent was warm and friendly. 'How are you doing? And 'ow's that lovely wife of yours?'

'Living in America,' said Skinner, even more shortly than before. 'I'm with another lady now. Don't you read the *Spotlight*? Have you been abroad for the last couple of weeks?'

'As a matter of fact, I have. But still, I mean, Jesus Christ, Bob. You and Sarah?' Adam Arrow was rarely knocked off balance, in any respect.

'No time for explanations, Adam. I need a favour, very fast.'

'If I can.'

'Let's hope. I want you to try a name for me. Peter Gilbert Heuer. Mixed German-UK parentage. A few years ago he was nicked in the Polish Consul's residence in Edinburgh with a gun and a bag which more or less had "swag" written across it.

'I was young and naive then, but now I don't believe for one second that he was a burglar. I need to know what he was there for, who sent him, and what his deal was meant to be.'

'Okay,' said Arrow. 'I'll try. Why's this name come up all of a sudden? Can you tell me?'

'Sure. Mr Heuer seems to have diversified into stealing politicians' children and selling them back to the Government for a million pounds a time.'

'I see. I've heard about that all right. Let's not hang about then. Where can I get back to you?'

'Use my mobile number. We've no time for niceties, even if the MI5 snoopers might overhear something that could be hazardous to their health.'

79

Noel Salmon was easy to find. There was no answer to the doorbell of his seedy flat, when Skinner rang it, but a single phone call to John Hunter established that the *Spotlight*'s former ace reporter could be found on most mornings in a pub called the Eastern, not far away.

Skinner knew it well. It was the type of place where knives were regarded as fashion accessories.

The journalist had his back to the door as Skinner opened it. The two men's eyes met in the mirror behind the bar, but before Salmon had time to react, far less to run, the policeman reached across, seized his collar from behind and hauled him out into the street, into the summer rain. 'Your place, or mine?' he hissed. 'Yours I think, this time. More discreet and I don't mind making a mess there.'

He hustled his helpless captive along the wet pavement as fast as he could, away from the Eastern, as the first curious morning drunks lurched out to see what was happening. Together they turned a corner, and found themselves almost at the stairway to Salmon's building.

The policeman was barely breathing hard when they reached the fourth-floor doorway, yet the little man's chest was heaving. 'Open it,' Skinner snarled. Salmon tried to obey, but he could only fumble for his key and poke it ineffectively at the lock, with a shaking hand. Impatiently, the detective tore it from his grasp, opened the door, and threw him roughly inside, sending him tumbling and falling along the floor of the hallway.

The quarry scrambled to his feet, completely terrified now. 'You . . . you . . . you . . .' he wailed. To Skinner's disgust, his former tormentor wet himself.

'Through there,' he ordered. 'The living room, if that's what you call it.' Salmon obeyed and collapsed, helpless, into a chair.

'There are no lawyers about now, Noel,' snarled the policeman. 'Not a soul in fact, just you and me, and this place being where it is, no-one will remember having seen us on our way up here.'

He crossed to the sash-cord window and pulled it up, tugging hard and opening a gap of around two feet. 'Know what defenestration means, cockroach?' he asked.

Salmon gaped at him, speechless.

'It means jumping or being thrown out of the fucking window. And that is just about where I am with you. You've given me grief, son, and now you're going to find out just how stupid you've been.

'I'm not going to thump you around or anything. It's as simple as this: you either give me the name of the person who tipped you off about Pam and me, and who gave you the info on this bribe set-up, or out you go. Splat. You'll be back on the front page again, only as a headline, not a byline.

'A drunken suicide, it'll be. There won't even be a Fatal Accident Inquiry.'

Skinner seized the reporter by the collar once more, jerked him upright and hauled him, whimpering, over to the wide-open window. 'I know it was one of two people. I think I know which, and I'm certain you do too. For your sake, I hope I'm right about that.

'So what's it to be?' he asked, and Noel Salmon found

himself with no reason to doubt the sincerity of his question. 'Are you talking or flying?'

80

Skinner was in his dressing-gown as he opened the door of the Fairyhouse Avenue bungalow. For once in his life, Sergeant McIlhenney looked nonplussed.

The DCC laughed. 'Relax, Neil, it's all right. I'm alone. I just felt the need of a shower and a change of clothes, that's all. Go into the kitchen and make us a couple of coffees. The milk in the fridge should be okay. I'll be with you by the time you're done.'

He was as good as his word. McIlhenney turned from the counter and handed him a steaming mug as he walked into the room, dressed in a black teeshirt and light cotton trousers.

'Did you get caught in the rain, boss?'

'No. Not for long, anyway. The company I was in made me feel unclean, that's all. I've seen the last of the wee bastard though. He decided to take a flight.'

The Sergeant looked at him curiously. 'Mr Salmon's going to make a fresh start in London. I persuaded him that Edinburgh was too small a place for his talents to blossom.'

'He'll be able to walk on to the plane, will he?'

'Walk! I reckon he'll run up the steps. So, Neil, how did you get on at Leuchars?'

His assistant beamed his satisfaction. 'Score one for us,' he answered. 'You were right. Or if you weren't, those planes were Russian. The CO up there was a bit coy at first, until I explained to him that if he didn't co-operate, you'd arrange for the Secretary of State to shit on him from a great height.

'From what he said, he had good reason to be coy. They've been running secret tests out of Leuchars at night, on a new radar system, using it to try to keep track of American Stealth fighters. You know, those Star Wars-looking things. It was one of them you heard on the wee boy's tape.'

'And was the course plotted?'

McIlhenney nodded. 'Oh aye, boss. Both by the radar system and by the plane's on-board system.'

He took a map from the pocket of his jacket and spread it on Skinner's kitchen work-surface. 'We timed the noise from the Big Ben chimes on the tape to within a couple of seconds. When the recorder picked it up, it was right here, travelling from east to west.'

He leaned over the map, and pointed to an oval, drawn in blue ballpoint ink, with an arrow indicating direction. 'This is a detailed Ordnance Survery map, boss. The flight-path at that point went over a valley called King's Gully. It's twelve miles north of your man Balliol's place, on Loch Mhor.

'There's nothing but hills between the two, but the map shows a couple of cottages in King's Gully itself.'

'Yes,' Skinner hissed. 'I think tomorrow morning we'll pay a call.'

As he spoke, his mobile phone, which he had laid on the counter, began to ring. He picked it up and answered, walking towards the back door and out into the garden. 'Skinner.'

'Me,' said Adam Arrow, tersely. 'Your man is known to certain people down here. If he's done what you say, then they are very, very angry with him.

'I'm authorised to tell you about him. Also I have a very specific request for you: a request, not an order. If you feel you'd rather not, then I'll come up to handle the matter, but the belief is that it should be dealt with locally if possible, and I've told them that you're more than capable.'

Skinner felt the hair prickle at the back of his neck. 'Is this your request?' he asked. 'Or does it come from someone else?'

'Oh yes,' Arrow replied. 'This doesn't come from me or my boss, or even his boss. It comes from the very top man. From everyone's boss.

'Now, let me tell you about your man.' The big detective listened, his face growing harder by the second.

Skinner was thinking fast when he walked back into the kitchen.

'I've been wondering, sir,' said McIlhenney. 'If we're going after this man, shouldn't we let the Northern Force know about it? King's Gully's on their patch.'

'You're right, Neil,' said the DCC. 'We should. But we're not going to.'

He took the kitchen telephone from its wall bracket and dialled the Head of CID's direct line. 'Andy,' he said, as soon as the call was answered, 'I want you to meet me at headquarters at six thirty. Don't discuss it with anyone, not even the Chief, but make sure that the sports field is clear. There's an army helicopter coming to pick us up . . . just you and me, that is. I'll be there sharp, but I've something to do between now and then.'

'Understood. Is there any equipment that you want me to draw?'

'No,' Skinner replied. 'The army's providing suitable clothing and boots. Your size and mine. Other items too. Everything we'll need will be on the chopper.'

81

He was in the bathroom when he heard the key in the lock. The door opened and closed quickly, then light footsteps crossed the living room.

He dried his hands, listening with a soft smile as he heard drawers and doors sliding, and general sounds of rushing around.

Silently, he stepped out of the bathroom, grinning as he stood in the doorway of Pamela's bedroom. 'Christ,' he chuckled, 'haven't you got enough clothes out at my place already? Did Andy let you go early? It's just gone four o'clock.'

With her back to the door, she jumped at the sound of his voice. 'Bob,' she cried. 'I almost died.' She turned to face him, looking flushed. 'What are you doing here? I thought you said you'd see me at Gullane.'

He shrugged. 'Call of nature, madam, like we used to say when I was in uniform. I was nearby, so I answered it here.'

'I didn't notice your car,' she said, recovering her composure. 'As you guessed, I just looked in to pick up one or two more things.'

He laughed. 'In a suitcase?' He shook his head. 'Love, why don't you just admit it?'

Her eyes narrowed slightly, and her face flushed again as she looked at him, quizzically. 'Admit what?'

'That you're moving in with me, piece by piece, dress by dress, shoe by shoe, tight by tight, knicker by knicker.'

Her face lit up as she grinned, gauchely, like any young girl in love. 'Well,' she said, 'now that I'm transferring to another force, now that, hopefully, I don't have to feel threatened by this madman, isn't it time that you . . .'

Bob chuckled again. 'Ah, you mean – like I said to Andy – that I made an honest woman of you . . .'

'Well?' she asked, with an expectant tone in her voice.

His grin widened into a broad smile. Then she looked into his eyes, and was hit like a hammer by the truth of something that she had been told, once before: that he was the most dangerous man she had ever seen.

'Pamela,' he said, quietly, still smiling, but deadly and cold. 'Quite literally, I couldn't make an honest woman of you to save your life. It's way beyond that.

'You're my implacable enemy, my so-called love. I was more baffled and bewildered than I've ever been, trying to find the person who wanted to finish me, and yet all the time, I was sleeping with her.

'Even though in the end he was desperate to tell me all about it, I didn't actually need Noel Salmon to admit to me that it was you who tipped him off about our being together, or gave him the bribe information.' He caught her gasp. 'Never underestimate anyone, even a weasel like him. Not even he is going to take an anonymous tip without at least trying to check the source.'

He pushed himself upright, off the doorframe. 'Remember, when you called him and dropped that note for him in the dustbin near the Norwegian Memorial in Princes Street Gardens? He went there early, and watched you drop it. He didn't know who you were, not then, until he saw the two of us together after he started watching us. When you dropped him the information about the bank account in the same way, he didn't need to follow you again.'

Skinner paused. 'At first, I wondered why anyone would pick a useless pissed-up wee twat like Salmon as a means of shafting me. But as soon as I knew it was you I worked that one out for myself. You were having it off with Alan Royston when I barred wee Noël from Fettes. You found out from him, on the pillow, which journalist hated me the most.'

His smile was all gone now. 'Come on, Pam, don't disappoint me. Protest your innocence.'

She looked at him, her once-soft eyes blazing. 'I can't. Because I can't believe what I'm hearing. I didn't realise you were so desperate that you could do something like this.'

'If you can't believe it,' he answered her, 'then why did you call KLM this afternoon and book a flight for Amsterdam at five forty-five this evening?' He eyed her evenly. 'Mario called me just afterwards, on my mobile, while I was in the garden at Fairyhouse.' He smiled cruelly at her surprise. 'Ever since I knew it was you, Special Branch have been bugging all your phones.

'That's what the suitcase is about, Pam.' She started to speak, but he silenced her with a single look.

'No. Don't interrupt me. You are in very great danger. Just listen.

'I knew it was you, my pet, because of two stupid mistakes you made. The first was when you slipped me a blank sheet of paper to sign when you were my executive assistant. For a second or two, I actually believed my own story, that I had given someone my autograph. Then I remembered that when I do that I always sign myself "Bob Skinner". The full Monty signature, "Robert M. Skinner", that's reserved for official letters and for cheques.'

He shook his head. 'I should have known from the first

moment that I heard of the bribe allegation that it was an inside job. But there are some things that not even I'll face willingly. And I didn't, not until Alex brought me back my own signature from Guernsey.'

Skinner sighed, then went on, in a cold, even voice. 'The clincher came when you used Carole Charles's typewriter to type that note. You never believed for an instant, did you, that anyone would match the note to that machine?

'It was handy, a standard electric typewriter unconnected with the force, so you used it. After it was recovered from the flat in Westmoreland Cliff that Carole kept as a secret office, Neil and I brought it back to Fettes, and I put it in your room. It was there for a day or so until it went off to the production store. You had that time to use it.

'In the same way, as my assistant, you had every chance to hide that receipt in my desk later.

'If Cheshire hadn't found it, I suppose that eventually you'd have dropped a hint that he should look there. It would have been a clumsy, accidental hint of course,' he said sarcastically, 'and you'd have been appalled by the way it turned out.'

He paused. 'The typewriter was a huge mistake, really – far bigger than the signature, because who else could have used it? I knew I didn't. Not Neil McIlhenney, in a million years. Not Ruth McConnell, in the same million. Not Carole Charles, because she was dead when most of this happened. Not Jackie, because he didn't even know about the Westmoreland Cliff office, let alone about the bloody typewriter. In fact when Jackie did claim to have typed the note, the whole thing screamed out at me, and the last of my disbelief vanished.'

Skinner grinned again, cruelly. 'Think about it, Pam.

When was the last time that you and I made love? Before that note was tied to that typewriter. Ever since then, I've managed to have a headache.

'No, lady, only you could have used that machine to type the note. I didn't want to believe it. At first I wouldn't let myself. Not because I'm deep in love with you, because I'm not. No, because I didn't want to admit to myself that you could con me, and maybe because I didn't want to find out why.'

He began to move slowly, menacingly, towards her. 'Then something happened,' he said, slowly, 'that made everything else insignificant.

'When Cheshire and Alex came back from Guernsey with the suggestion that the man who made the cash delivery might have been the same man who killed Leona and Catherine Anderson, and kidnapped the kids, at first I dismissed it out of hand.

'But when Peter Gilbert Heuer sent me this morning's tape, that outlandish idea turned out to be the truth. I made sure you were in earshot when I said that, out loud, in Andy's office this afternoon. I wanted to see how you'd react. It didn't take you very long to call KLM.

'Because you know, Pamela, that Heuer's involvement in both plots makes all of this a whole different game, one with lives at stake, and maybe yours among them.'

He was standing over her now, as she backed towards the window. 'That thing he let slip, my dear, that he knew of the Guernsey bank, means that you are linked to Peter Gilbert Heuer. It means that you gave him my unlisted number in Gullane, just as you gave it to Salmon. Most of all it means that you are linked to the murder of two women and the kidnapping of their children.'

He gripped her by the arms, just below the armpits, and

he lifted her up, clear off her feet, to stare into her eyes, cold, hard and with menace.

'You must tell me now, Pamela,' he said, evenly. 'You have no choices left.' He lowered her to the ground, turned her around, and pushed her firmly towards the living room.

'You will tell me everything, because you are standing on ground more deadly than you know. And most of all . . .' for the first time, his tone betrayed his hurt, and huge disappointment, 'you will tell me . . . why?'

When she looked up at him, her eyes were almost as cold, as cruel as his. 'Why?' she repeated, in a calm, hard-edged voice which he had never before heard issue from her lips. But it reminded him at once of one that he had heard before, and had thought was silenced for ever.

'To take away your life,' she said. 'That's why. And, to quote you back at yourself, to look at the wreckage afterwards and say, "Quite fucking right too".'

82

'Sorry I'm late, Andy,' said Skinner stepping out of his car, parked at the rear of the headquarters building. The time was fifteen minutes to seven, and a green helicopter stood on the sports field, its blades still and drooping.

'S'okay,' said Martin. 'Our stuff's on the chopper.' They began to walk towards the aircraft. 'Did you do the business you mentioned?'

He nodded. 'I won't be seeing Pamela Masters again.' Martin's head swivelled round in surprise.

'The lady's been a fucking roadblock in my life, pal,' Skinner said, vehemently. 'But not any more.'

'A clean break, I hope?' asked Martin, tentatively.

'Oh yes, as clean as they come.' The younger man looked at him, puzzled again by both his tone and his mood. 'I'll tell you all about it later; for now let's get away in this contraption. Hello, Gerald,' he said, recognising the young lieutenant who stood by the helicopter door, and shaking hands before climbing in.

'Where are we going, sir?' the pilot asked. 'Mr Arrow only told me to report here. He said you'd have further orders.' Martin looked at Skinner in surprise at the mention of Arrow's name.

'That's right.' He produced McIlhenney's map. 'We're going to pay a call on a man named Everard Balliol at a castle on the shore of Loch Mhor. He doesn't know we're coming, though. I always think it best to surprise Everard. He thinks I'm all right, though. Especially since I let him beat me at golf.'

The pilot looked at the map, then at a larger chart spread out on the seat beside him. 'Okay, gentlemen,' he said. 'It looks simple enough. I'll file a flight-plan with Prestwick once we're in the air. I'd guess around an hour and a half, two hours. I should warn you though, there's a restricted area just to the north. That might be a problem, if there's military traffic expected.'

Skinner shook his head. 'I don't think so. Let's go.'

Conversation was difficult because of the noise of the engines, but Skinner managed to brief Martin on the intelligence gleaned by McIlhenney on his visit to Leuchars. 'If the cottages are on Balliol's land, as I think they are, he should be able to tell us who the occupants are, and hopefully some more besides.'

'Yes, let's hope so. Who's meeting us up there? A squad from Northern?'

The DCC shook his head. 'Nobody.'

'Eh?'

'This is down to us, Andy, just you and me.'

They sat in silence for the rest of the flight, looking at the scenery, as they crossed Stirlingshire to Crianlarich, then swung northward, skirting Ben Nevis and Fort William to the west, and following the jagged coastline. Finally, just before eight thirty, the pilot began his descent, until Balliol's castle came into view, a grey speck on the horizon at first, but growing larger and larger as they approached, along the banks of Loch Mhor.

'Set it down near Mr Balliol's own helicopter,' Skinner ordered, looking down and seeing two black-clad figures run out on to the castle terrace.

As the aircraft settled in the grass and as the blades began to slow in their rotation, the DCC saw Balliol himself emerge, from a small door not far from his study. He jumped down from the helicopter, and ran towards him.

'What the hell's this, Bob?' drawled the American, yet with the air of someone who had not been truly surprised for a long time.

Skinner shook his hand and introduced Martin, who had followed behind. 'Sorry to drop in unannounced like this, Everard, but this is important and we have to move fast. I need to know, does you estate include a place called King's Gully?'

The billionaire looked at him. 'Sure, and the land for ten miles north of that, five miles east and all the way west to the coast.'

'There are cottages in the Gully – two according to the map. Who lives there?'

'Christ, Bob, I don't know that. My estate factor deals with all that stuff.'

'Is he here?'

'No, he lives on the far side of the loch. Come on in, guys; I'll call him, and tell him to get round here.'

'Thanks,' said Skinner, 'and ask him also, if he has any plans of the King's Gully cottages, to bring them with him.'

'Yeah, okay.' He led the way into the house, and through to the study. 'Set three more places for supper,' he barked to one of the Koreans. 'No, make that four: I forgot about the pilot.'

'No,' said the DCC. 'He has to stay with the chopper. I'm sure he'd be pleased if you took something out to him, though.'

They were still in the study, but ready to eat when the estate factor's Land Rover drew up outside the study window, twenty minutes after Balliol's telephone summons. A tall, grey, weatherbeaten, tweed-clad man jumped down from the driver's seat and strode purposefully into the house, carrying a briefcase.

'Hi, Don,' called Balliol, as the newcomer appeared in the doorway of the study. 'This is Donald McDonald,' he announced to Skinner and Martin. 'He was here when I bought the place, but if he hadn't been I'd have hired him anyway, for his name alone.'

The billionaire waved his employee towards a seat, as two Koreans followed him into the room carrying trays laden with hamburger rolls and jugs of coffee. 'Don, these guys are policemen. They need to know about the cottages up in King's Gully. Like are they occupied, and if so, by whom?'

McDonald gave a thin smile. 'I can answer those questions.' His accent, like his name, was pure Highlands. 'You may have seen two cottages on the map, gentlemen, but one has been derelict for years.' He turned to Balliol. 'I've been meaning to talk to you, sir, about either demolishing it, or refurbishing it for rental.'

'Later, Don, later.'

'Very good. The cottage which is in habitable condition is rented to a single gentleman. His name is Gilbert Peters.'

'How long has he held the tenancy?' asked Martin.

'This time, these six months past.'

'This time?'

'Yes sir. A few years ago now, when my father was estate factor here and I was his assistant, in the time of Lord Erran, Mr Peters also rented the cottage. When he gave it up, we assumed we'd seen the last of him, but when he turned up again, I remembered him well enough.

'I had no hesitation about letting him have the place once more. My father used to comment on how good a tenant he was. Always paid his rent on time, by bank transfer, and always kept the place spotless. He even made a few improvements.'

'Such as?'

'Well, when he was here the first time he had the telephone put in. Since he's been back, he's painted the outside, and he's installed a television satellite dish.'

'What sort of car does he drive?' asked Skinner.

'Last time he came to see me it was a Subaru,' replied McDonald. 'Silvery grey in colour, four-wheel drive. You really need that here.'

'When did he come to see you last?'

'About four months ago, to ask if he could paint the place and install the dish.'

'And when did you last call on him?'

'I don't,' said the factor. 'My father and I have always held that good tenants have as much right to privacy as property-owners. I've seen the place from a distance, seen the repainting and the dish, but that's all. If Mr Peters invited me to call on him, I would, but otherwise no.

'Last time he was here, he used to invite my father and me up for a malt, on occasion, but that hasn't happened since he's been back.'

'What do you know about him?' asked the DCC.

'I know that he was a soldier, because when he rented the cottage the first time, my father took up the references he gave. I saw no need to do so this time.'

'Did he tell you where he'd been since he left?'

McDonald scratched his head. 'Not directly. But he implied that he'd been on service abroad. He did say that he'd retired from the Army, though. He didn't say what he's doing now.'

'I don't suppose that you'll know when he's there, and when he isn't?'

'No. The last time I looked into the Gully I didn't see his car, but he could have gone to Fort William to shop.'

'When was that?'

The factor scratched his head a second time, as if to aid his memory. 'A week ago last Friday,' he replied at last.

Skinner nodded. 'Okay. One last question, Mr McDonald,' he said. He reached into the back pocket of his jeans, and took out a small photograph, taken earlier from the folder on Peter Gilbert Heuer. He held it up. 'Is this Gilbert Peters?'

The grey man peered at the picture. 'Oh yes,' he nodded. 'It's not recent, more like from his first time here, but that's Mr Peters, all right.'

The two policemen looked at each other. 'Plans, Mr McDonald,' asked Martin. 'Do you have any plans?'

'Oh yes,' the factor answered, delving into his briefcase. He unfolded an old sheet of waxed paper. 'This goes back years, to the time that the electricity was installed, but it's still accurate. There have been no internal structural alterations to the cottage since then.'

He spread the plan on Balliol's desk. The four men stood around it, studying the layout. Mr McDonald pointed to a direction symbol in the top right corner. 'The front of the cottage faces south, across the King's Gully,' he said. 'To catch the sun. It is built more or less on the Gully floor.'

He took them through the layout. 'This is the front door, here, with a window to the left. There is a small entrance hall with a living room to the right and a bedroom to the left. At the back of the hall there are doors to the kitchen, bathroom and second bedroom.'

'Where's the back door?' asked the Chief Superintendent.

'Through the kitchen. There's a wee garden to the back, with a wee burn running through it.'

Skinner and Martin leaned over the plan, studying it in detail. 'How wide is the floor of the Gully?' asked the DCC.

'About two hundred yards. The cottage is in the centre of the basin.'

'How is it approached, normally?'

'By vehicle, from a rough track to the east.'

'And what's the terrain?'

'Bracken,' said the factor. 'Tall green bracken. None of the estate workers ever go into the Gully. There's no point. It's no use for pasture, so you don't get sheep or deer going in there either. Only rabbits. Mr Peters is free to shoot as many of them as he likes for the pot. There's a wee loch just to the north. He can fish that for trout if he wants, too.'

'Does he shoot, do you know?' Skinner interposed.

'I've never seen him, but I've heard shots that could only have been him. If it had been poachers, the keeper would have found their signs.'

'What sort of firearm? Shotgun?'

'No. Rifle, it sounded like.'

'Mmm, I see,' mused the detective.

'One more thing,' he asked. 'Can you remember where the phone is?'

'The telephone, sir? Yes, it's on a wee table by the front door, beneath the window.'

'Is that the only one, or are there extensions?'

McDonald shook his head. 'As far as I recall there's only the one, unless Mr Peters has put in more. But it would not be easy to do that, because it's an old-fashioned installation, not the kind they have today that you can unplug and move about.'

'Right,' said Skinner, pointing at the plan. 'The phone's

under this window. Can you remember, is there a curtain or a blind?'

'No, sir, there is not, or at least there has not been. The front door is solid, so there is only the window to catch the light.'

'That's good. That's very good,' said the DCC, almost to himself. He picked up a hamburger, glancing at his watch in the process. 'It's nine thirty, so there'll be some half-decent light left. Could you take us up towards the Gully, now, to a point about a mile short? So that we know how to get back there in the morning?'

McDonald glanced at Balliol, who nodded.

'Thanks,' said Skinner, taking his mobile phone from his belt, where it was clipped. 'Before we go, I must call my daughter. Will I get a signal up here?'

'Sure,' Balliol told him. 'I had a cell specially installed so I can be contacted anywhere on the estate, anytime.'

He stepped to the study window and dialled Andy and Alex's number. The signal was strong and her voice was clear when she came on line. 'That's good, love,' he said. 'I wasn't sure this thing would work up here. Andy and I have had to go up north. We'll be back tomorrow.'

'Okay, Pops. I know better than to ask why. Tell him to bring back some salmon.'

'Venison, more like. We're off hunting. See you.'

He reclipped the phone and turned to see Martin follow McDonald from the study. Only Balliol remained. 'See here, Bob?' he asked. 'What's this about?'

Skinner looked him in the eye, debating with himself for a moment or two. At last he decided. 'Your Mr Peters has killed two women and kidnapped their children. He's holding them for ransom, in your cottage. Pay-day is the day after tomorrow. Andy and I have to get those kids out before then. That's if they're still alive.'

The billionaire's sallow face went pale. 'I have done some things in my time,' he snarled. 'But women and children . . .' His eyes narrowed. 'You want my Koreans? They're damn good. Mercenaries. Night fighters.'

'Not good enough for this guy. He'll have the area around the place wired with traps and geophones so's he'd know as soon as they were within fifty yards. He'd kill the children for sure at that, then your Koreans, and he'd be off into the night.'

The big policeman looked at the American. 'If you could lend us a Land Rover tomorrow morning that would be good, but I don't want your men anywhere near the Gully. I don't want anyone around.

'I didn't have a firm plan, before I'd spoken to Mr McDonald, but I do now. If everything is as he said, it'll work.'

'And if it isn't . . .'

'Then, Everard, I will simply wait, for as long as it takes.'

'For what?'

'For a clear shot. Then I'll just kill the fucker.'

83

It was 7.45 a.m. as they left the Land Rover in the small copse beside the track which Donald McDonald had shown them the night before.

On the slow drive from the castle, where they had spent the night, and breakfasted with Balliol, Andy had asked Bob about Pamela, and about their split.

'Later, man, later. I'll tell you and Alex together. But for now we have to concentrate completely on what's to be done here.'

There were no estate workers about as they made their way north, up the climbing, winding track, towards the Gully. Nor would there be any. On Balliol's orders, McDonald would direct them all to work on the south side of Loch Mhor.

The two policemen were clad in the green trousers and pullovers which the Army had provided for them. Pouches hung on their belts, and each carried a short stubby assault carbine. Skinner's weapon was fitted on top with a cumbersome, awkward-looking device, with an eyepiece.

Even in the early morning cool, they were both sweating as, after a thirty-five-minute trek, they reached the slope which, as their map showed them, led up to King's Gully. As the factor had described it they could see that, near the top, the grass gave way abruptly to wavy green ferns.

Skinner waved to Martin to stop just at the point where the bracken began, the two of them sitting down, heavily, at the edge of the open grass.

'Okay, Andy,' he said. 'Once we've got our breath back, we'll get into position. You're clear on the plan?'

Martin nodded. He wore a dark green beret to hide his blond hair, and his powerful shoulders bulged in the tight battledress pullover. 'I take up position to the north, behind the house, no closer than one hundred yards away.'

'Right. With your two-way radio on receive. Listen and do as you hear me say. It'll take you longer to get in position than me. I'll wait fifteen minutes before I move in.'

Martin nodded, and snaked off eastward, keeping below the ridge of King's Gully. Skinner sat on the grass and waited, hefting his carbine, testing and re-testing the device on top. At last, with a final check of his watch he moved off, up towards the crest of the slope, diving into the thick bracken before it opened out into the bowl of the Gully.

He snaked forward slowly and carefully on his belly, taking care so that any disturbance of the thick ferns would look like no more than morning breeze. After a few yards he stopped, and peered through a gap in the undergrowth. He saw the cottage, exactly where the map had promised, and exactly as Donald McDonald had described it. At the side stood a silvery grey car, a hatchback, with a slightly bulbous rear.

He changed course, wriggling to the left of his original approach, parallel with the front of the cottage, careful not to go too close. At last he was in his chosen position, around one hundred yards away from the cottage, directly facing the front door and the wide green-framed window. He smiled. The window still had no curtain or blind.

From the pouch on the left side of his belt, he took out his two-way radio. 'Ready to go, Andy,' he said quietly, into its microphone.

Next, from the same pouch, he took his mobile phone

and laid it on the ground in front of him. Finally he removed a small head-set, with earpiece and mouthpiece, which he put on before plugging its lead into a socket in the phone casing.

Taking a deep breath he switched on his phone, then pressed the short code for the telephone number which he had programmed in the night before: the number which Donald McDonald had given him, the number of the King's Gully cottage.

The mobile's display lit up, green amidst the bracken. Skinner pressed 'Send', then hefted his carbine up to his shoulder, looking through his very special telescopic sight, and training it on the window beside the black-painted front door of the house.

He heard the ringing in his ear, once, twice, a third time. On the fourth ring a tall, slim, fair-haired figure stepped into the hall, from the left. He was wearing glasses. Framed in the window, Skinner saw him pick up the telephone.

'Good morning, Mr Heuer,' he said calmly and evenly, before the man could speak himself. 'Please don't move a muscle, other than to look down at your shirt. Just left of centre, where you heart is.'

Through the sight, he saw the man look down slowly at a small red dot on his shirt, a dot which was not printed on, yet which stayed rock-steady.

'That's good,' said Skinner. 'I think you might know what that dot is. Nod if you do.' Very slowly, Peter Gilbert Heuer nodded his head.

'That's right, it's the trace from a laser sight, mounted in this case on an H & K carbine, not very far away. I am very, very good with an H & K. My name's Bob Skinner, by the way. It's my turn to phone you now.

'As I'm sure you've worked out by now, Mr Heuer, if

you drop the phone, or make any attempt to move from the spot on which you're standing right now, that nice wee red dot will turn all of a sudden into a black hole and you will be dead.

'Now.' His voice became rock-hard. 'Where are the children?'

'They are in the kitchen.' Heuer's voice was still flat and calm, but no longer assertive.

'Are they alive?'

'Yes.'

'And they are alone? There is no-one else in the house?'

'No-one.'

'If there is, you're dead, whatever else happens. You know that, Heuer, do you?'

For the first time, the voice was less than calm. 'There is no-one. I swear.'

Skinner raised his voice, so that it would be picked up by the radio lying in front of him. 'Okay, Andy. Kids in the kitchen. Kick the back door in. Go. Go. Go. Fire two shots when you're clear.'

He held the sight on Heuer. 'If there's any unpleasant surprise waiting in there for my mate,' he said, 'I'll shoot your eyes out. Are you religious?' he asked suddenly, almost conversationally.

'No.' The voice was flat and calm once more.

'I'd give it some thought right now, if I were you. There are a few ghosts waiting for you on the other side. I asked about you, Peter, and now I know what your obsession is.'

He paused, studying Heuer's face through the sight, seeing it twitch, and watching his eyes shift around as he peered through the window into the sunlight.

'You're a contractor,' he pronounced at last. 'Or you were, until you cocked it up. You did wet jobs in the

386

intelligence community. You were an assassin, Peter, back then, when our paths first crossed.

'You didn't go into the Polish Consulate that night to steal the silver, did you? You went in to kill the Consul and his wife. Those were your orders. Our people were going to plant documents to make it look as if the Pole had been working for East Germany, and that the Stasi had killed him.

'The whole idea was to create a big stooshie within the Warsaw Pact, and give Solidarity a big shove forward.'

The red dot wavered on Heuer's white shirt, as a sudden tremor went through him. 'Careful,' called Skinner, and it steadied immediately. 'I told you, not as much as a twitch, boy.'

He paused. 'But you made an arse of it, Peter. You didn't do your homework. You missed the second alarm. Or by your way of it, you weren't told about it.

'For you decided that you'd been set up. You expected your paymasters to have you released on some technicality. But they felt that would be too risky, and that you'd have to do time for your mistake. Naturally, being a psychopathic type, you took it personally.

'But what I want to know is why you took it out on me, you cunt. I was only a poor innocent copper doing my job when I gave evidence at your trial.'

In the sight, he saw Heuer look out of the window, his eyes searching the bracken. 'No you were not,' he said. 'You were part of the plot. It was your evidence more than any other which had me convicted, and you lied in the witness box, Skinner. There never was a second alarm. There was a last-minute change of plan; someone at the top got cold feet.

'My own people tipped you off. By then, it was the only

way they could stop me. So they did, and then they left me to rot.'

Skinner laughed into the phone. 'How long did it take you to work that story out, Peter? Careful now,' he warned as Heuer reacted to his taunt.

'There was no plot to get you. Your mission was meant to succeed, but you fucked it up. Of course there was a second alarm. It was even visible too. A small line-of-sight transmitter on the roof, aimed directly into our communication tower at headquarters. It looked like a radio aerial, and that's what you thought it was.

'You can't accept the idea that you're fallible, can you, Heuer? You never could. That's why you were kicked out of the Army. They let you off then, when you departed from an operational plan in Argentina in 1982 and had two of your men killed. They let you resign, because the op was secret and they couldn't have a court martial. And because you had a special talent for killing people, they passed you on to the intelligence community.

'How many people did you kill for our side, and for the Americans? A couple of dozen, was it?'

As Skinner paused, two shots rang out around the Gully. He smiled. 'Free and clear,' he said. 'Mission accomplished. You've cocked it up again, Peter. You'll probably blame the RAF this time.

'Face it, at last, man,' he went on. 'You got yourself caught in the Polish Consul's house, before you had killed him, fortunately. You were nicked by three carloads of our people. A dozen of them. There was no way, with that number of witnesses, that anyone could get you out of it.

'For fuck's sake, you were even paid when you were inside, even though you'd botched the job. To keep you loyal, they thought.'

His voice hardened. 'You've been planning this for years, haven't you? You did your time, five years with parole, and even took on a couple of jobs when you came out four years ago. Yet all the time you were planning to make your bosses pay big-time for the years you did inside.'

Unexpectedly, Skinner chuckled, startling Heuer, making the red dot jump. 'They are not pleased with you this time, not at all. Do you know, they even asked me to kill you. They don't want any of this coming out in a trial, you see, so they asked me to do you in, very quietly, resisting arrest sort of thing.

'What d'you think of that?' he said, a shocked tone in his voice. 'Asking me, a policeman, to kill you. That's how much they want you dead.' He paused. 'No, Peter, no,' he said sharply. 'Don't move yet. Not till Andy and the kids are well clear. And keep the phone pressed to your ear.'

Through his own earpiece, he could hear Heuer's breathing, no longer even, but heavy and ragged, making the red dot seem to ripple on his shirt as he watched.

'Imagine, thinking that I'd do that,' he went on. 'Even though you terrified two kids out of their wits, and did things that may well scar them emotionally for life. I mean, did you hear Mark's voice when he learned from the radio that his mum was dead? And what about Tanya, after you blew her mum's brains out right in front of her?

'As for Leona, would you have raped and killed her, if she hadn't been someone you knew I was fond of? You were watching her house that Friday night, Peter, weren't you?

'Come on, I want an answer. You were watching, and you saw the bedroom light go on, isn't that right?'

'Yes!' cried Heuer.

The detective drew in a deep breath. 'Boy,' he said. 'You

must be thinking that all your Christmas days have come at once, right now. You must be thanking your luckiest star that it's a straight, idealistic, career copper like me holding this gun, and not someone like my mate Adam Arrow, who'd kill you in an instant.

'Nod once if I'm right.'

Slowly, the man in the gun-sight nodded.

Behind the carbine, Bob Skinner's face took on a cold, terrible expression as the memory of Leona McGrath's abused, battered, throttled corpse appeared in his mind's eye. 'Wrong, Peter,' he whispered. 'Sometimes life hands you a luxury you can afford.' The red dot swept upwards to the centre of Heuer's forehead.

'Say hello to Ross for me.' He squeezed the trigger.

84

Martin and the two children were waiting at the foot of the hill south of the Gully as Skinner reappeared over its crest, after pressing Heuer's pistol into his hand, and squeezing off one shot into the wall beside the window just as Arrow had told him to do.

Mark came running towards him. 'Uncle Bob! Uncle Bob!' he cried out. 'I told Tanya that it'd be all right. I told her that you'd come to get us.'

Skinner swept him up in his arms, and carried him off back down the hill towards Andy and the white-faced, shocked little girl. 'And you were right, weren't you? Just like you always are.'

'Tanya's awful frightened, Uncle Bob.'

'She's had every right to be. So have you, although I don't suppose you were.'

'Well . . .' Mark began. 'What about the man, Mr Gilbert?' he asked. 'He won't come back, will he?'

'No, son. Mr Gilbert's dead. I told him not to do anything silly, but he did and I had to shoot him.'

'You mean he went back into the kitchen for his gun?' Skinner winced inwardly as he was reminded of the child's astonishing memory for detail.

'Yes, that's just the way it was.'

'What'll happen now?'

'Some Army people will come up to take him away.' In fact, he had begun the clean-up process with a phone call to Adam Arrow, from the cottage.

And then Mark asked the inevitable question, the one which his remarkable young mind had allowed him to block out until then.

'Uncle Bob . . .' he began. 'What it said on the radio about my mummy. That wasn't true, was it?'

Skinner hugged the boy to him. 'Let's sit down over here, wee man,' he said, 'and let's have a chat.'

85

'Mitch, does your firm handle property sales?'

'No,' said Laidlaw. 'But I can recommend good people. Why?'

'I'm selling the Gullane cottage,' said Skinner.

'You hardly need do that, Bob,' the portly lawyer beamed, 'since the Secretary of State has said that his office would fund your defence costs. He was pretty magnanimous in his statement exonerating you, after the line he took at the start.'

'He was told to be,' said Skinner.

The lawyer shot him a curious look. 'Fine by me,' he said. 'It means I can now add your daughter's time to the fee note with a clear conscience.'

The policeman laughed.

'I was surprised by what he said in the rest of the statement,' Laidlaw went on, 'that the allegations had proved to be spurious and that there would be no further enquiries.'

'He was told to say that too,' said Skinner, in a way which invited no further discussion of the matter.

'Still, Mitch,' he went on, quickly, 'despite the outcome, it was pretty hairy while it lasted. All your input and support was much appreciated, and I thank you for it.'

'Don't mention it. It's good to see you looking so relaxed after it all, and after yesterday's events. You've had no reaction to . . .' The rest of the question was unnecessary.

Skinner glanced at him. 'To having to shoot Heuer?' He

shook his head. 'No. It's a part of the job. Not an everyday part, thank goodness, but part none the less. Heuer made his choice when he killed Leona. Up the crematorium chimney's the best place for him.'

'Was he killed outright?' asked the solicitor, slightly awed by a side of his friend that he had never seen.

'Oh yes. When your brains are all over the wall behind you, everything else tends to stop working.'

Laidlaw shuddered. 'How were the children, afterwards?' he asked.

The policeman grimaced. 'Wee Tanya's completely withdrawn. It'll take her a long time to recover I think, if she ever does. I don't envy Bruce Anderson his job as a father. I think he may even resign his office to look after her.

'As for Mark, he's a remarkable and resilient wee boy. But he's still only that: a wee boy, orphaned by violence.'

'What'll happen to him?'

'He's with his grandparents just now, but they're retired. He'll need a different long-term solution. Still, I'm sure that one will be found.'

Laidlaw nodded. 'Let's hope so. Anyway, back to your house: you're serious?'

'Yes. I just fancy a change, somewhere I can build a new set of memories. I plan to sell the Edinburgh house too, and buy another place in Gullane.'

'Ah, so we won't be losing you from the Thursday night football club.'

'Shit no. That's my religion.'

'That's good. But after yesterday, I won't be kicking you again, that's for sure.'

Skinner laughed as he rose to his feet. 'Is my daughter available, by the way?' he asked.

Laidlaw shook his head. 'No, she called in and asked for the day off. She said that you and she and Andy had had a stressful time last night, unwinding. I told her I quite understood, and that I'd see her on Monday.

'She did ask me to give you a message, though. She said that a delivery service had been trying to reach you, about a package that's *en route* to you. She's told them you'll receive it at Fairyhouse Avenue at midday.'

Skinner frowned as he headed for the door of the lawyer's office. 'Delivery service?' he mused, aloud. 'Wonder what the hell that's about? The way my luck's been going lately, this one really will be a bomb.'

86

The package was explosive in its own way, but it was no bomb. It had arrived before he reached the bungalow.

He smelled fresh coffee in the kitchen as he stepped through the back door. He caught the fragrance of a familiar perfume as he stepped into the hall. He heard the rustle of movement as he turned into the living room.

'Sarah.'

He said her name quietly and calmly, as nervousness, relief and uncertainty struggled for mastery within him.

'Bob.' She replied coolly and cautiously, with no hostility, but with no hint of emotion.

'What . . .?' he began. 'What do you want? Why have you come back?'

'I've come back for a fight,' she said, her jaw set defiantly, holding her head proud and high, light glinting on her auburn hair.

Within him, uncertainty triumphed over relief. 'Oh my love,' he cried out, sadly. 'I don't want to fight with you. I never did, and I never should have, only I was too big a fool to know.'

She stepped towards him, skirt swinging, stepped right up against him, tall in her high heels, with her hands on her hips. 'I didn't say I was going to fight *with* you, honey.' She paused, still without a smile.

'After you called me, to tell me about you and the other woman, and to warn me about the *Spotlight* stuff, and I gave you that three-month ultimatum; after all that I sat down and I said to myself, "Hold on here a minute, Doctor. Have you ever stopped loving this man, since the day you met him? Would your life ever be the same if you lost him? Are you prepared to let some other lady enjoy your happy ever after?"

'The answers were "No", "No", and "Hell, no!". Right there and then I decided that you were not getting rid of me that easily, with just one phone call three months down the road.

'I'm here to fight *for* you, Bob, my love. That's if I have to.' At last, a tentative smile came to her lips, and into her wonderful eyes.

He shook his head as if to clear it, picked her up and pressed her to him. 'Oh but you don't,' he said, hugging her tight as relief, with an overwhelming counter-surge, swept everything else aside. 'My darling, you don't.

'I am so, so, sorry for the fool I've been. Please, please forgive me. I accused you of being disloyal to me, and I drove you away in the process. But it's me who failed the loyalty test, in a big way.' He set her back on her feet.

'Yeah,' she said, her smile gone once more, 'You sure did. But I have to tell you, husband, we're even on that score.'

He felt a punch, a hard, winding punch, in the pit of his stomach, but he rode out its force. 'This Terry guy, yes?'

She nodded.

'Well,' he sighed, 'you were entitled. As far as I'm concerned it never happened.'

'Oh but it did, lover,' she insisted. 'And you must listen to me. Like I said, I have to tell you why.

'It had nothing to do with entitlement, or revenge. I was evening the score between us, yes, but with a good motive behind it, I hope.

'I decided I should go to bed with Terry for one reason alone – and I'm telling you for that same reason – so that I'll never in the future, if ever I was stupid enough, be able to brandish my fidelity over your head like a club.' She laid her forehead against his chest, and spoke quietly. 'This is what happened.

'I invited him on a dinner date, and I even insisted on paying. Afterwards, I took him to a hotel room I'd booked, and I said, "Okay, Terry, now give me your best, and I'll give me yours." As it turned out, his was a lot better than mine – you'll be glad to know I'm lousy at casual sex – but it was nowhere, my love, nowhere near as good as yours.

'When we'd done it – once was enough – I got out of bed, took a shower, said "Thanks and Good Night", and went home, feeling guilty about using Terry, but leaving my banner of virtue behind me as I had set out to do. I didn't feel like a whore, though. I was relieved, because I'd been able to do what I believed was necessary, and most of all because I was ready to go home.

'I want to make a fresh start,' she whispered. 'Forgiveness on both sides.' She looked up to find his eyes looking solemnly into hers.

'If Terry had looked in my bag when I was in the shower,' she said, 'he'd have found the plane tickets there: Edinburgh via Amsterdam, one way.'

'Tickets?' he asked, hopefully.

'Of course we both came back,' she said. 'Jazz is with Alex.' She grinned. 'Hey, your gal's getting a touch broody, Pops. Maybe having her baby brother back will calm her down a bit.'

She hesitated. 'Alex told me all about Pam; she told me the whole story. That it was her who tipped off *Spotlight*? It was her who set you up with the bribe thing? And all because you put her brother away for something or other. How driven can a person be?'

Bob shook his head. 'Alex doesn't know the whole story, love. Neither does Andy. Only you can ever know it. Sit down.' He took her hand and led her to the couch, sitting her down and facing her along the leather cushions.

'I put Pam's brother away all right, Sarah love. Six feet deep.

'Remember the time we had the President of Syria here, and he was killed? Remember the man who shot him, and who was going to kill me, and you too, because I found out the truth?'

Her face went white. She leaned, suddenly and heavily, against the back of the sofa. 'The man you shot dead? That was Pam's brother?'

'Yes, that's who he was. His real name was Ross Masters. Just like Heuer, he was a soldier who'd become a professional assassin, and he worked within the intelligence community. He and Pamela were very close . . .' He hesitated, and she caught his meaning.

'Incestuous, you mean?'

'That's right,' Bob grunted, grimly. 'Incest, the game the whole family can play! Ross called her Polly, by the way. She came to hate it if that name was used by anyone else, even by her poor mug of a husband. The marriage was Ross's idea, she told me. Purely for show.

'The two of them were so close in fact, that she knew what Ross did, and the risks it involved. They had an arrangement. He always contacted her, in person or by telephone, within a three-month period. He told her that if ever he failed to do that, it would certainly be because he was dead. If that happened, she was to go to a private safe depository in London and present a key which he had given her.

'Just over three months after Ross and I had our fatal encounter, she made that trip. She was given a box which her brother had kept. Inside, she found a hundred thousand pounds, in Bank of England notes, and a letter.'

He reached into the pocket of his soft brown leather jacket and took out a folded piece of paper. 'This is it.' He began to read.

'My darling Polly
'You're reading this, so I'm dead. You can be sure of that, and you can be sure also that my end will have been unrecorded. The work I have been doing lately has been so secret and potentially calamitous for those who commissioned me, that if I fail or die in the act, it will be as if I have disappeared from the face of the earth. My real identity died a while back, as you know, in a genuine helicopter crash in Oman, in which Ross Masters was listed among the dead, burned to ashes in the process.

'Yesterday I met a man. His name is Bob Skinner, and he works in Edinburgh. I do not expect to die on this assignment, but if I do, then I know within myself and with a great certainty that it will be Bob Skinner who will kill me. He is a career policeman, but he has a certain quality too, one which only people like me can see in others. He may not even know it himself, but Mr Skinner is a killer, just like me. He is tenacious, he is very good, and it is possible that before this commission is complete, he and I will have a confrontation. Should that not happen I will have been in touch as usual. But should Skinner get too

close, then one of us will not survive, and you may have to read this letter.

'Polly, as you know, I don't fear death. But I am proud, as you are, and I am vengeful, as you are also. Take all the money in this box, most of my savings from my career as a contractor. I would like you to use some of it, at least, to ensure that Skinner accounts for my death in a meaningful way. Don't have him killed, though, unless you have no other choice. He does not fear death either, and in any event, you would have to be certain of success, or he would be very dangerous.

'You've always been a creative girl. Use your talents, and this money, to even my score with my executioner. Take Skinner's life from him, not in an instant, but in a way that will hurt him for as long as he breathes. But be careful, touch none of his, or he will hunt you down. Hurt him alone.

'There is a man who will help you. He is an acquaintance of mine, in the same line of work, and he has met Skinner also. His name is Peter Gilbert Heuer, and he is very bitter. He can be contacted by placing a personal ad in the Northern Echo on any Tuesday, under a Box Number, simply asking PGH to respond. Peter, with you and only three other people, knows my real name: ask him for it, to confirm his identity.

'Do this for me, Polly, as best you can. I leave you my heart and my undying love, for you and I are soulmates.

'Goodbye, Ross'

Bob folded the letter, put it back in his pocket, and looked again at his wife.

'So Polly, or Pamela, rather, took the money, took her marketing degree and experience, and joined the police, my force naturally, as a late entrant. Once there she took the service options which would bring her closest to me. She even had an affair with the Force Press Officer, who knows me better than most, as part of her preparation.

'When the time was right she contacted Heuer. When he heard that it was me she was after, he was only too willing to help her.

'She had her plan all along, and it worked better than she had ever dared to hope. Had it not been for a couple of mistakes that she made, I could have been convicted. As a minimum, if things had worked out, I'd have had to leave the force under a very big cloud.

'My splitting up with you was a tremendous bonus for her. She's a wonderful actress, is Pamela. She played it so well, so properly. She was there to lend me a shoulder to moan on, yet she refused to sleep with me before you and I were legally separated. She was in the final act of setting me up when it all went sour for her. She told me she wanted to get married. That's how confident she was.' His face was twisted with anger.

Sarah looked at him, almost fearfully. 'What have you done with her?' she asked. 'Alex said that all you told them was that she had left.'

'I haven't done anything with her,' he answered bitterly, 'or to her. I could hardly have her arrested and charged, in all the circumstances. With the national security interests that would have been involved, a trial would have been unthinkable.

'So instead, I signed the hundred thousand back into her name, I drove her to the airport to catch her plane, and I told her to get as far away from me and mine as she could.

I promised her also that I would let my contacts in MI6 and the CIA know that Ross Masters had a sister who is aware of the work he did for them.'

'And have you? Will you?'

'No, but she believes that I will. And that will keep her on the move, and will keep her mouth shut, for the rest of her life. She'll disappear like her brother, I guess. Like him, she'll find a new identity.'

'This man Heuer,' Sarah broke in. 'Didn't he kill Leona McGrath, and the Secretary of State's wife? Wasn't he the man you shot yesterday, when you rescued the children?'

Bob nodded. 'Yes, but Pam had no idea about that until Andy and I made the connection.

'She only used him as a courier to set me up with the bank in Guernsey. She swore blind that she didn't know he was planning the killings or the kidnapping. Eventually, she made me believe her.'

'And if you hadn't accepted it?'

He looked at the wall, suddenly cold as ice. 'I'd have handed her over to Adam Arrow,' he whispered, and she knew that he meant it.

'Anyway,' he said, softening in an instant, 'Heuer's dead and Pam's gone for good. Both of my persecutors are dealt with.'

Bob leaned back wearily on the couch beside his wife and drew her to him, to lay her head on his shoulder. 'I feel as if I've been haunted for the last few months, Sarah, my love, visited by all my ghosts and horrors from my past. God willing, now they're all exorcised, and the demons, the misunderstanding and the anger, which drove us apart are gone as well.'

She drew his head down and kissed him, for the first time in months, long and slow.

'Yes,' she said, 'they're gone. So if you've any more secrets to reveal, now's the time to do it. Nothing you say will be taken down, or held against you.'

He took a deep breath. 'Well,' he began. 'About Leona McGrath . . .'

She put her fingers to his lips. 'It's okay, I know. Alex told me that. I half-guessed at the time too. Although we were barely speaking, I remember that when you got home late that night, I thought that it was the first time I had ever seen you with a guilty look on your face.

'Poor woman,' Sarah sighed. 'No grudges borne. And, oh, her poor little boy.'

He looked her in the eye, so close to her that he was almost squinting. 'Speaking of Mark,' he murmured, 'I know this is a biggie, but how would you and Jazz feel about adopting an older brother?'

'I think we'd feel okay,' she replied, without a moment's hesitation. She leaned back and gazed at him for a moment. 'You know, Ross Masters didn't have a clue about the real you,' she said, smiling.

'Oh no? Which of us is dead?'

'And which of you was on the side of right, as almost invariably, my darling, you are?'

She was silent, contemplative, for a few seconds. 'One thing I learned from Ross, though,' she added, at last.

'What's that?'

'He told Pam that he and she were "soulmates",' she said. 'Until this moment, I've never really considered, far less understood, the meaning of the term.'

She looked up at him, and saw a glistening in his eyes. 'Oh Sarah,' he sighed, with the relief of someone who has stepped into a chasm in the dark, only to have his foot land safely upon a bridge, 'then maybe you'll know just how glad I am that you're back.'

'Cuts both ways, honey,' she drawled in her finest American, beginning to unbutton his shirt. 'Now let's give each other our very, very best. For today, Skinner's ghosts aren't all that's gonna get laid.'

Skinner's Round

Quintin Jardine

By the blade, by water, by the fire, by lightning, shall the desecrators perish . . .

A four-day tournament involving the world's leading golfers is being staged to mark the opening of Witches' Hill, a new country club created on his East Lothian estate by the Marquis of Kinture. But on the Sunday afternoon preceding, one of Kinture's business partners is found dead in his private jacuzzi in the clubhouse – with his throat cut.

The next day an anonymous letter is received by the local newspaper, containing a fragment of a legendary witches' curse upon anyone who desecrates their place of worship.

For Assistant Chief Constable Robert Skinner, the key to the murder is surely to be found in the here and now rather than in East Lothian's grisly past as a notorious centre for witchcraft. But then a second murder occurs, this time by water, and soon Skinner is facing the most challenging case of his career.

0 7472 4141 4

headline

A Coffin for Two

Quintin Jardine

After cracking their first case together as a private investigation team, Oz Blackstone and Primavera Philips find themselves simultaneously in love and in the money. And where better to lie back and contemplate life than the picturesque village of St Marti, on the rugged Costa Brava.

But is their new home quite so idyllic as it looks? Some very dark secrets begin to emerge as the inhabitants draw them into the intrigue which bubbles away beneath the surface, until suddenly, faced with a mysterious skeleton and an unauthenticated Dali masterpiece, Prim and Oz stumble across one of the century's most amazing stories . . .

'Entertaining . . . keeps you intrigued'
Carlisle News & Star

0 7472 5575 X

headline

Skinner's Trail

Quintin Jardine

First the joyous birth of Skinner's son . . .

Then the grim reality of murder in one of Edinburgh's prosperous suburbs. A man has been found knifed in a luxury villa.

The victim had run a chain of laundrettes, saunas and pubs throughout the city, but for some time the police suspected these to be the front for a drug-distribution network. As the murder investigation continues without result, it seems the killer was particularly cunning in covering his tracks – leaving no clues or leads to pursue.

But then another, seemingly minor, crime – involving property fraud – takes Assistant Chief Constable Bob Skinner in a new direction. Moving from Scotland to northern Spain, then back to a chilling climax in Edinburgh, this complex and suspenseful thriller follows a tortuous and bloodsoaked trail involving vice, corruption and the merchants of death.

0 7472 4141 4

headline

Autographs in the Rain

Quintin Jardine

As Bob Skinner takes an evening stroll with an old flame, glamorous film star Louise Bankier, a frightening shot-gun attack sends them diving for cover. Danger, it seems, has zeroed in on him once again.

Returning to her native Scotland to shoot her latest film, Louise Bankier is one of Scotland's most popular exports, except with the stalker who seems determined to scare her witless – and maybe worse. For Skinner, tracking down her tormentor isn't just business now. It's very personal indeed.

Meanwhile, the case of a pensioner found dead in his bath turns out to be anything but an open and shut case – especially when one of Skinner's closest staff is accused of murdering him. And a gang of thieves specialising in stealing items of a rather slippery nature is driving more than one police force to distraction.

On several fronts, Skinner is about to find out that nothing is quite what it seems . . .

Quintin Jardine is the author of ten previous acclaimed Bob Skinner novels: 'Remarkably assured . . . *a tour de force' New York Times*

0 7472 6387 6

headline

Now you can buy any of these other bestselling books by **Quintin Jardine** from your bookshop or *direct from his publisher*.

FREE P&P AND UK DELIVERY
(Overseas and Ireland £3.50 per book)

Bob Skinner series

Head Shot	£6.99
Autographs in the Rain	£5.99
Thursday Legends	£6.99
Gallery Whispers	£6.99
Murmuring the Judges	£6.99
Skinner's Ghosts	£6.99
Skinner's Mission	£6.99
Skinner's Ordeal	£6.99
Skinner's Round	£6.99

Oz Blackstone series

On Honeymoon with Death	£6.99
Screen Savers	£6.99
Wearing Purple	£5.99
A Coffin for Two	£6.99
Blackstone's Pursuits	£6.99

TO ORDER SIMPLY CALL THIS NUMBER

01235 400 414

or visit our website: www.madaboutbooks.com

Prices and availability subject to change without notice.